In Flight

In Flight

Dawn Leger

iUniverse, Inc.
New York   Bloomington

In Flight

iUniverse books may be ordered through booksellers or by contacting:

iUniverse
1663 Liberty Drive
Bloomington, IN 47403
www.iuniverse.com
1-800-Authors (1-800-288-4677)

ISBN: 978-1-4401-6989-2 (sc)
ISBN: 978-1-4401-6990-8 (ebook)
ISBN: 978-1-4401-6991-5 (dj)

Printed in the United States of America

iUniverse rev. date: 11/18/2009

For Nihat

Acknowledgments

Thanks to "my Turks" —family and friends—who helped (willingly or unconsciously) with the development of this book. After fifteen years of marriage to a Turk and almost as many annual trips there, I am indebted to my late husband, Nihat Özkaya, for so much more than just this novel. He introduced me to a culture and a people, both filled with history and stories, and for that, I am grateful. His encouragement to follow my dream still inspires and motivates me to continue writing.

Special thanks to several wonderful Turkish friends, both here in the U.S. and abroad, including Ayşegul and Naz Durakoğlu; and Fatma, Cuneyt, and my "research assistant" Nilufer Arslan.

First among my many readers is Pat Follert, a writer and friend whom I thank for her support. Many people at the Writer's Studio in New York contributed insights, and I appreciate the craft I learned during my time there, from Phillip Schultz and many others. Other excellent readers include, from various writing groups in Connecticut (and listed in no particular order): David Fortier, Don Paglia, John Charpie, Olivia Lawrence, Chuck Radda, Erin Pronicki, Marissa Blaszko, and Lisa Crofton. Other readers with helpful comments include Joanne West, Isabel Brady, Judy Giguere, Patti Ewen, Cathryn Addy, Cindy Scoville, Linda DiMatteo, Richard Lacey, Beverly Bain, Lorrie Glover, and Theresa Mastrogiovanni. Special thanks to Kelly Jensen Photography for the author photo. And, last but never least, my deepest gratitude to Alice Leger, my best editor, proofreader, and buddy.

Christina Baker Kline was one of several great teachers with whom I have worked. In her class at NYU, the first story about Marta was written. Christina has also been an invaluable editor and critic. Other professional assessments and advice came from folks at the Wesleyan Summer Writers Festival and the Iowa Summer Writer's Workshop (thanks Terri and Scot!). I appreciate the judges of the Amazon.com Breakthrough Novel Awards, who chose an earlier version of this manuscript to be a semifinalist in 2008. The comments of the judges as well as the public were very encouraging.

Every comment from readers, be they professionals or friends, helps a writer grow and manuscripts improve. When the advice conflicts (e.g., "You should never start a book on an airplane" versus "The novel should start when they meet on the plane"), it is the author's gut that has to prevail. Therefore, all errors or flaws are my creation, as are these characters, who remain alive and well in my imagination.

One

Shortly after boarding the plane, a glass of single-malt whiskey on its way to her hand, Marta had been disturbed to discover the seat next to her was about to be occupied by a nervous—shaking actually—and extremely elderly gentleman. "I was upgraded," he said, waving his boarding pass in Marta's direction. "My first time on an airplane, and I get first class."

"That's nice," she murmured, turning to look out the window while he stored his bag and jacket in the overhead compartment. Marta watched her own reflection in the glass, eyes falling in and out of focus, gazing sometimes at the scurrying airport personnel below and sometimes at herself, a woman who did not look her age at thirty-six. She had thick dark hair and slightly oriental, almond-shaped green eyes that were fringed with dark lashes under the curve of well-turned eyebrows and bracketed by sharp cheekbones covered with taut, unwrinkled skin. She flew weekly, sometimes more than once or even twice a week, some trips lasting less than a day. Always flying first class, she was a longtime member of the million-mile club—and the mile-high club, for that matter. She raised her eyebrow slightly when Denise, one of her favorites on the European circuit, leaned in to refresh her drink.

"Sorry, we're booked solid today. You won't be able to spread out this trip."

Marta frowned and sipped her drink. It was bad enough that she was bound for Istanbul, a place she'd left a lifetime ago. Now she was forced to share her trip with an elderly seatmate who insisted on referring to it as Constantinople, despite almost a hundred years of being known in the world with the Turkish rather than Greek designation on maps. Although she'd vowed never to set foot in that country again, a series of mishaps had landed her in this seat on a first-class rocket to the past to discuss none other than the international trade in pasta.

"Pasta?" asked the constant Constantinopler.

"Precisely," she replied, snapping open her laptop to circumvent further discussion of the topic at hand. After one partner contracted malaria (in New York City, no less, so who knew where that malady came from?), another had a skiing accident (this mishap taking place on the slopes in Vermont, but in early May, making it also suspect to Marta), and then the third and fourth were taken off the case to assist with the defense of an illegal nanny and gardener discovered working sans papers in the household of the firm's managing partner, well, it seemed that the planets had finally aligned themselves in such a way to compel Marta's return to Turkey.

"Short and sweet," she told the travel agent. "I want to get in there, do the deal, and get the hell out as soon as possible."

Marta was particularly rattled—and she never became rattled, particularly or not—by the prospect of returning to her homeland, a place she'd not seen since she left in 1985, at the tender age of twenty-one. Her colleagues were always vague about where Marta came from, although if pressed, the senior partners knew that she had arrived in their offices with a passport from Turkey, the ink barely dry on her Turkish law degree and the master's from Columbia Law School. After a while, in typical New York fashion, no one cared where she came from, including her.

New York was the perfect place to get lost, to reinvent oneself, to make a new history. This was precisely what Marta had done. And now, all because of a stupid legal tangle over pasta that was verging on an international incident, Marta was going back there.

"Book me in the newest hotel you can find," she told her secretary. "Schedule all the meetings there and make these guys come to me."

Marta was notorious for her liaisons with young associates, something that made her male partners uncomfortable and alienated her from the female staff. Marta viewed sex in the same way she followed a regular schedule of exercise—it was something necessary to keep her body functioning at its optimal level. Over the years, as she remade herself into the stereotypical tough New York lawyer, Marta had limited her emotional contacts until the only true devotion she allowed was to her physical trainer. She'd previously almost considered her hairdresser a friend, until the woman moved upstate without a word of warning. So much for friends.

While her intention for the trip was good—staying in a new hotel that would have no associations with the past—Marta would end up conducting the pasta negotiations in a spectacular, curved edifice overlooking the Bosporus, smack in the middle of the park in which she played as a child with a view not only of the legendary seaway but also the crowded slums of her youth. Oh progress, that decided to make a tourist destination from a decrepit villa and its bramble-ridden grounds! Oh fate, how it conspired to return Marta to a room with such a view, with only a pane of glass to insulate her from the smells and sounds of her past!

Mr. Vasilli Vassilios was not willing to recognize that Marta had no intention of engaging him in conversation for the duration of the nine-hour plane trip. When the plane reached its cruising altitude and people started to move around, Vasilli decided to try again.

"I need an attorney when I arrive," he said. "Can you give me the name of someone?"

Marta's hands stilled over the keyboard. "I don't know anyone in Istanbul," she said. "I wouldn't have the foggiest idea how to find one."

He looked pointedly at the legal papers entrapped in her briefcase.

Not being prone to feelings of embarrassment, even when caught in such an obvious falsehood, Marta smoothly continued, "The people my office deals with are all corporate lawyers. Believe me, they would know less than I do about handling a personal matter," she said.

"I see," he said. He nodded sadly and then put a gnarled hand over hers. "My brother just passed away, and I have been summoned to settle his estate."

"I'm very sorry for your loss." She counted to herself and focused on breathing. Why was she letting this old man interfere with her trip? "Mr. Vassilios," she continued, "I really need to get some work done. If you'll excuse me …"

"I haven't seen my brother since we were children," Vasilli said. "Now I'm the only one left. Can you believe it? All those years, children, maybe grandchildren even, and now, they call me. Look at me. I am an old man. But I guess I have to go back there."

Marta closed her eyes again. Vasilli's voice rambled, becoming soft and then, once or twice, guttural Greek sounds broke into the story like punctuation marks. It was hard not to be drawn into his tale, although at one point, she looked over at him. "What year did you say that was?" she asked.

"Around 1922, I guess," he replied.

"Just how old are you?" Marta marveled, turning to look at him for the first time. Up close like this, his cheeks resembled a photo of the Grand Canyon or a close-up of an elephant hide with some bristling hairs scattered over deep crevasses. It was a face that carried scars of more than eighty years of hard living. Watery brown eyes peered into hers, shaded by short but thick eyelashes and brows like two caterpillars readying for battle. His hair still sported more pepper than salt, especially the crop erupting from his ears and the tip of his prominent nose.

"Older than dirt," he replied. "Older than this *republic*, that's for sure. I was born at the end of the first war, in 1918. The Ottomans had backed the losers, the Kaiser, and everything started to fall apart for them in the next few years.

"We left, me and my father; we boarded a ship for America. My brother and mother stayed behind, waiting for Baba to send for them. We didn't have the money for everyone to make the trip. Yurgos stayed with Mama, since he was a bit older and could work ... He must have been ten or so, since I was about five at that time. Yes, he was old enough to help out.

"That was the last time I saw them, on the docks. We were in the boat. It seemed like we sailed for a year, but I suppose it was not so long. Baba was very sad, and then he became ill, but we both made it to America. But things happened during the war, I guess. The Greek families were moved out—relocated, is what they say now—and after that, we could not find my mother. And there was no word from my brother until now, this notice I received, you see? How did they find me after so many years when we could not find them?

"The letters all came back, you see, and when we finally heard from the others, my aunts and uncles, they were in Greece, in Thessaloníki, and they did not know where Mama had gone ... They said to Baba, 'Oh, we thought she was with you,' and he was so angry. That was the end, he said. No more family. It was just the two of us."

Marta picked up the onionskin papers, authenticated with a single gold seal and obviously typed on a manual machine with a thin ribbon that wrinkled occasionally and spit out a word or two in red. There was an elaborate but unreadable scrawl on the bottom of the page, in a style that Marta recognized from her youth, when all the college students—especially the males—worked hard to create a signature to match the elaborate style of the Ottomans. Her own still contained elements of this fashion.

"How *did* they find you?" she asked, more to herself than to the old man blowing his nose loudly into a frayed white handkerchief embroidered in the corner with interlocking blue Vs.

She could still read the Turkish, but she checked it against the second page, a bad English translation. She thought the signer would be a place to start, but she did not say it out loud. No way was Marta getting pulled into this old man's miniseries, his histrionics, his Greek tragedy. No way. If anyone's past life qualified for coverage in *Soap Opera Digest*, it was hers—and she had long ago changed to the *Law Review* and the *New Yorker*. She had no desire to go rooting around in personal history—her own or anybody else's.

"Is this all there was?" she asked. He nodded. "Where is the envelope?"

He pulled it silently from his breast pocket. There was no return address, and the postage mark was badly smeared. The stamps bore the familiar visage of Kemal Atatürk, the founder of the Turkish republic, and the address had been typed on the same machine as the letter, so that the "West" and both of the "Yorks" were red.

"Vasilli Vassilios. 384 West End Avenue, New York, New York. Hmm, good address," she said. "What do you do for a living?"

"Retired," he replied. And then, after a pause, he filled in the blanks. "Coffee shop, Seventy-second Street. Closed down last year when rents went up too high.

"I have no children, my wife is dead, and there is no one else, and now this. But I figured, what should I do? I can ignore it, or I can make one last trip. So I might find out what happened to my mother and my brother. And maybe there is more family there. Who knows? I can see."

"Yes," Marta agreed. "You can see."

Vasilli looked at her. "And what about you? You are going to visit family, yes?"

"No," she replied. "I don't have any contact with them. I'm just going for business." She absently fingered the locket hanging from a thin gold chain around her neck.

"Surely there is someone," he persisted.

"No, there is no one I want to see." She opened the computer. "I'll try to help you when we get there, but I'm not promising anything."

Vasilli nodded and closed his eyes, listening to the tapping of her keyboard until he slept.

Two

Marta arrived in Istanbul on a new highway from a new airport that was so different from the one she had left that she was momentarily able to trick herself into thinking that this was a different country. Billboards piled atop one another rested against apartment blocks so flimsy that it seemed that the advertisements surely provided more stability than decoration. But the smells and sounds of Istanbul swirled through her defenses. The view of the minarets and towers of Topkapi Palace and the winding waterway of the Bosporus clutched at her heart.

The Conrad Hotel staff greeted their new guest with speedy efficiency, ferrying her belongings into a suite larger than her first apartment in New York. Fruit platter, complementary champagne, and five-hundred-thread-count sheets awaited her in the Pasha Suite, which was reserved usually for high rollers in the casino downstairs. Thus distracted, Marta barely registered the location of the place on the edge of her old neighborhood before she was on the phone and then welcoming assistants and lawyers and consular officials into her lair.

She kept moving around the room, knowing that jet lag would soon threaten her sharpness. The windows, broad and curving and cool to the touch, beckoned her. Lights moved ahead of cars crossing the Bosporus Bridge, suspended like a necklace over the slower moving vessels crisscrossing the water below. Tired in her bones and unsettled in her soul, Marta was not used to the swirl of emotions that had been unleashed in her head as she struggled to control her thoughts. Her facial muscles clenched as she tried to concentrate on the legal negotiations and responsibilities that had compelled her return to Turkey. She turned her back against the busy traffic on Barbaros Boulevard. Shoulders tightly squared, her head resolutely turned away from the old neighborhood that lay across the street, Marta fought the impulse to reminisce as she focused her thoughts firmly in the present.

She watched a small fishing boat bob dangerously in the wake of a ferry that had passed too close to its path. The volume of traffic on the Bosporus had increased rather than decreased in the years since she had last watched the boats jockey at the piers. The hotel room, insulated from noise and smell, afforded a unique vantage point for Marta to observe the city of her youth.

"Istanbul," she murmured. She cocked her head, studying the landscape through the mist. So much for the tough New York lawyer, she thought. Only six hours in this city, and she was reduced to daydreaming at a window again, just like during her years in the public school that used to lie in the shadows of this hill. Was it still there, or had the hotel's construction obliterated more than simply the sandboxes of her childhood?

What else had happened in the fifteen years she'd been away? She pulled her hair harshly back into its elastic and willed herself to concentrate on the present, not the past. She turned back to the table and filled another glass with tea, trying to decipher the thread of argument in the rising voices. The meeting ended well past midnight, and Marta tumbled into a fitful sleep. A few short hours later, she descended to the lobby, seeking fresh air and coffee.

She paused and pretended to check her purse while rummaging through her short-term memory. *Of course,* she thought. *The Greek.*

Her traveling companion from the airplane was seated primly by the door. Dressed in a sharply-pressed linen suit, his white shirt punctuated by a brilliant blue bow tie, Vasilli Vassilios had watched the elevator for several hours in hopes of encountering his new friend. She sighed, walked over, and pulled up a chair.

"Mr. Vassilios, did you make contact with your family?" she asked.

He shook his head slowly. "No, I called ... but, no, I couldn't find anyone to speak with me." He clutched the folder of letters that she'd seen in the airplane. "Can you make a call for me?" he asked. "I hate to be a bother ..."

"Let's go for a walk, shall we? I need to get some air to clear my head. Then I will make a call for you. Come." She stood up, removed the folder from his hands, and handed it to the receptionist for safekeeping. The concierge provided a beeper that Marta hooked to her belt. She knew the best solution to the jet-lag headache was to venture out of the building for a walk and some fresh, unfiltered air. Walking a little slower to accommodate her companion, Marta took in the sights and smells of the old city. The wail of engines straining to make headway up the grade on the boulevard, accompanied by a streaming cloud of exhaust that pierced her nostrils with a familiar and unwelcome bite, competed with the horns, vendors shouting, the swirl of Turkish around her, and then, cutting through it all, the call to prayer that Marta had heard only in her dreams for the past fifteen years.

Midway down the hill, they stopped at a bench and Marta let it wash over her. The muezzin's call echoed over the hills, and then it was joined with others in a round of Arabic that was strange and familiar and known and untranslatable, and then came the blast of a ferryboat horn, the cruel groan of boat meeting pier, scraping too against her eardrums like the downshifting of the old busses making the tortured journey across the sprawlscape that was the new Istanbul, spreading out from the cramped city she once knew so well. Vasilli, perhaps sensing that the polished attorney was wrestling with her own demons, remained quiet and watched with interest as a man pulling a small bear on a chain crossed through the park and disappeared into the bushes.

"Gypsies," Marta answered his silent question. "I guess they are still here, abusing animals and conning the tourists out of their money." She paused. "Shame." They stood up and resumed their silent walk.

A new park along the water dressed up the old café she had frequented long ago, its second-story restaurant sending the odors of cooking fish to mingle with the brackish water lapping the shore. Students still gathered there, she noted, many with the black portfolios from the art institute that the young hopefuls filled with their aspirations, sketches, and watercolors. Some still wore the blue-blazered uniforms from the private school on the hill, white starched collars undone in the heat of the late May morning.

Marta settled at a vacant table, squinting into the sparkling waters as yellow-and-black-checked boats zipped across, "Taksi" emblazoned on their sides. How many hours had she spent gazing at this very scene? She'd loved this city, and at the idealistic age of twenty, she could not have conceived that anything would have made her leave it. Only a few hours in Istanbul, and something about the smell of the air and the cadence of the people had awakened in Marta the very blood that she believed had been frozen in her body.

She stretched and ordered çay for both of them. The tea was bitter, more so than she remembered, and she stirred a sugar cube with the tiny spoon that rested in the red-and-white plastic saucer. The melamine design and the sensation of hot glass between her fingers were so familiar. The scalding tea was better with the sugar. She looked around at the haze of cigarette smoke, recalling the first time she'd tried a cigarette, here in the park. She shook it off, too much of the memory stuff all at once. The rest of the tea was quickly consumed, the glass ready for replenishment.

She signaled for the waiter and noticed the many eyes watching her, watching each other. It was a land of gossips, of watchers, she knew. People looked at her, a tall slender woman with dark hair pulled back, her almond eyes and slightly Roman nose a confirmation that she was one of them, despite the lack of feminine wiles that so characterized other Turkish women of her age. She wore pants too, not quite as unusual today as it had been years ago. The falsettos of the women carried on the wind, as musical or irritating as the sound of the gulls clamoring for food. Marta's own mother, a village girl trapped in a city apartment with neither friends nor family to socialize with, had none of the airs of "city women" like this—silly women, Marta had always thought, although she knew that some of them were professionals like her. For them, the girlish affectation was so ingrained that they were no more capable of shedding it than of breathing underwater—another way in which Marta had always been different, since she'd never learned that behavior, never truly fit in with the other girls and boys.

"They probably think I'm your father." Vasilli chuckled.

"Hmmm." She was distracted by the sight of a group of little girls, walking hand in hand along the pier. The oldest one, at the head of the line of five, kept checking over her shoulder, looking at a woman jiggling a stroller who was clearly the exhausted mother of them all.

"She's got her hands full," Vasilli commented, trying another tack at conversation.

"Yes," Marta agreed. "Reminds me of my childhood. Me and my sisters, always connected to each other like that."

Marta's mother had lined them up every morning for the daily inspection, checking for clean hands, freshly tied headscarves, and minty breath. Sometimes one had a crumb or a dollop of toothpaste briskly removed with the corner of her apron, which had been dabbed in spit. A lock of hair would be tucked in, a scarf retied with head-squeezing precision while a stream of praise and admonitions came from Mother's nervous lips. Marta had no idea if they were still alive, her parents, and what had happened to the sisters who once followed her like matryoshka dolls, each garbed in a similar colorful combination of skirts and scarves and scrubbed faces. They grew up together, her mother like an older sister at times, and remembering this, Marta felt bereft for the first time in years.

She closed her eyes, and a scene played out like a movie behind them, as vivid as yesterday, the smells and tastes causing her mouth to water a bit.

Day after day, they had followed the same routine. It was a hard life, and they kept inside a very small circle, with no television or radio to bring outside influences into their quiet home. As Marta got older, she started to fight it, to fight her parents and the oppression of their narrow lives. Sitting in the park now, in the twenty-first century, the afternoon sun warming her face, Marta shivered as she recalled the first time she challenged her mother.

Every afternoon, they returned home from school to Mother's eager greeting. She would greedily empty Marta's books onto the table. By the time Marta had shrugged off her coat and poured a warming cup of tea, Mother would be examining the papers dumped from the book bag. She was short and thin with angular bones in her face and dark chestnut hair covered by a flowered scarf tucked behind the ears and knotted loosely under her chin. Mother always wore a floral-print housedress that clashed badly with the scarf, but she rarely noticed her appearance. Marta often shuddered at the thought that she would grow up to look the same way, and it bothered her, not because her mother was unattractive, but because Marta was fearful of living the same life. All the girls were smothered in some way by the force of their mother's personality, her neediness. She yearned for education and had taught herself along with her eldest child to read, write, and perform mathematics, all of it without the knowledge of her husband, and all the time pushing Marta to excel.

Watching her mother that night, Marta had reached up and pulled off the bland paisley scarf that covered her own hair and for good measure loosened the braid twisted at the back of her head.

As expected, the reaction was shock and disapproval.

"Why did you do that?" Mother demanded. "We're going to have to fix it before your father gets home, you know."

She snapped her finger at Marta's hairline in a stinging rebuke. Shaking her head, she pushed the math book toward Marta and opened her notebook. Marta hitched her feet in the rungs of the chair and took a long sip of tea.

"I don't have any math homework today. We had a test," Marta announced.

"Well, let's review the test and go over the material for tomorrow," Mother pushed.

Marta thrust her lower lip out stubbornly. "I don't need to review. I got a one hundred."

The four sisters looked up from their books at the change they heard in Marta's voice. Mother started fussing about ungrateful children and back talk, and Marta held the glass of tea and fixed a stare at her through the steam. As usual, Mother's speech ended up with the importance of education and the sacrifices she made for her girls.

"Why is it so important that I go to school?" Marta asked, for probably the hundredth time. "Father thinks that it is a waste of time." Red-faced, her mother ignored the question and started turning the pages in the math book.

"Let's go to work," she said. Marta sighed. It must have been the thousandth time she'd heard that announcement sitting at this table, and she rose to refill her cup of tea. Turning back to the table, Marta picked up a history book and sat down.

"You go ahead and study the math," she said. "If you have any questions, you can ask me. I need to memorize this history chapter." Marta avoided her mother's face but felt her sister's sharp kick under the table. Mother sat quietly looking at the math book for a long time, and the girls read in silence until little Nilgun—always curled in the window keeping watch on the street—yelled that their father was coming.

The books were swept aside as Marta hurriedly tied her hair back and pulled on the headscarf. She was laying out the silverware when Sevgi poked her hard in the ribs. Marta grabbed her arm, and Sevgi hissed, "Why are you being so nasty to Mother? Would it kill you to teach her that math?"

"You teach it to her," Marta said as she released her arm.

"She doesn't want to study with me, stupid, just you. She's not interested in learning the same stuff over again. She only wants to study with you." Sevgi turned back to the table as Father opened the door and greeted the family with a grunt. He went to the sink to wash up, and the evening ritual began. Marta sat quietly during dinner, absorbed and confused by the sudden surge of power that she felt over her mother.

Father rose from the table and left for his evening of bridge at the café down the street. The table was cleared and the dishes washed as usual. Mother pulled the history book from the pantry and sat down to quiz Marta on the dates. Her eyes sparkled each time Marta missed an answer, and Marta in turn challenged her mother to answer them without the book. Sevgi took the text, and the two began to match wits against each other.

The teapot hissed and jiggled in the background. Faces flushed from the competition, mother and daughter drank from the hot glasses until the little girls fell asleep and were carried to bed. Marta returned to the kitchen and, without speaking, opened the math book and began to work the problems with her mother.

Their relationship changed that day, Marta knew. Someday, Marta could leave and have her own life. While she still lived at home, she vowed to do what she could to help her mother improve herself. Maybe she, too, could find a way to have a better life. Education was the key for both of them, and Marta never again asked why she needed it, never again gave her father the power to veto her options.

The beeper went off, shaking Marta from her reverie.

"So you have sisters?" Vasilli repeated. "Are they still here in the city? And your parents?"

"I don't know," she replied and signaled the waiter. "I haven't spoken to them in many years."

"Shame," he said. Brightening, he added, "It's not too late."

"It is." She settled up with the waiter, and together, she and Vasilli walked through the clamorous farmer's market under the roadway, almost in a trance from the smells and sounds there—plums, peppers, tomatoes, fruits whose color and lushness she'd dreamed of and rarely come across in the Union Square marketplace. *I'll come back when I have some time,* she thought, her mouth watering at the sight of the crisp green plums next to a huge display of fuzzy apricots. Vasilli sniffed the tomatoes hungrily and reluctantly followed his guide back into the sunlight.

They climbed quickly. Marta kept her head down and did not look at the houses, old and new, aligned under the shadows. They jumped aside as squealing children on bikes rattled dangerously down the ancient cobblestone road. Vasilli mopped his brow and collapsed into the first open seat in the hotel lobby.

"I'll see you later?" he asked, watching her accept messages from the bellboy. She nodded absently, waved a hand over her shoulder, and then was gone.

Four

The pasta people had, rather unfortunately in Marta's opinion, begun to meet without her, and the tangle had become even messier than she'd anticipated when her travel began the day before. Marta called the New York office, giving a list of references she needed to be gathered and e-mailed. "I need this stuff before my meeting in two hours. Get everybody on it."

The phone rang, and the doorbell engaged. With the phone balanced on her shoulder, Marta opened the door to discover several boxes of legal documents piled next to two anxious young men. They were probably not more than twenty-five years old, handsome in that full-lipped, red-cheeked way that usually promised an entertaining evening to Marta. Today, however, with the smell of Istanbul clinging to her perspiring skin and a headache pounding behind her eyes, Marta directed them to bring the boxes inside. She disconnected the phone and turned to watch the young men struggling with the cartons.

"Who are you?" They were startled by her abrupt tone. Too much New York, she realized, forcing a tight smile and softening her voice.

They looked at her quizzically, trying to sort out the Turkish and English. "We are from the *makarna* company, Bombastini."

"I am Cem, and this is Murat," the green-eyed man said. He smiled nervously and shrugged at his companion as Marta turned away.

"Let's get to work," she ordered crisply. Marta started working the phones. The top government official in charge of trade and his deputy, a civil servant intent on covering his ass as well as the snafu that had brought the crisis to a head, brought Marta up-to-date on the breakdown in their negotiations. Any residual rustiness in her Turkish was quickly replaced by the familiar cadences of courtliness and cutthroat business tactics being exercised by the various parties. Hours passed this way, Marta slowly rediscovering the nuances of the Turkish legal dance.

"Let me get this straight," she urged at one point. "Tell me that you did not admit to flooding the American market with Turkish product ... Tell me you did not confirm that you violated the trade restrictions on the exportation of semolina products."

There was a too-long pause, during which Marta scribbled some notes. "Okay, don't answer that. Just get me all the documents right away, so I can review them before the next sit-down. And have the Barişkoy lawyers call me too."

Marta paced the room nervously, waiting for a call back from her contact. She wondered why the U.S. government was concerned with a dispute about trade limits and pasta importation. After a few hours on the phone, it became clearer.

The impatient Turks had decided to hold the Americans hostage by threatening to restrict airspace and close some American bases there. That got some attention, and Marta was soon busy calming things down. Negotiations to join the European Union had stalled again, and the Turks were in no mood to back off from their pasta business. Conservatives had taken control of the government too, and anti-Western sentiments were dominating the news media.

She'd been away a long time, and she had forgotten how cunning the Turkish businessmen could actually be. National pride aside, they were known to be ruthless and fierce and all those other adjectives that you hate to encounter in a courtroom. Fortunately, she was on their side. However, her clients' explosiveness did not lend itself well to the kind of clenched and protracted negotiations at which Marta excelled. They wanted this settled. They wanted to be able to export their pasta without trade limitations and by God—or, rather, Allah—they were going to do so. Throw in a mix of irate Italians, some dim-witted foreign-service fellows, and you had the makings of a long—and potentially very lucrative—legal tussle.

A conference call with the partners confirmed that they knew more than they'd shared with her. "Don't try to settle the case, for God's sake," Barry Lebenstein said. "We have years to get the thing hammered out, and frankly, I have my eye on a place in the Hamptons, so we can't afford to fast-track this."

"Just get them to back off the airbase thing, and we'll be back to status quo," added Clive Martinson. "We're counting on you."

"I can't guarantee anything," Marta said. "These guys want to settle— or go to war. It's not going to be easy to broker a stalemate here." The call ended with more instructions to drag it out, the partners unwilling to listen to Marta's analysis of the situation.

She wasn't entirely unhappy with getting a piece of this case. Everyone in the firm knew it was a potential gold mine. She had hoped to handle it from New York, far away from the delights of Turkey. However, since Marta's training in the law was actually accomplished at Istanbul University, she brought an "insider" sensibility to the case that made her perfect to take the lead. She was certain that she could handle the legal issues. What was more troubling was the unease that she felt at stepping foot in that city again. What if she ran into a classmate ... or a family member? Marta had left behind a bevy of sisters devoted to their mother and firmly under the thumb of their tyrant of a father. There were aunts and uncles and who knew how many cousins and by now, probably nieces and nephews; she did not want to deal with them.

She closed her eyes for a moment and then slipped into the bathroom to splash water over her face and wrists. She looked up and was startled to see how much she resembled her mother. The woman was always bent over the stove, constantly stirring, serving, cleaning, and urging her daughters to improve themselves. They had a little sorority, a harem of sorts, although the girls' presence seemed a constant affront to her father's need for a son. They were more like her sisters than her daughters, and Marta knew that Mother cherished the time they spent together.

Marta remembered blue school uniforms and lumpy cotton stockings, garish headscarves, and hand-tatted tablecloths stained here and there with oil and tea. The faces of the girls crowded in, too, Nilgun and Ayşe and Sevgi and Lale, the baby. They remained small in her mind, as young as the last time she saw them. The memory of their faces, distorted by tears, threatened to overwhelm Marta.

The memories of good times mingled with thoughts of the way she'd had to leave. For fifteen years, she had worked hard at constructing barriers to her past, walls that this trip was forcing her to breach. She was still connected to them, to her homeland, to her identity as a Turk, and it was becoming clearer with each passing hour that although she'd found freedom in her New York life, her heart had resumed beating to the rhythms of home. She fingered the locket again, her last connection to Mother.

She shook her head and glanced again at the mirror. Drying her hands, she returned grim-faced to the pile of papers awaiting attention.

Five

The next morning, Vasilli found Marta in the tearoom off the lobby, cell phone at her ear while she scribbled furiously.

"Evet, evet, evet," she repeated her agreement.

"Everything under control?" he asked when she folded the phone shut. She was not surprised to see him sitting across the table. They had formed a curious bond on the plane: the elderly man who would not stop talking, and the young woman afraid to open up her own life to scrutiny. Of course he was here, waiting for her help.

"It was a mess, but I think I've got it on the run," she said. "And how are you today? Rested well, I hope?" Their pleasantries were interrupted by the phone, several times, and the service of food and drink.

Vasilli took paperwork from his voluminous pockets. Before he said anything, Marta sighed heavily, and he pulled away.

"I won't bother you anymore," he murmured. The papers sounded brittle and waxy, and Marta softened.

"I'm sorry. There's just a lot of pressure on me right now," she said.

"About the pasta," he said.

"Yes, about the pasta." She reached for his envelope. The fact was however much she wanted to avoid the old man, Marta was intrigued by Vasilli's tale. In spite of herself, she found herself bored with the dry impersonality of corporate law and the men she had to deal with. Her temper was getting shorter while stockpiles of linguini and rotelli were growing stale sitting offshore in a retrofitted tanker. Vasilli's search was much more interesting.

"Let's take a look." She opened the thick pile of papers. Vasilli had pages of correspondence with the Greek consulate in New York, which cast more shadows and revealed little information about the issue at hand.

"Are we sure that your brother did not change his name, maybe if your mother remarried, yes? But then, if they moved back to Greece during the war ... I really can't tell from this what happened to him," she said. Shuffling through the papers, Marta found no answer in either the documents or the shrugging shoulders of her companion.

"Did they leave Istanbul? Or stay somehow?" She pushed the papers aside and folded her hands. "You must tell me what you know, or at least what you suspect."

"All I know is what happened to me in America," Vasilli began. "There were hundreds of people on the boats and then on that little island where they kept us until the doctors said we could leave. Ellis Island, it was. I guess my name is written there somewhere, along with my father's. He made a friend on the way, a woman whose husband was killed in front of her eyes. I have to say that she never got over that, even after fifty years of living with us, almost like a mother to me. And then her daughter, Effie, she was born on the ship and just passed away last year; she was like my sister. She was my sister. And then she was my wife, too."

"Excuse me?" Marta held up a hand. "You married your sister?"

"No, you're not listening. Don't look at me like that. It was nothing wrong. We grew up together, and when it was time, we married. So? So.

"We never heard from my mother again. We never found them. My father tried. He went back there many times, to Turkey, to Greece, but he never found them."

"Did you ever think about coming back yourself?" Marta asked.

"No, I made my life in New York." Vasilli took a long drink of water. "Shall I continue?"

Marta nodded. "I'm sorry, I don't mean to be rude ... I just wondered why you never came back."

"I could ask the same of you," he said. "So, Father never married again. No, he never would marry Elena. She lived with us. She took care of us, but they never married. Maybe there was just too much sadness in them. They couldn't get past it. And then Effie and I were married. She was just a girl, but we were happy together. We had a good life; we grew up in Paterson, New Jersey. You know it? Then we moved back to Manhattan, close to the coffee shop, back in 1974. But it was just us, no one else. After Father and Elena died, we were alone too, and then it was just me ... until this letter came." He pushed at the papers with a bent, darkly tanned finger.

"You say your father went back, looking for them? When was that?" Marta asked. He shook his head. "Are you sure he did? Was there a passport in his papers? Anything?" Once more, Vasilli shook his head.

"I wonder then how they found you after all these years. I wonder why they even bothered." She folded the papers neatly.

"I tried three times yesterday to reach this 'avukat,' Hidayet Kanti-something-or-other," he complained. "There are hundreds of lawyers listed in the phone book, and the concierge keeps telling me to call his cousin Zeki," he said. "Is that any way to hire a lawyer?"

"Well, it may be just as good as any other," Marta said. "Although I can see your point … but at least his name's not Attila … but maybe it would be a good thing to have a lawyer named Attila, not that it would make him more ruthless than someone named Zeki—"

"What?" he interrupted. The man sounded a little testy. "What are you saying? That I should find a lawyer named Attila?"

Marta had been rambling, she knew, and the old man was confused enough. "No, sorry, never mind," she said. "Didn't you say you had an appointment with the bank today? Why not just go there and hear what they have to say, and then you can decide about a lawyer later on."

"You think?" His voice was small, almost tiny, and Marta realized how frightened the old man must be.

"Why don't you call the U.S. embassy and ask them to recommend someone?" she offered. There was a long pause. *Dammit, here comes the guilt,* she thought. "I'll call them and see if I can get a couple of names for you."

She could hear the relief as he exhaled loudly and thanked her. She made promises then to call back or—better yet, he proposed heartily—join him for dinner later with names and ideas.

Her day passed quickly, the two assistants proving more competent than she'd initially believed. Together, they had sorted through hundreds of faxes and e-mails, convinced the Bombastini president to join a meeting with the Italian trade minister, and arranged payment to delay the shipping company threatening to dump fifty tons of macaroni into the Marmara Sea. Hopped up on too much caffeine and no fresh air, Marta desperately needed to take a break, and so she dismissed the lawyers and went to meet Vasilli.

Each time she stepped out of the hotel, Marta felt she entered a world transformed yet again from when she'd last laid eyes upon it.

"It's different," Vasilli finally said. The little Mercedes cab was jockeyed by its swarthy driver past signs with names that made Marta flinch—Şişli, Topkapi, Eskişehir, Edirne—until she narrowed her focus to the beaded toucan swinging from the rearview mirror.

"Yes, it is different," she agreed. "Where did you say this restaurant is?" she asked the older man, who handed her a piece of hotel stationary with an address scrawled on it. "Near the Hilton, okay." She leaned over the seat and rattled instructions to the driver.

Vasilli looked at her. "So, you remember?" he said.

She frowned. "I remember." The driver veered sharply and crossed over three lanes to an exit, narrowly missing several cars and causing a few more horns to be added to the cacophony around them. A turn and the city lay spread below them, dense red roofs and minarets rising from a brown haze of pollution with spots of green—a straggling tree or burst of flowers from a window box—as they passed acre upon acre of concrete. The meter clicked away as Marta accepted a handful of currency from Vasilli, and the cool allure of the restaurant beckoned.

The building was snuggled in a parklike corner of Taksim, a district whose streets were crowded with airline and travel offices, clothing boutiques, and computer stores. The wide boulevard, divided by a central strip with trees and jaywalkers, thrummed with industry, and, for a moment, Marta allowed a slip of memory—herself, walking arm in arm with classmates, laughter distorting their faces—before she let go of Vasilli's outstretched hands.

Six

Marta leaned back in the thickly cushioned booth. Vasilli was once again more voluble. Throughout the meal, he'd periodically attempted to get her to reveal something about her journey or her life in New York, but he was unsuccessful. She preferred to listen to his rumbling voice.

"Ellis Island, there's nothing like it, nothing. Imagine coming into the harbor, the Statue of Liberty huge against the skyline. We were filthy, stinking, and tired. And some people were sick, and others were dead. It was winter then, I think, at least I remember that it was cold and everyone was wearing piles of clothes and heavy coats. Maybe it was that we wore everything we had, I don't know. The wind was cold, and it tasted like salt. The sky was bright blue, and I can still see it when I close my eyes, that giant sitting in the water like an angel guarding the city.

"I've been back since then, one time. Effie wanted to go when they opened that big museum there, but it isn't the same. I can't tell you how it was, maybe because I was a child and we were so tired, sick and tired and almost dead when we got there. We were like a boatload of garbage, people running from something, people discarded from their homes. But we still had hope, some of us, and it came to me when I saw that statue, that there was hope."

He gripped his hands together like in prayer. Marta waited, and when he continued, it was as if years had been erased from his voice. He spoke with his eyes shut, the deep wrinkles softened as the tale unfolded.

"I was so hungry, always searching for food on the ship. I had a string with a hook on it that I fished with over the side of the boat, all the way across the Atlantic Ocean. They called me the fisherman, although I don't think I ever caught anything besides seaweed. I almost lost the line a couple of times. It got caught on junk or … wait, maybe that was just a bad dream, I don't know. I have this memory of looking over the edge of the boat, pulling hard on the line, but it was caught on something … turned out to be

20

a body, someone who'd been tossed overboard. I'm not sure I actually saw that, now.

"We had very little food on the boat, mostly dried meats and potatoes. That's what I remember. I remember sneaking peeks of Elena feeding Effie, and it made my mouth water to see the milk bubble out of the corners of her mouth."

Vasilli paused, licking his lips.

"The time on the island passed like a nightmare, so much poking and prodding and questions. We didn't speak English, no one did really, so the officers were harsh and it was confusing. My father kept me close to him all the time. I remember being under the flaps of his suit jacket, a heavy green wool that scratched and smelled like tobacco and wet animal. It smelled like the boat. And underneath, there was the smell of my father … what I always recognize as the scent of a man, really: musty and sharp, sweat and smoke and wool. Elena smelled that way too, actually, but there was that sourness about her, probably because of the milk. He sheltered me, and he ended up being her protector as well, stepping in and helping with the baby and talking to the uniforms.

"When we got out of there, it was spring. Father worked cleaning floors in a print shop, and eventually, he learned the trade. His hands were never clean after that, always stained with the ink." He stretched out his own digits, inspecting the knobby fingers capped with neatly trimmed nails.

Part of her, the cynical three-quarters, did not entirely trust Vasilli's story. It seemed almost too much like the PR repeated over and over, the Ellis Island "story" that everyone seemed to want to embrace. Marta, herself an arrival to the U.S. on a Pan Am flight via Frankfurt and then to the UFO-shaped terminal at JFK, was loathe to glamorize the immigrant experience in this way, reluctant to buy into the "huddled masses" mythology that somehow ended up making Americans feel even more smug about their country.

And yet, and yet … the man certainly looked the part. His story rang true, given what she recalled from Turkish history lessons. His bitterness about the fracturing of his family would come out, no doubt, once he allowed those feelings to rise. Marta, whose own exile had an entirely different character, would be curious to see its true expression.

"I spoke with that attorney," she said.

Vasilli looked up from his baklava, surprised. "You did? Oh, thank you so much!"

She put up a hand. "Don't thank me yet," she said. "I don't know exactly what's going on with these people, but they were very hard to pin down on the phone."

"What do you mean?"

"I think they were actually very surprised to hear from you. I don't think they expected anyone to show up in response to the letter. Did you try calling them from New York before you booked the trip?"

Vasilli shrugged. "It costs too much to make international phone calls."

Marta laughed out loud and clapped a hand over her mouth. After a pause, she said, "But you said you were afraid to fly."

"I know, I know," he said. "I should have called instead of paying a thousand dollars to fly halfway around the world." He shrugged again and sipped his water. "I hate using the phone." That made her laugh even more, to the astonishment of both parties.

Seven

Marta did some of her best work at night; she was a great insomniac, who turned her sleeplessness into an attribute. The most sparkling arguments, the most polished briefs flowed from her pen between the hours of midnight and 5:00 AM. Without the distractions of meetings and phone calls, which interfered with completing any actual work, Marta preferred the silence of her office after the staff cleared out. Leaving Vasilli on the tenth floor, Marta returned to her suite and tackled the paper with new energy. She took a few calls from New York, walking around the room and watching the constant traffic of boats on the move.

A pulsing light drew her eye to a spot near the shore, and she watched it for several revolutions before recalling the little island that sat at a bend in the Bosporus. There were as many versions of the legend of the *kız kalesi*—maiden's tower—as there were moustaches in Turkey. A small outcropping in the channel with barely land enough to circumnavigate the tiny lighthouse, it existed to warn approaching boats about the dangerous curves amid the swirling flow to and from the Marmara Sea. For a lawyer interested in international trade, Marta was well-versed in the history of her hometown. Strategically, Turkey and its imperial city of Istanbul—the only metropolis to span two continents—should have remained a superpower, given its control of shipping, where lumbering tankers were escorted to and from the Aegean Sea through the Bosporus, up the Marmara, and again to pass through the narrow channel of the Dardanelles before entering the Black Sea en route to that other empire, Mother Russia. After the fall of the Ottomans, however, the country never regained its place in the world.

If Turkish fathers were to be believed, however, the tiny maiden's tower was apparently constructed for a less benevolent purpose than merely warning of hazardous waters. The most popular version of the story was that once upon a time, a princess was told that her life was destined to end prematurely by a snake's bite. Her father, in the interest of protecting his pre-

23

cious daughter, constructed a tower on this little island, accessible only by boat and visible from his palace on the shore, and he placed his daughter in exile there. Of course, the story did not have a happy ending, as most morality fables do not, and the princess succumbed to a snakebite anyway. Some versions have her stolen away by pirates; others have her drowning in the currents while trying to escape the island.

According to local lore, it was the spirit of the princess that electrified the beacon to protect ships from impending danger. It was a story that continued to be told by fathers trying to caution their daughters about life, affirming their beliefs about the inevitability of death and the lengths to which men would travel to control their women. Marta's father had his own version of the tale, one more grounded in the betrayal of a daughter and his justified exile of her to the little lighthouse.

"See the light?" he'd ask the girls on the rare occasions the entire family was trying to catch a cool breeze in the park. "That's the bad princess sending a signal to her boyfriend to come and rescue her."

"And if he tries?" one of them would invariably ask, hope etched in their little, romantic faces.

"The boat will sink," Father would intone. "The boat will crash or burn and sink."

After their gasps, he continued, "The water around there is so dangerous because it is filled with shipwrecks. No boat can get close to the island now." He would pause for dramatic effect then and continue, "Every time a daughter disobeys her father, another boat sinks in the Bosporus."

Marta watched the light revolve, its reflection cast long on the water, illuminating various vessels and buildings, awake as she was late that night. What an ogre her father had been, so remote and threatening to his innocent daughters. How he had abused the good woman who was his wife. Marta shivered, thinking about the negativity that he exuded, the fear he had sown into their brains. It was the primitive way to simultaneously worship and revile women. No wonder Marta had rebelled against all things feminine and kept away from identifying with her country.

Marta sighed and turned back to the mountains of paper on the conference table. She'd eventually have to go to Ankara, it was becoming clear, to deal with the government officials there. Her goal to make this a quick trip was not going to be achieved, she knew, and the case was becoming more difficult than she'd expected. And then there was the puzzle of Vasilli.

Both of them were a little frazzled when they met over coffee the next day. Vasilli, acting on Marta's suggestion, had been given quite the runaround by the bank people and arrived at the hotel looking haggard and pale. He handed over yet another sheaf of papers and the business card of an attorney she recognized immediately. He saw that too and pushed for her help with his cause.

"You know this man, yes?" he'd asked. "Please, can you speak with him, just one phone call? I will go home then, I tell you. I will not fight these people, but I want to just find out what happened to my family."

His eyes seeped, blurry with cataracts and red-rimmed, and she picked up the phone to call her old professor. She left the hotel number and a message and then persuaded Vasilli to get some fresh air by the pool. She imagined the reaction to her call and wondered if the professor remembered her name.

Sami-bey, they'd called him, a young firebrand just a decade older than his students, but with a reputation far exceeding his years. He'd been imprisoned briefly and then for a longer period after the last coup but still managed to land on his feet. Marta was surprised that he had a private practice, but the years had probably mellowed his fervor for rabble-rousing and most probably, he had succumbed to economic realities.

It was not clear from his card whether he was still with the university, but the more she thought about it, the more certain Marta was that he would recall their friendship. She smiled, thinking about the sharpness and mental dexterity of her one-time mentor. Sami-bey—the attached "bey" was an honorific to show respect for an elder—had been one of the few people, male or female, who'd treated her as an equal, rather than just as another girl trying to score a law student for a husband. Despite their protestations to the contrary, there had still been a double standard in Turkey when Marta was in college. Sure, some of the professors were women, and there were many female physicians and scientists. But that was more because of a shortage of men after World War I and the war of independence that followed than from any true egalitarianism in the Turkish character.

Sami would be in his fifties now, and she wondered if time had been kind to the scrappy little man. He'd married and had a small child in the months before Marta left town. And he knew, and disapproved, of her relationship with Mehmet, that disastrous love affair that changed her life in so many ways. She suspected that he knew why she'd left Istanbul so quickly and quietly after graduation.

"What will you do?" he'd asked. Cornered while packing her satchel for the last time, Marta told him that she'd turned down all the job offers. He repeated the question, crossing his arms and leaning against the metal lockers.

"What do you recommend?" she'd countered, trying to deflect his questions, not meeting his probing brown eyes.

"Perhaps you should leave town," he mused then, startling her with his insight. "A fresh start might be just the thing—although you'd do well here. You know …" He stopped suddenly and grabbed her hand, an uncharacteristic move on his part. "The first year is all work anyway. You have no life of your own. You'll be buried in a library somewhere.

"Unless it is too late," he concluded, dropping her hand.

And now, thinking back on it, she was sure that he knew. She'd turned away from him then, not meeting his eyes, and when she looked back, he was gone.

Now, if it were to happen today, she'd stay, she was certain. Times were different, and although Marta appreciated that the pressures on young people had not much changed—and although she had the benefit of experience behind her certainty that she would be able to manage—she knew that she would not repeat the same mistakes. The pregnancy, her sudden exile to a small village where she gave birth to a child and handed the baby over to be raised by her barren aunt—all of it, she would have fought if she were not so afraid of her father. Her hand absently caressed the locket which enclosed the only thing she had kept from that time, a lock of her daughter's silken hair.

Marta paused before the window of her room to look out at the ferry traffic and the little white lighthouse. She sighed, turning away from the Bosporus to answer the phone and resume work on the case. Sami, whether he knew her secrets or not, should be pleasantly surprised to see his protégé in such a good position. The fact that he was representing the other side in Vasilli's case mattered less than, perhaps, it should have. But Marta would figure that out when she saw him.

Eight

Vasilli joined her for dinner. This time, they chose not to leave the hotel but rather convened in Marta's room over two plates of lamb, potatoes, and stewed vegetables. The bland hotel fare did not even attempt to capture the essence of the Turkish cuisine. They could have been in any hotel in London or Rome, if not for the view from the picture windows.

"Did that attorney call you back?" Vasilli asked.

"No, not yet," Marta replied.

"Harrumph."

They continued to eat in silence.

"How's your case going?" Vasilli finally asked.

"Fine. We're no longer on the verge of World War III. And I mean that literally. The Americans were getting ready to park a couple of aircraft carriers in the shipping lanes. I'm fed up with these 'diplomatic' types. And the Turks, all they think about is money and how they're getting screwed and how I'm the evil lawyer who is going to screw them even more. Let's talk about something else, shall we?" Marta grumbled.

"Tell me something about your family." In response, she leaned back in her seat and scowled at him. "Okay, never mind. Tell me about your life in New York," he prompted. "I told you about how I came to live in America. Tell me your story."

"Okay, you want the sorry tale of my introduction to New York? When I first arrived, I stayed in a rooming house near Forty-second Street. It was horrific—noise, bugs, rats, shootings outside—and this guy at the reception desk told me he knew a place for rent, that he'd help me get a decent place. But he wouldn't take me there without something in return. That was the first time I had to make that trade. It got easier. Does that shock you?"

Although he squirmed in his chair, Vasilli shook his head. "Is that what you are trying to do? To make me uncomfortable?" He coughed. "Go on. Tell me your story. The real story. I want to hear that."

27

Marta gazed at him for a moment, considering his request, before she spoke again. Her voice became low and choppy, as if she were reading a story about someone else's life. In a way, she was. Marta felt herself disengage from the memories she revealed until they felt like a movie she'd watched once, long ago, or a play on an off-Broadway stage. She could see the scene in her mind as she described it to Vasilli: the room she rented from a couple of sisters living in an enormous ground-floor apartment on Morningside Drive, next to what was probably one of the most dangerous parks in the city at that time, the two elderly sisters.

Marta lived with them for three years, in a small back bedroom that looked out on an air shaft. The apartment had five bedrooms, three bathrooms, two sitting rooms, a formal dining room, and a library that was darkly paneled and filled with leather-bound classics it would take a lifetime to read. Marta spent hours in that room, reading and studying, while other borders came and went without making an impression on the reclusive law student.

The sisters had two rules—no visitors of the opposite sex and no smoking. A list was posted in the kitchen of all the little things that "reasonable people" were supposed to respect, like washing out the tub, cleaning your own dishes, wiping down the countertop, never leaving an empty toilet paper roll, or putting unwrapped "female things" in the trash. The only thing the sisters asked was for the roomers to join them for tea every Sunday afternoon in the front parlor. Mostly, Marta was the only one who would sit with them. They served little English Pym biscuits, and they'd use the real tea set, with china cups and silver tongs for the sugar cubes.

Marta paid almost nothing to rent that room, which was ideal since she had nothing to spare. She ate salad picked up from a corner deli, cramming half of it in her mouth before going to the scales at the checkout counter. Once a week, she might have a burger, just to get some protein. In the beginning, Marta worked at the library, shelving books and answering questions, working on her English by listening to tapes and eavesdropping. When she got her degree and first job, Marta stayed on with the sisters for a while as she saved up some money to get a nice place. They were starting to fail, starting to depend on her too much, so she realized it was time to move on. They eventually had to have nurses living in, taking care of them.

"The last time I heard from them ..." Marta paused. "I'm not sure. I think I did see an obit just a little while ago. They both lived to be in their nineties. I wish ... No, not that I'd kept in touch. I couldn't help them, and they encouraged me to go out on my own." She sighed. "I just wish I knew what happened to all those books."

Nine

Marta was noted for her ruthless pursuit of a deal. She had climbed to the top of her class, became a partner at a very young age, and yet still felt the need to set herself apart from the other lawyers in the firm. They had families, golf, vacations—a life outside the office. She did not, by design. Even after all the years, the successes, the income she'd generated, Marta knew that the partners did not have total confidence in her ability to manage a case of this magnitude. She was being watched; she knew it, and she deeply resented it. And she was angry at herself because she actually cared more about Vasilli's case than her pasta dispute.

The *makarna* machinations—with faxes and e-mails flying between New York, Rome, Istanbul, and Ankara—were becoming more complicated with each passing hour. Time did not stop as the sun traveled around the globe and awakened new players in the controversy. In another uncharacteristic moment of whimsy, Marta thought about the Turkish taffy pulls from her childhood. As she watched the men's mouths work, she could almost taste the sweetness of caramel.

A taffy pull was one of thousands of food-related rituals that punctuated Turkish family life—a steaming caldron of syrup with a huge wooden paddle used to stir the caramel-colored treat. The heat infused the room with sweetness as rosy-cheeked girls pulled ropes of thick candy between hands covered in white cotton gloves that soon become waxen and stiff. Sweat flowed over cheeks distended by large bulbs of candy bulging there, candy that slowly melted and was washed down with periodic swigs of hot tea.

The voices droned in her ears, an endless conference call that was spiraling into a diplomatic morass. With each day that she spent in Istanbul, Marta found it harder to concentrate. She could not resist letting her mind drift back to scenes from her childhood, regardless of the setting. She tried to pay attention to the matter at hand, but it was as if a switch had been activated when she stepped out of the airport and she no longer controlled her own thoughts. She was in sensory overload, finding it impossible to focus.

And then there was Vasilli. While the Italian representative pontificated about poundage and packaging, Marta flipped through the notes she had taken at the notary public office earlier in the day. Not merely the sideline of a bank or public official, the power to notarize documents in Turkey came with a full-blown bureaucracy that required the establishment of offices with secretaries in smoke-filled second-story suites bereft of air-conditioning and, from all appearances, vacuum-cleaning services.

His passport was not sufficient proof of Vasilli's existence, apparently, and certainly not sufficient evidence that he was firstly, born in the Turkish republic and secondly, a relative of the person whose estate he was determined to settle.

"Just because it says on your passport that you were born here, doesn't mean that you were born here," argued a short, red-haired woman. She puffed on a cigarette so foul-smelling that Marta was uncertain if she could restrain herself from leaping across the desk to extinguish the butt tipped precariously atop an overflowing orange plastic ashtray.

Marta translated the problem to Vasilli. "So, how does one get a birth certificate?" she asked the woman with what she considered more patience than was warranted. With Vasilli by her side, Marta was compelled by some unseen force—stronger than gravity or even her own pounding headache—to behave nicely and politely ask questions that normally would have sent her into a tirade. "As you may notice, Mr. Vassilios is quite elderly and finding a birth certificate for a person who is older than this republic may be impossible. What would you suggest that we do about that?"

The woman tapped one hand on her keyboard while the other engaged in extracting yet another cigarette from her red-and-white pack of Samsuns. The influx of Marlboro Man advertising was so precisely geared to the Turkish macho sensibility it was a wonder they had any health warnings attached to smoking them at all, and yet here was a relatively young woman smoking the filterless brand of her father's generation. Perhaps the resurgence of nationalism had also manifested itself in the revival of Samsuns, along with the rejection of Coca-Cola and Lipton tea. She smiled, waiting for the woman's response, wondering if kids still believed the oft-repeated theory that Samsuns got their smell from camel dung.

"You'll have to speak with city hall," the clerk said eventually. "I can't help you."

Vasilli, whose hand-wringing had set Marta's nerves to tingle, let loose a string of invectives against Turks that threatened to excavate centuries of animosity.

Propelled by Marta out the door and to a bench under the shade of a freshly leafed tree, Vasilli gestured to a young Gypsy boy balancing a tray of pretzels on a filthy cloth donut atop his head. *"Yavrum,"* he called. He chuckled when Marta smiled.

"I haven't heard that in years." The label, used to call a boy or servant, was one of her father's most common putdowns of her classmates.

"I haven't said it in years," he agreed. Once established that the proffered fare was fresh, a round, sesame-studded bread stick was purchased and torn apart. The chewing had a calming effect on them that was usually only experienced by horses, cows, and recalcitrant babies gumming a zwieback toast.

"So?" he finally asked, weariness etched in his voice as well as his face.

"Where were you born, do you know actually?" Marta asked. She recalled that since Istanbul was divided into small districts, it might be easier to trace documents in one of the borough offices than the large morass of the main government facility.

"Buyuk Ada, the big island, we used to be there." Vasilli was thoughtful. "It was so long ago, all of it. Maybe I should just let it go. What do you think? I have my memories. I don't need any more."

Marta wiped her hands and pulled Vasilli to his feet. "I'm at an impasse with my case right now," she said. "Everyone needs to consult with their people so we're taking a break. Tomorrow's a perfect day to take a boat ride. We'll give it a shot, and if that's a dead end too, well, then you can feel like you really tried." They began walking back to the hotel. "And I still have to meet with the lawyers, so let's see what they've got to say."

An enormous green DeSoto lumbered to the curb, idling next to the taxi queue in front of the Conrad. "Look, a *dolmuş!*" Marta cried out. "I knew there was something missing."

"Isn't that a food, *dolmuş?* Some kind of stuffed cabbage or peppers?" Vasilli stopped to inspect the car. "Hmmm, no rust at all. How do they keep these things on the road?"

"The name comes from the dish, you're right. They called them stuffed because they would fit as many as ten people in one cab—look, here's the destination on the dashboard. So everyone going to that place would pile in, and when it was full, they'd split the fare. Much cheaper than everyone taking separate cabs." Marta sighed. "It's this kind of thing that I miss, the fact that you could have cars from the fifties, stretched out Fords and Chevys, taking you down to the ferries, and that short little subway that just has two stations and is only about five hundred meters long. I bet that it's still there. Quirky stuff, things that make so much sense, you have to wonder why no one else does them. Can you imagine these in New York?" They both laughed, the day's tension gone.

"I wonder if they still forbid cars on the island," Vasilli said. "Or if that's all changed too."

"We'll see," Marta said. She returned to her meeting, piping up during a lull in the conversation and once again getting the parties back on a track toward settlement.

Ten

Turks don't really eat much *makarna*, a rich pasta served with crumpled feta cheese and drizzled olive oil, except occasionally as a side dish. Their preference is rice, mostly plain white with the occasional currant or green pea thrown in for variety. A new bride, cooking her first dinner for the in-laws, is tested primarily on the quality of her rice. Is it clumped together unattractively? Heaven forbid a burned or watery presentation—the bride's failure is cause for immediate and justifiable intervention by the mother-in-law, with a correlating lowered status for the mother who trained her. After hours of negotiating linguini tonnage and angel-hair allowances, Marta eagerly tucked into her midnight room service delivery of pilaf and *patligan*—fried eggplant with ground beef and tomatoes, served with a snowball of rice.

The phone rang. "Yes," she answered, swallowing quickly.

"Ah, it is you. I wasn't sure, but I recognize the voice."

"Sami-bey?" A piece of rice caught in her throat, and she choked up a bit. "Excuse me." Covering the phone, she coughed and gulped at some water.

"Is this a bad time to call? I remember that you were always a night bird," Sami said. "I don't want to interrupt … let me call you tomorrow."

"Wait, wait, it's okay," she assured him. "I was just eating some dinner and you caught me with a mouthful."

"So, it seems we have some reason to meet again, after so many years. Let's take care of the business quickly, shall we, and then we can catch out with each other."

"Catch up with each other, yes." There was a silence, and Marta recalled how sensitive Sami was about his English skills, his use of the best "slang" expressions, and how proud he was to be cool in two languages. "Sorry. When can we plan a meeting to go over these Vassilios papers? The old man is having a hard time of it, and I'd like to get this squared away as soon as we can." More silence. "Do you have time tomorrow—oh, no, we're going

33

to Buyuk Ada tomorrow. How about the day after tomorrow? I can come
to your office, or you can meet me here if that's convenient." More silence.
"Hello?"

"Yes, I'm here." They settled on the date and time to meet, quickly, and
then there was another long silence.

Marta looked eagerly at her rapidly chilling dinner. "Well, if there's
nothing else, I'll see you then," she said.

"So, tell me, for what is it that you and the old man are visiting Buyuk
Ada? To see the cemetery perhaps? Or look at some property? We'll get
his problem squared off without you taking such a long trip." Sami's over-
inflection of "squared off" caused Marta to sit up a bit straighter in her
chair. "And maybe we should take some time to reunion with each other
first, eh?"

"Name the time," Marta answered. "I'll be in Istanbul for a few more
days." She could hear him flipping pages and scratching something, perhaps
a beard.

"I happen to be just on the corner to your hotel, which I understand
has an excellent lounge at the roof. Have you seen it? The view, they say, is
magnificent. All of Beşiktaş at your feet."

"And the Bosporus, of course," she added.

"Of course."

"I'll see you there in thirty minutes," she said. "And it's owl. Night owl,"
she added quietly before listening to the dial tone.

The conversation had been much more adversarial, with greater animosity than might have been a natural response to Marta's cliché correc-
tions. Sami had taken pains to mention the hotel's view of Beşiktaş, the
slum district that Marta had so scrupulously been avoiding since her arrival
in town, her former home and perhaps the place where her family still re-
sided. She was tense as she headed to the lounge.

Eleven

It was not a warm night, not cold either, but the same breeze that propelled a stream of diaphanous clouds across the brilliant moon also chilled any potential customers to the deserted outdoor patio where Marta first sat, huddled in her thin cashmere sweater. At close to midnight, only a few men clad in business attire sat sullenly around the bar, gazing at the view outside, or perhaps studying their own reflections in the doors and windows.

A glass of whiskey helped, although the chink of ice against the rim set Marta's nerves on edge. Half an hour passed this way, the warmth of the drink burning a trail to her belly that, in a few minutes, spread to her arms and legs. Nose dripping with cold, she finally moved inside, resisting the impulse to check her watch. The cell phone chirped at her hip, causing annoyed glances from the murmuring males around her.

"*Evet,*" she answered. "Yes?" Impatient at the interruption, she did not check the caller ID.

It was Carol, Marta's secretary in New York. "What? What did you say?" Carol sighed. "Don't tell me you've learned Turkish already," she said. "God, I wish I could learn just one language, and here you—"

"Carol, give it up." Marta interrupted the recitation of resentful respect that characterized Carol's feelings toward her boss. "I already knew Turkish." Silence. The revelation would not change Carol's report to her co-conspirators, the league of unfulfilled and underappreciated secretaries who met daily to share their observations in the lunchroom and by the copy machines. "So, what's happening there? Carol?"

"Um, yeah, Joshua wanted me to tell you that the client called to complain. About you. That's what he said."

"Dammit, that—okay, never mind. You tell Josh—and that's Mr. Barton to you, by the way—you just tell him that if he has a message for me, he should call me himself. And you tell him that I said everything is under

35

control. No, I'll tell him myself. No, you tell him that I'm ready to settle this thing, so he should just, ack …"

"What?" Carol was eager to be the go-between in this office feud. "What else should I tell him?"

"Oh, that's all, I guess. Just tell him you gave me the message and that I said everything is under control." Marta smiled. "Everything is just fine here."

"Uh-huh." Carol waited. "Anything else?"

"Tell him I'll be taking some vacation time as soon as I wrap up this case," Marta said. "Tell him I'll be back in New York when I'm damned good and ready and he can just cover my cases until I let him know otherwise."

"Are you sure? I mean, you're taking a *vacation*?" Carol said it like the word itself was contagious. "And you want Joshua … er, Mr. Barton to cover your cases? You know he'll steal your clients. You know that, right?"

"Carol." Marta laughed. "Don't worry so much. Everything is fine, really. I'm just going to take a little vacation."

She hung up the call, cutting off Carol's "Ah-ha" and speculation that Marta had found a handsome young man and was off on another hormone romp.

From behind her, a low rumble of laughter froze Marta's smile in place. She turned to see Sami slumped in a low chair next to the window, swirling a cloudy concoction of raki and water.

"I thought you weren't coming," she said, slipping into a kilim-upholstered companion to his chair. She raised her glass, one sliver of amber fluid caressing the diminishing ice cubes. "Cheers," she offered the glass to him, and he tipped the bottom of his own in her direction, nodding. His hooded eyes searched her face openly, while she studied the changes in him over the rim of her own glass.

Sami had never been an attractive man, and the years had not been kind. He had been a young, charismatic teacher, with a youthful exuberance that drew students and other professors into his sphere. Perhaps they had glamorized him, made him larger than life. Marta hardly recognized him. His physical appearance was almost a shock to her memories. He was short and thick around the middle, with only wisps of salt-and-pepper hair flying around a frog-like face, flat nosed with eyes bulging, the thin lips barely covering his snaggletoothed smile.

"Marta, you have grown to be a beauty," he said. "But wait, how many years has it been? Fifteen, twenty? You must be close to forty years old, but you barely look a day over twenty-five. I think you have hardly changed at all since I last saw you." His mouth smiled but his dark eyes remained cold.

"It's been quite a while," she agreed. "You're looking well." She raised her glass to signal the bartender.

"Oh, won't you join me in a little raki?" he asked, draining his glass. "I hate to drink alone." He put up one hand to silence her protest. "And whiskey does not mix well with the lion's milk."

He raised two fingers to the barman, who nodded and reached for another glass. *"Yavrum,"* Sami raised his hand again. *"Yavrum,* bring the bottle here."

Marta had not tasted the anise-flavored liquor favored by Turks since she left the country. A bit of water added to the glass transformed the crystal clear, ninety-plus proof booze into the so-called "lion's milk" that had ruined many a liver, including that of the republic's founder, Atatürk. She'd tasted it only once or twice in college, never at home, never to a good result—and never since.

"Şerife." They touched glasses again and sipped—more warmth, the familiar taste—followed by an obligatory sip of plain water. Cups of dried chickpeas and pistachios appeared on the elaborately carved table between them, more of the ritual associated with raki. Marta recalled the many customs associated with the drink, for example, how you must match your companion's pace because neither glass could be refilled before the other was also depleted. Sami's call for the bottle indicated either that he had a serious drinking problem or that he intended to challenge Marta to a gut-burning match of wits.

Sami busied himself with rolling papers and a small pouch of loose tobacco. His flesh strained against a tattersall shirt, a hand-knitted vest gaping open over his belly. Green woolen slacks matched a glen-plaid jacket whose leather elbow patches were only a shadow above the frayed sleeves. An expensive-looking Rolex peeked incongruously from one arm, but Marta wondered if it was the real thing or a knock-off sold at bargain prices in the Grand Bazaar downtown. There were no rings on his thickened hands, the heavy yellow nails attesting to his continued smoking and poor eating habits.

Sami brushed his thin hair behind one ear and leaned over the table to light his thin cigarette. Marta thought she saw a gold earring and noted his patchy beard flashing silver in the glow of the match. "Excuse me, did you want a cigarette? Sorry, I assumed you do not smoke." He shrugged as she waved away his offer.

"There are many things that you do not know about me, Professor," Marta said slowly. "You should be careful about your assumptions."

"Point taken." He nodded. "And may I say the same for you."

She nodded. Through the mix of smoke, they eyed one another. The hum of conversation mingled with low music and the clash of glass behind the bar.

"So, you've come all the way from New York to help this old man with his family business, eh? Must be a lot of money he is paying you to return here after so many years," Sami said, raising his glass again.

Marta was not biting. "I'm here on an international trade dispute."

His raised eyebrows were her only response.

"That's what I do, international trade. And usually, I am in New York, sometimes in Geneva or The Hague, London, you know, the European market." Marta grabbed her drink and held the cold fire in her mouth a few seconds before swallowing. *Shut up! Let him do the talking,* she admonished herself. He raised his glass again, and she took another small sip before reaching for the water glass.

"So you must be some kind of big-wing lawyer now, eh?" he asked.

"Bigwig, yes, that's me." Marta smiled.

"Big-*whig*." He blew out the "w" and grunted. "Or maybe big shot, how's that? Is that correct?"

She nodded, a flush of heat rising from her chest. A handful of leb-lebi cracked uncomfortably against her teeth as she recalled the alcohol-soaking properties of the dried chickpeas. "Yes, that's me all right," she tried to lighten the tone. "Just another big shot from New York, sorting out a fight over *makarna* exportation."

"*Makarna?*" Sami smiled. "Really? Fascinating." He did not seem to believe that was her true purpose in Istanbul.

"Yes," she repeated. "I'm here working on a trade case."

"And the old man?" he asked, eyebrows raised as he tipped the half-full bottle to her glass. "Is he part of the *makarna* case, too?"

Marta shrugged and reached for another handful of peas. "I thought we were just going to catch up with things tonight and talk business on Friday," she said. "So, tell me, are you still teaching at the university?"

He gazed at her a moment and then smiled. "Yes, I teach a course or two, but I am mostly doing the private practicing now. Things changed at the universities after you left, you know, and it was not so much a nice place to be for a while."

"And now?"

"Now it's like everything else here, all about money. Not the Turkish way. Just talk about money."

Marta almost laughed out loud. It was a common complaint, one that she remembered from her youth, that all everyone cared about was money. And in fact, it was true—and always had been—that the major topic of discussion among everyone, all the time, was money and the state of the economy. "More problems with the Greeks?" she asked.

"Ahk, these Europeans, they allow these lousy Eastern Europeans, these Serbs and Romanians, they can be in the European community—sure! Welcome!" He waved his arms around, resembling more and more the animated firebrand she remembered from college. "But the Turks, oh no, we don't want them to join our club—not those lousy Turks, they have no human rights. But the Serbs, that's okay, right?" He took a long pull from the raki and shook his head. "Don't get me started, okay?" He filled the water glasses and held up the empty pitcher until the waitress came over to take it from him.

"Kids, husband, have you got them yet?" he asked Marta, looking at her unadorned hands. "No rings, but that doesn't matter these days, does it? You're all liberated now, right?"

"I always was," she answered.

"So you say." He crimped up another cigarette and then settled the uneven bundle on his lip. The high flame of his lighter barely missed the errant hairs of his eyebrows, encouraged to bushiness by the legacy of Atatürk's mesmerizing eyes.

"And you, are you married?"

"Nah, once was enough for me. My kids are practically grown up now too, teenagers. We're all liberated." Sami smirked. "Have you visited your family yet, or have you been too busy?"

Marta pursed her lips and thought about how to respond to his provocation. *My family,* she thought. *Not a word in fifteen years, sure, she'd just drop in and say hi.* "I'm not in touch with my family any longer," she said.

"Ahh, yes," he said. "I was hoping you'd gotten past all that. I remember asking your sister about you once. What was her name now? Let me think …"

"You had one of my sisters in class?" Marta asked woodenly. She drained her glass, not looking at the older man. A smile played around his lips as he looked over her shoulder, pretending to study the view below.

Marta took a deep breath to quiet the buzzing in her ears. So Sami wanted to tease her, to play games about the past. She was not going to let him torment her. She opened her wallet and leaned over to place some bills on the table, ignoring his attempt to brush away her money.

"Good night, Sami-bey," she said. "It was nice to see you."

"Marta, you don't want to hear about your sister? About your parents?" he called after her. She did not turn around.

Twelve

The interesting thing about raki was that it did not leave a hangover, no headache or upset stomach, nothing to cue the drinker about the havoc it played on the liver. Its drinkers saw things more clearly, they liked to proclaim; they found the truth about life in brains clarified by the pure alcohol. Many Turks, already predisposed to pontification, became erudite philosophers under the influence of their native drink. Marta found neither the clarity nor the inspiration, but once she put aside her anger at Sami's manipulations, she settled in to do some research. She found the best source was the archives of several prominent Turkish newspapers. For the past dozen or so years, nothing appeared to have been written about Sami.

"Hmmm," she mused, pouring steadily from a thermos of tea. "Not much of a big shot any longer, are you?"

In 1988, just three years after her departure, there was but one article. And although short, it was indeed sweet enough to explain his reticence. It seemed that Sami's beloved wife, Seyyan, had run off with a prominent minister in the new conservative government. Sami had been jailed briefly for threatening and then released after promising to stay away from Seyyan and their children. If it hadn't been for his past imprisonment, no doubt the newspapers too would have overlooked the little domestic drama. But the final paragraph caught her eye—Professor Erdem had been removed from the university and his tenure revoked. Unless something had changed in the intervening years, Sami was no longer welcome on the university grounds. The knowledge brought a smile to Marta's lips. She wasn't ashamed of her cold heart, just the opposite—having information about someone's downfall or bad fortune that could benefit her client always made her smile. This time, since Sami had tried to use his knowledge—or implied knowledge—about her family, the smile was even sweeter.

Marta turned off the computer before temptation allowed her to type in her own family name on the search site. She'd had quite enough of the past. The sun was rising in the east, and the timer was still ticking on her pasta potboiler.

A flurry of early morning phone calls almost made her late to meet Vasilli in the lobby. She practically ran off the elevator, intent on the line of taxicabs outside the gleaming windows of the hotel, when she was stopped by the sight of the old man in the center of the lobby hectoring a shoeshine boy.

Vasilli smiled at her, lifting a finger for emphasis, and—mispronouncing every word yet with a very earnest inflection that made it almost endearing—exhorted the brown-faced urchin, "*Yavrum, haydi,* hurry up now, *haydi, haydi.*" The young boy, dark skin tinted by polish and dirt and Gypsy genes, squatted barefooted next to his elaborate brass stand. The ornately carved and gleaming box, equipped with all manner of polishes and brushes, sported a footrest and inlaid pictures of Atatürk on each side.

The old man's black lace-up gleamed under the ministrations of his buffer, who then administered a fast shimmy with a filthy rag, its edges stiff with wax. Although he looked no older than six, Marta knew he was probably a teenager, his development stunted by years of hard labor and malnutrition. These street boys polished shoes, sold filthy water in reused plastic cups, sat huddled over bathroom scales available for a quick weigh-in at one lira, and offered for sale an array of black plastic combs, three for the price of one.

Many roamed the streets of Istanbul, eking a living on the pedestrian bridges and staying one step ahead of gangs, the law, and death. They competed for the best begging spots with one-legged veterans displaying their stumps and scars, old women selling fortunes, blind men whose empty eye sockets haunted the dreams of sensitive little girls, and scantily dressed hookers offering comfort in a hurry. Better the shoeshine boy should earn his dollar the honest way, Marta thought as Vasilli began to haggle over the price.

Marta watched the older man trying to understand the foreign currency as well as the boy's insistent Turkish. Pulling a couple of bills from her pocket, Marta tipped the child as he backed away from the old man, staggering a little under the weight of his brass box.

Vasilli stood, admiring the shine of his shoes, and smoothed his gray wool jacket. His hand calmed any potential errant hairs on his freckled scalp; he practically clicked his heels together before speaking. "Thank you for waiting," he said.

She took his arm, hiding her smile. In New York—in fact, in any other city in the world—the tough attorney Marta Demir would never have allowed a client the opportunity to get this close.

When they arrived at the pier, a sparkling new catamaran gleamed in the morning sun, looming over the ancient and dented ferries also destined for day trips to the Prince Islands. "The fast boats get there in less than half the time." She tried to persuade the old man to take the new boat.

"Yes, but at more than twice the cost," he shot back. Marta silently moved ahead in the ticket queue, secretly happy to be taking the old boat but not willing to cede the point to her companion.

High-speed hydrofoils rocked the slower boats that still ferried thousands to work and back each day. Ferries named *Tuzla* and *Suadiye* were smoke-billowing vessels that raced across the narrow band of water and careened toward rickety piers only to cut and slide smoothly into place. Men waiting on the pier threw thigh-thick ropes alongside patrons who leapt from the ship and scurried toward the street amid vendors selling corn on the cob, pretzels, and freshly caught fish. These things had not changed. Many people before and since Marta's youth had found love and boredom and companionship on the waves, pressed together during rush hours and bobbing amidst the porpoises for a stolen day trip to one of the small towns along the shore. A typical day trip included a visit to one of the islands, places that still forbade cars and where most of the property—well hidden behind high stucco walls and thick hedges—was owned by the remaining Jewish and Greek families as well as some rich young Turks.

The day was perfect with a crisp spring breeze and a warm sun in a cloudless sky. How many times had Marta stood in this same line, checking the humidity and thinking about what the wind would do to her untethered hair? How many anxious moments had she spent watching the clock, sitting nervously on the deck, waiting for friends who, laughing, shouting, and waving their arms, jumped at the last possible moment onto the departing ferry? Marta waited to pay for the tickets, lost in her memories, while Vasilli wandered off to purchase fresh plums and a couple of *simit* from another brown-faced boy balancing a large round tray of the pretzels on his head.

Thirteen

After the seventh call, Marta turned her cell phone to "silent," tossing it impatiently to the bottom of her bag. Tying a scarf loosely around her hair, she closed her eyes to the soft sea breezes of the Marmara Sea and listened to the chatter of young families making the trip to the islands. Picnic baskets, the smell of suntan lotion and cigarettes mixed with the occasional plume from the belching smokestacks, and the happy vibration of the engine transported passengers and memories.

"You are happy today, I see," Vasilli interrupted Marta's reverie.

"Yes, I guess so," she agreed, opening her eyes under the shade of her hand. "How about you? How are you doing?" He shrugged and looked away. "What is it?"

"I don't know. I don't know what I'm doing here." He pretended to study something far on the horizon.

"What does that mean, exactly?" Marta asked. He shrugged but didn't reply. "Well, suit yourself then," she said. She leaned back in the wooden chair and turned her face up to the sun, eyes closed again. She felt the old man rise slowly and walk to the side of the ferry. He might want sympathy, or something, but he'd picked the wrong woman for that kind of dance. Marta knew he'd be back, ready to spill whatever was festering in his gut, but she was not going to beg him to share his "feelings" with her.

The boat slowed and then turned, making the first of its few stops along the coastline. Marta listened to the clatter of footsteps, the ringing buoys, the shouts of the men readying the boat for docking. Her eyes fluttered open, taking in the march of villas up the steep slope of the village and the old and new roads, little more than donkey paths cutting passage through the hillside.

A vendor selling orange soda and lukewarm tea jostled Marta's arm, and she scowled at him. An older woman sitting across from her smiled and continued her knitting. "*Yavrum,* watch the fancy lady," she warned the boy, pointing her knitting needles at Marta.

Nodding to show her comprehension, Marta acknowledged the woman. Too late, she realized that she'd opened the door for conversation.

"So, you are Turkish," the woman said. "I wasn't sure. You don't live here. I am right, no? So, you're here on a visit then. Going to see some relatives, eh?"

Marta just nodded lazily. The woman was content to spin her yarn without much more than a look of acknowledgement.

"You must be in New York," she continued. "The shoes are the give-away. The best shoes are in Italia, you know. New York has fashion shoes, but if you check the bottoms, you can see that they don't hold up on city sidewalks. You can tell everything about a person by checking their shoes," she said. Her knitting never faltered. "My niece is at New York University. Maybe you know her? Ayşe Özden?"

Marta shook her head. She was just about to make a comment about how everyone expected everyone to know everyone in New York City, when she observed Vasilli leaning precariously over the side of the vessel. "Pardon." She smiled at the woman as she rushed to his side.

"What's the matter? Are you seasick?" she asked him. He lifted a face gray with fatigue and shook his head.

"No, I'm fine, just tired."

Marta pulled him away from the edge. "What were you looking at? For a minute there, I thought you were going to jump." She forced a jovial tone and laughed uncomfortably.

He sagged then, leaning heavily against the high metal sides of the ferry. Shaking his head, he said, "I feel like I am starting to remember things, but I'm not sure that I want to. I'm not sure why I came back here."

"Well, join the club," Marta turned to look over at a large Russian freighter passing silently through the channel. "I don't want to be here either, and I definitely don't want to remember what I left behind. But here we are, so let's try to make the best of it."

He snorted and turned to lean over the side of the boat again. After a few minutes, out of the shadow of the freighter, he spoke again. "I have a hard time being on the water," he said. "You get mesmerized by the immensity of it. On the ocean, far away from any land, it seems like the world has gone away completely."

"Not necessarily a bad thing," Marta commented. He ignored her interruption.

"For a young boy, leaving the side of his mother, it was the worst thing … the distance that grew with every passing mile, the feeling that there was no way to go back."

Marta nodded as Vasilli closed his eyes and breathed deeply. She waited for him to speak, but he did a few little stretching moves and turned a forced smile toward her. "Do you think they sell lemon soda … What do they call it? *Gazoz?*" he asked. His eyes focused over her shoulder. "Do you want some?"

"They won't have it," Marta said. "They probably don't even make it anymore."

He was not listening but was already poking through the vendor's cooler. Some raised voices captured her attention—a group of college-age students huddled inside the ferry, boys perched on the back of the wooden seats, puffing mightily on cigarettes and squinting through the smoke as they flung hair, hands, and words around the group. Next to their energy, the females seemed almost invisible, silent and somber-faced. Three of the four girls wore headscarves; all had conservative knee-covering skirts and long-sleeved blouses buttoned high and tight. Marta strolled toward them feigning nonchalance and slid quietly into a bench directly behind the discussants.

"*Yok, yok, çucuklar,*" one of them chortled. "No, no, children," he said. "This is not the point … you are so naïve! The prime minister's report is not going to help; it's just going to provoke a reaction from the military. You'll see."

The other boys shook their heads, and one flopped heavily onto the seat behind Marta, causing the entire bench to vibrate. "Look at Ipek here." His voice was deep, with a bit of an eastern accent. "She is a modern woman, correct? Sitting here with her beautiful long hair, sitting with men—very modern, yes?"

The others were quiet, although Marta felt them nod as they fell under the spell of his deliberate, soft voice. She herself stifled an urge to turn and join the conversation, curious to see where he was leading them.

"So when our friend is faced with the unwanted advances of a man, say that she is attacked on the way home tonight, the modern explanation is that she is the victim and that she has no responsibility for what happens. Yes? I'm sorry, Ipek, I don't mean to pick on you, but let me say that in fact women are responsible for provoking the sexual response of men when they expose themselves like this."

No one answered for a moment. Marta heard a lighter and the inhalation of another tobacco hit. Just what year was it here? she wondered.

Instead of keeping up with the modern world, it seemed as if Turkey was deliberately trying to go backwards in time.

"Soooo," one of the other males began. "So you agree with the report? You know what it will mean for the republic, right?"

He laughed. "Just because something may contradict the precious republic doesn't mean it is automatically wrong. There are greater issues here—Atatürk was not a god, you know. And the prime minister has the votes now, so he can do what needs to be done."

Marta looked around anxiously, worried that someone might overhear this exchange. What strides the country had taken since the philosophical conversations of her youth—similar groups, perched around similar benches, arguing about the dangers of Westernization and the necessity of joining the European Union.

In her day, just fifteen years before, making a statement against Atatürk was grounds for imprisonment, and the girls wanted nothing more than to be able to wear jeans to class. She felt old and sad and suddenly worried about the other implications of these changes. It seemed like things had changed and were now going backwards—and quickly, if she understood the subtext of the headlines in the newspapers on display everywhere in the city.

"Want a Fanta?" Vasilli offered her a slender glass bottle filled with orange soda and a straw bobbing from the open top.

"Thanks," she said. "Feeling better?"

"I was not feeling badly," he said and then shrugged. "Okay, a little better. We're coming to the little island, it won't be much longer."

"Hmmmn." She sipped from the soda and watched the young people drift toward the prow of the boat.

"What was going on with that group?" he asked.

"You know, it's funny how everything can feel so different, and yet at the same time, it feels like nothing has changed in the years I've been away." Marta sipped from the orange drink. "Not so long ago, I was one of those young kids, thinking that I had all the answers. Now I know so much more, and yet I also know that I don't have the answers to anything at all."

Vasilli nodded, trying to understand. Finally, he gave up, shook his large head from side to side, and stuck his face near hers, laughing. "What?"

She smiled and pushed his shoulder away. "It's probably not the same for you, coming back here," she said. "When I left, I was an adult, more or less. And it was only a few years ago. So it still feels like home to me, even though I haven't thought about this place for years. But now, I feel like I don't belong here, and a part of me really wants to ... not the rational part." She smiled.

"I know. It's the little girl deep inside of you that wants to be home. But you have not let her out for a very long time."

Marta leaned back and looked closely at Vasilli. "Hmm," she said eventually. "Some of your coffee shop psychology coming out?"

"Don't make fun of that—I learned a lot listening to people's problems all those years."

"Well, you're right. I think your life experience is very valid." She paused for another sip. "How about you? How do you feel being here? Where you were born?"

"It's an entirely different world now," he said. Finishing the soda, he made a loud burp. "Sorry. I can't even begin to process how this city has changed since I was here. I don't even want to try. It would be a project for the History Channel."

"I suppose." Marta sighed. "I am not sure I would want my child to be growing up in this environment."

"What do you mean? Where did that come from—talking about children and the future generation? It's your turn to get all philosophical now, I guess." He stretched, stood up, and walked to the railing. "Come, let's just enjoy this beautiful day."

Fourteen

At least some things had not changed, Marta thought. The island, when the ferry had exchanged its passengers and left them on the road to town, looked much the same as it had back in 1985, the last time Marta had visited its pine-scented forests and pristine beaches. Older folks struggled with brilliantly striped satchels bulging with parcels from the city, and aside from the occasional bicycle horn, the prevailing sound was that of horseshoes on cobblestone. Mixed with the sea breeze, the smell of beer and seafood from the sidewalk cafés mingled with horse droppings and the scent of lemon cologne that was offered to every traveler who huffed into a metal chair on the roadside, looking for relief in a quick glass of tea.

Marta waited for the old man to take it in, watching as he turned in a slow circle near the buggy kiosk. She put up a hand to stop a peddler from approaching and again when a stableman summoned her with a click-click from the side of his mouth. She took off the cardigan piece of her yellow cashmere twinset and let the sun warm her bare shoulders for a minute.

"It has not changed," Vasilli announced. "Amazing." His face was lit with a childish wonder. "See that big white building there, on the hill? That was a magnificent hotel. I remember watching the fancy people going in and out of there. Oh my," he said. "It was all so long ago—the women in their long ball gowns and parasols, the men with tails and fez—they wore the fez back then, you know, for formal attire." He sighed again. "So long ago."

"Funny." Marta nodded. He looked at her expectantly. "When I was here last, that white hotel had been turned into a fat farm—a spa for rich women to come and lose weight."

Vasilli nodded. "I wonder what it is now? But at least it still looks magnificent, sitting on the hillside like that. I always wanted to go and sit on that big porch and watch the boats come in. I always thought that when I was older, and successful, I would be able to go there." He sighed and looked away.

"Shall we sit? Have some tea?" Marta led him gently to the least crowded café, away from the noisy children and mothers, to a place where silent men sat huddled over backgammon boards, smoking and slapping tiles. A television soundlessly replayed a soccer match; its quick tempo contrasted with the wailing music coming from a boom box near the kitchen door.

"I picked up a map this morning from the hotel concierge." Marta opened the colorful cardboard. "Let's see if we can find the municipal building ..."

"It's right there." Vasilli pointed over her shoulder. "The brick building, with the yellow doors. You know, the building with the big flag in front."

"Ah." She checked the map anyway. "You're right. What else should we look for? The church perhaps? The cemetery?"

"They're not here ... buried here."

"How do you know?" she asked.

He crossed his arms, stubborn again. "I just feel it. They're not here."

She looked at him for a second and then decided not to argue. "Well, I suggest that we visit the town hall and see what we can find. And then, maybe a buggy ride around the island, just to see what we can see."

"And lunch?" he asked.

"Definitely lunch," Marta's mouth watered at the memory of fried mussels smothered in a garlic sauce served on a hunk of fresh bread. "We will definitely have time for lunch."

Their tea consumed, the map restored to her bag, the couple made their way to the large brick structure sitting at the head of the intersection of five roads, a dirty marble fountain gushing in the center. The buggies were lined up on the north road, awaiting the next rush of travelers. A long bike rack filled with a variety of almost ancient conveyances was secured to the south side of the town hall, just next to the flagpole and a marble bust of Atatürk, standing alone on a pedestal near the front entrance.

After going in and out of seven offices, Marta's patience with the bureaucrats was ending. Vasilli, hopeless from the start, tagged along and tried to follow the conversations with his limited grasp of the language. Finally, thirty-nine minutes later, they exited the building. Marta's hair was no longer tightly coiffed, and Vasilli's jacket hung slackly from his left index finger. Without a word, they looked at the horses, sighed heavily, and turned back toward the restaurants.

"*Eki bira.*" Marta put up two fingers to signal a waiter, who brought frothy mugs of Efes Pilsen to their table, flourishing a menu and offering cologne from the large pocket of his apron. Vasilli cupped his hands for the splash of lemon, but Marta shook her head. She drank deeply from the glass, a bit of foam decorating her lip as Vasilli laughed.

"Thirsty?" he asked. "I didn't figure you for a beer drinker."

"I'm not," she confirmed. "There's just something about drinking beer here, in the salt air, with the mussels—it just all goes together. And after meeting with all those helpful public servants, well, I think we deserve a drink."

He nodded, intent on wiping his own frothy mustache. "Well," he said finally.

"Well."

After a moment in which they both sipped again, he continued, "That was a waste of time."

"Not entirely," Marta said mildly. "It got us here, sitting in this place on a lovely spring afternoon. Now we know that the answers are not here. So that is something, progress, right?"

"I never figured you for an optimist," he said dryly. The waiter brought over two huge sandwiches that stopped conversation for quite a while.

"What is in this sauce?" Vasilli finally broke the silence after the last bite of his lunch had been consumed. "I've never tasted anything like it."

"It's a secret recipe," Marta whispered. "But I think there's something in the water and air here that makes it taste special. I've had this in New York at some Turkish restaurants, and it doesn't taste the same. It's the whole package—the sun, the sea air, the beer—that can't be copied."

"Harumph." The old coffee shop owner was skeptical. "Everything can be made somewhere else, if you have the right ingredients."

Marta reached for the bill, but the old man stopped her hand. "I'll get this one," he said. "And someday, you'll come and visit me in New York, and I'll make this sauce for you. You'll see."

When they turned back to the stable, most of the horses were gone but an older dappled mare stood chewing on something deep in its feedbag. She looked almost mournful as her owner held the reins for the couple to climb into the small carriage. It was not a comfortable ride, up the steep hills of the main street. Aside from the fragrant diaper draped between the buggy and the horse, the cobblestone road was filled with deposits from previous trips.

Marta held a tissue under her nose, waiting for a breeze to give some relief from the heat and smell. "You can't see anything," Vasilli complained. "They didn't used to have all these big fences. This is not the same. Everyone's house was open to the street when I was a boy."

"Well, you know some things do change, right?" Marta lowered her tissue. "It was more than seventy years ago since you were here, right? So naturally, some things would be different."

He was silent, craning his neck to get a look over the thick hedges and catch glimpses of houses through the openings at gates and driveways. "Let's get out and walk, shall we?" he asked. "We need to walk off that heavy lunch and all that beer."

Marta reluctantly stopped the driver and haggled over the cost of a fraction of a trip and then suggested that the driver wait for them at the beach on the far end of the island. "At least we can be sure to get a ride back," she explained to Vasilli. "It's further than you think."

Fifteen

It was a magical place, a place inhabited by the fringes of Turkish society, a place where Greeks, Jews, and Armenians lived in a lovely exile from the big city. Mansions housed several generations behind pink, baby-blue, and beige walls. With pine and eucalyptus trees filling the yards and running almost to the sea, the air was fragrant and cool, the shadows deep as tree limbs danced in the light breeze. At the crest of the first hill, a faded white church sat directly on the roadside, no fence hiding its circular stained glass, ornate carved doors, and decorations that announced its Orthodox origins.

The doors were firmly locked against Vasilli's attempts to enter. Muttering, he tried to peer into the windows. Marta waited on the front stoop while he wandered around the building, looking for an opening. Signs written in a foreign alphabet were too obscure to decipher, and Vasilli was forced to admit that he knew very little written Greek.

"Shall we continue then?" Marta rose and wiped the back of her pants.

"No."

"What do you propose we do? Do we sit here all day and wait for someone to come?" she asked. "It might be days before someone comes here— maybe not until Sunday. Hell, they may not even use this church anymore. What then?"

"There has to be someone here." He sat down stubbornly.

Marta paced around and then decided to explore behind the building. A wall of overgrown hedges blocked access to the gardens, but finally, she found a gate along the side that was not locked, just rusted and hard to move. A six-foot tall hedge and an iron fence surrounded an old graveyard, filled with lopsided and fallen markers among coffin-sized hunks of granite, carved with the images of the dead.

She meandered around the large, sloping garden, stopping to read the occasional inscription in Turkish. "Fatma, excellent wife and mother, 1933– 1954." There were many children, alive less than a year, and then the old-timers, eighty- to ninety-year-olds like Vasilli, whose long lives broke all expectations in this relatively poor country. When she turned to walk a new row, Marta spotted Vasilli creeping along behind, searching for his family name among the dead. Instead of continuing her inventory, Marta headed down to the edge of the property, where an elaborate iron fence protected the visitor from a fifty-foot cliff descent.

Lost in her thoughts, Marta barely noticed the movement of the sun along the horizon and the mumbling of Vasilli behind her. Sparkling water carried sailboats across the blue expanse, crested waves rippling alongside larger pleasure craft that passed silently below. The trees rustled above, and a fly tickled her arm, provoking a sense memory that forced her eyes to glaze and wander. She'd been here before, long ago, with less noble intentions.

It was a time when all they did was look for a place to be alone. After months of traveling in a large group, Marta and Mehmet had found each other. Since the arrival of the warm weather, their only interest had been taking off on a cool boat and spending the day on an isolated beach, making love and planning their future together.

They were old enough to be sure, but not old enough to worry about the future—just foolish enough to think it would all work out. The day they ended up here, at the cemetery, was a real scorcher, pine trees popping cones that rained down on the parched picnic area. Every inch of the beach was covered; every hiding place they'd christened in the past months was hosting another couple or a family splashing among the slippery rocks. They headed toward the monastery, hopeful for a cool drink at least, and saw this old church. The graveyard behind was visible through the drought-dried shrubs, and they climbed over the fence, giddy with their discovery of the cool and private nook.

It was there, in the fragrance of the eucalyptus, that Mehmet gave Marta the ring—not the magical romantic ideal she'd fantasized about, no luxurious restaurant, no soft music and candlelight—but it was somehow more perfect. Sitting on the cliff edge, her blouse silky and undulating in the light breeze, tickling her naked body, which was still soft and wet from making love, Mehmet had proposed marriage to Marta.

Graduation from law school was coming fast, the final gasp of exams in the next few weeks. Apprenticeships were all arranged, the required year of work in a court or law firm before the new lawyers were allowed to take the licensure examinations and venture out to practice law. Mehmet and Marta had both signed up for work in the legal department of a large multinational, the first step toward an international practice. This ring, this marriage, was a logical progression in their partnership.

"Seni seviyorum," Mehmet whispered. "I love you. I want you to be my wife." Marta's tears mingled with sweat and saliva; their bodies intertwined again—it was all perfect. It was the last time it would be so right.

Marta shook herself out of the reverie when she heard a low moan and turned to see Vasilli laying supine on one of the graves. She could see his face contorted with what looked like pain, his hands clasped to his chest.

"What is it? Are you in pain?" She ran to his side, grabbing a hand and feeling for his pulse.

"No, no, no," he moaned, pushing his head into the grass.

"What is it? What's wrong?"

"They're all gone. They're not here. They're all gone ..." he moaned.

"Yes, well, that's not entirely true." Marta sat back on her haunches. "Someone is still here, and they sent you a letter. We'll meet them and find out what's what."

He was silent then, still as a corpse on the grass. Marta felt a chill as she looked at him, his eyes closed and his hands folded neatly on his chest. Was he ill or just overcome by the place? She watched him for a moment, until his forehead seemed to relax. Tears seeped from his closed eyes, but his chest moved rhythmically and so she decided he was not about to expire. She stretched out beside him, warmed by the sunshine that dappled her face. After a few minutes, she heard a soft snore, and she smiled. Clouds wafted past, quick enough to give her the sensation of the earth moving. She brushed away an ant and closed her eyes to the warmth.

They both slept, their eyes moving along with the dreams that passed through as quickly as the sun crossed from its position directly above to where it now beamed through the hedges on the west side of the cemetery. Marta awakened with a start. She was alone on the grass, although the outline of Vasilli's body was still visible on the plot next to her.

She stood up and saw him, standing with his back to her a few rows away. She approached, clearing her throat so as not to startle the old man.

"Did you see this?" He pointed to a newer stone, still white among its weathered neighbors. "Why would someone with your name be in a Greek cemetery?"

Marta fell to her knees before the stone, reading her mother's name there and the dates, 1947–1986. "No," she gasped. "This can't be."

"My goodness, she was young," Vasilli said. "Who is it?"

Marta looked at him blankly. "What?"

"She was young, only ... what, thirty-nine when she died," he said. "Who is it?" he asked again.

"It's Mother ... but it can't be her," Marta repeated. "Why would she be buried here? All the family is on the Black Sea. She's not even Greek.

Why would she be here? It doesn't make sense. It can't be her." Marta rose and paced back and forth at the foot of the grave. "This can't be," she kept repeating.

Vasilli sat down on the sarcophagus next to her mother's grave. His face was creased in thought, and he rocked back and forth slowly, searching the ground as if for clues to the mystery.

"Don't sit there," she scolded him. "That's not a place to sit." He ignored her and continued to rock while she paced.

"Why don't we go to the town hall again and get some information?" he suggested.

"They won't know anything," she scoffed. "Has any government office been of any help so far?"

"Well, they must have death records somewhere," he said. "There doesn't seem to be anyone minding the church or the cemetery, so maybe we can find something at the town hall." He rose, dusting off his trousers and adjusting his hat. "Let's go. Take a photo of the inscription and let's get out of here. We can come back later." She didn't move, just stood there looking numbly at the stone. He took the camera from her bag and hastily snapped a couple of shots of the inscription. "Come," he pulled her arm. "Come on now. Let's go before the office closes."

She looked blankly at his face, as if seeing it for the first time. "Go where?" she asked. "What are you saying?"

Clucking and coaxing, Vasilli led Marta back to the street, where they began the slow walk to the town square. Not lucky enough to capture an empty carriage on the way, the pair arrived sweaty and footsore just as the doors were being locked at the town hall. No amount of pleading could sway the officious young man pulling shut the door. He turned the sign face out, and Marta read aloud the hours posted for the following day.

"We'll stay overnight, then," Vasilli offered. "We'll find a couple of rooms and get some rest, and then we'll have plenty of time to get an explanation in the morning."

The tourist map showed several possible locations nearby, and with some effort, Vasilli returned key in hand to the tea table in the square where Marta sat in the deepening shadows. The camera was on the table, its film removed and delivered by a waiter to a nearby one-hour photo shop. They sat, grim and tired, silently watching the parade of visitors heading to the pier.

Sixteen

They switched to raki soon after twilight saw the last ferry of the day fade into the horizon, a final long blast of its horn echoing for a moment in the stillness of the evening. Plates of *meze* followed, little appetizers that soaked up and enhanced the taste of the alcohol. The waiter returned with their photographs, with a wad of colorful lira notes stacked atop an envelope. It sat untouched on the table between them.

"Tell me about your mother," Vasilli prompted. "If you'd like …" he quickly added.

She sighed and did not lift her head to reply. A long silence between them was punctuated by the wail of the muezzin and then the whinny of horses being led away for the evening. A television inside the restaurant chimed the hour and a news program opened with shots from a terror attack on the eastern frontier. Vasilli half turned in his chair to watch the flickering images, sipping slowly on his drink.

"My mother was just a girl, an innocent young girl," Marta began speaking softly.

"She had me when she was just fifteen, after being married off to my father the previous year. Her parents were dead; she was raised by an aunt and uncle who were happy to get rid of her. They had their own children, who were older and already out of the house. She thought of them like her sisters and brothers, but they were not close. So, as soon as she was old enough, they married her off to my father. He was much older than her, and he took her far away to the city. His first wife had died giving birth to their son, who had lived just a few hours. Father was a very bitter man, and he didn't understand what it meant to take my mother so far away from the village into the strangeness of a big city. She was always afraid, afraid of him, afraid of the city, afraid of doing the wrong thing, saying the wrong thing, of being ridiculed by the other mothers. She hid inside the apartment, only went out to shop for food.

"She never went to school, never had the chance. We learned to read together. We learned everything together. And she kept having girl babies, until she finally figured out how to stop them from coming every year. He was brutal to her; he beat all of us all the time, even when we had done nothing wrong. He probably killed her. He would have killed me if I'd stayed, I know. She protected me from that. I can't imagine … She died the year after I left. She was still so young. She was so young." She shook her head violently.

"I killed her." Marta spoke dully. Tears coursed down her cheeks, her stoicism lubricated by the liquor.

"How could that be so?" Vasilli reached across and took her hand. "You didn't do anything to harm your mother."

"I left. I left her alone. I broke her heart." Marta covered her eyes. "She had so much invested in me, in my success. I killed her."

Vasilli refilled their glasses quietly, adding just enough water to perfect the mix. "Here, drink," he urged. "Eat some of your cardboard things." He pushed the chickpeas to her side of the table.

"I'm so tired," Marta said, looking up at the old man. "I never wanted to know this. I never thought …" She shook her head again. "That's not true. I thought about her all the time. I just never thought she was dead, that she could be gone. I never thought that would happen. I always hoped she'd gotten away from him, made a life for herself somehow. I liked to imagine that she was happy somewhere."

Music started nearby, and a waiter placed a small candle on their table. "Merci," Vasilli said, handing the boy a folded bill. "How about some Turkish coffee?" he asked Marta, who lifted the raki bottle instead.

"I killed my mother," she said again.

Vasilli sighed with impatience and then shrugged. "Who knows, really, what happens when you leave people behind?" Marta did not respond, just studied the milky substance that she swirled around the glass. "My mother is dead too," he said suddenly.

She laughed sharply, a short and cruel hiccup. "Vasilli, you're eighty-seven years old. Of course your mother is dead."

"Well, who knows? … Maybe she was thirty-nine when she died too. I don't know. I may never know."

"Okay, I get you," she said, pulling her hands roughly through her knotted hair and retying it loosely with a band. "But really, I think my leaving killed her … No wait." She put out a hand to stop his interruption. "My father was perfectly capable of killing her, he was so angry when I left. That's probably what happened."

"So, you are still not responsible," he concluded. "What are you going to do now, call him up and ask him what happened?"

"Never." Her voice was deep and urgent. "I'll never speak to him again."

"What about your sisters? Can't you ask them?" he asked. She looked away, refusing to answer, her eyes closed and lips pursed tightly together. He sighed.

They leaned back in their chairs then, conversation suspended. Feral cats wound around their legs, crying for food, until Vasilli stamped his foot and the cats skulked off to another table. The soft glow of the candles competed for atmosphere with the green haze cast by the television, broadcasting a soccer match that prompted occasional outbursts from the men gathered near the set.

Marta swigged the last of her raki. "Let's get the check," she said. "I think we should call it a night."

They walked the short distance to a small hotel tucked on a quiet side street lit by old-style gaslights. They had only one room available, and Marta signed the register listlessly. They followed the porter to a large room, in which two twin beds bracketed an ornate carved desk with a lamp whose tasseled, ancient yellow shade cast a soft orange glow. Vasilli produced two oversized T-shirts, garish pictures of skateboarding action stenciled on the front.

"Your nightwear, mademoiselle," he said, bowing at the waist.

She laughed then, taking his outstretched offering. "Where did you get these?" she asked.

"On the street, of course," he said. "I asked for a couple of toothbrushes—yes, see, they're here in the bathroom. Everything a person could need. Would you like to use the washroom first?"

When she came out, the old man was already changed and tucked, snoring, into his bed by the wall. Marta sat next to the window and watched the sky change, stars moving in some magical pattern that she hoped would reveal the answers she sought. Rather than helping her sleep, the raki had sped up her mind, and she sat for some hours in the dark, sorting long-suppressed memories and feelings into new, manageable bundles. Vasilli's snoring proved a soothing backdrop, and eventually, her eyes weighted with fatigue, she collapsed across the short bed, her feet dangling and pillow tucked firmly into her chest.

Seventeen

"The question is why is she buried here, on this island, and especially, why in that cemetery?" Marta said. "I don't understand that at all."

Vasilli nodded, slurping his hot tea through a sugar cube held between his front teeth. Marta had started talking the moment they sat down at the breakfast table. It seemed that she had moved past the sadness and silence of the previous evening. She'd been on the cell phone since well before daylight, soothing clients in New York and making excuses to her team in Istanbul, who were concerned about her absence from the negotiating table.

"Everyone agreed to take a break from the negotiations, to think about the proposals," she'd repeated over and over. To Vasilli's surprise, Marta turned off the device and stowed it in her bag. "Battery's low anyway." She shrugged at his upraised brows.

"Well, what's the plan?" he asked. "How can we find out what happened here, if you aren't going to call your family?"

"I told you, I don't want to contact them, at least not until I have more information," she replied. Dark circles under her eyes were the only indication that she was suffering from this discovery. "I'd like to go back to town hall and see if I can dig up a death certificate—something to explain her presence on the island." She paused to nibble on a soft, cheese-filled roll. "You don't have to follow me around—maybe you can take a carriage, see some of the sights, and we can meet here for lunch later."

His head shaking slowly, Vasilli placed his hands side by side on the table. "I'd like to stay with you, if you don't mind," he said. "Unless you think I'll get in the way, I'd really like to help out, if I can." He lifted his palms to the air and smiled, almost shyly. "I don't know what I can do, but I would like to at least give you some moral support—and maybe another interpretation of what you find out."

Both of them knew that Vasilli's language skills would not lend themselves to actual assistance, but Marta understood what the old man was doing, trying to keep her calm and on track, and she appreciated it. "So, then, let's get there in time to open the doors. Maybe if we're the first instead of the last customers of the day, we'll have more success. And while we're there, you can ask about your mother," she added. She even smiled a bit, as Vasilli picked up his hat and bowed a little as he tipped it in her direction.

The search was easier this time, because they had an actual date and some information, rather than just a general query for the clerk in the town hall. For the equivalent of one dollar, they exited the building with a copy of a death certificate for Neslihan Demirci. Vasilli was once again frustrated in his attempt to find information about his mother, but he shook it off and followed Marta into the brilliant sunshine.

They hailed a carriage and gave the driver the address listed on the form. Marta perched anxiously on the edge of her seat.

"Relax." Vasilli placed a hand on the middle of her back. She could feel her muscles bunched tensely under her elegant attire.

They were both surprised when the carriage took a sharp turn just two minutes into their trip. It pulled into a large circular driveway, coming to a stop in front of the large white building that Vasilli had admired when they first arrived on the island. After questioning the driver and being assured that they were, in fact, at the correct location, the pair disembarked.

"This is bizarre," Marta finally said. They stood for a few minutes, inspecting the sign that identified the former Prince Hotel as the Buyuk Ada, Big Island, Spa and Women's Clinic. "This used to be a fat farm. Now the sign says spa and women's clinic," she translated.

"I remember that it was a hotel," Vasilli said. "But a women's clinic? What kind of clinic do you think?"

"I have no idea," she said. "Let's go and see what we can find out."

The lobby, still brilliant with its white marble and gold-encrusted moldings, featured an elaborate wooden reception counter and many smaller desks, staffed by matronly women talking quietly to a variety of clients, mostly young women whose girth filled the oversized chairs.

"Still a fat farm," Vasilli muttered under his breath.

Marta shushed him and took his arm as they approached a tall brunette whose blond highlights looked like they had been painted in chunks using a fat paintbrush. Marta worried that the woman's thick makeup might crack when she spoke. Her eyes were thickly lined with kohl, her cheeks emphatically blushed, and her lips outlined and filled in with at least three shades of red. She tapped her long, elaborately varnished nails on a computer keyboard and studied the screen, ignoring the couple despite Marta's polite, "Pardon?" Her subsequent, more insistent, "Excuse me," finally elicited a look.

"*Effendim?*" the woman asked, employing one of those Turkish words that was both question and statement, "Yes," and "What can I do for you?" Her badge said that her name was Semin.

"Yes, thank you, Semin. I would like to speak to the manager, please." Marta spoke in Turkish, and Vasilli tried valiantly to follow along.

"Are you a client?" Marta shook her head. "Is there a problem?" Rather than call her manager, the woman was suddenly interested in assisting Marta and Vasilli. "Perhaps if you tell me what this is about, I can help you," she offered.

"Well, several years ago, my mother died here, and I'd like to know what happened. I'd like to see her records, and maybe speak to someone who worked here at the time," Marta explained.

"Oh. Hmmm. Well, when did you say this happened? Because I don't remember ever hearing that someone died here." The girl lifted her hands in a prayerful way, gold bracelets rattling together across her thin forearm. "I am very sorry to hear this, but maybe you are mistaken?"

"It was in 1986," Marta said.

The girl blanched. "That was a long time ago. I don't know … The manager has only been here for a few years, like me." She looked around and then leaned across the counter. "Give me the name. I'll just look it up on the computer and see what comes up."

Many taps and one phone interruption later, she shook her head. "I don't see anything under that name here." She looked hopefully at Marta. "Maybe it wasn't here. Maybe it was some other place."

Marta slid the death certificate across the counter, her finger pointing to the address of the spa. "This is here, right?" The girl nodded, her mouth turned down in an expression of sadness. "So, do you at least know what this place was at that time? Was it just a spa or a hotel, or what?"

Vasilli chimed in. "Ask her, what 'women's clinic' means." Marta nodded and repeated his question in Turkish.

The girl stiffened a bit. "You're not a reporter or anything, are you?" she asked. "Maybe I will call the manager. Just a moment … Can you step away from the desk, please?"

Marta and Vasilli moved toward the entrance, flipping through brochures arrayed on a large table. There was nothing from the present location, only tourist offerings and promotional materials for weight-loss products. Marta strained to hear the quiet conversation that the girl was having with someone on the phone.

"Maybe I should tell her I'm a lawyer. That might get us somewhere," she said.

Vasilli shook his head. "Only as a last resort. She was already suspicious that we might be reporters. I don't know how people feel about lawyers in this country, but I don't think it would help your cause. Let's wait and see what the manager has to say." Marta huffed her objection but remained quiet.

A young boy arrived with a tray of tea glasses, and he motioned them toward a grouping of upholstered chairs. "I guess we're in for a long wait," Marta noted dryly, accepting the tea and raising her glass slightly in the direction of the receptionist. "Let's sit here until they decide what to do with us."

"Hey, maybe they called in their lawyers." Vasilli laughed.

"Well, at least they haven't sent out the bouncers."

"Not yet," he agreed. "That comes later."

For an hour, they sat, watching the parade of fat and thin, crying and defiant young women and their mothers. The combinations were interesting, and Marta stifled a chuckle when Vasilli leaned over and whispered, "Which one of these is the client?" A rotund pair, mother just as portly as daughter, struggled to fit into the proffered seating.

"Maybe it's a mother-daughter special," Marta whispered back. "I guess this answers our questions about what goes on here," she said.

"Was your mother, you know?" Vasilli puffed out his cheeks.

"No." Marta was horrified. "She was a tiny little thing, only about five feet tall, and she was thin, dangerously thin—she never ate, always made sure that we had enough first. She always said that she was full, from all the 'testing' bites she'd had while cooking."

"Hmmm." He stroked his chin. "Well, how about your sisters? Maybe she was bringing one of them here?"

"No, I'm telling you that would never happen. We were all thin, like her, and besides that, there was no money for a place like this. Are you kidding? Father would never pay for something like this, even if one of us needed it … which we didn't." She paused, watching the receptionist whispering in someone's ear. "I told you," Marta continued impatiently. "Mother was too scared to leave the house. She never left the neighborhood, unless Father made her go with him somewhere." She shook her head. "Coming all this way—no, it was not for the fat farm or for a day at the beach. There had to be some other reason for her to be here."

"Okay," he said. "Well, let me ask you this: Are we positive that it was her?"

"No, we're not positive about anything." Marta stood up in time to greet the older woman coming toward their chairs. She stuck out her hand, announced her name, and invited the pair to join her in the office. The diplomas on her walls showed that a Suzan D. Karagöz was a graduate of Galatasaray University, with certification as a social worker. Photographs of her with a homely-looking man and two sullen teenagers, a boy and a girl, adorned the credenza behind her massive oak desk. A silver wedding ring was her only jewelry, and the black shift she wore was as severe as the rimless glasses she placed on her nose. Dark hair cut in a pageboy style glimmered with gray highlights, which Marta interpreted as a modern gesture, since most women her age were already coloring their hair and it was highly unusual to see a Turkish woman with gray tresses.

Mrs. Karagöz studied the papers Marta handed over, listening silently to the explanation of how these travelers had found their way to the spa. Finally, she folded her hands on the desk and spoke.

"I must ask you, can I trust you to keep silent about what you learn here today?"

Marta flushed. "What exactly do you mean, 'keep silent'? Are you worried that I might sue you?"

"Sue? What do you mean, 'sue' me?" Her pleasant smile faded as she watched Marta's steely eyes flash. "I see from the television that people in the United States are always in the courts, suing each other, but I had never experienced this myself. Interesting." Marta still glared at the woman, who shifted nervously in her chair. "Okay. No, I am not worried about that, although obviously I should be. What I mean is this, we provide certain services here that we do not want to have public attention. Do you understand me now?"

"Services?" Marta echoed. She looked around. "Do you mean plastic surgery? Hair removal? What kind of services?"

The woman studied something on her desk while Marta's eyes searched the room for a clue.

"We do have certain clinical services for women here," the woman said softly.

"Clinical services … you mean birth control, abortion, that kind of service?"

"Among other things, yes."

"So my mother came here for an abortion and died?" Marta asked.

Vasilli reached out and put his hand on her arm, alarmed by the rising tone of her voice. He leaned over and asked, "What's going on?" but she brushed him aside.

"Just tell me if that's what happened," she repeated to the manager.

"Oh, I don't know for sure," Mrs. Karagöz said. "I just said that's one of the services we offer. I'll have to pull your mother's file from the archives. Can you wait here?"

"I thought the girl said there was nothing in the computer," Marta argued.

"The computer records are not so old," Mrs. Karagöz replied. "We have a file number, and I'll get it from the basement. It'll be just a few minutes." She rose, walking quickly to the door.

"Wait." Marta stood up. "Tell me what other 'services' you have here."

"Oh, well, you may not ... how should I say ... you may not need to know about the other ..." She shrugged. "Let's see what's in the file."

By the time Marta had satisfied Vasilli's questions, the manager had returned with a thin file folder and a grim expression on her face.

"What did you find?" Marta asked, leaning forward eagerly.

"Well, yes, your mother was here at that time," Mrs. Karagöz said slowly. "Now, do I have your assurance about the sensitivity of the information?" she asked. "I really must insist that you agree not to speak of this to anyone, especially in the newspapers." She crossed her arms and waited. Marta thought about reaching across the desk to take the file, but something must have shown her intention because the woman closed the file and put it in a drawer. "Do we have an agreement?"

"I can't agree to something before I even know what we're talking about," Marta began. Vasilli tapped her shoulder. "What?" she turned to him impatiently.

"What's going on?" he asked. "Let's just find out what the woman knows," he urged. "You're not here to expose the place or sue them, so just agree to her terms."

She sat back, eyeing the other woman and fuming about the options. "Okay," she said finally. "Do you want me to sign something, or will you trust me when I promise not to talk?"

"Your word is good enough," Mrs. Karagöz said. "I know that some of this will be very disturbing to hear—"

Marta interrupted her. "Listen. Don't play social worker with me. This happened a long time ago. Now I just want the facts. Please."

"As you wish ... Your mother was here several times. The first time was in 1985, when she came to ask about an abortion. We couldn't help her then; it was too late. We only do first-trimester abortions here, no exceptions." She looked up from the file to search Marta's face and then continued, "She came back, a year later, and this time, we were able to perform the procedure."

"And then?" Marta pushed, impatient with the slow recitation of information. "What happened, did she bleed out? Was there a problem with the anesthesia? What?"

"Um, no. The procedure was fine. But there was an ... interruption. Her husband arrived, ah, your father, I assume, and caused a great fuss. We had a hard time controlling him. We had a hard time getting him to leave. He wouldn't go without her—and so he dragged her away."

She studied the file, avoiding Marta's questioning eyes. "So that's it?" Marta asked. "Why does it say that she died here?"

"There's another thing we do here, a very, well, let me say, it is a very political thing. We had just started a couple of years before this happened, and it almost shut down the whole place. We tried to keep it quiet, but the whole thing is a word-of-mouth system, so we lost some clients for a while."

"What the hell are you talking about?" Marta asked. "Is this some kind of cult or what?"

"No, nothing like that," Mrs. Karagöz replied calmly. "We run a shelter here, a place that women can go when their husbands are beating them. You understand, in Turkey, this is not such a popular cause, especially for the politicians who don't want to offend the male voters. Don't interfere with family business, they say to us. You are undermining the authority of men, they say. Humph. No one is concerned about the women who are being beaten and even killed by their abusive husbands. No one." She stopped and looked at the shocked expression on Marta's face. "Should I continue?" Marta nodded.

"So, a few years ago, we started to notice that some of our clients in the weight clinic were coming in covered with bruises, some of them with broken ribs and noses, things like that. Some of them didn't even have a weight problem; they just came to recover from the beatings. We decided to try and help, for the ones that would talk about it and the ones who wanted to get away. Not everyone could. It usually took some time, but eventually, many of them realized that they had to escape, and so we helped."

"My mother was one of them," Marta said dully.

"Yes," Mrs. Karagöz replied. "She came back the next day. I don't know how she managed the trip. She was beaten badly, I remember. You could hardly recognize her face. There were many broken things, many injuries. And she was hemorrhaging badly from the abortion, I suppose. He must've done something ..." She stopped abruptly. "Sorry, I shouldn't say anything more. We have no proof that it was him. There was no police investigation. She died, as you know, and when we contacted your father, he refused to make any arrangements for her, told us to 'take care of it' since we killed her."

"So you had her buried here on the island," Marta said.

"Yes," Mrs. Karagöz said. "One of our staff at the time was the wife of the caretaker there, and she arranged it."

Marta opened her bag and removed the photographs of the grave marker. "Did you put the marker there?" she asked.

"Ah, no. That's an interesting story. The stone was more than we could afford, you see. A few years after your mother passed, someone with the same experience came to us, but that time, we were able to save her. Anyway, she was from a very wealthy family, and one of the staff happened to mention the similarities of her case to your mother's. Our social worker told me later that she only mentioned it because although this patient survived, she didn't seem to take her situation very seriously. When she realized how lucky she was to be alive, the woman gave a substantial donation to the clinic. One of the conditions was that we place a proper stone on your mother's grave."

Marta shook her head. "That explains it. Are you still in contact with that woman?" she asked.

"No, I'm sorry. We aren't," Mrs. Karagöz said.

Marta looked at Vasilli, his patient face etched with sorrow and confusion. "Can you pardon me for a moment? I need to translate this for my friend here." She spoke quickly to the old man, who drew in a sharp breath at her news and shook his head slowly when she finished.

"I'm so sorry," he murmured.

Marta turned to the manager again. "Mr. Vassilios here has been searching for information about his mother too. How can I find out if she was buried in the new cemetery?"

"Well, did you check at the town hall? They would have all the death records," Mrs. Karagöz explained.

"There's nothing there. We figure she must have remarried and changed her name at some point, but we can't find out what the new name might be." She paused, looking at the computer sitting to the side. "Where might we find marriage records? Maybe we can find her in there."

"Those are local too," Mrs. Karagöz said. "You'd have to know where she was married. If it was Istanbul, you'd have to know the district. It could be a very tedious search, since there's no central registry," she concluded. She watched Marta translate for Vasilli. She spoke again. "I'm very impressed with you, miss," she said. "You have just learned some horrible things about your parents, and here you are concerned about your friend. That's very admirable."

"Well, don't give me too much credit," Marta said, a lopsided smile on her face. "I just want him to get the answers he needs, like I did. There's nothing either of us can do to change what happened in the past, but at least we can know, right?"

"Yes, that's right. Now at least you know," Mrs. Karagöz agreed. "Here's my card, if you ever do want to talk more about this … and, again, I'm very sorry. We did try to help."

"Tell me something," Marta said. "Are you still doing this, running a shelter here?"

Mrs. Karagöz nodded. "Things are better, in some ways," she said. "It's still a big problem, and sometimes when you get a religious politician in office, things get, oh, more challenging …" She waved her hands around. "But anyway, you don't want to hear about politics, I'm sure."

Marta dug into her bag and produced a checkbook. "I'd like to help you, if I may," she said. "Who should I make a check out to?"

Eighteen

The big island was very hilly, almost like the tip of a mountain emerging from the depths of the Marmara Sea, longing for sunshine. The hills were covered with pine trees, the shore characterized by steep cliffs that challenged climbers and made access to and from the water treacherous. It was a good place for a fort, and the remnants of an ancient embattlement were still visible on the western side of the island. Now, a beach had been created on one end of the island, a jetty built on the other for the daily ferry traffic. From the air, one could see that the central peak of the island was encircled with a thick stone fence, with a shining white monastery perched like a pillbox in the middle.

Home of Greeks and Jews and Armenians, the island was also host, over the centuries, to generations of separatist monks whose presence was only noted during their annual delivery of jars of honey to a local grocer. Every few years, a young and pale devotee would arrive on the ferry and be met by a sturdy farm wagon piloted by a silent driver in brown robes. The young fellow, hoisting his bag into the back, would take one last, melancholy look at the secular world and then climb aboard the wagon, never to be seen or heard from again.

Marta remembered the monks as she paused at the end of the driveway to let pass a heavy wagon carrying several forlorn goats and a loudly bleating sheep. She slipped her hand under Vasilli's elbow to help maneuver the old man down a steep curve leading to the central square. His arm slipped around her shoulders, and he hugged her lightly. They sat wordlessly under an umbrella festooned with tiny lanterns. It was cooler under the green-and-white-striped cover, but Vasilli removed his jacket and wiped his neck with a large white handkerchief.

"Are you all right?" Marta asked, noting the elder's red face and shaky hand.

"Sure, sure." He waved off her concern. "And you, are you all right?"

Marta shrugged, stirring the cup of tea that had been placed before her by a silent waiter. "It's a lot to digest," she admitted. "Especially since it happened so long ago. There's nothing to be done about any of it now."

Vasilli nodded his agreement.

They watched, each lost in thought, as a boatload of ferry passengers walked by the restaurant. Some stopped for tea, and the resulting noise prompted Vasilli and Marta to finish their beverages. A nearby waiter dropped the check on the table, and Vasilli looked at his watch.

"What now?" he asked. "When's the next ferry?"

Marta consulted the schedule card. "Not for a few hours. Dammit, I should've checked earlier. We could've taken the one that just left." She looked impatiently at her watch. "Listen, I need to get on the phone with some people. Would you mind? Maybe you can take a carriage ride around the island while I do this. We can meet back here, have lunch, and take the 1:45 boat."

"I could just sit here with you and people watch …" he said, wounded by her dismissal.

Marta looked up from digging out her phone. "As you wish," she said shortly. With a notebook and her palm pilot opened, she waited, checked the phone battery, and sighed. "Not much charge left," she muttered. "I wonder if there is a phone around here … Oh, bother. I'll just do what I can."

Her contacts at the local law firm were "in conference" and couldn't be disturbed, but she managed to get one of the young lawyers to answer his cell and interrupt the meeting. "We're considering an offer on the table," he said.

"No, don't do that," she said. "Put me on with Kemal-bey, now."

Vasilli cringed at the sharpness of her voice. He turned his chair sideways and folded his arms across his chest, watching a group of tourists a few tables away trying to negotiate their maps, a menu, two guidebooks, and a small Turkish dictionary.

"Kemal-bey, what is the offer? What? When did this come in? This morning. Okay, so what's the emergency? We'll meet later to look it over and make a counteroffer." She frowned, listening intently to the speaker. "No. No. No." Another pause. "What's the deadline? One day? That's ridiculous. Everyone agreed that we would take some time … No. Don't worry about it. No, I'm telling you … What are they going to do? No, really, if they don't have an answer by five o'clock today, then what?" She covered her ear to close out the racket of chatter and glassware around the café. "Listen, we have a bad connection here. Don't do anything. Let's meet this afternoon and decide how to handle it. I'll call Bertolini about this deadline thing. No. No. Don't worry. I'll call you back if there's a problem. Okay."

She disconnected the line and looked around the patio. "It's too noisy here," she said. "I need to find a quieter place to do this." She squinted, looking beneath the cover of umbrellas. "I'm going to try the town hall. Maybe I can sit in the lobby or something. I'll be back." She picked up her materials and practically ran from the table, leaving Vasilli to signal the waiter and ask for a cold soda. Approached by a couple of middle-aged women whose accent he identified as Texan American, he invited them to sit and discuss their journey with him.

Marta returned to find the trio in deep conversation about religion and the differences between modern and Orthodox Christianity. She rolled her eyes and sat at an unoccupied table nearby.

Vasilli called over, "What happened?"

She held up the phone. "No signal in there."

"Come join us," he urged. The ladies smiled tightly.

"No, I'll try to work over here," Marta said. She pulled on her sunglasses and closed her eyes for a moment, allowing her mind to replay the conversation at the clinic. "Oh, Mother." She sighed, picking up the phone. The next time she looked up, when the low battery beeping halted all conversation, Vasilli was gone, along with the Texans. She checked her watch, groaned, and gathered her notes before embarking on a futile search of the surrounding stores and restaurants. No Vasilli.

Resuming her seat in the restaurant, Marta listened as the ferry announced its departure. "Shit," she muttered, picking up the dead phone. "Dammit." The waiter brought a phone and a glass of dry white wine that she sipped for a moment before using the café's phone to postpone the afternoon's meeting. "How did I get stuck with this old man?" she asked herself. The New York Marta would've been on the ferry, with or without the old man; the Istanbul Marta was screwing up a case in order to escort the guy back to his hotel.

"You're getting soft," she admonished herself. She checked her watch, checked the ferry schedule, checked her watch, and drank the remainder of the wine in one long gulp. "Shit." She crossed her arms and leaned back into the sunshine, removing her sunglasses and closing her eyes. The face of Mrs. Karagöz flashed, swimming along with visions of her mother, the social worker's words echoing in her ears. She pushed them away, trying to focus on distant, more pleasant memories. A light breeze tickled her face as the sun warmed it, and she shook her hair loose and settled deeper in her chair.

She remembered a day like this long ago, a perfect early summer day. The air was crisp and clean, the sharp smells of pine and seawater mixing with the sound of gulls and the clop-clop of horse hooves on cobblestone. It was a first, a day trip that Marta had lied about to her mother, the first time she and Mehmet had separated from their group to visit the island alone. His backpack bulged with a blanket, a bottle of wine, a loaf of warm bread, a hunk of *kaşar* cheese, and a bag filled with shiny purple kalamata olives. Marta was on edge, excited and happy and also nervous and scared. All of these things cast a glow over the trip, anticipation and guilty pleasure combined. They chattered idly on the boat, a tangled web of legal "what-ifs" that characterized the gang's usual discussions. It felt different this time, because they were alone, two minds challenging each other while their bodies sent different, urgent signals. A hand on a knee, the brush of an arm—the tension made Marta's breath quicken.

They'd been having long telephone conversations, planning this getaway. Most days, the pair would meet for lunch at the student center and then walk slowly to class. First kisses were exchanged in the library, the pair rejoining the others with red faces and swollen lips that they thought no one would notice.

It was the lie that bothered Marta the most that day, not the avoidance of the gang, not the fear of the unknown. She was ready to take the next step with Mehmet. He was older, more experienced, and she trusted him completely. She believed they were in love, that they would marry, and she thought that was all that mattered.

They had arrived early to the island, practically running to the horses awaiting passengers. They rode up to the topmost point where the grounds of the monastery lay open to exploration and picnicking. After walking for about half an hour, looking for a secluded spot to picnic, they came upon a little clearing in a ring of large cypress trees that swayed with the breeze. Even fifteen years later, Marta could still remember the roughness of the blanket on her bare skin, the slow and tender movement of his hands on her body for the first time, and the sharp pain that reminded her of the reality of what they were doing.

"It'll be better the next time," he had whispered. "The first time is always the worst."

Marta had nodded, reaching for her shirt and surreptitiously wiping away the tears that pooled and overflowed into her ears. She was disappointed but felt older and wiser after the brief lovemaking. Mehmet's breath deepened as he slipped into sleep, and Marta lay next to him, watching the birds dipping and soaring overhead. Her body felt new, split open and altered, and she was confused by the feelings of shame and pride. She looked

at him, her first view of the naked male form, hairy and muscled and punctuated with the curl of wet penis that lay shining against a thatch of dark
hair. *What a strange thing this is,* she had thought. What a wondrous and
strange thing the human body was, and how curious the way it worked.

The sun was high overhead when he awoke and reached for her again.
Afterwards, they pulled on swimsuits and picked their way carefully down
the steep path to the beach. Mehmet was very talkative, and Marta barely
heard him, although they walked closely together.

It would be a long time before she could relax and enjoy the intimacy.
She'd trusted him with her future, and she was surprised at the vulnerability
of that choice. Marta realized that intellectually, she didn't like the feeling,
the exposure both physical and emotional. She was right to feel uneasy, and
she would never let another man get that close again.

Nineteen

The sky had that fragile, glittery look that happens just before twilight, as the sun shoots out its last hurrah of the day and the warm sky tries to absorb as much as it can. It was later than she'd planned when they headed back to the city, both tired from the late heavy lunch, the cold beer, and the emotional wringer of the past two days. Marta had spoken sharply to Vasilli when he finally returned to the restaurant, arm in arm with the two Texan tourists. His beaming smile froze as she berated him for making her miss the afternoon ferry, and he said a hasty farewell to the ladies.

Now on the boat, they sat silently on the hard deck bench and watched the sky change. Wake from dozens of other boats lapped the ferry like the sensitive fingers of a blind man checking his surroundings. The wind favored their position, sending away the billowing black smoke from the ferry and instead cooling their sunburned cheeks with a light, slightly salty caress.

In the distance, the water broke suddenly as a porpoise flashed in the sun. Vasilli grunted, too tired to be impressed with the show. "There was nothing out here when I was a boy," he said finally. "Look at all those houses … Where did all the people come from?"

"Oh, a lot of people moved from the villages, thinking that life would be better here," Marta replied. "My parents too." She was silent as the horn from another ferry signaled its passage across the bow. "Most of these new developments are illegal. They appear overnight, like mushrooms, just people throwing up a shack and settling in there. No heat, no running water, nothing. But you know how it goes here—a little payoff, the officials look the other way, and nobody gets hurt. Eventually, the shacks become houses, the power lines get spliced, and the city throws some asphalt on the path to make a road."

Vasilli grunted again. "It's sad."

Not really, Marta thought. "It's progress."

"Oh, I don't care about that. It's just that these hills used to be green. You could hike for hours and never see anything larger than a rabbit. The birds, they probably don't survive here anymore. I once saw an eagle. And the water was full of fish, and you could actually eat it and not get sick." He sighed.

"We used to swim in the Bosporus when I was a kid," Marta said. "If you didn't take a hot shower right away, you got this terrible rash all over. And you never ever drank the water—if you got dunked and had a mouthful, you'd get such bad diarrhea. What a thing to remember." They sat in silence again, as the boat turned and the city came into view. "It's funny what we remember, isn't it?"

Again Vasilli huffed out his reply. The trip to the island had been a roller coaster of emotion for both of them. Once they were finally on their way back to the city, she put aside her anger at the old man's disappearance and allowed herself to be invigorated by the views.

"I know you're disappointed that we didn't find out anything about your family," she said. "We'll get to the bottom of this thing, trust me." He crossed his arms in reply, and she decided to enjoy the last quiet before stepping back into the city's chaotic tempo.

From the east, the cry of a muezzin cut through the motor's steady rhythm. "Allah-ah …!" He sang the evening call to prayer.

Vasilli started to speak, but Marta touched his arm. "Shhh, listen." The voice echoed down the hills and across the water, and in a moment, another joined it, further to the west, "Allah-ah!" as if in a round. Behind them, another started up, and then, following the progress of the boat, too many to distinguish chanted their summons to the mosque.

The sun dipped below the hills, casting the water in gold. The minarets of the Blue Mosque and the towers of Topkapi Palace were outlined in robin's-egg blue, streaked through with a brushstroke of rose. Her hand still on his arm, Marta felt a loosening in her chest—the walls melting with the onslaught of memories, perhaps. It was entirely possible that she had sat in this very spot years ago, listening to the fading echoes and memorizing the golden wash of light over her hometown.

"Why do they do that?" Vasilli asked, impatience sharpening his tired voice. "Can't they coordinate the timing better?"

"It's not like a clock chime," Marta replied. "The prayer begins at sunset, which moves along the path of the sun. So each mosque starts a few seconds later than the one to its east." Her explanation was received with something like a horse's snort of air, venting Vasilli's frustration with the vagaries of Turkish culture.

"Just a jumbled mess," he said eventually.

A jumbled mess … like everything else, Marta thought. She leaned her head back, the music playing again in her head. "Wait a minute!" she exclaimed. Vasilli started awake, coughing to cover his snort.

"What? What? Are we there?" he asked.

"No, sorry, I just thought of how to settle the pasta mess," Marta said. *These guys are all singing the same song, just starting out at different points in time,* she realized. She pulled out her palm pilot and jotted some notes, her mind racing ahead of the boat.

The ferry slowed to make its groaning approach to the first of several stops on both sides of the Bosporus, inching its way to the central depot area at Galatasaray.

Vasilli was on his feet, leaning over the edge of the ferry to watch the skilled maneuver, while Marta relished the last thrumming feel of the boat behind her back. As a mode of transportation, despite its slow pace in the hectic city, Marta imagined that taking the ferry to work must be a wonderful thing. She shook off the reverie as Vasilli shouted her name, already poised on the gangway. *Ah, who am I fooling?* Marta could hardly stand to wait two minutes for a subway, preferring instead to hail a cab whenever she ventured out of her Midtown neighborhood.

Jostling across the tarmac to the waiting red-and-tan buses, Marta pulled Vasilli toward the cabstand. "We can just take a bus. It'll be cheaper," he protested.

"When you're on your own, feel free to take the bus," she said, pushing him into an idling Mercedes sedan. It took less than a block before the sweaty scent embedded in the fake-fur-covered seats overtook the calmness induced by a day on the water, and Marta practically growled when the driver reached to turn up the volume on the latest earsplitting wail emanating from the radio. *"Lütfen, hayir,"* she said. "Please stop it."

It seemed like every inch of every public space was sold for advertising, from the tops of the cabs to the sides of the buildings. Ads were draped in banners across the street and embellished the bus stops, news kiosks, and trash cans. Marta noted the plethora of American—all right, international—companies hawking their wares here. Some standouts included European appliance manufacturers, some signs in Arabic for who knew what purpose, and many Turkish companies, some familiar but most new to Marta's eyes.

"What is Toyota-Sa?" Vasilli asked.

"The S.A. is like Co., or Inc.," she said. The cab lurched to a stop in the heart of Şişli, close to one of the oldest churches in Istanbul—and nearly in front of the familiar sight of her best friend's apartment building.

"Look, a church." Vasilli leaned across her lap to read the sign. "Saint Panasios. Hmm, Orthodox."

"Istanbul is the seat of the Greek Orthodox Church, you know," Marta reminded him. He straightened back into his half of the tight back seat.

"That's Constantinople," he corrected her. "No self-respecting Greek is going to call it anything but, when referring to the church."

"Ahhh." There was nothing more to say, nothing that needed to be shouted over the cacophony of car horns, police whistles, and raised voices. Most of the intersections contained no signal light, sported no stop sign—there was not even a yield sign in sight—and so the pair experienced a typical Turkish rush hour. It was a free-for-all unmatched in the Western world, except perhaps for in Rome.

"Watch it … tssssttt." Vasilli sucked his teeth as the cab nearly ran over the toes of a crisply dressed police officer standing incongruously in the center of the northbound traffic lane.

"Vasilli, do you think that your brother may have changed his name, or shortened it somehow?" Marta asked. She suddenly had the light-headed feeling that signaled the arrival of a brilliant legal argument. With everything else that had happened, she had not taken the time to analyze her strange meeting with Sami. Why would someone like Sami be involved with this little probate matter? Marta wondered why she detected a sense of urgency behind his casual offer to settle, an offer that had raised the proverbial red flag in her mind.

"See that school—look, there too, the skyscraper—and there, that billboard on the side of the road." She pointed. "It's all the same, Vaso S.A. Can that be a shortened version of Vassilios?"

Vasilli scratched his chin.

"Look there, the Vaso Bank S.A. I'm telling you, this could be it. They want you to take a settlement and go away, before you figure out that the family is worth millions," Marta said.

"No, you're reaching. No way could that be my brother," Vasilli said sadly. "He would never change his name." He was silent for a full minute, eyes scanning the signs. "It can't mean anything …" He paused again. "When we were little, that's what he called me. Vaso. But it just doesn't seem possible. Anyway, if this is true, then why would they contact me at all? That doesn't make any sense."

"I'm going to check it out," Marta insisted. "If I remember my family law, they probably have to show the court that they made a good faith effort to find any other siblings. Hell, they probably didn't expect you to still be alive. And I bet they changed the family name from the Greek in order to survive those early years." She paused. "Look, don't get all upset about it. You're probably right—it's just a shot in the dark. But it seems like a very big coincidence, doesn't it? I'm going to look into the corporate records and see what I can find out."

"Just don't charge me for it," he groused.

She rolled her eyes and opened her wallet to shell out the stack of lira this little tour had cost.

Twenty

Some time apart seemed in order, after the intensity of their visit to the island. Vasilli took a stack of *Herald Tribunes* to a poolside chaise, his bony knees poking out below voluminous safari shorts, into which he had tucked a brilliant white button-down oxford, complete with pocket square and red polka-dot bowtie. Marta followed him to the patio and hunkered down at a table in the shadows with her files and a telephone. Vasilli was not aware that Marta was sitting nearby, her hair covered with a scarf and large sunglasses perched on her nose. The pair sat in their separate worlds, delving into mounds of paper, periodically pausing to process some portion of the events on Buyuk Ada, both with their eyes fixed on a distant vista, lips pursed, hands nervously strumming a beat on the table.

Marta could not stop thinking about her mother—and her father's violence. She blamed herself, certain that her pregnancy had been the catalyst for the fatal confrontation. He had a temper, a violent one, which was why as soon as her baby was delivered, Marta had been packed away to New York by her mother. Wallowing in her own losses, Marta had never before considered what she had left behind. She looked out at the Bosporus, imagining once again the brilliant explosion that she still associated with her broken engagement.

One of those events that mark time—akin to the birth of Christ or the death of Kennedy in the way that it seared the memories of every resident of Istanbul—the tanker crash in Istanbul was a cultural milestone for most Turks, even those living in the eastern part of the country whose lives were affected by the economic and political fallout for years afterwards. For Marta, the event coincided with the explosion of her own life and the end of her grand plans for the future.

Relationships end, sometimes quietly, sometimes with a huge blowout. Ships sink, sometimes spectacularly, sometimes causing great damage as they erupt in flames or crash into other vessels or structures. The bow of the tanker whose wreck was marked off with buoys that tolled a warning to other travelers was still visible, more than fifteen years after it collided with a small tug and its cargo burst into flames that lit the city for hours and singed the fronts of villas along the shore for almost a mile in either direction. Paint peeled from these venerable homes, whose windows shattered with the explosion.

The tanker fire coincided with a huge battle between Marta and her parents and the demise of her first and, ultimately, her only true love affair. The night sky was illuminated with white sparks and billowing smoke that was pink with the reflection of flames shooting perhaps fifty feet into the air. Things had been tense in the apartment after Marta's engagement was unceremoniously ended and her lover failed to stand up to the objections of his parents. While Marta prepared the tea—leaving the room for the families to negotiate the marriage agreement—Mehmet's mother had refused the offer of sweets. She had looked critically around the room and then said to her son, "You didn't tell me they were peasants."

Marta's father erupted and unceremoniously threw the woman, her meek husband, and the unsuccessful fiancé into the street. He would not allow any further discussion, instead ruminating on the damage to his reputation and family honor. These were not good thoughts in a man of his temperament.

Marta was at loose ends for several days, waiting for her fiancé to return. He called her once, said his mother threatened to cut him off if he married into the Demirci family, and whispered his apology before hastily hanging up the phone. Marta never got the chance to tell him about her pregnancy but had to agree with her mother's assessment: It probably wouldn't have made any difference to Mehmet. Marta worked on her résumé, fielded job offers, and studied the calendar, while her mother spoke about the need to make "arrangements."

"It's the best solution for everyone," she said frequently, but it was a plan that had to be kept from the man of the house, in order to save lives and preserve the family.

"Aren't you being a little dramatic?" Marta asked her mother. "Save lives? I mean, this is my life we're talking about here, my child, and you're acting like the fate of the world rests on my decision."

"The fate of my world does, and your world too," Mother said. "You know your father."

Yes, Marta knew her father, but by age twenty-one, she'd spent what felt like an eternity being subservient to the man, kowtowing and cowering and sugarcoating life, as if he couldn't stand any fuss, as if the knowledge of his daughter's mistake would be the end of everything.

"It's the Laz," her mother said quietly. "You know."

Marta had shrugged then, frustrated, and stood up before her mother, proclaiming boldly, "Well, I'm not afraid of him, Laz or not."

The Laz were a people from the Black Sea coast noted for their short tempers and murderous rages. Turks compared the region to the American Wild West, where family honor superseded the law and even the police and army respected that code or died trying to argue against it. Those men, the Laz, did pretty poorly in an urban setting. They were not well suited to living in close proximity to others who did not value their code. They did not thrive in corporate life and usually ended up where Marta's father did, working in a small shed as a blacksmith, barely eking out a living because of his inability to deal with a boss telling him what to do. It was hard enough to listen to the simpering of customers, asking for impossible ironwork designs and then trying to stiff him out of the payment when a curlicue was not precisely symmetric. But his ranting at those indignities was nothing compared to his reaction to any damage to his family honor. That was an integral part of the weeks of fighting that followed the rejection of the marriage offer and her father's perceived insult at the hands of one cocky little Turkish woman, Marta's would-be mother-in-law.

"You will be the death of us all," her mother announced, clutching her heart. She ranted. This daughter, the one for whom she'd taken innumerable beatings so that she could go to high school and then college, this daughter was going to push him over the edge. Marta had been protected from his rages, she said. Mother had tried to protect all her daughters, so they'd rarely felt the sting of his physical fury, and now this. Her mother finally hushed Marta's bravado.

"Remember when we used to go to the farm every summer?" she asked quietly. "Remember why we stopped?"

Marta sat down, respectful of her mother's somber tone. "Not exactly … I vaguely remember some things, but I'm not sure why we stopped going."

"Remember the chickens?"

Their eyes met, Marta's large and scared. "That was just a story, right? A scary story one of the cousins told," she protested, although suddenly she shivered. She remembered the chickens and felt a cold fear clutch at her bowels.

Twenty-one

It had been an especially hot and sticky summer day, tempers were short and chores were piled on all the females of the family. After lunch, Marta and her sisters hid in the cool shade under the back porch. Every time someone slammed the door, a shower of dust fell on the four girls. The sweat ran down their backs and burned their eyes. A frog peered between the wooden slats. Cicadas shrieked. The high-pitched voice of an older woman, *Bubba-anne*, Marta's paternal grandmother, wafted out the open window, and Marta moved her head closer to the floorboards trying to listen.

The smallest girl curled into a pile and napped, sucking her filthy thumb noisily. A tabby cat squeezed into the cool space, rubbing against each body in turn, tickling arms and legs. In the darkness, the girls listened to the cat crunching on something, probably a mouse. Giant black flies buzzed around. A chicken squawked nearby, and a black rooster approached. Sevgi made soft clucking noises and wiggled a finger at the chicken. The rooster crowed and danced toward the chicken, and Sevgi lobbed a pebble to frighten him away. It bobbed and dodged the gravel.

The door flew open, and footsteps crashed overhead. Loud men's voices boomed above and Ayşe awoke with a start. She sat up abruptly and hit her head on the floorboards, but no one heard the sound over the shrieks of the aunts and the growling voices of the uncles. Animals raced around flapping their wings, and the rooster took the opportunity to mount the chicken. Marta pulled away from the opening and covered her face to block out the sight. The ground seemed to shake with anger. The tiny grandmother cast a long shadow across the porch as she paused, her cane tapping a random rhythm that loosed dust and bugs on the girls below.

Father's voice roared suddenly. Everyone else was quiet, even the cicadas seemed to take a breath. The chicken clucked softly, and the rooster began to crow. Marta pushed her face against the latticework, trying to see what was happening. A curious strangling cry was followed by a loud gasp. Bub-

81

ba-anne's cane fell to the floor loudly, and Marta craned her neck around just as the rooster's feet hit the ground. Its head dangled from a broken neck. For a few long seconds, it ran in a circle, blood spattering the clothes of everyone standing around. Marta turned away and reached a hand to cover her sisters' eyes.

"Don't look," she whispered. There was a moment of hot silence, where everyone seemed to stop breathing.

Bubba-anne spoke quietly. "Get out."

A waft of lemon cologne penetrated their dusty hideout as Bubba-anne bent down to retrieve her cane. She muttered something that sounded like either a prayer or a curse—maybe a little of both—and her slippers scuffed across the porch. The door slammed. In a moment, Father spat on the ground and stomped off to the barn.

The other men stood around in a circle speaking in quiet voices. Slapping noises echoed as fists smacked open palms, and then their footsteps moved away. The youngest, Uncle Musafer, brought the rooster to the porch where he sat heavily on the step. Casting a dark shadow, he began plucking feathers. The sour smell of blood and sweat filled the air. Three white chickens rushed to peck at the feathers cast aside, and the cat crawled out to survey the scene.

Doors slammed inside the house. A chair crashed, and Mother called out the window looking for the girls. The girls all looked at Marta, and she shrugged. A feather tickled Sevgi's nose, and she sneezed. A heavy hand rapped sharply on the floorboards. "Your mother is looking for you."

One by one, the girls squirmed out of the opening, where they stood blinking in the bright sunshine. They were covered with dust. Marta slipped out the other side, crouching low until she reached the shadows. She waited as the other girls climbed the porch, single file, mutely looking at the bloody rooster lying pink and speckled on the stoop. The youngest sneezed again, and the door slammed behind them.

His job done, the children out of the way, Uncle Musafer kicked aside the feathers and wiped his hands on a dirty cloth as he walked slowly to the barn. Marta followed him at a distance, stopping to look at the rooster. He was hardly recognizable, but she knew it was Bubba-anne's favorite, the one she called Pasha. She walked quickly around the building until she could hear the men inside.

"I've cleaned up your mess again, Brother," Musafer said. There was only a grunt and the clanking of iron in response. "I don't think you should come back here anymore. It upsets everyone, especially Mother. Every year you come here and stir up trouble …" His voice stopped in a choking noise.

"You, you piss-bed boy, you don't tell me to stay away from my home." Father's voice was dangerously quiet. Marta tried to peek between the slats, but it was too dark inside. Flashing sparks, coughing, another sound, and then, the familiar smack of hand to flesh.

They roared a language she did not recognize, other voices joining as footfalls raced into the barn. The air seemed to crackle with energy, *twinnt*, metal hitting metal, *shaah*, fist hitting face, *pwack!* Grunting, animals rustled amidst their straw beds; the horses beyond, in the barricade, snorted restlessly too. There were shouts, curse words Marta recognized from the school yard.

No sound, no person came from the house—it seemed empty, like a deaf-mute witness. Suddenly, Marta's cousin Umut threw himself down next to her with a huff of breath.

"What have you heard?" he whispered.

"Lots of noise, yelling, but I can't make out anything," she replied.

They waited, straining to hear more. It was quiet, except for the whinny of a horse. Umut said, "*Bitti*, I think the fight's finished. *Gel bureya.* Come here."

The pair slid along the backside of the building, to a low-hinged door used to release the pigs into the enclosure. Blinking to adjust to the darkness, they crept inside. Marta's cotton stockings were caked with mud and pig shit up to the knees.

Suddenly, Father's voice rang out. "Anyone else? Does anyone else say that I am not welcome in my father's house?" He took a deep, ragged breath and then slapped his chest. "I will not be disrespected in my own home."

Marta and Umut peered over bales of straw and saw the men in a circle of dust-filled sunlight, all of them with metal pipes gleaming in their hands. Uncle Hamzi, a schoolteacher in the village who brought games and stories to the farmhouse, stood by the door, bent over and retching quietly.

In the center of the men was a heap of clothing; Marta caught a glimpse of flesh. And from the silent pile, a pipe stood erect. A black shadow spread larger, pooling toward the door. Father spit once again and then in one quick gesture, pulled out the makeshift sword and flung it to the side.

"*Gel.* Come here and pick up his legs." He rapped out orders as the others dropped their poles and moved forward.

The children ducked down behind the straw, eyes leaking and mouths hanging open, breath coming in little gasps. "Let's get Bubba-anne," Umut whispered.

Marta shook her head slowly, eyes narrowed and cold. "You must never tell anyone what you saw here," she said. He shook his head, incredulous. "I mean it, Umut. If you tell, my father will be in big trouble."

"But, he … he … he … he killed Uncle Musafer. You saw it too." He grabbed her hands. "We have to do something."

"I didn't see anything, and neither did you." Marta leaned over and grabbed his throat, squeezing lightly around his neck with her thumbs. "Nothing happened, you hear me. Nothing." She pushed him aside roughly and then squeezed his shoulder again as she drew close to his face. "If you're not careful, the same thing can happen to you." Marta looked down at the dampness spreading across his crotch and sniffed in disdain. "You pissed yourself again, Umut. You better go get cleaned up. Maybe your momma can give you a bath."

Umut gasped and ran then, fear and confusion all over his face. He ran straight to Bubba-anne, crying and shaking, the mark of Marta's hand beginning to redden on his neck. And so began their exile from the family.

Twenty-two

Marta sat back in her chair, shaking off the bad memories of her childhood. She noticed a young brunette giggling behind a fashion magazine held high enough to cover her chin. The girl walked toward Vasilli, and Marta could hear her ask him, "You like I do you?" in a falsetto as she perched on the chaise near his hip.

Marta watched the girl shake her long brown hair, bending to expose her breasts to the older man. Vasilli shifted slightly on the chair to allow her more room, and she relaxed against his thighs. Vasilli loosened his tie with one hand and cleared his throat. "So," he rumbled. "What's your name? Where are you from? What are you doing in the hotel?"

She giggled again. "I am Elif," she said, tossing her hair over one shoulder. She picked up a bunch and inspected the ends. "I live nearby, come here to the hotel for using the pool. Okay, now your turn."

"Oh, yes, ahem, my name is Vasilli, and I am visiting from New York."

"Ooooh. New York." She fairly shimmied with delight. "I am thinking to go to New York and become famous model. What do you think? Can I be famous fashion model?" She lifted her nose into the air, pooched out her lips, and thrust her chest skyward.

"Oh my, yes, you could be a model," he agreed. "You are a very pretty girl."

"You will take me with you?" She leaned closer, her hand brushing the front of his shorts before coming to rest on his hip.

Okay, that's enough, Marta thought. She stood up and walked over to Vasilli. She shaded her eyes for a moment. Marta knew the girl was most likely a pro, one of a crew that worked the hotel bar, patio, and casino in search of johns and—gold mine—a sucker to sponsor their emigration to America.

There's one born every minute, she thought as Vasilli mopped his brow with a voluminous handkerchief. "Hi!" she called cheerfully.

He stood up abruptly then, swaying a little on his feet. She rushed to take his arm. "Are you all right? Come sit at this table in the shade." Marta settled the old man and then herself. She watched as the girl hesitated in her approach to their table.

"I ... I wasn't expecting you for hours," Vasilli said.

"I have been sitting here, working, for quite a while," she said.

"Oh. I didn't notice you." He played with the ends of his tie, which dangled sloppily from his undone collar. "I just ordered some water." He looked around. "Oh, I left my newspapers." He started to stand up.

"I'll get them. You just sit here and relax." Marta walked slowly across the patio, scooped up the newspapers, and then raised her head toward the girl. "*Gel, çucuk,* I want to talk with you for a minute." Elif walked toward Marta, eyeing the older woman warily. A trace of defiance was still present in her stance, which quickly evaporated as Marta whispered a few sentences. "Listen, *orospu*, whore, I want you to stay away from my friend over there. If you don't, I'll call the concierge and have you banned from this hotel. Do you understand me? Keep away from him."

Although he leaned forward, Vasilli could not catch any of the exchange. By the time he had dealt with the waiter and the elaborate ritual of signing and tipping that accompanied the check, Marta was back at the table and Elif was nowhere to be seen.

"What did you do?" he demanded. "I bought her a Coke."

Marta reached over and took a sip of the sweet beverage. "Thanks. I needed that." She tipped her head and studied the man; his lower lip was protruding like that of a petulant child. "I'm sorry I chased away your little friend. But you should thank me. I just saved you a lot of money and probably a series of penicillin injections."

Vasilli's mouth opened and closed silently. He shrugged. "Listen, I've been thinking a lot about yesterday."

"So have I." She nodded. "I'm sorry we didn't find out anything about your family—but I made an appointment to meet with the lawyers for the estate."

"Okay, thanks." He leaned forward, his hands covering the sweaty water glass. "That's not what I wanted to talk with you about. There was one thing that Mrs. Karagöz talked about that has been bothering me, and I wanted to ask you about it."

She hesitated one minute. This was not a topic she wanted to get into right now. He watched her face and then spoke again. "I was wondering ... you remember that Mrs. Karagöz said your mother came the year before, and they couldn't do anything for her because she was too far along? Well, I was just wondering ... You said that your mother had stopped having children after five girls and, well, did she have another one? Just before you left?"

Marta studied her hands. The nails were straight and unpolished. She thought idly about getting a manicure and wondered where one might find a Korean nail salon in Istanbul. Her ears buzzed. She looked up when Vasilli touched her hand. His mouth moved, but she did not hear anything except the lonely echo of a ferry horn in the distance.

She shook her head. "Mine," she said finally. "It was me. Not her. She went there to get an appointment for me. But it was too late."

They sat in silence for a few moments, each processing the words hanging in the air between them like cobwebs, symmetric and fragile and yet strong enough to withstand the weight of important revelations. Marta studied the flight of the swallows, still dipping into the water and returning to thick mud nests cemented under every corner in the overhangs surrounding the pool area. They worked silently, methodically reinforcing the nests where occasional loud peeping could be heard. The perfect turquoise of the pool rippled in the slight breeze, fluttering wings and sea-salt air barely marring the perfection of the day.

Marta looked down to realize that Vasilli's hand covered her own hands, which were clenched and working nervously as she tried to avoid his eyes, this subject, that memory. She shook her head slightly. "Look, I—"

A waiter interrupted, rushing toward the table with an outstretched telephone. "Pardon, a call for you, sir," he said. Vasilli fluttered his fingers toward Marta, and she took the phone from the boy.

"Evet, effendim ..." She launched into a string of Turkish while Vasilli handed the waiter a few lira and rebuttoned his collar. The boy leaned down and handed Vasilli a folded piece of paper. "For you, sir," he whispered.

Vasilli slipped the paper into his shirt pocket without opening it. Marta frowned at him, held out her hand, and made a snapping motion with her fingers. He looked away, shifting on his chair to watch the arrival of a family laden with towels and toys. The children ranging in age from preteen pouting to drooping diaper, their voices ricocheting in the canyon of the patio, the troupe settled onto loungers that had been scraped loudly across the concrete.

Marta concluded the call and then placed the phone on the table between them. "Aren't you going to read that?" Her look grazed his pocket and avoided his eyes.

"Who was on the phone for me?" he asked.

"You first."

He sighed heavily, pulled the paper from his pocket, and handed it to her without opening it. She unfolded the square, skimmed the message, and placed it on the table near the phone. "It's a phone number," she said. "No name, but I guess we know who it's from." He shrugged. "Well, are you going to call her, make a date for later? Oh, do you want some privacy? I can go sit over there …" She pointed toward the pool.

"Never mind, I'm not calling her." He crumpled the paper and tossed it at a nearby ashtray. "Who was on the phone?"

"It was the lawyer for your brother's estate. They've asked to meet with us today. They're coming here, to the lounge downstairs, at 4:00." Her mouth formed itself into a smile, although her eyes were distinctly not involved with the sentiment. "Is that convenient for you?"

"That's fine. I don't suppose they said anything else … what's the reason for the meeting, or anything like that?" She shook her head. "Okay. Listen, we were interrupted, and I think you were going to tell me something. Do you want to talk about it?" Marta shook her head again. "All right then, we'll talk later. Maybe after we see what the lawyers have to say." He stood up. "I think I'll go in and have a little rest before then, if that's all right with you."

She shrugged, looking away as Vasilli left the patio. Her eyes squinted against the flash of sunshine reflecting off the white patio and brilliant blue water. A large, ungainly bird flew overhead, almost in slow motion, and Marta stood to follow its progress toward a decaying tower behind the hotel. It looked like it might have once been used as a minaret, but now its bricks were worn and loosened by years of hard weather and pollution. Marta scarcely noticed when the door closed behind Vasilli, although he watched her for several minutes from the coolness of the hallway.

She watched the bird, which she believed to be a stork. It had been years since she had seen one, for such exotic animals were never spotted in Manhattan. She remembered the small hotel near the Istanbul airport, her last stop before leaving the country and heading to a new life in New York.

Marta had been in a trance, a stupor, for the week that she had to wait for a visa to come from the American embassy. Her plane ticket to New York was in her luggage, which was packed snugly with all the belongings she had been able to take. Staying in a cheap hotel near the airport, Marta spent days and nights huddled on the balcony, drinking in the smell and sound of Istanbul. For days, she focused her attention on a family of storks nesting on top of a nearby chimney. There was a mother and four or five chicks. The flight of the big bird seeking food was majestic, almost prehistoric. Marta watched them like scenery in a movie that was playing in front of her eyes, a backdrop to the drama inside her head. On one chilly morning, her last in that limbo, she drank a glass of bitter tea and snuggled in a heavy sweater, waiting for the sun to reach her shadowy hideout.

The mother stork left, searching for food while Marta warmed her lip against the rim of the cup. Her attention wandered but then snapped back to the chimney where a large cat was carefully perched and ready to pick up a delicacy for breakfast. Before Marta could react to this event, the mother stork dropped out of the sky and attacked the cat, which was sent flying to the cobblestones below. Marta leaped to the railing, grasping the cold metal, watching the drama. It all happened in a flash, and yet everything seemed to be moving in slow motion. Marta watched the mother feeding her chicks. Her hands grew cold. The body of the cat was splayed on the cobblestones below. She looked away, watching the birds until the sun blinded her, obscuring her view of the nest.

Marta had remained on the terrace all day, watching the stars appear as the sky darkened and the lights were extinguished one by one. Although she could not see the nest, for the rest of the evening, her mind replayed the stork's diving save of her young. She felt no sadness for the cat, the predator whose remains had been unceremoniously scraped into a bin by a shop owner. When the muezzin sang his early call to prayer, the stork stood, stretched its wings, and surveyed the city below. Marta left the country later that evening, with no intention of ever returning.

Now, a lifetime later, Marta watched a stork settle on its nest, stepping gingerly in a circle until it plopped awkwardly atop the pile of sticks that jutted from the jagged edges of the brick. She turned away as the bird tucked its head under a wing. When she looked at the door, Marta thought she saw the shadow of a man there—Vasilli perhaps, still lurking in the shadows. She turned to cover the movement of her hand as she retrieved the note he'd tossed away, slipping it into her own pocket.

Twenty-three

A packet of papers in a sealed envelope awaited Marta's return to her room. The services of a private detective, at a cost that would be laughable anywhere else in the world, had in a single day generated a substantial, albeit superficial, report on the Vaso dynasty. Marta skimmed the paperwork, eyebrows rising occasionally. She jotted some notes on a pad, shuffled through her copies of Vasilli's letter, and absently fingered the locket around her neck.

Its filigree design was worn off on the backside, after years spent first on her mother's neck and then, for the past fifteen years, on Marta's. A faint design remained on the gold heart, which Marta wore on a long, thin chain so that it hung deep between her breasts, never visible to prying eyes. She seldom opened it anymore; she didn't need her eyes to envision the smudged photograph inside or the tiny bundle of dark hair secreted there.

Putting aside the papers, Marta unfolded the note she'd retrieved. It was a phone number, but not one that Marta herself could call. She tapped it impatiently on the table and then picked up the phone to summon one of the junior associates she'd been working with closely on the pasta case.

"Cem, I need a favor," she began. "No, this is personal. I need you to help me with something, something very confidential." She paused, listening, and then smiled, recognizing the prize she'd need to offer this young Turk. "How about we have dinner in my room later?"

Quickly changing into a loose cashmere tunic over a pair of snug black pants, Marta brushed her hair back into a tortoise shell clip and dabbed a smear of gloss on her lips.

Vasilli had taken more care with his attire, although Marta pretended not to notice his shiny pinstripe suit and crisply knotted pink bow tie. "Ready?" she asked. He nodded solemnly and summoned the elevator.

As the machinery glided to a smooth stop at the lobby, Marta watched the older man's face in the mirrored door. "Nervous?" she asked him. Her tone was gentler; she felt bad about their misunderstanding by the pool.

He lifted his chin and met her eyes. "Yes, yes, I am." He hesitated as the doors began to open. "I'm not sure I want to hear what they have to say, after all this."

"Let me handle it for you." She stepped toward the door. "If it gets to be too much, or if you want to discuss something with me, just say so." He grimaced. "What?" she asked. The doors opened and then slid shut again. "Just tell them you'd like to have a moment to speak with me privately. It's no big deal. We lawyers do that all the time ..."

He shook his head again. "I don't want to look like ..." The door slid open with another discrete *ding*. He turned to face Marta as the door slid closed again. "I don't want to look like I need a woman to take care of my business," he whispered, reddening slightly around the collar.

Marta quickly swallowed her retort as another couple entered the elevator and pushed the number five. "Which floor?" the man asked.

"Ah, five is fine," Marta said. They rode in silence and watched the pair leave the elevator. When they were alone and headed once again down to the lobby, Marta turned to Vasilli. "Look at it this way, most powerful men in this part of the world have staff—including lawyers—who do their talking for them," she explained. "You're not losing face by stopping the meeting to give me directions."

He sighed heavily. Reaching into a pocket, he removed a crisp twenty lira note and handed it to Marta. "Okay," he said. "Now you work for me." The doors opened. "Let's get this over with."

She folded the bill into her pocket and led the way to the lounge.

Although only Sami and another man rose to greet them, Marta knew that the other gray-suited men sipping tea at the next table were probably also with them, on hand in case their particular expertise was needed. Sami's Cheshire Cat smile did not conceal his appraisal of her casual dress. "*Effendim*, please sit here, Mr. Vasilli-bey." He pulled out a chair and then nodded for Marta to occupy the other. Sami was using the Turkish "Bey" or "sir" to flatter the old man, but Marta was not impressed with his smooth manners.

"We have Mr. Refik Ulu here with us, to represent the family." The younger man took Vasilli's hand, kissed the top of it, and then touched it to his forehead in a gesture of submission and respect. He did not speak.

Vasilli looked at the young man and then asked, "How are you part of the family?" Everyone shuffled around, finding seats and ignoring the older man's question. Vasilli, a bit unnerved by what he felt was a very rude beginning, accepted a cup of tea from the elaborate tray on the table. "I assume you know my attorney, Miss Marta Demir. She will be happy to answer your questions," he said. Marta detected a bit of an accent in his voice as he took on the guise of a mogul.

"Ah." Sami shuffled his papers and leaned over to whisper into the younger man's ear. "Yes, well, we simply require some confirmation that you, Mr. Vasilli-bey, are in fact related to the family." He spoke careful English, directing his remarks toward Vasilli rather than Marta.

Marta smiled at him. "Mr. Vassilios was contacted by your law firm, so obviously you have reason to believe that he is in fact the brother of the deceased. We have received notification that the estate is being settled, and Mr. Vassilios is here to comply with that legal notice. As far as I can tell, there is no court date that has been set for this probate. Is there a problem with the court?"

"No, nothing like that," Sami said impatiently, reverting to Turkish. "We understood that there was a brother, long ago, and we made every effort to find this person. As you know, we contacted Mr. Vasilli-bey because there was a possibility that he was, well, perhaps he was on the same boat as the missing brother ..."

"What? You mean to tell me that you had this man travel halfway around the world because he might have been on the same boat as your client's brother in 1923? Really?" Marta shook her head. "Just tell me, what is it that you want from Mr. Vassilios?"

"Can you provide some proof of his birth and citizenship?" Sami turned and spoke in English to the older man. "Sir, how well do you remember the boat trip you took to New York when you were a child? Do you remember any of the other children on the boat?"

Marta put up her hand to stop Vasilli from answering. "Wait just a minute. Before we go any further, I insist that you reveal the identity of your client."

"That may not be necessary," Sami said.

"Well, I believe it is essential." Marta crossed her arms and stared at the two lawyers. Vasilli accepted another cup of tea from a hovering waiter, and the only sound was the slurping of the hot beverage between his pursed lips.

"My brother's name was George, Yurgos in Greek," Vasilli said. "My brother was born in 1913, so he was ten years old the last time I saw him. He stayed with my mother—her name was Anna—and I went ahead with my father to America. It was just after the war, and by the time we got to New York and sent a letter back to Constantinople, the Greeks were mostly gone." Vasilli waved away Marta's frowns as he watched the attorneys scribble the names and dates on a sheet of long yellow paper. "Before that, we lived on the big island, in a small house, and my father worked as a barber, and he fished, just like all the other Greek men. I don't know anything else. I was only about five at the time."

"And your mother's maiden name?" Sami asked.

"I don't know." Vasilli sighed and stared out the window. "There was one thing, maybe it is important, I don't know. My brother had a mark on the inside of his elbow, a dark half moon about the size of a quarter. I remember the old women talking about it, that it was a sign. But I don't remember what kind of sign it was. Just that my mother got very red in the face and told the women to hush about it." He fingered his own elbow. "I have a shadow, just a darker patch of skin there. Not like Yurgos. His was very dark."

Vasilli looked at Marta. "I had forgotten about that until just now," he said. "I remember seeing it when we were in the bath, or when we were getting dressed." He sat up and replaced the teacup in its saucer. "So, gentlemen, did your client have a birthmark like that on his arm?"

Marta had been watching the men's faces throughout Vasilli's recollection, and she was sure that he had correctly identified the man as his long-lost brother. Even Sami had lost a bit of color when the birthmark was described. Sami was bent close to his companion's ear, his hand obscuring the rapidly moving lips. Refik slowly raised his eyes until he and Marta were locked in a stare.

"Well, Sami-bey?" she asked in Turkish. "Are we talking about the same man?"

"I ... ah ... I'm not in a position to answer you now. First, I need to have some paperwork from Mr. Vassilios that will officially corroborate his claims. And then we can talk further."

"No," Marta said. "That's not how this is going to work. You are going to tell me what you know and exactly why my client was contacted in New York City. And you are going to tell me the name of your client and provide me with some proof about his parentage."

Sami sat higher in his chair, at least an inch taller, by Marta's estimation. *He must do a hundred butt crunches a day to be able to get that much lift,* she thought, a smile flitting across her lips. Her amusement seemed to infuriate her former teacher, whose neck reddened and eyebrows bristled with energy.

"I can see that you are not going to be cooperative," he said. Papers were gathered and snapped into a file folder. "When you are ready to talk in good faith, please give me a call. Otherwise, we're just wasting time here." He stood, extended a hand to Vasilli, and made a small bow across the table.

"Good day, sir," he said. He leaned over to the older man and stage whispered, "I think you should reconsider your choice of *avukat*."

Vasilli smiled and waved the men away. He clicked his own heels together and prepared to rise. "Brilliant," he said.

"Excuse me?" Marta put down her lukewarm tea.

"You heard me. Brilliant performance. I think we've got them," he chortled. "Worth every cent I paid for you."

She looked at him, and they both burst out laughing.

"We didn't get any answers, you know," she said finally. "So there's your nickel's worth of legal counsel."

Twenty-four

Marta arranged for Vasilli to take a shopping excursion with an attractive young woman contracted by the concierge. After he left, Marta sat by the window, working the phones until the darkness overtook the room. Before turning on the lights, she watched the ships making their way through the Bosporus, the ferryboats cutting in and out around the larger ships. Cars, boats, airplanes—all manner of vehicles cast colored threads through the twilight sky.

The phone rang, breaking the reverie. "Have you lost your mind?" The voice of her senior partner cut through the airways. "Do I need to come out there and handle this myself?"

"Calm down, Barry," Marta said. "I've got it all under control."

"That's not what I'm hearing," he said.

"Really? Well, you gave me this case and so you have to trust that I'll take care of it," Marta said. "I know what I'm doing."

"You better not screw this up," he said.

"I'm going to take a little trip to Ankara, and after that, we'll be all set," she said. "Don't worry."

"I always worry," he grumbled.

Marta hesitated a moment and then disconnected the call. Although there was no formal agreement between herself and Vasilli, technically, she should have shared the information about this potentially lucrative new client with her boss, but for the moment, she delighted in keeping that little tidbit to herself.

A few moments later, after a quick call from the young associate she'd put on the trail of Vasilli's poolside paramour, Marta called room service, changed into a cashmere pantsuit, and turned down the lights. There were too many things clamoring for attention in her mind: the awareness of her mother's violent death, her precarious hold on the pasta deal, and Vasilli's potential—no, probable—relation to the most powerful family in Turkey.

Marta needed a time-out, and the best way she knew how to relax involved a cold bottle of champagne and a warm young man to share it with. Both needs were satisfied in short order.

Cem had proved a quick study, both as an assistant and a lover. Marta smiled as she felt a delicious tickle along her abdomen, Cem's tongue lapping around her navel.

"Let me," he said. "Close your eyes, and just relax." He continued to murmur, taking her breast in his mouth and playing with the nipple, flicking his tongue and then engulfing the entire globe with his mouth. She moaned, covered her head with a pillow, and reached for him, only to have her hand firmly pushed away.

Slowly, his hand traced her body. The skin was tan velvet covered with fine hairs that rippled when he moved over them. His hand moved over her hip, under the back to cup a firm buttock. He pulled her body forward, moving his mouth from navel to the line of fine black pubic hair.

She gasped, her head rising above the pillow. "Slow down."

"No." His reply was muffled with the taste of her.

She twisted, reaching, grabbing at his chest, running her finger around his nipple, moving her leg between his, and pushing gently behind his balls with her knee. He swam up then, his finger taking the place of his tongue, moving his mouth over hers. His hand stopped, steady pressure building between his forefinger, pushed deeply inside of her, and his thumb, covering the clitoris.

"Listen to me." He grabbed her hand and removed it from his penis. "I want you to relax."

"But, I want you—"

"Marta, I think you forgot how to be a woman. Relax, and let me show you how a man makes love to a woman."

Okay, kid, she thought. *Show me what you've got.*

Around midnight, Marta was awakened by urgent knocking on the door. She pushed aside the slumbering male whose legs were trapping her in the bed, grabbed a thick terry robe, and flipped on the light in the entryway. Vasilli, being held up by two heavyset bellboys, was leaning heavily on her door.

"What happened? Why didn't you take him to his own room?" she asked, pulling the older man into her suite.

"He insisted to come here," the one name-tagged Ali said. "The police, they dropped him at the door."

"And where is the lady who was paid to escort him tonight?" Marta asked as she struggled to settle Vasilli on the couch.

The two men were silent, taking in the sight of a naked man entangled in her bed. Marta snapped her fingers impatiently. "Never mind that … Help me here. Get his jacket off … Has he been beaten? What is all this blood?"

Vasilli righted his head, moaned, and shook off Marta's hand. "I'm fine, just had a bit of a tumble on the street … No matter, no matter," he mumbled. "Pay the boys something there, Marta, won't you?"

Checking his pupils quickly, Marta determined that the old man was not badly hurt after all. She handed the porters a few lira and then shut the door firmly behind them. She handed a wet towel to the old man and then issued a quick tap on the exposed shoulder of her evening companion. "Cem." She shook him gently. "You have to leave now."

It took a few minutes, both men grumbling and eyeing each other, before Marta had her room restored to some order. Promises of another date accompanied Cem's delivery of a thick envelope that Marta secreted in her voluminous pockets. When she turned back to Vasilli, he was crouched in front of the minibar, pulling several small bottles of brown liquid from its cache.

"Let me." She pulled him into the chair nearest the window. Two glasses, some ice cubes, and the pair settled into a quiet drink contemplating the view.

"So," she began.

"Don't start with me," he muttered.

"Wait a minute … you got deposited at the hotel door by police, dragged up to my room in the middle of the night covered with blood and dirt, and you tell me not to 'start' with you?" Marta poured another shot into her glass and then did the same for Vasilli. "You owe me an explanation. The last time I saw you, you were off on a shopping spree with a pretty woman. What happened?"

"I'm not exactly sure," he said eventually. "But what about you? I thought you were working, and here you have some young Turk in your bed."

"And that is truly none of your business," she said. "So? What do you remember? Did you make it to the famous mall?"

"Yes, yes, I bought some things—a new suit, some shirts. Yes, they were going to be delivered, I think. And some other things, silk ties, I don't know. We were there for a while."

He rubbed his lip, which Marta noticed was swollen slightly. His right eye was puffed up, but Marta was reluctant to turn on more lights and inspect the damage. He held up the empty glass and shook the ice.

A couple more bottles were liberated from the bar, the warmth of the liquor easing some of the tension between the pair. "And then?" Marta prodded. "Did you have dinner? Where have you been all evening?"

Vasilli shrugged. "Not sure." He finished the drink and gestured for more.

"I don't think so." She took the glass out of his hand. "I think maybe you need to get some rest, and in the morning, we'll figure out what happened to you." She looked at him for a minute. "Are you hurt? Is that your blood all over your shirt?"

"I'm not sure—it might be. I think I might have had a bloody nose or something." He stood up unsteadily. Marta looked at her rumpled bed. Well, if he complained, too bad. She pushed him down into a seated position on the edge of the bed and gently pried his shirt off. He raised his head and pushed her hands away. "I'll do the rest, thank you." She stood up and went into the bathroom. There was another bathrobe, but nothing suitable for an old man's nightwear. When she came out with the robe, however, he was already buried under the covers, his soiled suit in a heap on the floor. She picked it up gingerly, returned to the lighted bathroom, and emptied the pockets onto the counter.

His room key was there, along with a clip of money and his wallet, still containing credit cards and other identification. There was a folded receipt from a high-end tailor shop, some other small slips she couldn't identify, and a monogrammed handkerchief with bloodstains dappled across the fine linen.

Marta folded the clothing into a dry-cleaning bag, slipped into her own discarded clothing, and went down to the lobby. At three in the morning, however, the "C" team was definitely behind the reception area, and no one knew anything about anything that had happened—or not—in the lobby that evening. At the very least, she got Vasilli's clothes into the dry-cleaning hopper and determined the name of the escort who took him shopping.

The old man was deeply asleep when she returned to the room, not even flinching when she turned on a light and inspected the swelling around his eye, cheek, and lip. Aside from a little crust of blood around one nostril, it seemed like the damage was minimal. She extinguished the lights and resumed her vigilance over the Bosporus. Unfolding the contents of the envelope from Cem, Marta confirmed her suspicion that Elif had been hired by Sami's firm and sent to the Conrad pool with the intention of seducing and possibly drugging her target, Vasilli.

Why go to all this trouble? Marta mused. *Why bother to contact the old man in New York at all? Bring him all this way, deny that he is a relative, then set him up with a prostitute and later, a mugging?*

As always, she pulled out a legal-sized notepad and started jotting her thoughts, creating columns of possibilities, linked by sharply drawn arrows to other scenarios and characters. As her right hand moved steadily on the paper, her left fondled the locket, tracing the design and finding little comfort in that last connection to her own past. There were too many contradictions, too many mysteries—too many things that Marta had tried to avoid for too many years.

Twenty-five

The day was bright and warm, but neither Vasilli nor Marta was in the mood to enjoy it. He'd awakened early and returned to his room for a shower. When Marta arrived at his room at 8:00, he hardly raised his eyes in response to her questions.

"I'm fine," he said finally. "Why don't you just leave me alone?"

"Oh, okay, that's what you want," she said. Shiny shopping bags were toppled on the rumpled bed, crisp cottons and linens peeking from the striped tissue paper. "Don't you think you should hang these things up?" She poked at a bag.

"Leave it, would you?" He coughed. "Don't you have work to do, some lawyers to bully?"

"Actually, not for a couple hours," she said. Marta sat on the edge of the bed and inspected the bruised eye and slightly swollen lip on the old man's face. He pulled away, but she grabbed his chin and forced eye contact.

"Listen, we need to talk about what happened to you last night. It's obvious that someone set you up, but this time, they only intended to scare you. I'm not sure why …"

Vasilli rubbed his unshaven chin, avoiding her eyes. Taking in his wrinkled khaki pants, the unbuttoned top button of his blue-and-white-striped oxford shirt, Marta realized her companion was deeply shaken by his assault. She picked up the phone, ordered breakfast, and then placed his wallet and money clip on the table.

"Here's your stuff," she said. "They didn't rob you and obviously didn't hurt you too badly, although the message is clear that they could have."

"Yes, that's clear. Thank you for pointing that out."

"Do you remember anything that happened last night—anything at all?"

He shook his head. "I just remember coming back here ..." His eyebrows rose. "And finding you ... with that boy." He actually seemed to blush, again rubbing his face.

"I was getting information from him, if you must know, but that's really not your concern." Marta rose to answer the door.

"That's how you do business? You sleep with young men for information? I thought you were different. I didn't think things like that ... well, obviously, I was wrong," he said, his voice strengthening a bit as his comments continued. The waiter pushed his cart into the center of the room, eyes lowered, while the couple continued to argue.

"Like I told you last night, that's none of your concern." Marta closed the door firmly and returned to stand in front of Vasilli. "I did learn that your little friend at the pool was hired by Sami, probably not for your enjoyment, but since you didn't call her to make a date, they went to plan B."

Vasilli uncovered a plate of scrambled eggs and began to eat hungrily, turning his face away from Marta.

She sighed, took a piece of toast, and watched him for a moment. "Are you going to pour the coffee?" he asked, reaching for a glass of thin orange juice.

"Sure," she said. "Anything else you need?"

He grunted. "Why don't you just leave me alone for a while?"

Marta pushed a coffee cup toward his hand. "All right, I'll get out of your way. Just do me one favor." He reached for the cup, and she stopped his hand. "If you leave the hotel, let me know so I won't send out a search party for you."

"Fine." The coffee sloshed slightly when his shaking hand raised it to his lips.

Fine, then, Marta thought. *Stubborn old man.*

A note delivered to her door at one o'clock brought Marta out of her work stupor. "I am joining a tour to Topkapi Palace. We will return at 5. V."

She reached for the phone, connected with the desk, and was assured that Vasilli had joined a legitimate tour with twelve other Americans who were just then leaving the driveway in a van. Marta surveyed the tabletop, which was covered with sheets of yellow legal paper, each heavily inked with her distinctive tight black handwriting. Arrows and circles connected some of the paragraphs, while other pages were completely black with writing. Sitting back in her chair, Marta sighed and absently twirled a hank of hair into a loose knot that fell out when she dropped it.

Topkapi, the center of the Ottoman Empire, had been the repository of the country's wealth and culture. Its famous harem was still a draw for tourists. The spires of the complex dominated the hills of Istanbul, more so than any high-rise office tower or statue. The city that straddled the East and West, Europe and Asia, was defined by the majestic towers of Topkapi.

Every child went there, almost annually, as did every tourist and pilgrim. It was a symbol of the lost empire, still standing even after the calamitous last years of the Ottomans, even after the establishment of a republic that denounced the spoils of the royals, even after the demise of the turban and fez in favor of the fedora and Western ways. The city was littered with these remnants, the pride of long-lost glory and the contradictions that characterized the modern Turk—so many palaces, now museums. Behind the Conrad was another small palace. Down the hill was the magnificence of Dolmabahçe on the water, close to the restored hulk of the Çirağan Palace, now a luxury hotel with some of the best shopping and dining in the city.

Marta's inventory was interrupted by a knock on the door, and she was surprised to see Sami's face through the spy-hole.

"What a surprise," she said as she opened the door. There was no pleasure in her voice, as she mentally made a note to reprimand the staff for allowing a visitor upstairs without forewarning.

"I hope I am not interrupting." He smoothly moved toward the table, standing with hands clasped together at his back. "Ah, working hard, I see."

Marta quickly assembled the scattered papers and placed them in her open briefcase. "How can I help you today?" she asked. "We didn't have a meeting scheduled, did we?"

"Oh, no, I was in the neighborhood, and I thought I would come by and see how your client was doing today."

"Really? And why would you be concerned about my client?" Marta sat comfortably on her chair, crossing a leg and indicating with a nod that Sami should occupy the other seat.

"He seemed a little … how shall I say, shakened up after our meeting yesterday?"

"Hmmm. Well, no, he's fine. He's actually out doing some sightseeing today. No problem at all." Marta smiled and crossed her arms.

"And you, how are you doing?" Sami pulled a cigarette case out of his pocket. "Do you mind?" he asked. "Will you have one?" Marta lifted her eyebrows and clicked her tongue, one of those curious gestures by which Turks respond negatively. She moved an empty ashtray from the windowsill to the table, still keeping her eyes on his unreadable face.

"I'm fine, thank you. My business here is going well, although I think I may have to make a short trip to Ankara to settle the final deal."

"Ankara." Sami rolled out the name like a chest-clearing cough. "Not my favorite place."

"It must be different now," Marta offered. "All the ... politics, that was a long time ago."

"Not so long, really. You've become like an American, I guess. The world began for the Americans only a couple hundred years ago, and no one remembers what happened last year ... even last week."

Marta smiled. "Have you visited the United States then?"

"I don't have to—it's all over our lives. Our television, books, magazines—even the music and food are becoming Americanized. It's a shame."

"You almost sound like one of those conservative religious leaders, Sami-bey," Marta chided. "You used to be such a raving liberal."

"Yes, well, my dear, we both used to be something else, didn't we?"

There was a pause while Sami extinguished his cigarette and waved away the smoke with an impatient hand. He teased a bit of tobacco between clenched lips and picked it off with the long yellowed nails of his right hand. "Do you have any soft drinks, a soda perhaps?" he asked.

Reluctant though she was to serve him, Marta rose and displayed the array of bottles in the minibar. "What's your pleasure?" she asked, knowing full well that there would be no soda without a dash of whiskey to lubricate the professor's agenda.

"You know best," he replied, sniffing. "So, let's get to business, shall we?" He placed both hands on the edge of the table, apparently inspecting his nails. "What does your client want?"

Marta placed a glass filled with amber liquid at the center of the table and then sipped her own glass of sparkling water. "That's an interesting question. Really. My client came to Istanbul in response to a letter—he's not the one looking for something. You are. And I'd like to know exactly what it is that you want."

Sami grinned as he sipped through clenched teeth, the ice cubes splashing a cold spume on his nose. "Yes, your client replied to the letter. Yes, that's true. And why? What does he want from this little adventure—aside from the obvious benefits of spending a vacation with a glamorous lawyer from New York?" The glass was empty. He swirled the ice, but Marta merely lifted her chin toward the bar.

"Help yourself." As he pushed out of the chair, Marta noted the frayed edges of his collar and cuffs. "Let's just say that all my client wants is knowledge; he wants some closure about his family. He wants to know what happened to his mother and brother, and frankly, I think he'd like to know if he still has family. He's been alone for a long time, you know, and maybe he just wants to know that he's not, that he still has family somewhere."

"Nice sentences, nice." Sami nodded as he settled back into the chair. "Not here for money or property then, just to see if there is 'family' left, eh?"

"Why is that so hard for you to believe?" Marta asked.

"Yes, why?" Sami tapped the glass against his teeth again, an annoying habit that Marta suddenly recalled from their days arguing after class. He reached over and opened a package of leb-lebi, spilling the chickpeas across the table and then quickly scooping a handful into his mouth. "Some people, they don't want to know what happens to their family. Some people leave and never look back. And then others, when there is maybe some money, they come running to have reunite with their long-lost brother. It is interesting."

"And for this, you would frighten an old man?" Marta's cell phone rang, and she looked quickly at the caller ID and then silenced the mechanism. "Try to trick him with a prostitute, have him beaten and robbed on the street?"

"What?" Sami put his glass on the table sharply, with an almost comical display of outrage. "When did these things happen? We certainly had nothing to do with any … any … any kind of damages that Mr. Vasilli could have done."

Marta shook her head slowly. "Listen, I'm telling you. He doesn't want anything—he just wants to know what happened to his brother. You can tell your people to leave him alone. He won't hurt you; he doesn't want anything."

Sami paced before the window, sputtering about honor and trust. "How can you make these accusations?" He wrung his hands and then flung himself back into the chair, cigarettes and lighter at the ready.

"Please, just give them the message," Marta said. "I can't guarantee that he won't change his mind, if something else should happen …"

Sami blew a long stream of smoke directly in her face. "Is that a threat?"

She nodded. "Yes. It is."

Twenty-six

The phone's incessant ringing finally helped Marta remove Sami from her room, after which she placed a call to the desk complaining about their security measures. After threatening to move to another hotel, Marta asked the manager to arrange for Vasilli to be escorted to the waterside bar at the Çiragan Palace at 6:00 PM.

More yellow sheets were covered with her analysis of Sami's comments, until finally the entire bed was covered with names, dates, arrows, and large question marks circled in red ink. She sorted the sheets and drew another pad to her knee. Number one: It was clear that they never expected Vasilli to come to Istanbul. Number two, she wrote: It was clear that they wanted him to go away, quickly and quietly. Number three: Why?

A knock on the door signaled another unannounced guest. Marta flung the door wide, hinges protesting, and startled Vasilli in his retreat down the hall. "I thought you weren't here," he said. His voice shook a bit, and she was startled by the pallor that had appeared on his face. He held a note. "Is this from you? An invitation for dinner?"

"Yes, I want to show you something special," Marta said. "Are you up for it?"

He waved his hands, about to deny the fatigue that was obviously taking a toll. "No, I think I'll stay in tonight, get some rest. Maybe tomorrow. That Topkapi Palace, what a place. But I'm beat." He smiled a little. "I'm just very tired tonight. Thanks anyway." He walked down the hall and then turned for a moment. "Was there anything important you needed to talk with me about? Anything new?" he called out.

"No, that's fine. Tomorrow will be good. We can talk and make some decisions."

Marta listened for the elevator bell and the slide of the doors. She padded down the hall in her stockings, slipped up the stairwell, and cracked the door enough to watch Vasilli slip his key card into the track once, twice, three times before it finally engaged and he was able to open the door. The "Do not disturb" sign was hung on the handle, and Marta retreated when she heard the locks click soundly into place.

It was four thirty, still light and inviting outside when Marta left the hotel and crossed the busy boulevard. Despite the green light, a taxi squealed to a stop at her outstretched hand. "*Çiçek Pasaji,*" she ordered. It was time for a visit to the Flower Passage, once her favorite shopping spot in the bustling city. Sami's office had been there, along with numerous cafeteria-style restaurants, stationery stores, bookshops whose wares tumbled from ancient shelves, and Gypsies whose illegal flower sales caused merchants to occasionally run into the streets, wielding short-handled brooms and cursing like sailors.

They'd come here often, as students, seeking out the cheap food and hunting through stacks of books looking for something different, a forbidden political tome or racy American novel. Harold Robbins had been a big draw, Marta recalled. She'd watched the others as they flipped pages, looking for something, anything titillating. None of these had any appeal for Marta; she was so in love with the law and its intricacies. Not even Mehmet's sharing of sexual passages in *The Godfather* could draw her into their reading frenzy. But she held herself apart and watched—and learned.

Those same books seemed to cover the tables still, the same group of fresh-faced idealists poring over the battered bounty. She turned away and entered a *lokanta*, a long room filled with high tables and bar stools and the distinctive odor of *kokareç*, which she ordered on a hard roll from the first available waiter, that and a glass of *ayran*. Nothing like some fried goat intestines, set off with a thick, salty drink of yogurt, to stimulate the sensory memory she hadn't experienced from the Westernized kitchen fare at the Conrad.

Once she'd eaten her fill, Marta resumed her wandering. She noticed that the area had become a tourist curiosity. Cameras obtrusively snapped photos of old men washing their feet before entering the mosque, chased covered Arab women down alleyways cluttered with cars and feral cats, and sought the artistic shot of Gypsy women selling brilliant purple clusters of sweet william, the colorful flowers clashing with their garish headscarves and mismatched outfits. Colors layered over colors, patterns challenging florals, all in the cacophony of a hundred-year-old covered alleyway in a thousand-year-old borough, in an ancient crossroads, where religions bloomed, where art and culture flourished and died along with the empires that supported them.

Marta pushed her way into a stationery store so cluttered with product that it was hard to imagine the walls behind the display. An old man hunched too close to a tiny television, its familiar flickering green screen a microcosm of the heart of every true soccer fan. Before she could touch the pile of legal pads obscuring the countertop, a young girl slid in front of her.

"May I help you find something?" she asked, her polite query delivered in English with a fairly aggressive tone.

"Fatma," the old man barked out in guttural Turkish. "Be nice. Sell something today, for Allah's sake."

Her face reddened. Marta ignored the exchange and simply asked the price of the yellow paper. "This is the price. But really, miss, this is not a good paper for you. Here, this one is better, see? You can feel it. And look at the yellow, it's much nicer on the eyes, yes?" She practically rubbed the paper on Marta's cheek. "See here, you can see the lines in a better way, much better for an important person like yourself. See, you cannot make a hole in this strong paper. You can only write brilliant words on this paper."

The girl glanced over at the television. "I give you discount if you buy ten pads," she whispered. "One free. How's that? I wrap for you? Anything else, you must need pen to go with the paper, yes? We have thousands of them. What ink is your preference? Black, I think."

Marta smiled, slightly alarmed when the young woman opened a case to reveal what must be one of every possible kind of writing instrument ever manufactured. She shook her head.

"Ballpoint, roller ball, cartridge, fountain pen? Pencil then, erasable ink? I have Parker Brothers. I have Pentel. I have Waterford, the best for you." The girl was on a roll. Marta put both her hands on the stack of legal pads, pulling them slightly toward herself. "I just want these," she said. "Please wrap them for me. I'm in a hurry … important meeting, you understand."

And so, walking back toward the covered flower market, Marta realized she'd paid for ten pads what a gross would cost in New York. A smile of admiration crossed her face. "Sell just one thing today," indeed. It had been so long since she lived here, Marta was ashamed to admit she'd forgotten the cardinal rule of commerce: always bargain. Never pay the first price. She was really a foreigner here after all. She veered quickly into a bright pastry shop, pointing to a creamy white dessert that was served with a cup of Turkish coffee, a small folded and shiny paper napkin, and a thin tin spoon.

Kazandibi. The improbable result of hours of boiling chicken breast created the smoothest pudding, a favorite that was never served in the up-scale Turkish restaurants she'd visited in the States. They preferred to dazzle customers with baklava and *kadiyif*, pistachio concoctions, and soft almond cookies. But the simplicity of the pudding made it Marta's comfort food, another touchstone to childhood—steaming kitchens and her mother's back, always hunched over something needing her attention at the stove.

An offer to read her fortune in the coffee cup was rejected in favor of continuing her journey through the passage. While a colorful bunch of mixed wildflowers was being wrapped, Marta allowed her gaze to wander over the signs swinging on arms from second- and third-story windows: *avukat, avukat*, an occasional doctor, dentist, or translator. Some had illustrations to catch the eye—a giant tooth, a stethoscope, or the eternal symbol of the law: scales weighted with coins and books. One, a psychiatrist specializing in fertility treatments, featured the leering face of a giant baby tethered like a balloon to the doctor's outstretched hand.

Marta paid for the flowers and moved quickly toward the avenue. She stopped short and recoiled into a doorway. Waiting a moment to be sure she'd read it correctly, she was pale and breathless. She searched the street for a cab, fairly running from the sight of Sami's name on a large billboard nearest the intersection. It wasn't his name that shocked her so; it was the sight of a familiar face gazing through a window above his sign. She moved closer to the curb to get a better look and saw a face that was so close to her own image that Marta reeled backwards off the curb into the path of a cab. She didn't hear the screeching brakes or the horn over the sound of her heart beating frantically in her chest. She moved back against the solid building again, shading her eyes, and tried to get a better look at the woman in the window, but the fading daylight and reflections of neon signs made it impossible.

She finally walked a block to a larger intersection and hailed a cab. From the backseat, she turned to look again at the window as it slid by. She was certain, wasn't she? The face in the window, so like her own. And there, under Sami's name, she had clearly seen her sister's name painted on the sign. Marta knew that the woman in the window was her sister, *Avukat* Sevgi Demirci. *My sister is a lawyer,* she thought. *A lawyer who works for Sami.* The food rumbled threateningly in her stomach, and she leaned back against the seat as the cab careened onto the busy boulevard.

Twenty-seven

Cem was back, waiting in the lobby when Marta arrived, wild-eyed and shaking from her discovery. "Let's get a drink," she commanded, pulling him into the elevator. When he reached a hand toward her shoulder, Marta absently handed him the sheaf of flowers. He looked at them, unsure of what to do with the bouquet. Marta had turned away, clutching the package of notepads to her chest. She smoothed her hair, checking her image in the mirrored walls.

"I've got the information you called the office for," he said. "Are you okay? What happened? Do you—"

She cut him off as the doors opened. "Later," she said. "Let's just sit for a minute. Here." Before her bottom hit the seat, she'd ordered a whiskey from the waiter hovering near the tables. *"Dub-le."*

Cem put his briefcase on the floor next to his chair, placed the flowers on the table, and watched Marta. "What's going on?" he asked. "You seem upset."

She snorted. Her words were clipped, her tone abrupt. "Nothing. No, I'm all right. Nothing happened. So, tell me, do you know anything about Sami Erdem?"

"What about him? I know he's the lawyer who hired that girl, but I never heard of him before yesterday."

"Hmmm." She drained the glass and raised it, the waiter swooping in to remove the empty one. A plate of nuts appeared on the low table. The strains of music were competing with the low chatter of a group of young Asians seated near the windows. Cem reached over and grabbed a handful. His raki was still untouched.

"Who is he? What else do you want to know about him?" Cem asked.

"Never mind. He's just one of the lawyers; that's all." Her second drink arrived, and she sipped it slowly, sinking deeper into the club chair. "On second thought, can you run a check on him, see if you can find out anything?" She tossed a handful of leb-lebi between her two hands, aiming for nonchalance.

"No problem."

"Okay, thanks." She sighed. "What did you get for me?"

"You're not going to believe this," he said, pulling out a large envelope. "Look."

He handed Marta the top sheet, a grainy black-and-white photograph reproduced from a newspaper. She sucked in her breath.

"This is his obituary?" she asked.

"Yes. Doesn't it look like—?"

She interrupted him again, holding the photo closer to the small lamp at the center of the table. "Exactly." There was no question; this was Vasilli's brother. The man in the photo could have been his twin.

"What else did you get?" she asked, wiggling her fingers in his direction. He had pages and pages of articles copied from the financial pages of the Turkish newspaper *Hürriyet* and other international newspapers. Reports estimated the wealth of the family, of the Vaso empire, at trillions of lira, before revaluation—the equivalent to billions in Euros and American dollars. The articles referred to hefty charitable donations made by Vaso and his late wife, the endowments, the buildings, and the fortune left to his heirs. Marta smiled, finally, the whiskey having smoothed over the tension she'd brought into the bar.

"Excellent," she whispered. "We've got them."

"But, the thing is—" he began.

"What? What is the thing?" Marta asked. He bit his lip. "Well, what do you have to say?"

"The thing is, all of this is public knowledge. I mean, anyone could get this information and the picture—the guy's face is plastered all over the place," Cem said. "So do they think we're, um, you're stupid or something? That you wouldn't figure out how much this family is worth? I mean, even an illiterate taxi driver knows who Vaso is."

"That's true. It is strange. The only thing I can figure is that they never expected such an old man to come here in response to the letter. But they had to send it; they have to show that they contacted every possible relative before the children can inherit the fortune."

"And when he did show up, they tried to smooth talk him ..." Cem mused.

"... not figuring that he'd have hooked up with an attorney who could actually put two and two together ..." Marta continued.

"And so then they turned to intimidation to get him to back off."

"Right."

They both reached into the bowl and tossed handfuls of leb-lebi into their mouths. Crunching, they nodded.

"Now what?" Cem asked. He took a sip of the raki which he followed with a water chaser and then looked up at Marta.

"I don't know," she said. "It depends on what Vasilli wants to do, I suppose. I don't think he really cares about the money, but if it were me, I'd be pretty ticked off right about now. I mean, all the old guy wants is to meet his family and talk about what happened to them." She straightened the papers and drained her glass.

"Coming?" She stood up, offering a hand.

They waited a few minutes by the elevator, standing close enough to share body heat and the promise of more. The doors opened, and Marta stepped back quickly.

"Vasilli," she said. "What are you doing here?"

He was dressed in a gray business suit; his shirt was a bit rumpled but the pastel tie obscured the most obvious wrinkles. "I thought I might find you here," he said. "Hello, young man, my name is Vasilli." He extended a hand, which Cem shook gravely.

"Sir," he said.

"Can you excuse us for a moment?" Vasilli took Marta's elbow and steered her back into the bar. "I just wanted to thank you and say goodbye."

"Good-bye?" she blinked. "Where are you going?"

"I'm going home," he said. "I'm tired, and I just want to go home."

"No."

"No? Why not? I'm not going to get any answers from these people, and I'm sick of hanging around here, getting in your way ..."

Marta pulled Vasilli to a table and gestured for him to sit. "Come on, just for a minute," she said. "I need to show you something, and then if you want to leave, you can leave." She pulled the photograph out of the pile and placed it in his hands. *"Yavrum,"* she called the waiter. "Bring a light for the man."

Vasilli blanched, and Marta watched his eyes scan the image over and over. "Are you okay?" she asked. He nodded. She called Cem over from his perch on a bar stool. "Can you get us a couple more whiskeys here?" she asked. "I'm sorry; this will only take a few minutes. You can leave if you like." She gave him a smile and held his gaze for long enough to ensure that he'd stick around, and he retreated to the bar.

"This is Yurgos. This is my brother." Vasilli finally spoke.

"Yes, that's pretty obvious," Marta said. She handed him the cold glass and sipped from her own. "So. Now we are sure this is your relative. Do you still want to leave?"

"No." He took a drink. His faced reddened. "Yes. Dammit." He smacked the glass hard on the table. "I do want to leave. Why should I stay here? These people don't want to have anything to do with me; they are trying to scare me into leaving, for God's sake. I should just … just … I don't know what to do."

He shrugged, his hands dangling helplessly between his legs. "I got another 'message' at Topkapi today; someone almost pushed me down a flight of stairs, but luckily, one of the ladies on the tour grabbed me before I lost my balance."

They sat in silence for a moment. "Okay, listen," Marta said. "Tomorrow is Sunday. Let's have a nice day, relax, have a good dinner. Then I have to go to Ankara, so you come with me. Get out of town. They won't follow you. We'll go to the airport; they'll think you're heading back to New York, and we'll take a little side trip."

"Why? Why don't I just go back to New York? I don't want to go to Ankara. Why would I want to go to Ankara?" He put his head in his hands.

"I need to do some business there, and apparently, their business is headquartered there, and the family compound is somewhere in the vicinity," she said. "Just sleep on it, okay? Don't make any hasty decisions. We'll meet in the morning. We'll talk it over then, okay?"

Marta put her arm around the older man, lifting him gently onto his feet. Cem scrambled to his feet and followed them to the elevator. *"Bir daka,"* she whispered in Turkish. "One minute, and I'll meet you at my room." She passed him the key, her arm still firmly around the older man's waist.

Vasilli leaned his body into hers, his head drooping a bit. She was unsure if it was the whiskey or fatigue or if he was acting, but she grimaced at the "accidental" brush of his hand against her breast. At the door, she had to grope in his pockets for the room key and thought she detected a smile pass over his lips.

"Okay, here you are." She turned on the lights and led Vasilli to the bed where he sat down heavily. "Please don't leave before we talk in the morning, okay?" she asked. He nodded, struggling to pull off his jacket. He threw it on the floor.

"I'll be here, at least in the morning," he said. "Leave that photo, will you? … Before you toddle off with that youngster again." He pulled the tie clumsily, a button flying off the collar and pinging the wall.

When Marta looked back, he was studying the picture, one hand fumbling with the buttons of his shirt. "Good night," she said. He waved a hand in her direction, and she closed the door.

Twenty-eight

Neither Marta nor Vasilli looked well when they met in the lobby for a breakfast of rolls, cheese, olives, and sliced tomatoes. Their silence was interrupted only by the crackle of pages turning in newspapers, the click of spoons against tea glasses, and the vacuum slide of doors opening to release or welcome hotel patrons.

"So." Vasilli cleared his throat and folded his newspaper. "What argument are you going to make to persuade me to stay here?"

Marta laughed, a strangled attempt to lighten the older man's mood. "Let's just agree that we will have this one day to see a little bit of the city and relax. No talking about family problems—your family, my family, nothing like that. No pasta business. Just two people spending a quiet day in a beautiful city. Can we do that?"

"And then what?" he replied. "What about tomorrow and the day after that? I'm telling you, I just want to go home and forget about all of this."

"Do you really?" Marta leaned back in her chair and looked at her companion. "I don't think you want to leave. I think you are actually having a good time here." Vasilli shook his head and started to rise from his chair. "Now, listen, I know that you've learned some difficult things about your family. So have I. But we both need to stay a little longer and see things through. Now we know who your brother is and what happened to him. Don't you want to meet the family and find out what you can about them?"

Vasilli snorted. "If they don't kill me first."

"They're not going to do that."

"How do you know? You don't know. You weren't there." He sniffed, pulling a voluminous white handkerchief from his pocket and patting his nose.

Marta signaled the waiter, who brought cups of American coffee and removed the remains of their breakfast. She watched Vasilli straighten his pale-blue chevron-patterned tie, adjust the seersucker jacket sleeves, and replace the white fabric in his pocket. Eventually, he looked up, and she spoke again.

"I am not trying to ignore what happened to you; I just think that you can't run away from it. You came here for a reason, and you shouldn't leave until you get some satisfaction." She sipped the coffee, watching his face for a reaction. Only his cheek muscles moved. "And besides that, you can't let these people scare you away. You are entitled to some respect." This elicited a small lift of the mouth in the corners; she had almost gotten a smile out of him.

"And what about you, you're pretty adamant about my family, but you haven't talked about your mother since we found out how she died. Aren't you going to get in touch with your father or your sisters? And you haven't said anything about your child …" he said. A shadow passed over his face. "Ah, we have company. Your young man has decided to join us." He crumpled the linen napkin onto his plate and began to rise. "I'll speak to you later. Excuse me."

"No, please, just sit here for a minute." Marta leaned over the table and took his hand. "I just need to talk to him for a second, and then we can go." She increased her grip on the old man's large mitt. "Come on, you know you want to …" she cajoled.

Cem arrived at the table and sat down, oblivious to the interchange between Marta and Vasilli. "Good morning," he said, turning in his chair to signal the waiter for a plate and cup. "What's up?"

Vasilli slid back into his chair, a sparkle in his eye lightening his expression. "I'm going to just finish my coffee. Don't mind me." He unfolded the paper and hid behind its colorful pages.

"Did you get the stuff I asked you for?" Cem handed over a slim brown envelope. "Thanks, Cem," she said. "I'm going to take Vasilli out for some sightseeing."

"Okay, I can take you," he offered. "I have my car just down the street—"

"That's not necessary … but, ah, hmmm." Vasilli lowered the paper a bit and watched Marta. She weighed the options: a private car versus a series of cabs. It would be another demand on her attention but also a free form of security. "Okay," she agreed. "You can drive us." She stashed the envelope in her bag and followed the two men into the bright spring sunshine.

Cem waited in the car while Marta and Vasilli walked through the gardens and toured the famous Blue Mosque. They spent more time at Aya Sofya, the St. Sophia museum, where Vasilli marveled at the ancient layers of Christian and then Islamic symbols exposed in the museum. "How could they deface a church?" he asked, his voice echoing through the vast open space.

"History, you know, it has many interpretations, depending on where you sit," Marta replied.

Vasilli walked away, muttering to himself in Greek. She watched him stop, make some kind of religious sign, and then return his gaze to the decorated walls. After a moment, she turned and walked out into the bright sunshine. Cem joined her on the grass.

"Are you having a nice time?" he asked.

"Yes, thank you," she replied absently, missing the sarcasm in his voice.

"Tell me something," he said. He coughed, stretched his neck, and pulled on his earlobe. He was nervous about something.

"Mmmhmmm." Marta seemed oblivious to his discomfort, but she took it all in and leaned back casually. A busload of tourists threaded their way through the entrance. "Hey … have you noticed anything suspicious? Anybody following us, hanging around, anything like that?" He shook his head. A motorbike roared by, and he waited for it to pass before speaking again.

"Are you going to get me a job in New York?" he asked. "Or are you just strumming me alone here?"

"You mean, 'stringing me along'?" She almost laughed, but his expression was too serious. "No, I told you I will see what I can do when I get back to the city."

"Really? Because I am thinking you are just using me, and you will forget about me as soon as you get on the plane."

"First of all, you are being paid for the work you do, right? So I'm not using you; I'm employing you to do some research for me. And second, I never promised you that I would bring you to New York, did I? We've had some nice times together; that's true." He pulled some grass and flung it at a pigeon hovering closely. "So, I'll bring your résumé to New York and see if they have a position for you, but I told you, you'll have to get another degree if you want to practice law in the United States."

"I know. I will do it," he said. "Thank you. I just … well … it seems like you are more interested in the old man than you are in me—"

Marta stood up then, brushing the back of her slacks. "Don't be silly. He's a client."

"And what am I?" Cem asked.

"You're … well, right now you're a colleague." She coughed. "We have a good time together; that's true. But don't go making this into some big romance, all right?" She tapped his shoulder lightly. "I'll go get Vasilli, and we can get some lunch. Do you know a good place around here?" She had not noticed the older man hovering in the shadows and was surprised when he appeared at her elbow. "Let's go," she said, leading the way to the parking lot.

More idle time passed easily. It was another perfect day with no clouds in the brilliant blue sky, when the smell of exhaust and pollution was masked by the scent of flowering trees and a slight hint of the sea, when the wind turned just right—not too many tourists, not too many noisy children. The gardens were resplendent with perennials, bumblebees, and birds doing their part to create idyllic scenes. In the grounds surrounding Dolmabahçe Palace, Marta took Vasilli's arm and pointed out the other magnificent villas, palaces, and battlements that could be seen from the edge of the Bosporus.

"This was the last home of the last Ottoman emperor," she said. "They had wonderful parties, beautiful people wearing silks and satins and covered with jewels. All kinds of food and drink … and through the gardens, turtles crept around with candles stuck on their shells. Can you imagine that scene? That was the end of the empire. Atatürk actually was living here when he died. When we go inside, you'll see all the clocks are stopped at the same time, the hour of his death."

They stopped and turned back toward the building. "I think I'd rather not go inside," Vasilli said.

"Really? Why not?"

"I think I've had enough of palaces and gold and china and all that," he said. "What about a drink?"

"Yes, that's a good idea." Marta began looking around for Cem. "Where is he?" She pulled her cell phone out, but Vasilli put his hand on her arm.

"Don't call him," he said. "He's bored. I'm sure he had somewhere better to go, and we don't need him hanging around anymore. Do we?"

Marta laughed, folding the phone back into her bag. "Follow me," she said, pulling Vasilli along the shore. "This building was just a shell, gutted in a fire, but then some investors, Japanese or German, I forget which, restored it. Wait until you see …" She smiled. "Don't worry; it's not another museum. It's got wonderful little shops inside, and there's a hotel attached. All the ritzy people stay here: foreign dignitaries, rock stars. And there's a terrific bar, right on the water."

"How come we're not staying here?" he asked. "Aren't we 'ritzy' enough?"

"Too rich for my expense account," she explained. The Çırağan Palace Hotel, glowing in the soft light of the coming dusk, was a polished jewel box on the water's edge. Beside a disappearing pool, the pair sat at a tiny table that barely held their sweating glasses of gin and tonic, with the obligatory nut assortment in a small bowl at the center.

"Where will you go next?" Vasilli asked.

"What do you mean, 'next'?"

He coughed. "When your legal business is wrapped up, then what? Will you go back to New York and forget all about this?"

Marta played with the swizzle stick in her drink, pink plastic that ended in the shape of a tulip. "Did you know that tulips originated here in Turkey? They were named after the turbans that the sultans wore. Then they exported a few to Holland, and the Dutch made them into an industry. But they come from here." Vasilli was silent, watching Marta's face in the changing light. He waited for her to speak again. Both of them turned to watch an oil tanker slide silently through the deep blue water.

"I don't know what's next," she said finally. "I can't go back and pretend I don't know what I know. I know that I should get in touch with my family. I know that. But a big part of me wants to get back on a plane, go back to New York, and forget all of it." She chewed on the stick again. "But I've … I don't know."

"You've changed," he said.

She looked at him. "Yes."

"And?"

She sighed. "And … and what? I don't know. It's easier for me to focus on your family issues than think about mine." Her phone trilled; she looked at the caller ID and switched it off. "Cem. He must be wondering where we are. Oh well."

"Are you going to bring him to New York?" Vasilli asked.

She smiled and shook her head. "They always want to come to New York. No matter where you go—Rio, Singapore, Milan—they all want to come to New York."

"And did you ever bring anyone back?"

"Only once. When I first started traveling for the firm." She snorted. "Big mistake. Never did that again. So, Cem … I don't know. If he comes over, I'll try to help him. But I'm not sponsoring him." She tipped her head and wagged her finger at Vasilli. "You were eavesdropping."

He smiled. "Maybe a little bit." He looked up and signaled the waiter. "Another round?"

"You've changed too," Marta commented. "You're much more comfortable now. Younger, even."

"Oh yeah." He laughed. "That's what getting beaten up has done for me."

"Well, a little adrenalin never hurt anybody," she said.

A companionable silence settled over the pair. Boats passed, some ferries disturbing the peaceful sound of seagulls with their horn blasts. Water taxis and oil tankers, large rusted vessels with foreign names and not a human in sight, added to the ambiance. Piped music began to play softly in the background as the sun slid toward the horizon. They emptied their drinks just as the call to prayer began to echo through the streets. Marta smiled.

"Time to move," she said.

"Tomorrow—" he began.

"Tomorrow, we get out of town."

Marta reached for her wallet, but Vasilli raised a hand to stop her. "Please, let me pay for the drinks," he said. "So, out of town. Just where are we going?"

"Ankara."

"Oh, no," he wailed. "I don't want to go there. I think I'll go home."

"No, you'll love it. Just for a couple of days. I need to wrap up this stuff, and we can try to meet your family."

"In Ankara? Are you sure? I thought they were here, with those lawyers, you know," Vasilli said.

"No. The company's headquarters is in the capital, and apparently, they live in a little town just outside the city. So it'll be perfect."

He frowned. "Did I mention that I can't go on airplanes?"

Marta crossed her arms and looked at him with raised eyebrows. "How did you get here then?"

"I was a little nervous. My neighbor gave me a valium, and I had to take half just to get on the plane."

"So take the other half."

He shook his head. "I think I'll just stay here."

"We'll talk about it in the morning." Marta sighed. "Why does everything have to be so complicated?"

"Well …" Vasilli puffed up his chest, ready to argue. "I don't see why we both have to leave."

"Never mind. Let's go."

They rose and started walking toward a cabstand near the hotel entrance. "You just want to leave Istanbul without seeing your family," Vasilli pointed out.

She shrugged. "Maybe. But I have an aunt near there, and, well, I need to check on some family business in Ankara too." She refused to elaborate and changed the subject once inside the cab which took them toward Ortaköy and a dinner of fresh fish and raki.

Twenty-nine

"Let's go for a walk." First thing in the morning, Vasilli appeared at Marta's door, rolling suitcase and carry-on bags piled neatly in the hallway.

"What?" She was brushing her hair back into its usual tight bun.

"Oh, leave it loose," Vasilli begged. "It makes you look so much younger."

"Thanks a lot." She put down the brush and shook her hair. "With all this humidity ... I give up. You'll help get the knots out later, right?"

Vasilli bowed comically, his hands together at chest level. "It would be my pleasure to untangle you." He maneuvered into the room, placing his bags next to her pile. "So, shall we get some exercise? We're going to have a long trip, and it'll be good to stretch our legs a bit beforehand."

They walked out into the bright morning, refusing the offers of cab rides and instead walked around to the back of the hotel. Another abandoned palace, a faded reminder of past glories, surrounded a lush courtyard filled with roses and dwarf trees. A uniformed guard approached, and Marta spoke with him briefly.

"We're not allowed here," she told Vasilli. "They were working on a museum, but with all the budget cuts, they closed it down." She turned back toward the hotel.

"Let's at least go through the park," Vasilli said, taking her arm. He pulled her gently toward the sloping green, a few small benches placed randomly along a crushed rock path. At the center, a statue of a seated man pondered the Bosporus.

"Who is this?" Vasilli asked.

Marta stood silently, almost reverently at the foot of the statue. Vasilli touched her shoulder, waiting for her to speak.

"It's the poet, Yahya Kemal," she replied. "We worshipped him when I was in school. And now, I don't even know why. I don't remember what he wrote." She studied the figure for a moment and then walked to a nearby bench.

They sat, the blur of car and truck traffic, ferryboat horns, and children's voices enveloping their quiet contemplation. Suddenly, a flock of pigeons rose like a flag over the Toyota repair shop across the street. They crossed the sky and dropped suddenly toward land. The sun reflected on the underside of wings that appeared to shimmer, and then the birds seemed to disappear as they turned, only to reappear momentarily, moving across the horizon like the dark shadow of a plane. At a certain point, it looked like they had stopped, wings glittering, and both Marta and Vasilli held their breaths and then exhaled when the birds swooped back toward the earth. Vasilli looked at Marta and saw a youthful gleam in her eye.

"Aren't they lovely?" he asked. She nodded.

"I had forgotten them. I wonder if—no, it can't be the same man. He was ancient then." She laughed. "Well, everybody over thirty was ancient to us, I suppose." The pigeons crossed over the street and then cruised to the ground near their bench. Mostly a dove-gray color, the birds were well cared for, each with a yellow tag on its leg. They pecked at the dirt nervously and then suddenly took flight again as one, as if hearing a silent summons, and flew back toward the rooftops. A turn, a shimmer of light catching their wings again, and they were gone.

"I used to play here, when I was growing up," Marta said and paused. "But you figured that out, didn't you?" He didn't reply, just settled back onto the splintered slats and crossed his arms and ankles.

"I grew up across the street, behind those businesses. There's a whole little ghetto back there—lots of working-class families, living on top of each other, everybody knowing everybody else's business. Not exactly the sophisticated city you've seen in the past week."

"Show me," he said.

She shook her head. "I can't go there."

"You can, and I think you must," he said. "You're not going to see anyone this time of day, I'm sure, but you need to go there just to … oh, I don't know how to put it … to update the images in your head … to get it out of mythology and back to reality."

"It's been too long," she argued. "I don't see what good it will do."

"Humor me," he urged again. "I want to see where the real people live in this city."

They walked across the park, waited for traffic to stop at a pedestrian crossing, and then left the asphalt to climb a steep, one-lane cobblestone road. It was unclear who was supporting whom; was Marta being pulled forward by Vasilli, or was she serving as a crutch for the old man's unsteady climb?

The only thing different on the street, narrow and heavily shadowed by the three- and four-story buildings crowded along both sides, was the vintage of the cars pulled helter-skelter onto what was only the suggestion of a sidewalk here and there. Feral cats appeared, lean and hungry, mewling and complaining, from open or broken windows, the smallest alleyways, or the abandoned shells of old wooden houses.

Vasilli paused to catch his breath, discreetly pushing cats aside as he looked up at an ornate three-story house. "This must have been something," he noted.

"I suppose," Marta replied. "It looked exactly the same when I lived here, and that was fifteen years ago."

"Why doesn't anyone fix it?"

"I don't know … too expensive? Usually there's a fire that takes care of it."

Vasilli shook his head, and they continued along the narrow street.

"Wait, look there." Vasilli pointed up at the old wooden house. "There's someone living there."

A white curtain fluttered out an open window. When she looked up, Marta caught a glimpse of a face in the "modern" apartment building accented with hundreds of turquoise tiles and fronted with a row of sliding-glass windows. The shades were pulled down hastily as Marta turned away.

"Where did you live?" Vasilli asked.

"There, the gray one on the left." She coughed down a laugh; all the buildings were some shade of gray. "Well, the gray one with the wrought-iron doors."

"Hmmm. It looks nice."

"Just keep walking." She grabbed his arm. They moved ahead a few steps and then stopped when a bag of trash was dropped from an upper window, barely missing Vasilli. She muttered some Turkish "blessings" and sidestepped the aromatic pile of refuse.

"It's not so bad, really," he observed.

She snorted. "You should see it at four, five o'clock, when the kids are screaming from one end of the street to the other, the mothers are hanging out the windows bargaining with peddlers and Gypsies, and then the fathers come home and the televisions start blasting. It's a real nice neighborhood."

"Just like most working-class cities."

She shook her head.

A toddler appeared around the corner, his pants dragging in a puddle. He stooped low, patted the water pooled in the chasm of a couple of missing cobblestones, and rested on his haunches as three kittens appeared from an open casement window.

"Kedde, gel, kedde," he crooned. Shiny brown eyes darted eagerly, and he wiped his nose on the back of a sleeve. The cats edged toward the boy's outstretched hand.

A short-handled broom appeared around the corner, stirring up a tornado of dirt, followed by a squat woman covered head to toe in unmatched floral-patterned clothing. Humming, eyes downcast, she did not see Marta and Vasilli until they were practically engulfed in her cloud. She shrank against the wall, called her son in a low tone, and pulled his head into her skirts when he ran to her.

They passed a tiny store on the corner. Eggs were arrayed in a display in the hot sun, and wine bottles lined the windows where sausage links, garlic braids, and dried red peppers hung from a blue-and-white plastic clothesline. Fresh breads were piled in a basket near the door.

"I suppose you used to shop there." Vasilli tried to loosen Marta's grip on his upper arm. A car roared to life, and the driver blasted his horn as the pair stepped out of the road.

"Sure, for emergency stuff, fresh milk, a pinch of sugar. Too expensive for regular groceries." She pulled him across the road, avoiding the sharp turn of a motorcycle roaring over the crest of the hill. A scraggly park filled the block diagonal to the store.

"This is nice," Vasilli commented. Boys flung balls at naked metal hoops at both ends of the concrete courts. Dogs sniffed the trunks of ancient oaks, yelped, and ignored the whistles of their owners, seated on peeling wooden benches along a dirt pathway.

They walked in silence, avoiding conversation along the way, until they arrived at the juncture of three roads. The hill dropped off steeply; the tiered sidewalks presented more of a challenge than navigating the roadway. All manner of small businesses lined the road, their wares spilling onto the limited frontage.

Marta stopped. "Let's go back."

"Why? Let's just go down this way." He turned and gestured down the hill. "Look, there's a steeple over there. Is that a church? Come on, let's look."

Marta looked around. "I don't want to." She crossed her arms, and Vasilli raised his eyebrows at her childish pose.

"What? Tell me why you don't want to go down this street."

She pushed her hair back angrily and caught it loosely in a fabric-covered elastic. "I don't—can't we just go back this way?" She pointed toward the left fork, which led back toward the hotel.

Vasilli looked around, taking in the workshops and sounds of tradesmen coming from the storefronts. "Your father worked here somewhere, didn't he?" She did not respond, just turned away. "Come, we'll walk quickly and go look at that nice little church. Come."

He pulled her arm until they reached the first cross street. A couple of trucks forced them against the buildings to avoid being clipped. Engines raced to make the steep climb, horns blaring to avoid stopping or even slowing when obstacles appeared in the distance.

"This must be something in the winter," Vasilli commented. His feet slipped a couple of times on the worn cobblestones, but Marta's firm grip on his arm kept the older man from falling.

"You have no idea." Marta chuckled a little. "You should try going up, with your arms full of schoolbooks or groceries or a baby or two. Now that's a challenge."

The road twisted a bit. A street opened to an alley on the left, and the white stucco of an old church beckoned. It was Armenian, seemingly abandoned but still pristine, its stained-glass windows sparkling with deep cobalt and ruby colors.

"I don't remember ever seeing anyone here," Marta said.

"Well, it looks like someone is still taking care of it." Vasilli led the way around the tiny structure, which was barely twenty-five feet square. Its steeple listed a little, but the Orthodox cross was intact.

The closer they got to the bottom of the hill and the more the slope flattened out the more retail businesses appeared. The fish aroma from an open-air market filled the air; more cats waited patiently along the sidewalk for morsels flung by merchants inspecting and shuffling their product. The smell of freshly baked bread competed with the tang of coffee, an overlay of perfume, and exhaust emanating from the junction of another alleyway. Men's clothing stores, women's shoes, children's toys, and housewares competed in display windows. A prominent corner was engulfed by a huge restaurant, its open kitchen visible from the street. Small pizza-like creations were being pushed and pulled into the flames on long wooden pallets.

"*Lahmajun,*" Marta said. "You want to try one? It's kind of spicy."

Wrapped in wax paper, the rolled dough contained spicy meat, parsley, and onions, which she topped with a red spice.

"What is this red stuff?" Vasilli wiped his mouth ineffectually with a slippery napkin.

"Sumak," Marta replied.

"Like the poison bushes?"

"Yeah." She laughed. "I'd definitely make you eat poison sumac."

After eating, they continued along the twisted street. The boulevard was crowded even in the middle of the morning with motorists, beggars, police, and buses.

"We can't cross here; we have to go down to one of the bridges," Marta said. "Unless you're too tired."

"No, I'm good." Vasilli tossed his napkin into a bin. They joined a stream of people walking single-file along an ancient wall onto a pedestrian bridge that crossed over nonstop traffic. On the other side, Marta grabbed Vasilli's arm again as they elbowed past long queues waiting for buses, ferry transport, and *dolmuş* cars. Every few feet, beggars sat with outstretched hands, faces turned in supplication toward the crowd. Marta and Vasilli stepped carefully around them, slowly descending the slippery stairs on the other side of the bridge. The sounds of ferryboats called them to the water-front, but they turned up the hill toward the hotel.

On the quiet back road, away from human and vehicular noise, Vasilli stopped and mopped his forehead. "Give me a minute," he said. They looked around at the little houses nestled under wide-limbed trees. "So, your father, he was a laborer?"

"Yes, ironworker. I told you that before."

"And his shop, it was there on the hill." It was a statement, not a question.

"Yes."

"Did you see it today? Is it still there?"

"I wasn't looking." Marta untied her hair and busied herself with its rearrangement.

"I don't believe you. But that's okay." Vasilli pocketed his handkerchief and straightened his jacket. "No one ran after you, calling your name. No one threw anything at you, right? So it was okay to go there. Right?"

She took a step, turning away from his questions. "We'd better get going. It's time to head to the airport."

Thirty

Marta sat in the front seat of the taxi. Vasilli was in the back surrounded by baggage. Pretending to fix her makeup in a small mirror, she watched a car pull onto the street behind them and follow their progress toward the airport.

"Anything?" Vasilli asked.

"Yes, we've got a tail; this will be perfect." She turned and spoke for a moment to the cabdriver, whose questions forced a wearying repetition of the request. "Maybe I should've been more careful about picking a cabbie," she muttered. Finally, she opened her bag and showed him several large denomination bills. "Okay?" she said.

"Okay," he agreed, stepping heavily on the gas pedal.

The "new" airport, a large structure that had just opened when Marta left in 1985, was a cinderblock monstrosity surrounded by a convoluted roadway. Unsmiling army personnel lined the entryways, guns at the ready, squinting into each vehicle that slowly rounded the driveway. Marta checked her mirror again; despite the challenges of the traffic, their tail was still two cars behind.

"Ready?" she asked Vasilli. He nodded and hoisted a small bag onto his lap. "Ready?" she asked the cabbie in Turkish. He held out one hand in response, and Marta deposited some bills. "The rest you get on the other side," she said. *"Tamum-a?"*

They jumped from the cab and avoided the entreaties of porters seeking to make money carrying their bags the fifteen feet to the door. She waved her ticket at the officer in charge of the door, Vasilli following her example. Inside, they stepped to the shadows and watched two men rush the doors, pushing aside police officers threatening to tow the car abandoned at the curb. They were not as brazen dealing with the army personnel who moved in at the first sign of aggression. In short order, their pursuers were searched and placed flat on the ground, rifles trained on their bodies.

"Great," Vasilli said.

"I hope they'll think we've left the country," Marta said. "Now let's see if our friend kept his word." They bumped along the corridors, periodically stopping to ask for directions, Marta doling out paper from her dwindling stack of currency. Noticing that Vasilli was dragging his bag and his feet, Marta allowed a short coffee stop at an overpriced café.

"I'm going to buy some candy," Vasilli said. "Would you like some?"

"Don't buy it here. This place is a tourist trap."

"But ... isn't it duty free?"

"Listen, where we're going, you can get all the candy you want for the price of this little coffee. Save your money. Okay, let's get out of here."

A polyester-suited young woman wearing an earpiece showed them to a side door, which was used only by employees. Several utilitarian blue vans idled outside, and she gestured to one of them. "*Bodrum!*" she shouted over the din of an arriving plane.

"We're going to Bodrum? Where the heck is that?" Vasilli yelled in the vicinity of Marta's ear.

"They think we are and that we got dropped off at the wrong airport," Marta said. "Just a little diversion for our pursuers, in case they get this far."

A bumpy ride to a smaller airport, used for domestic flights only now, resulted in their deposit on the tarmac where they watched another screaming plane make its descent.

"Now what?" Vasilli asked, looking around at the deserted terminal entrance.

"Just a moment." She reached into a bag and pulled out a bright red baseball cap, which she handed to Vasilli, and a brilliant yellow and blue scarf, which she tied over her own hair. "Put it on," she said impatiently. He looked down at the cap, lip curling slightly. "It's a signal, put it on for a minute. It won't kill you."

Their cab rolled up, the driver's hand extended for his payment. "*Haydi,* let's go." Marta made sure Vasilli was fully in the vehicle before urging the driver to move. "Take off that hat now. Duck down a little back there if you can," she told Vasilli. "Just in case they're looking for us."

"Is this really necessary?" he huffed. Turning sideways so his bony knees had room to fit, Vasilli hunched down in his seat.

"Kămel Koç," she told the driver. "The bus depot outside the city, on the Ankara highway." She handed him the remaining stack of bills. "*Haydi,* let's go."

"The buses to Ankara run in the evening," she explained to Vasilli. "We'll have some time to kill at the bus stop."

It was more than a little while before they were finally aboard a double-decker bus heading eastward toward the capital city. Too many cups of tea and fried sandwiches left both slightly nauseous and totally awake. Stomach gurgling, Vasilli hunted through his carry-on bag for a roll of Tums.

Marta dug in her bag for the cell phone, studied the list of calls she'd missed, and prepared to dial up New York. "Paper, pen," she muttered and then more rummaging. "What's this?" She pulled out the brown envelope Cem had given her.

"Let me see." Vasilli plucked it out of her hand. "Ahhk, it's all in Turkish," he groused, handing the envelope back to her. She was dialing New York, checking her watch to calculate the time difference.

"Hello, who is this?" she asked. She sat up a bit straighter. "Yes, I'm on my way to Ankara, and I'll take care of everything when I get there. Yes. Yes, I know. Well, I'm sorry about that ..." There was a long pause. She tapped her foot in the aisle, the only sign of her anxiety. "Yes, I know. But—" Another interruption. "Okay. Okay. Yes, I know. Trust me. This is how it works here. No. I don't think anyone else would be able to ... Well, that's your choice. I'm just saying, I know these people. I know the language and the culture, and I'm telling you ... Okay ... Well ... All right. I'll call you tomorrow. Fine. Good-bye."

Silence. Vasilli studied his newspaper while Marta folded the phone back into her bag. "Everything all right?" he asked.

She snorted in reply. Closing her eyes, she let the rumble of the tires take her back to a simpler time.

In her childhood, the buses for the eighteen-hour ride to the Black Sea coast were always old and crowded and smelled of greasy cheese sandwiches and sour diapers. On every trip, Father sat in the front seat near the driver and smoked until a putrid cloud obscured his head. They made the annual trip to the farm as soon as school ended, trekking north each year until the fight between the brothers, when Marta was about ten years old. She recalled a trip, perhaps when she was seven or eight, when she was just beginning to understand her place in the family. The girls and their mother crowded into three seats in the back of the bus, luggage stuffed under and between them. The bus wheezed along the coastline stopping at filthy little gas stations where bitter tea was 1¢ a glass and the children preferred to pee in the bushes rather than the restrooms. Father usually walked by himself to the roadside, his hands busy working the strand of amber worry beads that always jangled in his pocket. He grew quieter when they returned from the village, becoming once again the silent man they recognized from the dinner table.

Marta stood with him once when the bus stopped in the middle of the night for fuel. Mother and the other girls slept, but Marta had always been a light sleeper and so she bounced off the bus and surprised her father as he stood smoking. Neither of them could sleep on buses, and the pair walked silently to the canteen where he bought the girl a cola as a special treat. They stood gazing at the stars and the quiet woods surrounding the brightly lit service station. The bleary-eyed driver opened the luggage compartment and rolled himself inside wrapped in a blanket. The assistant shut the door, and the new driver drank cups of steaming coffee. A boy in rubber overalls hosed the dead bugs off the window and gave Marta a look as she gulped the cola. She quickly turned away, her heart pounding as she waited for her father to step forward and kill the boy with a single twist of his neck. Father ground out his cigarette and inhaled deeply of the fresh, cold air. He hadn't seen the look.

Father bought two packs of Samsun filterless cigarettes in the familiar white box. Marta grabbed the empty box as he removed the last flat tube. He watched as she traced the red letters with her index finger. "Can you read that?" She did, and he grunted as the man gave him his change. "Girls learning to read." He shrugged at the clerk who nodded and turned away.

The bus driver revved the engine, and they boarded the bus in a cloud of exhaust. Marta walked slowly back to her seat with the box clutched in her hand. Her sisters had spread out so she pulled a bundle into the aisle and sat there, leaning against her mother's leg. Ahead, she could see the flash of a match as Father lit a new cigarette for the next piece of road. Marta opened the box and inhaled the heavy scent and then licked the loose tobacco out of the corners. She let the leaves sit there for a while, trying not to swallow but to feel the pleasure of the strange taste in her mouth. The girls hoarded these boxes whenever they could retrieve them from the trash bin under the sink at home. Various collections of rocks, bottle caps, and marbles were secreted inside. Periodically, Mother found them and threw them out, especially after finding one filled with dead bugs in Ayşe's book bag one afternoon. Women did not smoke, she lectured the girls. Although she wanted them to be educated (and herself as well), she remained a traditional woman from the village.

"Where did you get that?" Marta was startled as she hunched over the box. The bus rolled through a dark forest, and the sky was brightening through the dusty windows.

"Father gave it to me." She covered the box with both hands.

"Don't let anybody see you carrying that thing," Mother warned. "Only bad women smoke, and only evil women let their children smoke." She gently tugged Marta's hair to show that she was not angry. Marta slipped the box into her pocket and rested her chin on her mother's knee. The baby was nursing hungrily, and Mother's breast shone like silk in the glowing light from the rising sun. Marta reached up and touched the locket she always wore.

"Tell me about the locket," she whispered. The bus rumbled up another hill, and the baby smacked and moaned with pleasure. They rocked along, and Mother recounted the romance of her parents.

"They were engaged, but he had to go fight in the war. She promised to wait for him, no matter what, and he pledged to bring her a special gift to celebrate their marriage. She waited for years without word, tending goats on her family's farm and embroidering sheets and tablecloths. After a long, long time, he returned and they married. He gave her this locket with his picture inside, and she wore it every day. Less than a year later, she died in childbirth. Father never smiled after my mother died, and he barely spoke to me, but I know he loved me because he gave me the locket." She paused to adjust the baby. "One morning, I found him hanging in the barn."

She spoke in a very soft voice, and Marta was surprised at the ending. Mother had never mentioned her father's death before, usually ending the story by talking about her hastily arranged marriage. She was quiet for a long time until the baby whimpered and she moved her. Patting the baby for a burp, she looked at her daughter. "I never took off the locket either. Someday, it will be yours." The bus lurched on a bump, and the baby vomited. "Give me a diaper." The smell filled the close space, and they wiped it up, folding the soiled cloth inside a newspaper.

The baby was already asleep on her lap as Mother closed her dress. She hesitated, fingering the locket. "Did I ever show you their pictures?" Marta leaned in over the warm bundle on her lap. "This is my mother," she said, indicating a dim photograph on the right. "I keep her next to my heart, even though I don't remember her. And this is my father." There was a grainy black-and-white picture of a severe face dominated by a huge mustache and eyebrows. "He is next to her, but not next to my heart." She snapped the locket shut and polished the deeply etched design with her sleeve. Marta looked at her pinched face and for the first time noticed the tiny lines around her eyes and mouth. "Love is not always a romantic fairy tale," Mother said sadly.

Marta laid her head on the armrest, and her mother stroked her downy cheek. Marta's mouth was sour with the taste of tobacco and her stomach grumbled loudly. Her head was full of questions, but she kept quiet, disconcerted by Mother's sad expression. They passed into morning that way, listening to the snores of the other passengers. Marta watched the sun rise beyond Father's profile in the halo of smoke ahead.

The squeal of brakes brought Marta out of her reverie. Her hand was cupping the locket gently, as she often discovered upon waking. She looked over at Vasilli, who was snoring softly, and pulled the envelope from her bag. She took out the four sheets of closely written text, smoothed her hair down, and prepared to read all about Sami.

Thirty-one

Cem's dossier on Sami had little to add to what Marta had already surmised. The facts of his professional decline and sell-out were clearly obvious from his threadbare wardrobe. Why, then, had he been hired by the Vaso family, who certainly had entire law firms at their disposal? His was not among the names on the document Vasilli had received in New York. No, it was not until she became involved that Sami had appeared on the scene. These people were clever and dangerous … and smart. But so was she.

She turned pages quickly, scanning the client lists and cases, until she found it. Her sister's name was listed as one of his "associates." Since there were only three people in the firm, that designation held little importance. She and the secretary made up his entire staff. Marta was pleased that her little sister had become a lawyer too. How long she'd been working for Sami was not clear. Was this a recent hire, or had she been there since graduation?

The bus, alone on the two-lane highway, was making good time. Stars spotted the clear sky above, mirroring clusters of lights scattered along the road. At the front of the bus, the driver and his porter spoke softly. After a while, the bright oasis of a rest area cast a glow on the horizon. It was time for a stop. The porter shuffled into his shoes, folded the jump seat away, and leaned out the open door directing the bus to an empty spot near the restaurant.

It went like this all through the night: smooth periods of driving that lulled the passengers to sleep or melancholy interrupted by quick stops at preordained areas that featured fetid restrooms that charged one lira for a square of shiny toilet paper and served overpriced glasses of bitter tea, thick meat stews served with day-old bread to sop up the heavy gravy, and toast that was washed down with barely cold and mostly flat cola in old-fashioned glass bottles. Soon, the sky lightened, both from the approaching dawn and the haze of city lights ahead. Sleepers awakened. Marta folded away her laptop, having done her best to construct a convincing legal argument to present to the minister of trade in Ankara. How to make a compromise sound like a victory? In most cases, Marta was a master at that task. Here, she just hoped for the best.

"You get any sleep?" Vasilli asked, after taking care to slick down his hair and wipe the sleep crumbs from his eyes.

"No."

He studied her for a moment and then looked out the window. The suburbs of Ankara were swallowing up the road. "How much further?" he asked.

"Not long."

"Where shall we stay? I think we—"

She cut him off. "I've made some reservations; don't worry. We'll go there first, have a shower and breakfast. Then I've got some business to take care of."

And so it went. The new Sheraton was a short walk from Embassy Row and a quick cab ride from the AkBank where Marta headed shortly after their arrival. Vasilli was left in the lobby with a newspaper, a cheap cell phone purchased at an exorbitant cost from the concierge, and instructions not to wander. He didn't wander, just followed Marta as she walked quickly down the road.

From her passport case, Marta extracted a well-used, multifolded piece of paper that listed her bank accounts. Years of automatic wire transfers had taken place since these accounts were established, shortly after Marta obtained her first full-time job, briefcase, and apartment. Thousands of dollars had been sent, in accounts set up under her mother's and aunt's names. With automatic deposits and an accountant who handled all the paperwork, Marta had never paid attention to the quarterly bank envelopes she had stacked in an envelope for each year's taxes. Now that she had discovered her mother's premature death, there should have been thousands still in the account. There weren't.

She studied the balances printed on the two slips of paper. "This can't be right." She pushed one of the papers across the desk. "Let me see all the activity on this account." As she had anticipated, an argument ensued. Marta pulled out her palm pilot, cell phone, passport case, and, for good measure, her hotel room key. She hoped that something in that assortment would intimidate the clerk, so she held her ground until a manager was summoned and more high-level denials were issued.

Finally, a young woman emerged from the elevator and took Marta into her plush offices. When the situation had been explained, she began tapping on a computer keyboard. "Okay. Now we have you opening the account in 1989. Automatic deposits were made every month, first for $1,000 and then increasing to $5,000 and so on. The balance on the account is presently $20,347.38 at this time." She sat back in her seat. "Now, what is the problem?"

"Miss … excuse me, what is your name?"

"Öznur."

"Okay, Miss Öznur, my problem is this: The account was established in 1989 for my mother, Neslihan Demirci. She passed away in 1986, but I did not know that. I continued to send the money every month. So, where is it? There should be over $1 million in this account. Who has been taking out the money?"

Miss Öznur blanched a little, her dark tan fading around the edges. "Ah. Let me see, hmmm." She made a lot of those soothing noises that just set people on edge. "I … um … I'm going to have to check on this."

Marta nodded. "Yes, you are." She pushed the other paper forward. "And this account, I'd like to see the balance sheet for it please."

The young woman squinted at the paper, her smile thinning. "Why don't you just tell me what's wrong with this one?" she said.

"There's too much money there."

"Well, miss, maybe you have the two mixed up. Maybe this number is the one your mother never touched, and this one is the one where money was being withdrawn regularly. What did you say the name was on the second account? And who is Mrs. Uzun?"

"This is my aunt, who was the only signatory on this account."

"Is she dead, too?"

"Not that I know of," Marta replied. "There is some money gone, but not nearly what should have been withdrawn. So, again, I'd like you to print out all the transaction records for this account."

"That will take some time," Öznur said.

"I'll wait."

"It's not practical. It will take a long time."

"How long?"

"I don't know. Weeks maybe."

"I don't think so. We have computers now. You should be able to locate the records in a few seconds and print them out for me immediately."

"Let me ask the manager to come and speak with you."

The young woman excused herself. Her white crepe suit rustled against Marta's arm when she passed, the scent of cologne lingering long after she had left the room. Marta moved behind the desk, where she studied the unfamiliar Turkish keyboard and screen for a few minutes. When Öznur returned, Marta was comfortably navigating the bank's innermost record systems.

"You need to get some security systems installed here," she mumbled as Öznur pulled her away from the screen.

"Excuse me, miss." Her voice had a shrill and anxious tone. "You can't be doing this. You have to leave now."

"I thought you were going to bring me to see your boss." Marta sat back in her chair. "Or is he coming here? Even better."

"No, he's busy right now. He can see you perhaps tomorrow. Call this number and make an appointment."

"No."

"No?"

"I'm not leaving here until I see someone in charge, and I get an explanation for what has happened to my money."

"Your money is right here." Öznur pointed to one account.

"It shouldn't be." Marta checked her watch. "Listen, I have a meeting to attend at the trade ministry. And then I'm coming back here. And you will have my information ready. Okay?"

The woman avoided meeting her eyes. "I'll see what I can do."

"No." Marta shook her head. "No, you will have the information for me at, let's see, one o'clock."

"We close between noon and one—"

"Fine. I'll be here at 1:30."

Marta was not surprised to see Vasilli sitting in the bank lobby. She nodded as he rose to join her departure.

"Everything taken care of?" he asked, falling in step beside her.

"No. What would give you that idea? Has anything gone smoothly since we arrived in this country?"

"Oh." They walked to the corner, where traffic separated them from what looked like a delightful little park, its borders of cheerful red geraniums and daylilies bursting behind a low brick wall. "Care for a coffee?" Vasilli pointed to a small café whose empty wrought-iron tables spilled onto the sidewalk.

He tried again at conversation. "We seem to spend a great deal of time eating and drinking, don't we?"

"Why are you here?" she asked.

"Nothing else to do." He shrugged. "And this message came just after you left." He held out a pink note, which Marta looked at and then folded into her pocket.

"What is it?" he asked.

"The case. No, not yours," she added when his face turned pale. "The pasta mess. I've got to go and deal with this." She glanced at her watch and then abruptly finished the Turkish coffee in front of her. A mouthful of grounds caused her lips to pucker, and she sucked her teeth uncomfortably. "So. Now I have to go to this meeting, and then I will come back here for round two with this bank person. And what will you do?"

Vasilli shrugged. "Maybe I'll just hang around this park for a while. Unless you think I can come with you to your meeting. I won't say a word, I promise."

"No. That's not a good idea. And anyway, you'd be bored."

"No more than I will be sitting here all morning. I'd like to see you in action." He threw in a little flattery, knowing she was not susceptible to it.

"I wanted you to stay at the hotel, remember? We don't want the Vaso people to know that you are here in Ankara. And if you're tagging along with me, I'm sure their little spies will report that you're here. So we'll be back where we started." She cast a steely look at the older man. "Why go through all this clandestine stuff to get out of town and then have you waltzing into meetings with me?"

"Oh. Okay." He finished the coffee and pulled a handful of bills from his pocket. "So, I should have just gone back to New York like I wanted to in the first place," he argued, following Marta out of the café. They stopped at a corner where a cab appeared as soon as her arm was raised to call one.

"Please go to the hotel, let me take care of this meeting, and then we can spend some time together. We have to figure out a way to get in to see your nephew," she concluded. "Now, please go and stay out of sight. I'll see you in a couple of hours." She rattled off directions to the cabbie, shut the door on Vasilli's protests, and turned to flag another in the cab's wake.

Thirty-two

Marta had been to the capital city only once before, but she was comfortable navigating its well-ordered streets. As a high school student, she had traveled to Ankara to take the university admission exams at the Middle East Technical University. Some teachers had advised their better students to take the exam in Ankara because of a rumor going around that they had a greater chance of getting into the school where they took the test. Marta traveled with three other students and a teacher chaperone. An elaborate ruse convinced her father that it was part of a class trip, nothing to do with the university examinations. He was not easily convinced but eventually relented. The teacher arranged for a short tour of the city, including visits to Atatürk's tomb and a couple of museums, after the examinations were done.

Ankara was an unnatural capital, a city transformed from an ancient, sleepy village into the seat of a new government when Atatürk took power. Grand boulevards, majestic parks, and a mediocre architecture turned Ankara from a backwater into a capital city modeled after Paris and Washington. Ankara had no natural beauties, none of the special characteristics that distinguish most European capitals. There was no major port, no important trade intersection. It had evolved into a bureaucrat's city, with legions of paper-pushers and their middle-class aspirations filling nondescript apartment blocks in nondescript neighborhoods.

Until the late 1980s, private universities were unheard of in Turkey. In a system that accounted for numerous stress-related suicides, students applying for the limited class slots in the public universities were assigned majors at specific schools according to the results of a national examination given each spring. The money issue was central, especially to those middle-class families whose aspirations for their children did not usually include the thousands of dollars necessary to finance an overseas adventure. Of course, rumors of corruption helped fuel the righteous indignation of those with children whose scores were too low for one of the few slots. Then, even the most upright citizen would look for any way to raise money, corrupt or not.

These issues had not been of much concern to Marta when she was younger. She was certain of her intellectual capability, although her teachers warned her that the competition for university places was steep. She knew that she would be accepted somewhere. But she also knew that her fight would be with the father who did not even want her to take the test, let alone step foot near a place of higher learning. He was against high school for girls, preferring instead to market his daughters for marriage to a good family in the village. In his outdated world vision, if his daughters married well, he might have some chance of getting what was owed him: the devotion of a dutiful daughter and the adoration (and financial support, in his old age) of a loving son-in-law. Instead, he periodically beat his wife because of her advocacy for the girls' future education.

Marta's only apprehension about the exam itself was that she would be assigned to one of the medical schools, rather than her first choice of the law. Not that she would be a bad doctor, quite the contrary, she was not at all squeamish and often assisted with the removal of splinters, the treatment of cuts and scrapes, and the revival of fainters. No, Marta wanted to use her brain to advance larger causes than the health of individual patients. She loved the law for where it could lead, into the political arena where she would be able to change the country itself, if not the world. Oh, she was idealistic.

The evening before the exam, she left her companions in the hotel cramming one last time and embarked on her own preparation. From the old Dedeman Hotel, she walked down the wide, tree-lined boulevard to the nearby parliament. The building was at once larger and at the same time less intimidating in person, its reddish-brown stone façade seeming open and yet also formal. No one stopped her from walking the halls there; no one asked any questions as the teenager gazed respectfully at all the statues, read all the tablets affixed to the walls, and stood in awed silence in the spectators' gallery above the silent government chamber. This was it. This was the place where history could be made and where a strong woman could become a leader. Marta was certain of this, just as she knew by the time she left the building that she would get a place in the law school. She returned to the city only once again, when she was in the final year of law school interviewing for jobs.

Now walking those same streets, Marta tried to focus on the case at hand. She needed to concentrate and forget where she was. She shook her shoulders back in place, almost willing her body and mind to reform the steely walls that had protected her for so many years in New York. She needed them back, now. Leaving Istanbul had strangely brought her closer to the confrontations she'd been avoiding, even though her roots in this city were shallow and seemingly insignificant.

"Not now, not yet," she muttered, climbing out of the cab and into the landscape of the past. She pushed open the door to the trade ministry and scanned the directory. A voice called her name, echoing in the cavernous lobby. She turned.

"Sami-bey, what a surprise to see you here," she said slowly, although her chest was clenched with anxiety.

"Quite so," he replied. "Unexpected business. You know how it is."

"Yes."

Other patrons of the ministry streamed around them; elevators opened and closed while the pair studied the directory.

"I don't see ... ah yes, there it is." Marta turned to Sami. "If you'll excuse me."

"Certainly." He smiled agreeably but did not move. "May I ask where is your elderly friend?"

"I'm sorry, I have an appointment." Marta exposed her watch, tapping on its face. "So nice to see you."

She stepped around him and glided into the nearest elevator just as its doors were closing.

"What floor, miss?" Marta started at the question and then looked at the paper in her hand. "Three, I think," she replied. Her hand shook, and she shoved it into her pocket. When the door opened, she encountered another disturbing sight, that of her associate chatting casually to another attorney. "Dammit." She stepped forward, hand outstretched again. "Josh, what a surprise."

Barton turned and revealed his sharp teeth in what he probably meant to be a smile but looked more like a shark's invitation to dinner. "Marta." He introduced the Turkish attorney with whom Marta had been working for a week. "Do you know Mr. ...? I'm sorry, can you pronounce your name again for me?"

Marta brushed past him. "We've met, Josh, that's okay." She smiled at the other man. "Would you excuse us for a moment? I would like to speak with my colleague before we begin our meeting. Just a moment, thanks."

When they were alone, she grabbed Josh by the arm and hissed, "What the hell are you doing here?"

"Martinson sent me." He pulled away and shook his suit jacket back into place. "What's going on here? Word is this deal is about to go down the tubes."

"No, it's not. Dammit, why don't you guys trust me?" She glared at him.

"It doesn't look good—"

"Bullshit. I know how these people work, and I am telling you, there is no problem. This is the way they play it here. First, you go to the brink, then you close the deal. Your arrival may have just erased all my groundwork. Dammit." She walked away and then returned and leaned close. His after-shave was too strong, and she detected a hint of liquor on his minty-fresh breath. "If you blow this deal, so help me …" She took a deep breath and spoke softly. "Okay. Here's what we're going to do. You hand me a file, yes. Open your case and give me something. I don't care what it is. Fine. Now, you will turn around and leave. Don't you dare argue with me. I need them to see you as a messenger; that's it. What hotel are you in?"

"Hilton."

"Fine. Leave now. I'll call you after this meeting." She dropped the file into her portfolio. "Go now."

"What am I supposed to tell Barry?"

"Tell him I'll deal with him later. No, better yet, tell him he'll be lucky if I come back after this little stunt. Now get out. And don't talk to anyone else."

"But Barry said—"

"Listen, if things don't work out today, it's all yours. I'll step aside, what-ever you guys want, but let me have this meeting. If I don't deliver, it's yours. Okay?" He nodded, adjusted his tie with a glance over her shoulder, and walked away.

Marta watched him leave and then opened her date book. After pre-tending to make a note there, she turned and marched into the meeting. Sami's appearance may have temporarily unnerved her, but she was well past that now. The anger she experienced upon seeing a junior partner sent over to "save" her case had kicked in, and she was ready to take on the Turks, the Italians, and the entire European market.

Just as she had predicted, in short order, an understanding was ham-mered out with Turkish companies retaining their share of the interna-tional pasta market, in exchange for an agreement to funnel some Italian leather products through their ports to circumvent export restrictions to the States.

Ink dried on the papers spread over the table while delicate crystal glass-es of steaming tea cooled on gold-plated saucers. Marta leaned back in her chair and quickly drank the scalding beverage, and then turned to the men arrayed around the table. "Any chance that this is a first step to overcoming opposition to Turkey's admittance to the union?" she asked. The men sighed and shifted uncomfortably in their chairs, but the Italian minister moved closer to her and sighed.

"It's not us. It's those northern countries—the cold places—they don't like the Turks," he confided. "For us, no problem, everybody is welcome. It's the Mediterranean way!" He lifted his glass and held it out for a toast. "To the future—money and success to us all!" He started to drink and then stopped and tapped his glass with Marta's. "As we say in Italy, *Auguri e centi anni!*"

Marta smiled and watched the man empty his cup. "Drink, drink," he urged.

"What does it mean, *'Auguri e centi anni'*?" she asked.

"Well, congratulations, of course, and then, roughly, I wish you a hundred years."

"Ah." She nodded and drank. "Same to you then, I'm sure."

The group continued its congratulatory outpourings, each knowing that none of the proclamations had any chance of happening. Liquor soon replaced tea, and Marta knew it was time to get out of the room gracefully. There was an outbreak of laughter when one man wished the other would enjoy "only male children" and "plenty of asses." For her part, Marta just hoped that the agreement had more shelf life than a pound of pasta. But it was signed, it was sealed, and when she gave it to her "friend" at the Hilton to carry back to New York, it would be delivered.

"What is next on your schedule?" the Italian minister asked. "Another international deal? Will you stop in Italia before returning to New York? I would be pleased to show you around my country." His eyebrows danced with the invitation as his stubby fingers fumbled with the hot tea glass.

"Yes, I think I will take a little vacation," Marta announced. "It's been a while."

He leaned forward eagerly. The room began to clear out as papers were sorted and each party given a folder with their signed agreements tucked inside. The Turkish ministry staff left the room. The lawyers mumbled to each other, and the Italian staff stood patiently behind their leader. No one was particularly interested in the conversation, but Marta continued to surprise herself. She never engaged in personal discussions in a business setting, unless the charm was necessary to make the deal happen.

"I may do some traveling here in Turkey, visit family, that kind of thing, you know." She shrugged. He sighed. "But I may find myself in Rome sometime. Perhaps you can leave me your business card. It has been a pleasure working with you; maybe we can do it again sometime."

Thirty-three

When she arrived at the hotel, Vasilli was waiting in the lobby, their bags near the door and the bill, such as it was, already paid. Marta had called him from the cab and informed him that they had to leave the hotel. He had asked no questions and greeted her with a smile on his face. She scribbled a note and handed a large file folder to the concierge for delivery to the Hilton. A hundred lira note assured its speedy passage to Josh Barton.

"Let's go." She took Vasilli's arm and stepped toward the curb where a taxi slid into place.

"Where to now?" he asked.

"We're going to stay in a little town on the outskirts of the city." She spoke rapidly to the driver and then turned to look at Vasilli. "What happened? You look, well, you actually look happy."

He smiled again. "I don't know. I just feel better getting out of that hotel." He shrugged. "Why did we have to move anyway?"

"I ran into our friend Sami-bey," she said. "I have no idea how he knew where I would be, someone from the other firm must have told him about our meeting here today, and I suppose he took a shuttle, which is a hell of a lot faster than the route we took. But anyway, he's here, and I don't want to deal with him, so I'd like to move."

"Oh, it's okay with me. I didn't feel comfortable in that place." He crossed his arms. "You know, I saw this man who looked like a prince or something, walking through the lobby followed by all these poor creatures in black veils from head to toe. I tell you, I did not like the sight of that." He shuddered and checked his watch. "What about your bank? Didn't you want to stop there this afternoon?"

"Oh, shoot, you're right. Do you mind?" She laughed, a sound that made Vasilli turn and look at her wide-eyed. "I know, I can just run in and harass the woman for a minute, while you wait in the cab. Is that okay?" She leaned over and tapped the driver on the shoulder when Vasilli lifted his hands in consent.

It was not so smooth inside the bank when Marta encountered a senior manager ready to block her questions in every way. "Our records show everything is in order," said a Mr. Osman from behind his massive desk. "We cannot inspect every single transaction for so many years."

Marta smoothly explained the discrepancies again, but he was not impressed. "You must speak with the family to find out what happened to the money," he insisted. "We cannot control who had access to this account, only you can decide that."

"But surely you have records of who made withdrawals?"

He looked at her blankly. "No. Someone with proper identification came and removed the money. That's all I need to know." He leaned back in his chair, fingers laced across an ample belly. "Didn't you look at your statements over the years? Now, after so long, you notice this was happening? Didn't you ever check on these accounts? You know, you have thirty days after each statement is sent to challenge its contents." He shook his head. "I can't help you, really. You can close the accounts now, if you like, or change the access numbers. But that's all I can suggest."

They stared across the table for a long moment. Finally, Marta stood. "Thank you. I believe I will be closing both accounts, so I will come back another time and take care of that."

When she slipped back into the idling taxi, Marta asked Vasilli if he was ready for lunch and perhaps a little sightseeing.

He pulled a straw boater low over his eyes and smiled. "I'm all yours."

Winding through streets crowded with embassies, Marta directed the driver to a stop near an overgrown, six-foot-high brick wall. Pushing through the massive iron gates, the pair entered a fantasyland of blooming tulips, gaudy animal-shaped bushes, and dwarf fruit trees covered with pink, white, and yellow flowers. Tables were interspersed throughout, shaded by pastel umbrellas and occupied by well-heeled patrons.

"Oh my." Vasilli breathed his appreciation as they were seated at a corner table. "This is exquisite."

Marta waved away the menu, speaking rapidly in Turkish to the slim waiter. "Some wine?" she asked. Vasilli nodded, smiling as Marta rattled off another barrage to the waiter.

"There is a vineyard near here that makes the best wines, and you won't believe how inexpensive they are." She corrected herself. "Or they were. I don't know what a bottle is going for these days. Oh well, we'll find out." She laughed, giddy. "We have to celebrate. My case is settled. I'm finished with macaroni!"

Vasilli crowed his pleasure, clapping his hands until three waiters ran over. "Whoops, sorry." He blushed. "No, we're just … I didn't mean for you … Oh, never mind." They laughed, and he grabbed her hand and planted a kiss on the knuckles. The wine arrived and was poured. Vasilli raised his glass in a toast. "To your successful business. As we say in Greek, 'May your work bring much satisfaction and many goats to your family!'"

Marta drank deeply of the young vintage. She looked over the menu. The trill of her cell phone interrupted the ordering process. She listened to the speaker, said a few words, and then tossed the phone into her bag.

"Your colleagues calling to congratulate you?" Vasilli asked.

"Not exactly." She grimaced. "After all their worries that I was not on top of things here, now they're saying that I've blown it. Apparently, I was not supposed to settle the dispute, just calm everyone and avert a disaster. They're upset in New York because they wanted this case to last a while, so they could make a lot of money from it."

He tapped her hand, lifting his glass. "And so you did a good job. You're not extorting money out of your clients. Congratulations! An ethical lawyer!"

She drank some more of the wine, trying to smile. "I think this trip is going to have some long-lasting effects on my life, whether I want it or not."

"Well, I don't know what you're so glum about. You did a good job, and now it's done, and you deserve to celebrate. Let's order something fantastic, shall we? Just look around at this beautiful place …" With his soothing voice and enthusiasm, Marta eventually relaxed. Now officially on vacation, she pushed away all thoughts of her partners and turned her attentions to the wine and food and Vasilli's entertaining chatter.

After their leisurely meal, the pair officially embarked on their search for Vasilli's family. The simple country roads Marta remembered had been replaced with impressive highways that moved traffic smoothly in and out of the city. Marta could not believe how extensive the development was, how many new high-rise apartments and cooperative villages now surrounded the center.

"Where are we going?" Vasilli asked after the congestion of the capital was behind them.

"We're going to find your relatives," Marta replied. "And then, maybe we're going to find mine too."

In reply, Vasilli simply raised his eyebrows and watched the countryside take hold. Their taxi was soon held captive behind a truck filled with young women dressed in voluminous pantaloons of wildly colorful fabric. Their heads were loosely covered with kerchiefs, and their ruddy complexions were creased with dirt and laughter.

"Are they Gypsies?" he asked as the driver sped up and tried to pass the lumbering vehicle.

"No, I don't think so," Marta answered. "Although there are plenty of Gypsy families in the area, I'm sure. No. These look like typical farmwork-ers." The cab rushed forward to pass, revealing an elaborately painted scene on the side of the truck. Depicting a brilliant sunrise over a field speckled with poppies and populated by cattle, it was almost a mirror of the view that presented itself at the next turn. Large bales of hay were rolled along a meadow deeply green and bisected with a small stream where groups of animals, sheep and an occasional cow, bent for a drink.

After another hour, the taxi pulled into a service area, where the driver jumped out and began arguing with the attendant over the price of gaso-line. Marta and Vasilli headed to a set of weathered metal tables arranged alongside a stream. A boy brought tea, placed it in front of them, and smiled crookedly. Marta handed him a coin and then leaned over to sip the bitter beverage.

"At least it's hot," she said.

"So." Vasilli put down his glass and leaned back in his chair. "Where are we?"

"Almost there. Another thirty-forty minutes, I think. From what I could get out of the articles Cem collected for me, the Vaso family compound is out this way. Of course, it's heavily guarded, so I don't think we'll be able to walk up and knock on the door."

"What's the next move then?"

"I propose to send them a note by messenger, like in the old days, and ask for an audience. What do you think?"

"I think we might end up waiting a long time for a reply," Vasilli said.

"You may be right, but I like the direct, 'old country' approach. In the meantime, we try other avenues. We'll hire some locals to gather informa-tion, maybe. I don't know. Worst-case scenario, we walk up to the door and knock." She shrugged.

"And what about your 'family business'?" Vasilli said. "Will you go to your aunt?"

She did not answer. Vasilli watched her fiddle with the tiny spoon, avoiding his eyes. He stopped her hand with his gently. "You must, you know. We're both on this journey now. We can't go back until we know."

"There's so much more to it," Marta said.

"Nothing can be worse than not knowing."

"Once you know ..." Marta sighed. The boy came over and refilled their glasses. The driver sprawled at a table nearby smoking and watching the pair.

"You can't go back." Vasilli finished her sentence.

"You can't. Ever since I set foot in this country ... I don't know. It's like all the toughness I built up all these years has just evaporated." She leaned over the tea glass, watching a lump of sugar melt. "But you're right, I know you are. I have to find out what happened." She sighed again. "And so do you." She stretched. "Then we figure out what to do afterwards."

Thirty-four

The small town of Afyon had not changed; it still looked as if the houses and roads had been carved from the yellow stone that broke through where trees ought to be. There was dust everywhere, and the sunlight filtered through a gauzy haze. Old Chevrolets, belching smoke, idled at intersections that had no stoplights. Horses were tied to light posts covered with notices, their hooves tapping an impatient rhythm on the cobblestone roadway. The street was full of wagons, most with elaborately painted panels depicting life in the countryside.

Not very many people around, Marta thought, and the ones who were scurrying in and out of stores looked to be about the same age as Vasilli, although she knew that they were probably closer to her age than his. It was a hard life in these towns, with high mortality, low literacy, and a life expectancy hovering below sixty for both men and women. Most of the young people headed for the city as soon as they could escape to work in a different kind of servitude for hotels, restaurants, and construction companies.

An unremarkable *pension* on a narrow, unpaved side street proved to be exquisite inside. It had been decorated in soothing shades of coral and saffron. Two rooms up a narrow staircase shared a bathroom overfilled with a giant tub that made every other activity almost impossible. The facilities included a water closet, a gas water heater, and a washbasin so cracked it resembled a mosaic of white porcelain with yellow and rust-colored accents. A chain dangled from an ancient water tank held to the wall with two rusted metal bands. A hard yank with two hands was necessary to activate the flush. A tiny window, its glass encrusted with either dirt or paint, hugged the ceiling and cast nothing but a yellowish shadow throughout the room. Its single light fixture added little to the dimness.

"Cheery, isn't it?" Vasilli poked his head around the door as Marta wiped her hands on a square of terrycloth that had probably held color when the thread count was above fishnet.

"Charming. How's your room?" He shrugged. "Let's look around, shall we?" Marta led the way to the common room downstairs where the telltale scent of scorched tea filled the air.

"What is it about Turks and their tea?" Vasilli asked. "I thought the drink of choice was coffee."

"Nah, coffee is for the rich, or for dessert, like a special occasion. Tea is locally grown. Everybody drinks it."

Vasilli crinkled his nose as the bitter liquid arrived in glasses rattling on the ubiquitous red-and-white melamine saucers. "I feel my teeth turning brown just looking at it," he groused.

"At least here it's the real thing. The Lipton tea bag invasion has just about decimated the locals. There's this prejudice against Turkish tea—that it's not pure enough for the big companies, like Twinings. The Turkish farmers might as well just grow poppies. At least there's a market for that."

"You're sounding a little bitter yourself," Vasilli said.

"Too much time with the macaroni people, I suppose," she agreed. "And I guess my deep-seated national pride is coming out now too." She laughed. "That's a sign I've been changed on this trip. I spent fifteen years pretending to be anything but a Turk, and it all comes back to me in ten days."

They settled on the lumpy couch, looking through a picture window at the human, horse, and automobile traffic passing by.

"What makes that smell? Is it the type of tea or the way it is prepared?"

"Do you really want to know, or are you just making conversation?" Marta asked. He smiled. "Okay, you asked for it. There is a tea ritual in this country, just like the Japanese. It's a double-boiler system, really. A larger pot is filled with water that is brought to a boil. The small pot on top has just the loose tea in it. When the water boils, you pour it from the bottom into the top pot, add some more water to the bottom, and let it rise to a boil again. Then you pour about a third of a cup from the top through a small strainer and cut it with the plain water. The smell you have in the houses is the loose tea being heated before the water is added to make the drink. The pot is replenished throughout the day, kept under a cozy or on a low flame, little bits of loose tea added once in a while to keep the body. By the end of the night, the top pot is full of tea leaves. In the morning, the old leaves are dumped into a flowerpot or garden and the ritual repeated. Makes for good compost."

Vasilli sighed and put down his cup. "Sounds too complicated."

"Ah, but one of the tests of a potential bride is her ability to make a perfect cup of tea. The other one, in case you're interested, is making a perfect pot of rice. But I won't tell you about that one—it's too Byzantine." They both laughed.

"I can't imagine you in such a domestic role," Vasilli said.

"Oh, I am my mother's daughter—or at least I was. Skilled in all the necessary female roles: cooking, cleaning, servitude. Actually, I wasn't very good at that last one. But I learned a lot of other things from her—lying, scheming, manipulating. All the things she had to do to manage my father. Turns out she wasn't as good at it as I had thought. But it was a good foundation for becoming a lawyer." She grimaced and played with the sugar bowl.

"Well, you seem to be a very good lawyer," Vasilli offered. She shrugged.

Their empty glasses were refilled with the fresh, steaming beverage. The landlady slammed the kitchen door on her retreat. Sounds of cooking and child abuse emanated from the kitchen.

"Nice place."

"Reminds me of my first place in New York, ironically," Marta said. "When I lived with the sisters, the super's apartment was the only other one on that level, and the screaming that came from those rooms was incessant. At first, I was concerned, but then I realized that no one ever came out of there with bruises or broken bones, so obviously, it was just their form of expression. And since it was all in Spanish, I didn't understand a word of it."

Thirty-five

The spring evening was perfect, a Camelot at 73 degrees with light breezes carrying the scent of familiar but unidentifiable flowers. Children played in the street, an occasional car skittered by, and the glow of television sets illuminated windows in the near-dusk hour. Most of the stores were closed or closing. A few late shoppers juggling bags with garish smiley faces printed on flimsy yellow plastic hurried past the couple strolling along the main road. A municipal building, distinguished only by the ten-foot-high bronze casting of Atatürk on its front façade, dominated the intersection where the "centrum" sign pointed left. It looked like the bus they'd rode in on was returning to the bus station, probably after completing its run to the nearest large city, Bursa. Vasilli jostled Marta's arm with his and nodded at the bus.

"Leave anything on it?"

"No, I'm just glad we don't need to get on one of those again for a while." Marta slowed down as they passed a café. It was overflowing with men, most in work attire and hunched over games of backgammon. Cigarette smoke hung thickly over the room, wafting around the heads of the taller men. A swarthy man whose girth was wrapped in a sparkling white apron stood in the doorway and nodded. The riotous sounds of a soccer game erupted from the room, although only a couple of the younger occupants reacted to the television.

"Looks like a fun place," Vasilli said.

"Things never change."

"What do you mean?"

"Those places. Men's clubs—men's hideouts, actually. My entire childhood, my father spent most of his waking hours playing cards in a place like that." She laughed, a short bark. "Probably we were better off, him not being at home yelling or beating anyone. But that whole generation of men, they had no connection to their family, no role in raising their own children." She shook her head.

The quality of the light changed perceptibly as they rounded a corner. At the end of the block, a white building was illuminated and seemed to glow. Its spire was an ornate helix of bricks capped with a roof painted bright blue. Men walked briskly past them now, and Marta pulled Vasilli into the shadow of a doorway. "Look, up there." She pointed. "The muezzin, he's going up to the top. I thought they only did that on Friday ..."

Vasilli squinted and tried to follow her gaze. He shook his head and then, "Ah." He spotted the white-clad man emerging into the small open area. A microphone dangled from the ceiling, and he grasped it. They heard him cough and then begin to call.

For the entire message, Vasilli and Marta remained hidden in the darkness. More men rushed by, some pulling at their shoes and hopping. "They have to take their shoes off and wash their feet," Marta whispered. "There's running water and a trough outside every mosque."

"Why is it in Arabic?" Vasilli asked when they had resumed their walk, staying close to the buildings opposite the plain front of the mosque.

"I guess it's some kind of sacrilege to translate," Marta replied. "I was never that interested in religion, to tell you the truth. It was something for my father, different from the praying that the women did at home, but the two never seemed to be about the same thing."

Another corner and they had almost completed the promenade. They came to a small restaurant, where tables were pushed onto the sidewalk and waiters were setting utensils on fabric-covered tables. "Welcome!" the host shouted. "Can I interest you?"

"Hire, yavrum." Marta smiled at the boy, who blushed when he heard the Turkish. *"Teşekkür."* (No, thanks.)

Vasilli paused to look at the list of specials displayed by another ground-floor establishment. "I am getting kind of hungry again," he said.

"Wait—look." Marta grabbed his arm and pulled the old man away from his temptations. "What does that say?" An enormous iron fence stretched to the corner, its embellished gate looming ten feet overhead. On a plain square next to an intercom, a single word was carved. "It's Greek, isn't it?"

Vasilli pursed his lips, pocketed his hands, and studied the sign. "Yes," he said finally. "It's Greek."

"Well, what does it say?"

He walked a couple of steps, peered through the gloaming, and turned back to face her. "You know, there are thick hedges here. You can't even see any buildings." He looked toward the driveway and then extended his hand between two of the bars. "I think this takes up the entire block. I—whoops! Here comes the welcoming committee!" Spotlights flashed from several directions, until the entire street seemed bright as day again.

The sound of rushing footsteps preceded the appearance of two burly men dressed in elaborate faux-military garb.

"Step back from the gate," the shorter of the two ordered. The other ran a nightstick along the bars, raising a racket.

"Oh, pardon." Marta grabbed Vasilli and backed quickly across the street. When they reached the sidewalk, they waved at the men and walked back into the shadows. Around the corner again, they exchanged barely a glance before heading into the little bistro they'd just passed a few minutes earlier.

"*Su*, please," Marta asked the boy holding menus. "Water."

A quizzical look on his face, the waiter shrugged and snapped napkins over each lap before heading toward the kitchen. Marta's and Vasilli's eyes met, and laughter erupted.

"'Whoops, here comes the welcoming committee'?" Marta mimicked. Water arrived, in glasses too full of ice.

"Order?" The boy had his pen poised and ready.

"*Bir daka*," Marta gasped, holding up a finger. "Just give us a minute to look over the menu." He retreated again but remained standing just inside the curtained doorway. His teeth gleamed in the darkness as he spoke softly to someone behind the curtain.

"Who was it?" Marta finally asked. "What did the sign say?"

"Why, Vassilios, of course." Vasilli chuckled. "We found them."

Two men dressed in dark suits entered the restaurant and slid into chairs on the opposite side of the room. The waiter started forward and then saw the upraised finger of one of the suits and retreated to his doorway. His eyes darted between the two tables, and suddenly, loud music began playing from speakers suspended in every corner of the room. A sharp gesture from the other table, something like a knife cut across the throat, and the boy vanished behind the curtain. The music stopped.

"They found us," Marta said.

"I wonder if they follow every person who happens to stand too close to the gate." Vasilli reached for his water. "Or maybe they were expecting us."

"Let's eat," Marta said. "All this intrigue has got me famished."

After a rather merry time spent ordering, drinking a good local wine, and then devouring small plates of hot and cold appetizers, the two settled back to contemplate the steaming cups of Turkish coffee placed on the table before them.

"I'll read your fortune in the cup after you finish it. Be careful not to drink the grounds," Marta instructed. Vasilli reached for his spoon. "No, you don't stir it. Just drink the liquid part and try not to get a mouthful of grounds."

"Do you think our friends ..." Vasilli nodded in the direction of the two men. "... enjoyed their meal as much as we did?"

"I don't know. They certainly didn't have much to say."

"Not to each other. Did you notice that they spent the entire time on their cell phones? I am really surprised about that," Vasilli said.

"About them talking on the phone?"

"No, that everyone here has a cell phone glued to their ear all the time, much more than in New York," he said. "And I complained about them in New York."

"As I recall, regular house phones were very few and far between here. We didn't have one at home, not until I was just about through college," Marta said. "There was something like a three-year waiting list—"

"Shush," Vasilli interrupted. "They're talking to each other now ... I think it's Greek, but I can't pick it up clearly."

"Can't you turn up your hearing aids?"

He shook his head. "Give me your phone." She hesitated. "Give it here. I'm going to pretend to make a call. Go to the bathroom or something, just be quiet and let me try to listen to them."

When Marta rose from her seat, the waiter appeared silently from the curtained doorway. "Can I help you?" he asked and then held the curtain for her. The men continued to talk. Vasilli played with the phone, peering at the tiny screen. He held it to his ear just as a phone trilled across the room.

"'Alo?" A bad connection forced his voice into top volume, his Greek slow and loud enough for Vasilli to discern clearly. "What? What? Yes, he's still here. No, no, they just had dinner. Dinner. Yes. Yes." He covered the phone and spoke rapidly to the man across the table who then got up and went outside, flipping open his phone as he slipped out the door. Vasilli could see a flash of light as he lit a cigarette. Vasilli turned his attention back to the tower of sugar cubes he had created on the tiny saucer.

"Okay." The man nodded vigorously. His phone beeped, and he held it from his ear for a moment. "Sorry, another call coming in. No, not important. Just my wife. Go on. Yes, they're still here. The old man is on the phone, and the lawyer went somewhere. I don't know. Probably the can. Nah, she wouldn't leave him here. He's helpless. She's been leading him around all day. Okay. We'll stay on them. Nope. I'll check in at 10:00."

Vasilli jumped when Marta's phone rang in his ear. He studied the buttons while the machine trilled. Finally, he answered, "'Alo?"

"It's me," Marta whispered.

"I can't hear you."

"Sorry, it's me."

"Then why are you whispering? No one can hear you."

"Sorry. Are they still there?"

"One is outside smoking; the other is watching me. Probably wondering why the phone rang in the middle of my imaginary conversation here."

"Sorry again," Marta hissed. "I thought the phone was set on vibrate. Anyway, I'll be right back."

"Vibrate? What the hell? I'm glad it didn't vibrate." Vasilli continued to talk until Marta returned to her seat, reached over, and took his phone. "Shall we settle the bill?"

"Not until you read the coffee grounds."

"You're kidding. I don't know how to do that."

"But you said …"

She looked around and then signaled to the ever-watchful waiter. A few quick words, a shake of his head, and then she turned to Vasilli and snapped her fingers. "Give me some money."

The boy took the bill and backed into the darkness again. "Drink your water." Marta pushed the glass across the table. "This might take a few minutes."

Their surveillance team called the waiter, the two men obviously not moving until their quarry headed home. "Did you hear anything?"

"No, just that they've been watching us all day," Vasilli said.

"How the hell did they find us?"

"Apparently, you're not the sleuth you thought you were."

Marta grunted. "Or we've got some kind of tracking device on us. I don't know."

The door opened. An attractive dark-haired woman swept in on a breeze of spices. She twirled out of a camel-colored cape, smoothed her unruly curls, and pulled a chair toward their table. Before speaking, she picked up each cup, covered it with the saucer, and then flipped the two over.

"I am Lana," she said in perfectly enunciated English. "My brother said that you are looking for a reading. Twenty lira each." Fingers wiggled at the end of her outstretched hand. When the bills were folded into her skirt pocket, she pulled Vasilli's cup toward her and tapped lightly on its bottom.

"You ready?" She leaned over and squeezed Vasilli's knee, causing him to jump awkwardly under the table. He blushed and smiled. "Ticklish." She did not acknowledge his words, nor did she seem to notice his embarrassment.

"Let's see." She picked up the cup and began examining it. "Hmmmm. You have traveled a great distance, see here? This bird? Flying over the water. And here, a fish. So once by sea and once in the air." She smiled, raised her eyebrows, and continued to turn the cup in her hands. Silver rings adorned every finger and thumb, some with stones and others with intricate designs cut into the metal. Her nails were long and perfectly manicured, and except for a long scar along the curve of her jaw, which was mostly hidden by her loose hair, she was quite exquisite. Red lips parted to reveal more insights, her black eyes flashing and occasionally winking at the older man.

"You are a lonely man. You are traveling alone. No wife, no children … is this right?"

Vasilli nodded eagerly. Oh, he was buying it. Marta groaned internally. *Pretty soon,* she thought, *the Gypsy will warn him that he's in danger and tell him to return home before it's too late.* Marta shook her head, focusing again on the woman's words.

"You have come a long way, but you must go home immediately. There is a problem that only you can solve there!" The woman put her hand dramatically on her heaving chest.

"Can you show me where it says that?" Marta asked, using the sugary voice affected by most Turkish women. Vasilli's head snapped up when he caught her tone. A quizzical expression crossed his face.

"Oh, I cannot explain how I see these things; it is a gift," Lana replied. "Sometimes it is a curse, when people don't listen to me." She sighed. "Do you want to hear more?" she asked Vasilli.

"Ah, no. I … No. Thank you. That's quite clear to me," he stammered.

"Okay. Now yours, miss."

"Oh, I think I will pass," Marta said. She switched to Turkish. "You are *Rom,* right? Tell me, how did you learn to speak English so well?"

"Oh, miss, I speak many languages, and I see many things." She picked up Marta's cup. "Let me see—"

"Don't." Marta spoke sharply. "I'm not interested in hearing your rubbish, *falcı.* You can't scare me like you did the old man. Now, maybe you can tell me something useful, like who sent you here tonight. Or maybe you can share some insights with me about our friends over there."

The woman put down the cup, although she continued to study it. "You really should see this; it's very interesting."

"No."

"Perhaps the cards then …" She pulled a deck of tarot cards wrapped in a length of green silk from her vest and handed them to Vasilli. "Just cut the cards once, please," she instructed in English.

He did, in a sort of stupor, before Marta reached across and took them from his hands. "No, we're not doing this." She looked at Vasilli and then spoke softly to him in English. "She's a charlatan, don't you see? She was told to come in here and frighten us with her Gypsy mumbo-jumbo."

"I am not Gypsy." Lana retrieved the cards from Marta and began placing them on the table. "Touch again, mister," she said. "Thank you. Hmmm, you see what card has come first. This is what I saw in your coffee grounds. There is not much time left for you. You are on your last journey, and soon you will be joining your wife."

"Jesus, just stop it." Marta slammed the table with her hands. The cards jumped and then settled back on the table. "Come on, Vasilli, let's get out of here." She looked over her shoulder. "The men have gone. They must be waiting for us outside. Let's pay the bill and call it a night."

Vasilli was a curious shade of yellow, with a little green around the eyes. "I just need to use the bathroom first," he said.

Watching him leave the room, Marta grabbed Lana's wrist, taking care not to touch the cards again. "Can you help us, or are you owned by them?" she asked.

Shaking off the other woman's hands, Lana calmly continued to lay out the cards. "You have no idea what you are doing here. See—look at this card. It is the water carrier. You are shouldering the burdens of this old man, a stranger to you. Very kind, but ill advised. Soon you must tend to your own demons. Here she is, the abandoned child. You have much more trouble ahead, trouble with your own family. Leave the old man. He is done with you. You brought him as far as you can. Now you must tend to your own business. See, this is the cups."

Marta placed money on the table and walked to the door. She watched the street until Vasilli appeared at her side, and they left without another word to the fortune-teller.

Thirty-six

"She's right, you know," Vasilli said. "I'm on my last journey here."

"Don't be ridiculous. She's a fraud."

"I know that. Most of what she said was just common sense. Look at me. I'm an old man, so obviously I'm not going to be hanging around forever. And by the way, you sent for the Gypsy, not me." He turned to look at her, eyebrows bristling over soft eyes. "I understand it's just entertainment, not the word of God."

They veered into the hotel lobby and headed for the sitting room. One of the children appeared and asked, in a small voice, the ubiquitous question, "Çay?"

Marta nodded and then leaned forward, elbows resting on her knees. "Listen—" she began.

"No, for a change, you listen to me." Vasilli spoke slowly, softly, so Marta had to lean forward to hear him. "You brought me here. I found my family. I can't tell you how much I appreciate your help. But now I have to finish this myself. And you have to go on and find your own family and deal with your own past. I'd help you if I could, but I think you have to do it alone."

"No."

Vasilli looked at her, waiting. She leaned back in her chair, crossing her arms and looking out toward the kitchen. The boy came then, carrying two cups and a small brass pot on a melamine tray whose elaborate floral motif was scarred with cigarette burns. Marta smiled at him, reached for the sugar bowl, and clamped a cube firmly between her teeth before sipping the steaming tea.

Vasilli dropped two cubes in his tea and stirred them lazily with a tiny silver spoon. Still, they sat in silence, only the distant murmur of the television set breaking the quiet.

"So, if you say 'no,' then what's your plan? Hmm? Are we going to travel around the country together, seeing the sights and dodging imaginary

157

enemies until something happens?" Vasilli asked. He clucked his tongue. "That's not what's going to happen. I'm tired, Marta, and I am going to make some kind of peace with my family. Once they know that I don't want anything from them, they'll be okay, I'm sure." He slurped the tea. "I want to find my mother's grave. I want to visit my brother's grave. I want to meet his children. That's all I want here."

"And then what?"

"You know."

"What? You're going to die? That's just ridiculous. You're healthy as a horse."

Vasilli laughed. "More like an eighty-year-old ass."

"All right." Marta poured some more tea into their glasses. "Let's say you're right. Have you made any arrangements?" She shrugged at Vasilli's uplifted eyebrows. "You know, to have your body transported back home, to be buried, to execute your estate? Stuff like that?"

"Well, actually—"

"I thought so. I mean, most people don't think about this stuff, but believe me, it has to be done. You don't have any survivors, so what do you think is going to happen? Do you think the American government is going to arrange to ship your dead carcass home?"

"Well, you don't have to be so crude about it." He sniffed. "And now that I found them, I do have survivors: my brother's children."

They stopped to listen to the muezzin make his final call to prayer of the day. When it was over, the sound echoing along the narrow streets and rocky shelf, Marta clasped her hands on the table and began speaking again. "Your brother's children don't acknowledge your relationship. But that's beside the point, right? So, you want to be buried here? What about your wife? Don't you want to be buried next to her?"

"I will be."

"What?"

"She's here, with me. Well, in my suitcase actually." Vasilli chuckled. "I think Effie would like to be buried here with our people."

"And your father? Effie's mother? I'm sorry, I don't remember her name."

"Her name was Elena. You understand … my father hated the Turks. He would never have wanted to come back here. He'd come back from the dead if I tried to bury him here. And Elena is by his side, as she was for all those years. But I want to be here, with my mother and my brother. And my wife would want to be buried with me."

"I can't believe you carried human remains on an airplane."

"And in a bus and a taxi … What's the difference? It's just ashes in a little cardboard box."

She shook her head. "Oh my God."

Vasilli laughed. "It's not that big a deal. I've had her ashes on the dining room hutch for quite a while. Good dinner company."

Marta shivered. "I don't want to hear this. It's just too … weird." She paused, peering into the darkness. "There's someone out there. A limousine just pulled up."

"Well, maybe they'll come in and have some tea with us," Vasilli said. "It'll save us a trip to the big house tomorrow."

They sat waiting for several minutes, Marta tense on the edge of her seat and Vasilli sprawled loosely in his. Marta jumped up, looked out the window several times, and then huffed back into her seat. "I don't know what they're doing out there."

"Maybe it's not them. Maybe it's someone else. Maybe they're picking up another guest at this establishment and taking them to the airport." Marta snorted. "All right, I'll admit that's unlikely. Probably not a whole lot of limos wandering around this town. But they'll come in—or not—when they're ready." He smiled. "Unless you want to go out and knock on the window to invite them in?"

"So, then, here we sit." They looked into each other's eyes, until Marta looked down into her empty cup and then into the empty teapot. She clanged the lid shut loudly, hoping to provoke a response from the kitchen. Only the loud laughter from a sitcom on television came from the other room. She crossed her arms and met his gaze again.

"All right then, let me be a lawyer for a minute. Do you have a will? Have you made any provisions for the disposition of your property in New York?"

"Yes. I've left my keys and a letter with instructions with an old friend, one of my bridge buddies. He knows what to do. And there's not much to it. I pretty much cleared out all the personal stuff before I left."

"Well, let me raise something else with you. You've obviously come into some money here, with the death of your brother." Vasilli raised his eyebrows and nodded.

"Yeah, that seems to be the motivating interest of our friends in the car out there," he said.

"So what about that?"

"I don't care."

"I realize that. But maybe you should. Look, there's a lot you can do. You could set up a foundation, give scholarships, sponsor a museum. Lots of good works could be done with all that money."

"My brother apparently did enough of that for both of us."

"Yes, here he did. But what about in New York … You're not interested in going back and doing something there?"

He shook his head. "The money was earned here; it should be spent here. Why? Do you want some of it? I can ask …"

It was her turn to shake her head, just as the boy peered around the curtain. "No, no, I wasn't shaking my head at you … Dammit, he's gone. You want some more tea? Something stronger?" She got up and headed to the kitchen.

"No. I'm okay for now."

"We're not done talking," she said.

When she returned, Vasilli was not at the table. She sat down heavily. The flesh on the back of her neck tingled when she noticed someone sitting in the dark corner of the room. When she turned, a hand reached up and pulled the string to illuminate a lamp.

"Sami-bey."

"Marta, how nice to see you again."

"Why are you here?"

"You know. I want to talk with your gentleman friend."

"Oh. He went to bed. Come back tomorrow."

"I don't think so. I'll wait here until he finishes in the restroom." The boy brought another steaming pot of tea and then looked at Sami. "*Yavrum,* I will have a glass of raki and some water."

The boy bowed his head slightly and scurried from the room.

"So, how are you enjoying your vacation, Marta?"

"It's fine."

"I am interesting to hear your observations about how the country has changed since you left. What are you thinking about the new Turkish republic?"

"I hadn't really given it much thought," she replied. "It looks fine to me."

"You think so? You saw the girls with their heads covered at the university? You saw all the women in chador walking around downtown Istanbul and in our supposedly Western capital, Ankara? I would think those things would bother you. Not to mention the journalists in jail, the *askers* on every street corner, the *imams* on the cover of every newspaper? You used to be such a liberal. Have you read the newspapers since you've been here? I think there was something about a consultant that went missing … Some woman raped and beaten in Erzencam, for not wearing modest clothing. Doesn't that just get your blood running?"

"You know it does. And you know that I'm not afraid of you, so don't bother with the little threats. I'm not buying it. What happened to you in jail to make you so bitter? And now you're working for a bunch of *Yunan*?" Marta whispered the word for "Greek" and then poured some tea and blew on the hot liquid. "Is there some coup in the works? That's why the *asker*— the army—is everywhere?"

"I don't know about the army. You know that's the national pastime, complaining about the economy and the government and trying to predict when the army will step in." Sami sipped his raki and then chased it with a gulp of cold water. Ice cubes clanked on the glass, the only noise in the room besides the ticking of a glass-domed mechanical clock on the mantle in the dark corner of the room.

"Still, Greeks." Marta shook her head.

"They are more Turkish than you," he replied. "That family has been here for generations. They stayed when others fled and made this their home. Vaso has given away more than most countries spend on education. And I am happy to do what I can for them."

"I'm sure you're being well compensated too," Marta noted dryly.

Sami sat straighter in his chair. "Let's get down for business, then. Your friend, Vassilios, how much does he want?"

"He wants nothing."

"Really?"

"He simply wants to meet the remaining members of his family and learn what happened to them after the war. That's it. He's fairly well off too, and he is past the age of needing more money."

"Hmmm."

Marta saw Vasilli come into the room, look around for her, and then retreat when he saw Sami. She hoped that Sami had not noticed, but he jerked his head in the direction of the door and said, "Tell him to come in."

"He'll just tell you the same thing. Simple man, simple request. You don't need to threaten him with thugs or fortune-tellers. Just let him meet the family, let them see that he is a harmless old man who just wants to know what happened to his mother and brother. That's it. Can't you do that?"

"I don't think so. I think you should go find your own family and take care of your own business."

"And I suppose you have something you want to tell me about that too." Marta finished her tea and folded her hands on the table. "So. Go ahead. Tell me your version, your 'truth' about my family. Tell me how my sister came to be working for you. That's some coincidence. Go on, tell me. You've been dying to talk about it ever since I arrived in Turkey, so go ahead. I'm all ears."

Sami took another sip of his drink and then tipped the glass in her direction. "Are you sure you don't want a glass of this? I remember you had a taste for raki back in college."

She shook her head. "That wasn't me. Your memory is not clear on everything, I guess."

They sat in silence, Sami toying with the fringes of the woven cloth covering the little round table. Marta watched him, silent. Each lawyer was trained to wait for the other to speak, to reveal truths just to fill uncomfortable silences. Neither was willing to give up, neither willing to leave the table first.

After five minutes, Vasilli stepped out from the shadows. "Marta."

"Yes," she replied without looking away from Sami.

"Come here, please. I want to talk to you."

"I'm busy right now. I'll see you upstairs." She crossed her arms. "You go on ahead."

He sighed, looked around the room, and then walked quickly to the door. Marta looked out the window and jumped out of her seat. "Dammit." She was outside and behind him on the sidewalk in a few seconds, but not fast enough to stop him from tapping on the back window of the limousine and leaning in when the glass was lowered.

Thirty-seven

Vasilli swatted away Marta's hand on his back and spoke softly to the dark shadow in the back of the car. His body blocked her view inside the vehicle. She noticed Sami slide into the front seat of the car and heard the door close with a quiet *thwunk*. She pulled on Vasilli's arm, but he twisted until she ended up squeezed firmly to his side, his large hand spread across her lower ribs and abdomen. Rather than fight, she leaned into him and tried to see or hear something.

"Okay." He stepped back, continuing to hold her firmly to his side. Together, they backed away from the car and watched it glide away, tinted window sliding into place. She felt his heart beating against her side.

"Come," he said. They walked into the hotel, and he let her go only when they could not squeeze up the stairs side by side.

He turned on a small bedside lamp and then indicated that Marta should sit on the only chair in the tiny room. He shook off his jacket, hung it neatly on a hanger behind the closet door, and loosened his collar.

"Phew, it's hot in here," he commented. He rolled his sleeves up and made a quick blot of his face with the ubiquitous white handkerchief. Shadows moved across the ceiling when a car crept along the narrow street below.

"You're not having a heart attack or anything, are you?" Marta asked. He shook his head.

"It's been a long day. I'm too old for this stuff," he said with a smile. "Do you mind?" he lifted a leather shoe, which was promptly removed along with its partner and stowed near the door. Only then, wiggling his black-nylon-clad toes, did Vasilli launch himself onto the bed, resting his cheek against a fist as he lay sideways. "You can join me if you want," he said.

Marta settled deeper in her chair, kicked off her own shoes, and propped her feet on the edge of the bed near his knees.

"Who was in the car?"

Silence.

"What did you just agree to?" Vasilli smiled but did not answer. "Come on, don't play games with me. Okay. Obviously you set up some kind of meeting with one of the family. You know I don't think that you should go alone, but you can do what you wish."

"I know."

"That's it? That's all you have to say?" She remained in her casual pose, but her voice was steely. "Fine."

They sat in silence, listening to the distant sound of owls and other nocturnal creatures, some human, as they settled into the night.

"I'm going to bed then," she said finally. "Will I see you in the morning, or is this good-bye?"

"I'll be here," he replied.

And so he was, cheerfully greeting her in another crisp suit the next morning. How he managed his wardrobe was beginning to be a mystery to Marta as she rinsed, rotated, and accessorized her small repertoire of outfits.

"I'm meeting with my nephew at twelve," he announced. "You are welcome to join me, or you may wish to stay here and continue your conversation with Mr. Sami. He's over there, in the corner, behind the newspaper."

Marta drank something powdered that was probably supposed to be orange juice and then tried a badly burned piece of toast and signaled to the waiter. "What kind of tea is this?" She held up a Lipton tea bag dangling from a lukewarm pot. She switched to Turkish. "*Yavrum*, my boy, what kind of breakfast is it that you are serving here? You should be ashamed of this mess."

The waiter blushed. "It's an American breakfast, miss," he replied.

"Do me a favor, bring me the Turkish version." She turned to Vasilli. "What kind of meeting is this going to be? With the family or the lawyers?"

"Probably a little of both," he replied. "You can come as my friend, or my lawyer, or whatever." He glanced at the back of the room. "I find it fascinating, these Turkish newspapers. All that nakedness on the front pages. You wouldn't think that in such a conservative environment, the papers would be allowed to put all those naked women in the newspaper."

"Yes."

"Yes?" He frowned. "What's the matter with you today?"

She shook her head and then stood up and walked over to Sami's table. "What do you want?" she asked, sitting opposite the offending newspaper. He did not lower it.

"Look, Sami-bey, I don't have time for this foolishness. Either say what you've come to say, or get out and leave me alone." The waiter brought her a proper cup of tea and placed it on the table. There was silence from behind the newspaper.

"Fine." She took her cup and returned to Vasilli. "Let's go for a walk after breakfast, shall we? I need to clear my head."

"Good idea." They ate in silence, fresh bread having replaced the blackened toast. Olives and cheese in small plates had been arrayed on the table. "Your friend is leaving."

"Humph."

"Don't you want to talk to him, follow him? Beat some information out of him?" Vasilli was smiling. She smiled back.

"No, I'm good."

He pushed some papers across the table. "Remember this? The letter I showed you? I thought you might want to look at it before we go over there. And these, I wrote a few things down last night, if you can take a look. Sort of an amendment to my will."

Marta looked at the handwritten pages and then pushed them back across the table. "You can't do this. It won't hold up."

"What do you mean?"

"If you have a will in the United States, you can't amend it here. It's not defensible."

"So just do a new one, and the other one is void."

"No."

"Anyway, who's going to compare the one in New York with the one here? This legal system is completely different and separate. So what's the problem? We get this notarized, and it's all set."

"As you may have noticed during the past few weeks, it's not that simple. The law works differently here for inheritance. Blood trumps everything. You can't disown a family member. You can't give money to a charity instead of your second cousin. It just doesn't work the same way as it does in the States. Sorry." She pushed the papers back to him. "I appreciate the gesture, but you can't do it."

He looked at the table. "Marry me then."

"You have got to be kidding me."

"No, I'm dead serious. I thought all night about what you said about the money, and I do want to use it, not just leave it for this giant corporation. And I want you to have it, so you can make sure that it is used for good, like for that women's shelter on the island, things like that. I want to do that. And I want to make sure that it happens, even if I am gone."

"That's very noble, but—"

"No buts." He wrapped up the papers and stored them in his jacket. "Take a look at this before we go, just to refresh your memory. If you'll excuse me, I have to use the facilities."

Marta poured more tea. She looked briefly at the papers on the table, not needing to read them in order to recall the content. She finished her tea, watching the two men in the car opposite the hotel watch her. After a moment, she checked her watch. Looking over at Sami's table, Marta saw the folded newspaper was still there. She walked over, picked it up, and discovered a manila envelope tucked in its pages. When she returned with the paper, Vasilli was being served another cup of tea.

"Can I have an egg?" he asked. "Boiled, hard or soft, doesn't matter. I'd just like to have an egg, please."

They laughed at the waiter's expression as Marta translated the request. "You'd think I was asking for gold," he commented.

"Perhaps you are." He looked quizzical. "By now, I'm sure that everyone in town knows who you are. And I'm also sure that they don't know exactly what to think about you, or me, for that matter. We must be the object of a great deal of speculation."

"Precisely why we should marry," he announced.

"I'm not seeing the connection."

"They probably think you're a paid companion anyway, might as well make it legit," he said.

She ignored him and opened the envelope. In it, she found a compilation of press clippings, some old and yellowed, some obviously reprinted from the Internet. "What the …" She held up a rather tattered page. "This is an article about my graduation from Columbia. How the hell did Samibey get this?" She riffled through the pages, eyes narrowing, occasionally shaking her head. She closed the file. "Well, that's interesting," she said.

Vasilli reached for the file. "May I?" He placed tiny reading glasses on the tip of his nose and squinted at the pages, while Marta tapped her nails against an empty cup.

"Graduation, one of the loneliest days of my life—although, no, there were worse days," she said. "Probably what made that day bad was that I was completely alone, had no one to even tell. That's when it hit me. I was really alone. I had been buried in my books for months, working and studying night and day, keeping busy so I wouldn't have to think. But on graduation day, there it was. I was alone, surrounded by hundreds of happy families. And there I was. I don't know why I went, really. I guess I thought you had to go, or you wouldn't get the degree. My Turkish educational indoctrination, I suppose. So I walked through the ceremony like a zombie, went back

to my room, and slept for twenty-four hours. When I got up, it was over."
She smiled, showing the mask back in place.

"How do you think he got all of these?" Vasilli asked. "And why—although I suppose that is obvious. The man had a crush on you."

"Please. I was his student. That was fifteen years ago. I … no, I don't think so."

"How else do you explain this? He kept a file on all his old students just in case they turned up as opposing counsel? A little far-fetched, no?"

She shrugged, took the file, and put it in her bag.

"You don't want to talk about it," Vasilli said. She crossed her arms and looked out the window. "Well, let's take that walk then, shall we?"

The streets were busy at mid-morning with trucks and pedestrians negotiating the narrow roads. They headed to the centrum, where a massive bust of Atatürk had been carved from the yellow rock and stood balanced on one corner.

"You know, there's probably a mountain of rock underground there, holding that thing up." Vasilli pointed.

"It's a pretty good likeness," Marta said. "How did they get his eyebrows to look so bushy in the rock?"

"He's a pretty popular guy, this Atatürk."

"You might say that. Every town has a giant statue like this, every classroom a painting—sort of like George Washington."

"I don't think George is as popular as he used to be." Vasilli chuckled. "When I first attended school in Paterson, yeah, they had his portrait right over the chalkboard in every room."

They rounded the park, waited for the light to change, and entered the commercial district. Shops displaying clothing, shoes, and housewares vied with banks and bakeries for attention. Vasilli stopped in front of a children's clothing store.

"I've been meaning to ask you, what are those little uniforms all about?" He pointed to a brilliant green satin military-style suit, complete with sparkling silver fringe, a baton, and a hat trimmed with more of the silver stuff. A similar ensemble in blue was on display.

"Oh, those. They're for the circumcision parties."

"For what? No, don't tell me. I can imagine. They make them wear those ridiculous outfits and then, oh my! I thought this was a civilized country."

"Don't be judgmental. Every culture has its little idiosyncrasies." They walked away from the display, Vasilli catching Marta's hand as they crossed a busy intersection.

"No lights," he noted.

"No—traffic signals are for sissies. Even when they bother to install them, most Turks treat the lights as a suggestion. You saw that in Istanbul." They watched a Mercedes pass a bread cart and narrowly miss hitting a taxi. "Hey, maybe I should rent a car," she said. "Wouldn't that be fun, driving around in this?"

They rounded the block and could see the hotel name in bright white letters on the dark awning over the sidewalk. "Do you think our friends enjoyed the parade?" Vasilli asked. He looked back at the limo edging down the street behind them. A long line of cars snaked down the block. Horns blew as cars attempted to pass. They stopped and watched.

"They look happy, actually." Marta raised her hand, entwined with Vasilli's. "What are you doing, trying to send them a message? Or just playing a game?"

He moved his free hand to cover the others. "I am not playing. I think it would be a good thing, for you to marry me. It would be a very good thing." He released her hand, opened the door to the hotel, and followed her inside.

Thirty-eight

The meeting with the clan was set for noon, the "shoot-out at high noon" according to Vasilli. They walked back to the ornate gate, which opened automatically upon their approach. No person was visible, but the whir of cameras followed their every move toward the house. The gates clicked shut. Marta nervously looked over her shoulder at the solidity of the sound.

"I hope we can leave as easily as we came in," she muttered. Vasilli took the opportunity to reach for her hand again, both of them surprised that she allowed it.

"Welcome, sir, madam." A black-clad servant appeared at the door. "Please follow me into the library. Can I offer you some tea? Splendid. Please have a seat. Someone will be with you shortly. Oh, you may feel free to look around." He slid out of the door, leaving it slightly ajar.

His footsteps echoed on the parquet floors.

"Look at this." Marta turned in a circle, taking in the twenty-foot ceilings and thousands of books. The wrought-iron mezzanine ran along three of the walls, with spiral staircases at each end. Leather bindings cast a muted glow over the windowless room, which was furnished with heavy leather club chairs and a single, massive, leather-embossed desk. Silk carpets covered the hardwood floor.

"Wow. These carpets are amazing! These books. Man. The leather. Think of all the animals that died to outfit this one room."

"You're not one of those wacky animal rights nuts, are you?"

She smiled. "What do you think?"

"Okay." He moved to take one of the chairs. "Are you going to sit down?"

"No, I want to look around. Think it's safe to climb these things?" Without waiting for an answer, Marta began climbing the stairs, stopping to shake the railing a bit. "Seems pretty sturdy," she noted.

"Be careful," Vasilli said.

The door opened. A small boy entered and spotted Marta walking along the mezzanine. "Hey!" he shouted. "Did my father say you could go up there?"

"Who is your father?" Vasilli asked. The boy spun around at the sound of his voice and put his hands on his hips.

"Who are you, mister?" he demanded. "Who let you in here?"

"My name is Vasilli. I was invited to meet someone here."

"Huh. My name is Yurgos. I live here." He jumped into the chair next to Vasilli. "Are you here to see my father? How old are you? You look like my grandfather. He was very, very old, and now he is dead. Are you going to be dead soon too?"

"I hope not." Vasilli chuckled. He leaned toward the little boy. "How old are you? Five. Wow. You are a big boy. Do you have big muscles? Can I see them?"

The boy pushed aside the sleeve of his T-shirt and made a muscle that Vasilli admired with the appropriate ooohs and aaahs.

"Can you hold out your hands? That's right." He put his own hands out over the boy's, and the child squealed in delight as several coins appeared in Vasilli's fingers.

"How did you do that? Do you know magic? Do some more."

Vasilli looked up at Marta, who was resting her arms on the railing above them. "He has the mark. Can you see it from there?" She shook her head. He pulled a small whistle seemingly from inside the boy's ear and handed it to him. "Is this yours, Yurgos?"

The boy laughed again and then began to toot on the little whistle and march around the room. "It's a half-moon birthmark, inside his elbow. Just like my brother's."

He sighed. "It is true then. That confirms it. This is my brother's family." He made eye contact with Marta again, smiling sadly. "We found them."

She nodded and then lifted her chin toward the door, where a slim man with salt-and-pepper hair was standing. "Yurgos!" he spoke sharply. The little boy continued his noisy march around the room. "Yurgos, come here and be quiet." He clapped his hands, and the boy turned, startled, and then dropped the whistle into his pocket.

"Come here." The man held out his hand. "Give it to me. Good boy. Now, did you say thank you to the man? Yes? Okay. Now give it back to him. Go on."

"He can keep it." Vasilli stood to greet the younger man.

"Nonsense, sir. The boy is not allowed to accept gifts from strangers. Yurgos? Give it back to the man. Now go and find your nanny." They watched the boy leave, and his father closed the door softly. He stood holding the doorknob for a moment, and Vasilli and Marta watched his shoulders rise and fall with a deep breath before he turned to face them.

"Please, sit." He held out a hand toward the chairs. "Tea will be delivered shortly."

They sat, each looking appraisingly at the other. "So." Vasilli broke the tension with a smile. He stretched out his hand. "I am Vasilli Vassilios, brother of Yurgos, and son of Anna and Konstantin Vassilios. I am your uncle." His gesture was not returned, and slowly he dropped his arm. "What is your name, Son?"

More silence. The younger man, his ruddy complexion darkening a bit, frowned.

"Look, I mean you no harm. I am not here to stir up any trouble. I don't want anything from you or your family. But it is clear to me that we are related, and I am pleased to see the son of my brother, and his son, and to know that our family name will live on long after my brother and I are gone," Vasilli said.

"My name is Konstantin. And I do not believe that it has been established that we are related."

"Your son has the mark. Here, inside his arm. And you probably do too."

They were interrupted by the clatter of a tea cart being wheeled into the room. A small gold-plated samovar topped by an ornately decorated porcelain pot sat in the center, surrounded by plates, glasses, and a triple-tiered tray of small sandwiches. The servant began pouring and then with a slight motion of his head signaled to his employer the presence of the silent woman on the mezzanine. Konstantin nodded. "Miss, will you be taking tea with the gentlemen?" He handed the first glass to Vasilli.

"Yes." She stood up and made her way slowly to the other end of the mezzanine and then down the stairs. She perched on a chair and accepted a glass of tea. Konstantin, a smaller version of a younger Vasilli, looked at her with his dark eyes under heavy knitted brows, but he did not speak. Pursing his full lips, he blew softly on the tea in the same way Marta had watched Vasilli do every morning for the past ten days. He had the same large hands too, the long pink nail beds, the gentle wave in his short hair. Even his ears were the same, Marta noticed, with the flat auricle ending in a slight point. She turned and looked at Vasilli and confirmed a similar bump on his slightly longer lobed ear. She smiled.

Several minutes passed. Each man concentrated on his tea and openly inspected the other.

Finally, Vasilli put down his cup and cleared his throat. "I am here because you sent me a letter. I did not search you out, and I mean you and your family no harm. But I was informed of my brother's death, and I came to pay my respects to his family. That's all. I don't understand why you are so hostile. Well, maybe I do now that I know who you are, but I have not changed. I am Vasilli Vassilios, and you are my nephew. That's all I know." He leaned forward and tapped the other man on the knee. "And it makes me very happy to know this and to see you and to see your son. It makes me very happy."

Konstantin's face reddened. "Listen," he started to speak and then stopped, covering his face for a moment. "I told the lawyer to send letters to anyone in New York with the name Vassilios. We are Vaso now, but I knew from my father's papers that his name had been changed after the war. And I discovered some photographs of him, with his parents and a brother. So I had a legal obligation to look for you, but I never imagined that you would still be alive." He cleared his throat and looked around the room before continuing. "That is, ahem, if you are who you say you are."

"I have the letter you sent right here. Would you like to see it?"

"No, I believe you received the letter. Did you know there are seventeen Vassilios living in New York City? And only you have arrived here. The other letters either came back or, well, they must have been thrown out."

"That's because I am the brother of your father. There is only one Vasilli Vassilios. And I am here."

Konstantin ran his hand through his hair. The rolled-up sleeve of his cotton shirt did not rise above the forearm, and he reddened again when he saw Vasilli looking at his arm. Slowly, Vasilli removed his jacket, with Marta helping from her perch on the arm of his chair. He rolled up the left sleeve of his thin white cotton shirt, pushing it above the elbow and turning his arm out to show the mark.

"Mine is just a shadow, see? And it's smaller, just so. Your father had the true mark. It was dark, almost black, like your little boy's. And I bet you have it too."

Konstantin shook his head. "I don't have it," he said. "My father did, but not me."

"I see," Vasilli said softly.

"It proves nothing. You could have read about it—"

"I don't think so. At least when we were young, the adults never spoke of it and always made my brother keep his arm covered. They thought it was a mark of the devil, not something you wanted anyone to see. I would be surprised if many people know about it. Am I right?"

"I have to go." Konstantin stood up.

"Wait a minute." Marta broke her silence. "We're finally here, talking. Aren't you going to answer some of his questions?"

"No. I told you, we need the lawyers to—"

"No, you don't. If you want, we'll have a DNA test. How about that?"

His hands gripped the back of the chair. "Why do you want DNA? Are you coming after us? I thought you said you didn't want anything. So now, you want DNA?"

Vasilli stood as well. "The DNA is for your benefit, not mine. I don't need it."

"You will sign papers giving away all claims to the estate?"

Marta held up her hand before Vasilli could answer. "Not so fast. Are you acknowledging him?"

"No."

"Then why would you want papers?"

"This is ridiculous," Vasilli interrupted. "Nobody needs papers. I'm not here for a legal claim."

"I need papers," Konstantin said.

"Then we need DNA," Marta replied.

"Then you sign?"

"I'll let you know after we see the results of the test," she answered. She put her hand on Vasilli's arm to stop his protest. "First, DNA. Then we talk about the rest."

Konstantin walked to the door. He turned back, one hand on the knob. "I am here without lawyers, to speak with you man to man."

Vasilli rushed forward. "I just want to get to know you. I can ask her to leave if you like."

Konstantin shrugged again. "If she keeps quiet, she can stay."

They returned to their chairs. Vasilli popped a small sandwich into his mouth and made appreciative noises.

"Wonderful," he murmured. "Reminds me of these little pastries my mother used to make, rolled dough with fillings—oh, cheese, potatoes, spinach, meats. We would eat them right out of the oven, and she'd swat us with a towel. How many times I burned my mouth!" He chuckled.

Marta moved back into the shadows, settling into a chair slightly behind Vasilli, as he began to talk.

Thirty-nine

Vasilli started to speak. "We had a simple life, a happy life. Like all the men we knew, Father was a fisherman. When he was home, he sat in the yard mending nets. He didn't talk, just sat and watched the sky. My brother was like that. He was older, and he crouched next to father, imitating his movements over the nets, pausing to watch the sky."

He laughed and shook his head.

"What's funny?" Konstantin asked.

"I was just remembering," Vasilli continued. "Father chewed tobacco, and Yurgos would stick his tongue in his cheek to make the same lump there. He did that all the time, even in school, and he was always getting in trouble for it. 'Spit it out,' the teacher would say, holding her hand in front of his mouth. But there was nothing to spit."

Konstantin nodded his head. "He always did that when he was working on something. You'd see his tongue working the side of his cheek." He laughed softly. "I never knew where that came from. I thought it was some kind of compulsive thing, like the counting. But I'm sorry—continue with your story. I want to hear all of it."

From her position in the shadows, Marta watched Konstantin struggle to control his emotions as Vasilli resumed speaking.

"Counting, you say? That also comes from childhood. Mother made us count aloud all the time. How many eggs? We had to shout out the numbers from inside the henhouse. 'One! Two! Three!' Both of us yelling. And her yelling back. When we came out, she'd have the total and make us count them all over again to make sure we hadn't missed any. We had to count the fish while we sorted them. I think she felt bad for keeping us out of school so often, to help with the chores, so she made us count and read aloud all the time." He paused again, taking a sip of the chilled tea.

"Yurgos was five years older than me. So when I remember him, it was always me running after him, tagging along, trying to keep up. He hid from me, ran from me, but when I wandered off, he was always the one to run around looking for me, and he was usually the one to find me. Once, I was sleeping in the laundry basket with the cat and apparently everyone was searching up and down the street looking for me. Yurgos found me. He screamed so loud, I remember it clearly: 'Oh, Vaso, you are found!' The way he said it 'Va-So.' Va-So. I had forgotten that he always called me that name. Such a long time. Va-So. Hmmm."

Vasilli shook his head and rubbed his chin. "Vaso," he repeated softly. "Well, that was more than a lifetime ago, no?" He looked at Konstantin, whose eyes were glassy as tears streamed silently down his face.

"Uncle," he said finally, wiping his cheeks with the backs of his hands. "I am sorry."

Vasilli tapped him on the knee. "You're a good boy. You meant me no harm. I know it."

Konstantin laughed, a sharp hiccup. After a moment in which Vasilli sat back, amused, Konstantin reached over and tapped Vasilli's knee. "This. Tapping. My father also did it—for good and bad, but mostly for good. Tap, tap, tap. 'You're a good boy,' he would tell me. The best praise. A tap on the knee. Ha." Konstantin rubbed his hands vigorously over his face and shook his shoulders. Marta could see the muscles in his jaw clenching as he sat back in the chair.

Vasilli coughed. "Can I get some water, some ice perhaps?"

Konstantin jumped up, opened the door, and shouted something. In a moment, the servant reappeared and then returned again with a pitcher of ice water and some melon slices on a delicate china plate.

"Please, take your time."

Vasilli walked to the other side of the room, rolling his shoulders. When he turned, he was smiling. "So many memories I had forgotten!" he exclaimed. "Thank you for helping me remember those happy times!"

He walked over to Marta's chair and placed a hand on her shoulder. "Isn't this wonderful?" he asked. The question seemed to echo as he gazed around the room, a wide smile on his lips.

"Are you all right?" Marta asked. "We can take a break and come back later." She took his hand. His skin was dry and papery. "Why don't you sit and have some more water?"

Konstantin sat forward, elbows to knees, and spoke quickly. "What else can you tell me about him, my father? What else do you remember?"

Vasilli returned to his chair. "I'm not sure if this is a real memory or a dream—Yurgos falling from an olive tree, like in slow motion, landing with a thump that knocked the wind out of him. Father prodded him with the oar he used to shake the olives out of the tree. 'Boy, you okay there, boy?' he said. Yurgos just huffed, got up, nodded, and went back up the tree, I think. Later, his arm was all crooked, and Father pulled it straight and tied it to a board. Can that be true? Did he have a broken arm?"

"Yes, it must be," Konstantin said. "His left arm was a little crooked, and he'd rub it when the weather changed. 'Olives' was the only thing he said. When I was little, I thought he was allergic to olives. Later, I figured he'd fallen from a tree, but I never knew it was during a harvest. He didn't talk about his childhood. Not at all. And Yaya—my grandmother—never spoke of the past. She barely spoke anyway. She lived with us like a ghost, always in black, always sad."

Vasilli drank another glass of water. A servant came to the door, and Konstantin excused himself.

Marta moved to the side of Vasilli's chair and touched his cheek. "Vasil-li, are you okay?" she asked.

He put his hand over hers, smiling dreamily. "Marry me," he whis-pered.

She checked his head and looked into his red-rimmed eyes. "I think we should stop now. We can come back tomorrow, and you can talk some more." She stood up, and he grasped her hand. "I'm worried about you. I think you're getting dehydrated."

"I'm fine."

"Really? You don't look fine to me."

"Thanks a lot." He sat up straighter. "Now? Do I look better now?"

"No."

"You're just saying that."

Konstantin came back into the room. Marta began to speak, but he waved a hand to stop her. "Sorry, I have to leave. There's a little problem I have to take care of." He leaned closer to the old man. "Uncle, would you like to stay here with us? I can have your things brought over from the hotel. We have plenty of room here."

Vasilli looked up at Marta and then turned to Konstantin and cocked his head in her direction.

"Oh, of course, you too, miss. You are also welcome. We'll be happy to keep both of you here with us." He stood up, almost clicking his heels to-gether. "So, it's settled then?"

Marta rose as well, shaking her head. "No, I think we'll stay in the ho-tel." She was impressed by Konstantin's rapid transformation, back to be-ing in control and businesslike after the emotion he'd displayed in the past hour.

"Wait, I think it's a good idea," Vasilli interjected.

"I'll have my man bring your things over, if you give me the keys, then," Konstantin said, stretching out his hand.

Marta turned to Vasilli, shaking her head. "I have a problem with this. I don't think it's wise for us to stay here until we get everything settled." She turned to Konstantin. "Can you give us a moment, please?"

When he left, she crossed her arms and looked down at Vasilli. "I don't want to scare you, but have you lost your mind? I don't trust these people one bit. I won't stay here, and I don't think you should either."

"I have to trust him. I know he's my nephew, and I don't think he would harm me," Vasilli said. "I wish you would stay. You can keep an eye on things."

"I'll do that from the hotel. One of us has to be objective about this."

"Fine. But I don't think you'll be any more secure in the hotel, you know. I think they own the entire town."

Marta turned as Konstantin stuck his head into the room.

"Will you be staying, miss?" he asked.

She shook her head.

"No? Well, we can have a car take you back to the hotel later. In the meantime, please excuse me. I have business to attend to. Make yourselves at home. Walk around the grounds. Go for a swim. We have peacocks in the garden. They're quite beautiful this year." He backed out of the room.

"This is not a good idea," Marta began again.

"Oh, posh." Vasilli jumped to his feet.

"Posh?"

"Yes. That. Let's go scare up some peacocks, shall we?"

Forty

They walked through grounds as lush as those at Dolmabahçe and Topkapi, the homes of the sultans. The Greek version had small arbors here and there, ornate structures laden with grape vines. Stone fountains spewed water from fish mouths. At the edge of a thick hedge, they found a small church, which resembled a child's playhouse with a tall steeple. As they approached, they realized that it was just large enough for one or two adults to enter. Marta watched Vasilli as he peered in the windows; his color was better. She could see that he had almost recovered from the session with Konstantin.

"This looks like—Wait. It is, isn't it?" Marta asked. "This is a replica of that church on Buyuk Ada, where my mother is buried."

"Yes," Vasilli replied slowly. He moved away from the entrance to the corner and then stopped short as a horrible wail rose from the bushes. Several large peacocks marched out then, one crying loudly. Marta covered her ears.

"God, I hate that noise," she muttered. "Sounds just like babies crying. Ugh."

The birds surrounded the pair, two of them with their tail feathers fully fanned.

"They are beautiful," Vasilli whispered. "Look at those colors."

"Hmmm." She shivered. "Make them stop."

"They'll settle down in a minute … Hey, what's the matter? You're not afraid of them, are you? They're just birds. And they're putting on a beautiful show for us." He rubbed her shoulder. "There's a bench over there. Let's sit. So, tell me, another bad association? Some childhood trauma where you were chased by wild peacocks?" There was a teasing tone to his words, but he kept his arm lightly around her waist.

"Oh, you don't want to hear any more of my sad stories."

"Sure I do—and I think if you tell them, they won't have any power over you anymore."

178

"Are you a psychologist too?" She looked at him and smiled ruefully. "Sometimes it is best to keep your memories to yourself."

"Look, my place wasn't a bar, but I heard more sob stories behind my counter every day—"

"And did the telling make everything better for your customers?" He didn't answer. "That's what I thought. Same story, over and over, right? So what good did it do?"

Vasilli stood up suddenly and walked around to the rear of the building. Marta called over to him.

"I'm sorry—I didn't mean to imply that you didn't help people." She got up and followed him, still talking, until she rounded the corner.

A large fenced area enclosed several gravestones, looking like twin beds in a dormitory room. They were gray from years of exposure to the wind and had simple Greek characters carved on the headstone of each. One pristine white box dominated the center of the area, an almost full-sized angel looming above the inscription.

"My brother," Vasilli whispered. "And next to him, this must be his wife. Where is—? There. Mother." He fell to his knees and rested his head on the granite. Marta stood back and then walked over to place her hand on his shoulder. "I'll leave you alone," she said.

"No, stay with me," he said. "Oh, Mother," he cried softly. "I missed you. I never forgot about you. Mama." He rocked back and forth. Marta rubbed his shoulder lightly. The peacocks' cries and a ruffle of feathers broke through the moment. She shivered at the sound. Vasilli took several deep, calming breaths and leaned against the stone.

"Yurgos loved to hunt. Did I tell you that? He was only a little boy, and he was a great hunter. His gun was taller than he was." He laughed, shaking his head. "In the fall, he'd go out early in the morning, before light, and come back hours later with a bunch of pheasant. I don't know how he learned to hunt. My father never went with him. I don't even know where he got a gun, but that wasn't so unusual in those days. Everyone had a gun. If only the Turks knew, when they came to evacuate, that every Greek had a gun in his closet ... Trick was, no one used them anyway." He sighed, shifting a bit against the cold stone. Marta slid to the grass beside him.

The birds, tail feathers lowered, came closer and pecked at Vasilli's shoes. He jiggled a foot, and they backed away, mouths open but no sound coming out.

"Don't make them cry again," Marta said. "Please. I hate that noise."

"Okay." Vasilli crossed his arms and looked at the sky. "So this is the place I will be buried," he said. "It's nice. I can even live with the birds. Effie will like it too."

Marta shuddered. "I think you better talk to your nephew before you go digging any holes in here."

"Don't worry." He smiled. "I'm all set."

She looked at him. The lines in his face were softer, his eyes clear. Relaxed? Happy? He looked happy, finally. But she was concerned. He had the faraway look in his eye that people got when they were getting ready to die.

"Oh no you don't," she said, grabbing his arm. "You're not going to die on me. Not now."

"I've finished my journey," he replied. "I'm content to spend the rest of my time here, getting to know my family."

"You have got to be kidding," she said and then clamped a hand over her mouth. "Sorry. I can't believe I said that." She sat back against the cold stone. "I'm sorry. You're right. You found what you came here for."

He laughed. "Marta, you know that I'd like you to stay here with me, help me settle things with the family. And then, when I'm gone, you can do whatever you wish. I trust you to do the right thing." He took her hand. "Marta, I want to help you find your family too. I'll do whatever you ask. Just let me help you."

She looked at him for a moment. "I appreciate your offer, I truly do. But I married once for the wrong reason, and I'm not going to do it again," she said. "I hope you understand."

"The wrong reason?"

"Green card. Even back in those days, it was not as simple as I thought it would be. It was still a legal marriage and not easy to end," she said. "I know I must sound like a romantic to you, which is clearly not my nature, but some institutions should be respected. Marriage shouldn't be just a business contract … or at least, not all the time."

He wiped his hands on the side of his trousers. "You're right. I know you're not a gold digger. And I didn't propose to you just to have someone to leave my money to." He sighed and started to rise. "Someday, I hope you'll tell me about the man who hurt you so much when you were young. And I hope you know that I would never do anything to harm you." He groaned. "Right now, I think I'm too old to be sitting on the ground. Maybe I'll go in and have a little rest. Do you want to join me?"

Marta dusted off her slacks and looked back toward the house. "It seems that we have a visitor." She nodded toward the garden path, where a short figure was approaching the church. "You go on up to the house. Let me talk to him. I'll join you in a minute."

She returned to the bench and waited for Sami. Vasilli nodded at the other man as he passed and then turned and watched him. He waved once at Marta and then disappeared into the hedge.

"Sami-bey."

"Marta. What a lovely day. Aren't the gardens magnificent? Have you seen the peacocks? Such lovely creatures."

"Let's skip the niceties, shall we? I want you to tell me about my sister."

"Which one?"

"You know perfectly well—okay. Sevgi. She works in your office, remember? She must be the one who kept those clippings about me, right? Why'd you give them to me? Just so I'd think that you've been watching me. I know it wasn't you. Why doesn't she come to see me herself?"

He sighed dramatically. "Your sister, she is in the mind for justice. This makes a good lawyer sometimes, but then she is too angry about other things to be effective. She had a hard life after you left. You should know that. And it made her a hard person."

"I don't know what she told you, but my father was not a good person. He brutalized my mother—"

Sami chuckled. "Don't be so dramatic, Marta. It's not a soap opera."

"He's Laz. You know Laz? Do you know what family honor means to them?" She stood in front of the little man. "Let me give you just one example. When we were kids, one of our cousins came to stay with us for a few months during the summer. I guess he must have gotten into some trouble at home, so they sent him to the city for a while. I took him out with some friends once; a whole group of us went to a Luna Park. He was clowning around, trying to dance with one of the girls, trying to tickle one of the others. And he grabbed one of the boys and did a little jig around with him. We were laughing so hard. No one took offense, at least that's what I thought. The next day, when Father came home, he took my cousin outside and beat the crap out of him. One of the fathers had complained that he better keep his 'pouf' nephew under control. Can you imagine? The kid had a broken arm and probably a lot worse … He was on the bus back to the village before we could even say good-bye. That's my father. Family honor above all."

Sami, wide-eyed, made a careless gesture with his hand. "Your story is not so unusual, you know. Your father was no different from most."

"Well, anyway, that's not the point. I need to talk to my sister."

"All she knows is that you disappeared. You got your diploma, and no one ever heard from you again."

"That's not exactly true, and she knows it." Marta sat down. "I just figured it out. She took the money, didn't she? That's how she went to college. She took the money I sent Mother."

"Your mother died the year after you left." Sami had a triumphant smile on his face.

"I know." She searched his face. "Disappointed? I can see that you wanted to be the one to tell me, but it's too late. I know the whole story—maybe even more than Sevgi. I know what really happened to Mother, and I know that it was my father who killed her. Just like he would have killed me if he had the chance. That's why I had to leave."

"Well ..." Sami shifted in his seat.

"I'm sorry that I had to leave them, but I couldn't protect them from him. Maybe now I would stay and fight, but then, I was too young and afraid. My mother gave me a way out, and it was the only choice I had."

"Your mother?"

"She helped me get away from him."

"But why?"

"Oh, you don't need to know. The only person I owe an explanation is my sister—actually, all of my sisters. Do you know where they are?"

"They're around. You'll have to talk to Sevgi and see if she wants ... well, if she wants to see you, if she wants to hear your sad story, if she wants you to know where your sisters are. That's up to her, like you said."

They sat in silence. From the distance, children's voices could be heard. "I still don't understand what your relationship is with the Vaso family."

"Simply business."

"Really?" She cocked an eyebrow and looked at his threadbare wardrobe. "From the looks of your office, and you, business has not been that good lately."

"I do all right."

"Really?"

Sami stood up. "Yes. Well, I would like you to come to the house so we can talk about some paperwork that needs to be done."

"What kind of paperwork?"

"We have some papers for your client to sign, very simple things, to settle the estate, you know."

They began to walk through the gardens. "Uh-huh. So, you think that my client is going to sign a waiver, don't you?"

"He said he doesn't want anything. I'm taking him at his word. So he signs, everything is settled. He can stay here as long as he wishes, spend some time with his nephew, whatever. But he must sign the papers."

"No more DNA, no more pretending that he's not a relative?"

Sami laughed. "No, he seems to have made a pretty strong impression on Konstantin. We're satisfied that he is Yurgos's long-lost brother."

"I'll need that in writing first then." Marta stepped through the door Sami held open. "When you give me that sealed affidavit, we'll look at the other papers."

He bowed and then held out a card.

She shook her head. "I have your card."

"It's your sister's. I thought you might want it." She crossed her arms and studied the floor. "Well, fine, I'll leave it on the table here, just in case you change your mind. Good day."

Forty-one

Marta went looking for Vasilli and found him asleep, stretched out on top of a huge canopy bed, his long body covered lightly with a butter-yellow cotton throw. Marta stood next to the bed, watching his chest rise and fall. She rested her cheek against the newel post and then curled into a window seat, legs tucked under and arms hugging her torso. Still, he slept. She sighed.

She studied the room. Heavy silk fabric covered the walls. It was hand painted with brilliant yellow flowers, honeysuckle, trailing greens, and the occasional exotic bird perched on a petal that seemed to sway with his weight. The bottom of the walls was paneled with heavy mahogany, the same rich-toned wood of the furnishings. A large bureau, covered by a delicate lace runner, also held two ornate ceramic lamps. At the center, reflected in the heavy mirror, a cut crystal vase was bursting with yellow forsythia.

Two windows were framed with luxurious satin drapes. The outer layer was embroidered with a floral pattern that matched the wallpaper but in shades of spring green. The liner, near Marta's hand, picked up the butter color that soothed the eye as well as the hand.

A movement outside caught her eye. Sami, in the driveway, was gesturing angrily at another man, someone Marta recognized from their first days in Istanbul.

One of the real Vaso attorneys, she thought, the one who probably hired Sami and brought him in to threaten Vasilli and rattle Marta. She watched them. The man turned back to the house, Sami kicking up dust as he returned to his little Opel parked by the gate. It started up with a roar of smoke as the gates opened and closed on his departure.

The sky was dusky, pink clouds streaking across larger gray billows. Marta watched a flock of pigeons rise and then fall sharply across the sky. She waited, but they did not reappear. The red-tiled roofs glowed under the salmon dusk. From the vantage point of the house, which was set on a rise and clearly taller than any other building, Marta could see the entire town as it spread around the base of the rocky mountainous outcroppings. The yellow rock seemed hard and sharp next to the small red-roofed houses snuggled against it. She imagined the shadow cast by this house, its brick walls and gray roof totally out of character with the rest of Afyon, just as its owners kept themselves apart. She frowned, searching the sky for the pigeons, but they were gone.

When she turned back to the room, Vasilli was watching her. He turned on his side and tucked an arm under his head. His stomach grumbled loudly. "Those little sandwiches didn't last." He smiled. "When do you think we'll get dinner?"

"It's still early," she said, glancing at her watch. "Oh, no. I stand corrected. It's almost 7:00. I was planning to go back to the hotel to change."

"We've got time. Tell me what Sami wanted."

"Oh, Sami-bey. You know, he's all dodging and weaving, won't give a straight answer to a direct question. Your typical lawyer," she joked.

"Just like you now?" He sat on the edge of the bed. "Tell me what he said to upset you."

"I'm not upset." And so she told him about her sister.

"But none of this is a surprise, is it?" he asked.

She shook her head. "We should go down for dinner."

"I'm thinking about having a suit made." He sat up and swung his feet over the side of the bed. "A white suit, for our wedding."

She laughed, a sharp hiccup, and then stopped. "You're not serious?"

"Oh yes, I've noticed that they have some very nice suits here. And perhaps you can get a dress, something simple. Doesn't have to be white of course."

"Listen, my friend, I'm not marrying you. That won't help your cause with your nephew, and I'm sure they'd challenge my position anyway." She walked to the door. "I am very fond of you, you know that. But you have to stop this fantasy about us. We're going to be great friends, hopefully for a long, long time. Okay?"

"No. But I'll wait for you to change your mind." He stood and straightened his collar in the mirror. "Do you think I need to change for dinner?" He leaned forward, inspecting himself in the mirror until his eyes caught Marta's.

She opened the door. Before it closed completely, he called out, "Marta, the white suit, you think it would be too much? I could go for linen, but I always wanted to wear a white suit like that Mark Twain fellow."

She stuck her head back into the room. "You can definitely carry it off."

He laughed, pleased with himself and her and the world in general.
"Yes, I can," he announced to his image in the mirror.

Outside the dining room, Marta perched on a settee and waited for
Vasilli. When he arrived, in yet another fresh white shirt, Marta said, "There
is one little problem with Sami-bey that I should tell you about. He wants
you—they want you—to sign an agreement giving up any rights to the family fortune. I told him that before we even talk about that, you require a
sworn affidavit that they acknowledge your relationship and right of inheritance. So we may be at a stalemate."

"Nonsense. Konstantin will not require such things from me, and I
won't ask him either. We are family. Didn't you see that this afternoon?"

"Well, it appears that there are others involved, people he has to answer
to, and they are playing hardball."

"Don't worry; everything will be fine." He smiled and held out his arm
for her. "Shall we?"

"Back into the lion's den," she replied.

Dinner was preceded by an elaborate cocktail ceremony in which Konstantin introduced his wife, Serpil, and their three children. The two older
girls, dressed alike and severely controlled by their mother, were in stark
contrast to the ragamuffin Yurgos. The little boy bullied his way to the
cracker-and-cheese table, popped several olives into his mouth at once, and
chased the cat under a console table covered with crystal glasses and carafes.
His father watched him, pride swelling his face, and when one of the crystal
glasses crashed to the floor, he defended the boy while snapping his fingers
for the maid to clean up the glass shards.

"He's a real boy, this one. You know how boys are." He shrugged at
Vasilli. "You shouldn't make them into sissies; they have to be free to explore
and learn."

Marta coughed. "And your daughters? Are they free to explore and
learn?"

Konstantin glared at her. "No. That is not the way to raise young ladies.
They must be protected and learn proper behavior. Respectful, and silent,
that's the way for girls to behave." He looked her up and down, taking in her
pantsuit and loose hair. "Otherwise, they grow up to be … ahem … wild.
Like harlots. To shame the family. No proper marriage is possible if you let
a girl get too … how shall I say? Too smart for her own good. Wouldn't you
agree, Uncle?"

"Um, well, I never had children myself, you know, but it is a new world,"
Vasilli replied. "Even here, I understand there are female professors and doctors and lawyers … Wasn't there a female prime minister a few years ago?

Educated in the States, I believe, wasn't she? So there're other things for women besides marriage, right?"

Konstantin barked a command in Greek, and his wife bowed her head before escorting the two girls from the room. Yurgos continued to torment the cat, pulling his tail from where it protruded at the edge of a couch.

"Thank God they don't understand English. Mr. Vassilios, you must understand that we are different. This family is not the same as everyone else; we have to protect our children and raise them in a way that will protect the family name and the family business. Thank God I have a son, who will be my partner when he is old enough."

"Good for you that you got your male heir after only three tries," Marta interjected. She turned to the liquor table and replenished her gin and tonic, adding a bit more gin than the bartender had provided in her first drink. She watched Vasilli in the mirror as he tried to make conversation with his nephew.

"Your family, are there other brothers and sisters? Or is it just you?"

"We have many siblings, my sister and I. Father married a few times, so there are half-brothers and a couple of other sisters. They are not involved in the business. Father made sure of that. It is only my sister and I, and her husband basically takes care of her interests."

"What is her name? Does she live here? Does she have children, too?"

"All in good time," Sami answered as he came stealthily through the door. "You'll meet the rest of the family when the time is right."

"Mister, I think you have underestimated me." Vasilli stood up, looming over the squat attorney. "I am the brother of Yurgos Vassilios, and I am the uncle of your employer, Konstantin Vassilios. I will demand your respect. And if you do not give it to me, you will get out of my sight. Now." He turned to Konstantin. "Do you understand me? I will not be treated like some poor relation. You will respect me as your elder and call off your flunkies who are trying to undermine me." He held out his hand, his eyes locked with Konstantin. "Come here and pay your respect to me, *Yavrum*."

After a moment, Konstantin gestured for Sami to leave the room.

"No, he stays," Vasilli said. His hand was still outstretched. Konstantin stepped forward, took the old man's hand, and kissed the top of it and then brought it to his forehead in a gesture of supplication.

"That's a good boy. Now. You ..." He pointed to Sami. "I want you to get out of here, and don't come back unless I call for you. Do you understand? I don't want to see your face here again. Now ... *git*." He turned away and clapped Konstantin on the back. "Let's get some air." They walked to the open patio doors and stepped into the dusk.

Marta spoke softly to Sami. "I'd get out of here, if I were you. He'll ruin you for sure." She held up her glass. *"Şerife,"* she toasted him. "And you can tell my sister I would like to speak with her whenever she's ready to hear my side of the story."

Sami smiled as he left the room. "We'll see about that."

"Don't threaten me …" she muttered at the closed door.

From his position outside the room, Vasilli watched Marta prowl around the sitting room. Filled with the kind of ornately carved and stuffed furniture that was as uncomfortable to look at as it was to sit on, the room offered no place to rest. Another painted mural depicted pastoral scenes that existed nowhere but in the artist's imagination. Stiff bouquets of bright magenta coxcomb were arrayed on every glass-topped surface.

Marta jumped as Yurgos popped up from behind a love seat. "Do you like my cat?" he asked. "His name is Tekir. He is the same age as me, but in cat-years, that's really old. Did you know that?" He babbled facts about his cat and his amazing feats, and soon Marta was compelled to lower herself onto a short chair. Her knees poked up at an uncomfortable angle. The little boy came over and dropped his cat on her lap.

"Oh, no, take him away," she said. "I think I'm allergic."

"What is that?"

"Cats make me sneeze."

"You're not sneezing." He stood back and looked at her. "You're lying to me. You sure are tall. Where's your husband? Oh, he's outside talking to Father. That's right. You should not be listening to the business talk. That's not for ladies."

Marta began to object and then sighed. She took a swig of her drink and then held up the glass and jiggled the ice cubes at the barman who rushed to replenish. *"Duble,"* she said. "Make it a double."

The cat kneaded at her cashmere sweater. Fortunately, he had no claws, but just as she relaxed into the steady vibrato of its purr, the back paws dug into her legs and the cat went sailing over the back of her chair. Yurgos had pulled his tail again.

"Why do you do that?" she asked.

"He's my cat," he said. "I can do whatever I want to him."

"That's not right. He's a helpless animal. You should be kind and gentle with him."

Yurgos looked at her like she'd grown horns. "That's not the way to make animals obey. You have to show them who's boss."

She shook her head. "And here I thought you were such a nice little boy," she said.

"Who wants to be nice? Nice is for sissies and girls. I'm not nice." He crossed his arms and gave her a swift kick in the shin. Fortunately, her hands were empty still, and she grabbed him by the shoulders.

"Don't do that. That is not … acceptable." She shook him slightly. She let go of his shoulders when Konstantin stormed into the room.

"What is going on here? Let go of my son!" he shouted.

Marta rolled up her pant leg. A large red egg appeared where the boy's hard-sole shoe had connected. "Is this the way that you teach your son to treat guests? To be rude and then physically aggressive?" She accepted the drink offered by the silent servant and glared at Konstantin. "Did you know that mistreatment of animals is the first sign of a major psychiatric disorder in young children?"

"In your country, maybe. Here, it is normal for young boys to play rough with their pets. It teaches them control. Helps them understand that men are the rulers of the world."

"You certainly have no self-esteem issues," Marta commented. "I suppose men are the rulers of women too?" She turned to Vasilli. "See what your brother has raised? Very enlightened attitude. So all your philanthropy, all those schools and museums that you support, that's just a public relations ploy?"

"My father was a very generous man."

"And that's not your style, is it?" She rubbed her leg. Yurgos clutched his father's hand as she rose out of her chair. "Don't worry, little boy. I'm not the one who is going to hurt you." She turned to Konstantin. "Your company will not succeed if you try to follow some antiquated code of behavior. You just won't make it in the modern world. And you'll end up a very lonely person. I'm sorry for you, that you can't understand the importance of giving. The more you give, the more you get. It's a basic thing. And that's why your father was so beloved, and why his company was such a success."

Vasilli took her hand and helped her sit down. "Perhaps some ice?" he asked the barman.

Marta accepted an icepack. She leaned back against the chair unsteadily, perhaps more because of the gin than the throbbing on her leg.

"I'm all right," she said.

Konstantin led the boy from the room, pausing to announce that dinner would be served shortly.

Marta pulled Vasilli close. "Watch what they serve you. Don't eat anything that you don't see served to the entire table," she whispered.

"Now you're getting paranoid," he said. "They're not going to hurt me. Konstantin is a little rough around the edges, I'll admit. I'm sure his father would never have tolerated this brutish behavior."

"Well, we don't exactly know that. I mean, he may have raised his son in the same harsh way, for all we know. But judging from his record of philanthropy, he was truly a generous man. He definitely gave more than his share, and I don't think it was all for public relations. I think it was genuine."

"I'll make Konstantin appreciate the responsibilities that come with this kind of money. It's obvious we'll have a lot of work to do to counteract his crazy ideas about women." He chuckled as he led her to the door. "He's really going to love the money we'll give to that women's shelter, don't you think?"

Marta looked at him with a serious face. "You think he beats his wife?"

"Oh, I don't think he has to; she looks frightened enough that he probably never has to raise a hand to her. He picked the right girl to be his wife; that's for sure."

"Well, her life would've probably become very difficult if she continued to deliver girl babies."

The meal, while sumptuous, was quiet and uncomfortable. A quartet of musicians played in the corner of the large dining room, negating the need for any conversation beyond the occasional request for salt and announcements of a new course. Konstantin glared at the children whenever one or the other ventured to speak, and eventually the three were removed from the room by a uniformed nanny. The service of a flaming dessert was greeted with appreciative comments, and before long, the table was cleared and the guests excused.

"See, no poison," Vasilli joked when he led Marta to the car waiting to return her to the hotel.

"Not yet," she replied. "Be careful. And have a good night."

Forty-two

Once in her room, Marta fell asleep quickly, the effect of the long day and all the alcohol she'd consumed. Her dreams were interrupted by the disruptive tones of a cell phone demanding attention. In the shadows, she slipped across the room, looked at the phone, and shut it off before tossing it into her bag. Fully awake now, she stood before the open window.

Something moved below, and she noticed two men in the shadows looking up at the building. Retreating into the room, she turned on a small lamp and looked at the clock. She'd only been asleep for an hour. She picked up the hotel phone and asked to be connected with the Vaso estate. Vasilli was still awake, and he filled her in on a short conversation he'd had with Konstantin after her departure.

"He's worried about money, the business, that kind of thing," he said.

"Probably wants you to think there is no money left."

"I don't care about that," he replied. "How are you doing? Recovered from your encounter with Yurgos?"

"Little devil," she muttered. "I never got along with children."

He chuckled. "Really? What a surprise."

She stifled a yawn. "By the way, there's someone watching the building from the street."

"Good," he said. "That way, you'll be safe. So, will you be here for breakfast?"

"Mmmhmmm." She yawned again. "Sorry."

He coughed. "Listen, there's something I want to say to you." He hesitated. "I know I'm old. I'm too old for a gorgeous creature like you. I've been having fun with you, talking about marriage and all that. But I want you to know that you are very important to me." He paused and cleared his throat. "I need you to listen to me. You have not been living your life. You've been selling yourself short—all those clichés are true. I hope that someday, you'll know what it's like, a real love between a man and a woman, not some

191

wham-bang with a pretty boy. I wish you would find it. You deserve to be happy. I want to help you, the way that you have helped me."

There was silence. "I don't know what to say," she finally said.

"Your daughter, where is she? Do you know?"

"I was forced to give her away, to be raised by my aunt. I know where she is, or at least I think I know. Since I got here, I realized how little I do know about things."

"Well, I think it's time you found out the truth, and I hope you'll let me help you," he said. "And since I am speaking frankly, what about the girl's father? Do you know where he is?"

There was no response. Vasilli continued, "Look, I know I'm butting into your business now. You obviously had feelings for this man, and I know he gravely disappointed you. But I think you should see him, too."

"No." Marta sighed. "He doesn't know anything about the child. I told you, he disappeared after the engagement was broken, and I never heard from him again. I have no idea where he is."

"You could find him."

"For what?" She shook her head. "It's hard enough trying to reconcile with leaving her behind. I don't think it would help anything to try and find him too."

"All right," Vasilli said. "But don't you wonder about him?"

"No, I can honestly say I don't."

"Hmmm." It was his turn to pause.

"What?"

"I, well, I don't want to make broad generalizations about this country, but …"

"Go ahead …"

"So far … how do I say this? The males we have encountered these past few weeks, either directly or by association, all have been angry and even violent, especially toward women. Your father, your uncle, and my nephew, is this the norm or the exception?"

She paused. "I don't know. I don't think I'm the right person to ask."

"Well, that's fair, I guess," Vasilli said. "All I can do is try to do what I can with Konstantin. But it may be impossible to change him." Marta could hear him rubbing his face.

"You're tired," she said.

"Yeah. It's been quite a day. I'll have them send a car over to fetch you in the morning. Have a good night."

Marta found Vasilli seated on the patio when she appeared at the house the next day. "Coffee or tea?" Vasilli asked, raising his cup in a salute.

"Look at this gorgeous fruit salad." Marta filled a small bowl and topped it off with a dollop of yogurt. "I'm famished."

They sat side by side at the glass table, sipping coffee. The smell of honeysuckle mingled with the aroma of freshly ground beans. Vasilli skimmed a Greek newspaper, trying in vain to make sense of it. The sound of footsteps approached, and then Konstantin emerged with his briefcase in one hand, cell phone in the other.

"Oh, they're both here," he said into the phone. "Yes, both of them. Fine, I'll call you later." He put the briefcase on a chair and folded the phone into his pocket. "So, a late start to the day. How are you, Uncle, miss?" He looked at Marta. "A little hungover, perhaps?" he asked. She smiled.

He studied her face and then shrugged.

"Anyway, Uncle, I have some papers to go over with you this morning. That is, if you have no other plans." He opened the case and produced an accordion file and then settled in the chair opposite Vasilli and removed several sheaves of paper. "Now. Here we are. This is what I spoke with you about last night." He pushed the papers toward Vasilli on the far left side of the table, away from Marta on his right.

Vasilli pulled his half-glasses from the pocket of his seersucker jacket. "Ah, yes. These are in order. But where is the other thing, the statement that your man Sami promised to bring today?"

"Which statement is that?" Konstantin crossed his arms.

"The one that acknowledges Vasilli as your uncle," Marta interjected. She smiled when he glared at her.

"Well, that's right here. See, it says here that as brother to the deceased, which is my father, Uncle repudiates any and all claims to the family business. See? Once this is signed, everyone will know that you are my uncle."

"I'm sorry. I want the other paper first." Vasilli handed back the documents. "Your man Sami said—"

"He's not my man. He's just a hired … hand." Konstantin placed the papers back on Vasilli's side of the table. "Please, Uncle, be reasonable."

"Why is this so important to you? You are in charge of the business. Who is making you do this, disown your own flesh and blood?"

"It's not me. It's my brother-in-law. He's very adamant about this." Konstantin threw his hands in the air. "I have to respect the husband of my sister, you know?"

"Really?" Vasilli gave him a hard look and then folded the papers into his jacket pocket. "I would not think that you … Well, you see, I guess I don't know you well enough to make judgments on your character. But please don't play games with me, blaming your brother-in-law for decisions that you have chosen to make." He shook his head. "So, I have some business to attend to in town, and we can discuss this later. When you have the other papers ready, we can talk about this further."

The pair rose from the table and left Konstantin glowering at their empty seats. As they walked away, Marta heard Konstantin shouting into his cell phone.

"What the hell did you promise the old man? Nothing? Nothing … well, get your ass over here right now. He's not going to sign. I knew it. I knew he wasn't going to give it up so easily. And that bitch lawyer of his, you'd better do something to get her under control."

Forty-three

They walked down the main thoroughfare, followed again by a security vehicle. They stopped to window-shop, holding hands and laughing at some
of the displays along the street. At a tailor shop, Vasilli urged her through
negotiations for a white suit, which, with the appropriate financial reward,
would be ready later that day.

Tea was being served as they wandered into Marta's hotel, so they sat
for a cup. Marta moved languidly, her body more relaxed than it had been
in recent memory.

"Marta," he repeated. "What's up with you today? You didn't hear a
word I said, did you?"

"No. Sorry." She shook her head. "Please say it again."

"I was asking what you think we should do now. I doubt that Konstantin is going to give me the agreement you requested."

"Probably true. Well, we can either wait it out, or draw up our own
papers and try to get him to sign. It won't be hard to get DNA tests done,
either. We can get a sample from you and then probably find something of
Konstantin to send for a match. It will take time; that's the only thing. We
can FedEx it to a lab in the States, but it will take a few days to get results,
even if we pay for a rush job."

"Let's do that—both of them. Can you?"

"Sure—you have no idea how many tricks I have in my little black briefcase. Come upstairs, I can get my laptop and we'll find out what we need
to do."

When she opened the door to her room, Marta immediately saw a small
figure sitting in the window seat, posture perfect and holding a cheap faux
leather briefcase.

"Sevgi," Marta breathed. "Is that you?"

"Yes." She coughed softly. "Can you open a window. It is so stuffy in
here. This room is a mess ..."

In two steps, Marta pulled back the curtains and flung open the French doors. She turned and pulled the spread over the bed and then sat down across from her sister. "There. Satisfied? If it offended you so much, why didn't you wait downstairs instead of intruding on my privacy?"

Vasilli put an arm around her shoulder. "English, please," he said softly. "Calm down. Take a deep breath." He stepped forward and offered his hand to the other woman. "I am Vasilli Vassilios. Pleased to meet you."

She looked at his outstretched hand and then back to Marta. Continuing to speak in Turkish, she spoke in a harsh voice. "So, you are a slut then, just like I imagined, just like Father said. All these years, I thought, no, it can't be true. My sister is too smart to be like that. She would never sell herself. I was wrong." Her face was a paler version of her older sister's, her hair a darker shade streaked with white.

"Tell me what else our father shared with you." Marta's voice was back to the steely tone of a litigator.

"He told us that you ran away," Sevgi said, picking at her nails. "Then, about a year later, Mother went to look for you. She never came back. Father told us you were both killed in a car accident." Sevgi raised her eyes to look at Marta. "I believed it, for a long time. You have no idea how we grieved for you. Poor Marta, led astray by some bad man, and Mother had to go and rescue you. But then, tragically, you both died on your way home. What a load of horseshit. All of us, we believed him." She snorted.

"And then?" Marta pushed. Sevgi glared at her. "And then the money arrived, right? The report from the bank. All you had to do was make sure that you got the mail first, which was easy, wasn't it?"

"Easy? You think it was easy what I had to do? I had to step up and run that household." Sevgi returned to studying her jagged nails. "I had to quit school. Does that sound easy to you? I stayed home. I cleaned. I cooked. I raised that baby. You think he was angry before? Just imagine—his wife was dead, his oldest daughter run off somewhere. I had to do this for years, until Lale was old enough to go to school." She looked into Marta's eyes.

"You bet I took the money. I deserved it." She looked away again, hands folded tightly against her body. "A few years ago, I met your professor, Samibey. I was in his class. I think it was some boring contracts thing, and when he read my name, I saw the recognition in his face. He's been good to me, really. I bought an apartment, near the Çiçek Pasaji, and when he retired from teaching, he offered me a job in his firm. We do mostly corporate stuff, nothing glamorous like your career."

"And do you sleep with him? Is that part of your job too?"

"No, I'm not like you." Sevgi straightened her skirt, making sure it covered her knees.

"So, why are you here? If you know everything and you hate me so much?" Marta studied her sister's face. Years of anger had permanently creased her brow and dug frown lines between her eyes. Her hunched shoulders and plain dress spoke volumes about her career as well as her personal choices.

"Sami-bey told me that you wanted to see me, so here I am. Say what you have to say."

Marta smiled. "If you must know, Father forced me to leave the house because I was pregnant. After I had the baby, Mother brought me to the airport, and she gave me this." Marta held the locket between her fingers. Sevgi gasped.

"Give it to me," she cried.

"No. Mother wanted me to have it. Sorry. It's the only thing I have left, and I'm keeping it." Marta fingered the locket, not meeting her sister's eyes. "I'm sorry for what happened to you. But let me tell you one thing, Mother was not killed in a car accident. He did it. He beat her so badly that she died."

"I don't know anything about this. Father said ..." She sobbed. "Father said that there was a fire after the car crash and the bodies were incinerated. He used that word, *incinerated*. So there was no grave, no burial. He told us."

Marta looked on coldly as her sister wept. She turned to translate for Vasilli, but he shook his head sadly. "I understand enough," he said. "You should comfort her."

Marta held up her hands and then dropped them on the bed.

"Yes, Sister." Sevgi spoke clearly in English, mockingly. "Why don't you comfort me? Hmm?"

"Why are you so angry at me?" Marta continued in English. "I didn't do this to you. In fact, if I hadn't sent the money every month, you would still be living in his house, washing his floors and cooking his dinner."

"And what else?" Sevgi laughed, clutching her throat. "Yes, he made me do that, too. He ruined me, so I could never marry, so I could never leave. You're right." There was a long pause as she looked around the room, not wanting to meet Marta's eyes. "We had a good life, a nice family. Mother was ... wonderful. Everything was fine until you ... until you went and got yourself in trouble, just like he said you would. Why couldn't you have been better than that? Why'd you have to go and prove him right?"

Sevgi stood up and slapped Marta sharply across the cheek. She picked up her bag and walked to the door. "If there's anything else you want from me, call Sami-bey. He'll give me the message. I don't want to see your face again." The mirror and sconces tinkled as the walls reacted to the crash of the closing door. The carpet muted her stamping progress down the stairs. Vasilli heard her yelling at the porter, and then a shudder ran through the building as the door was slammed.

"Phew. That's one angry woman," he said finally.

"I suppose she has good reason," Marta said ruefully, rubbing her cheek. She moved to the window seat and peered out the window. When she spoke again, Vasilli turned to look at her in surprise. Her voice had returned to its usual matter-of-fact tone. "What she said—about Father—do you think …? Did she mean …? Was he …? No, that can't be." She rubbed her hands up and down her arms. Taking a deep breath, she turned to Vasilli. "God, what a mess," she said lightly. "Thank God she got out of there. I'm glad she took the money. I'm glad *he* didn't get hold of it."

Vasilli looked at her for a moment. "Are you upset? Should I get you some aspirin?" he asked.

"No, I'm fine." She laughed, holding out her hands as if to convince him. He was silent. "What's the matter?" she asked him.

"You seem so cold." He shook his head. "Aren't you upset by this?"

She stood up and walked past him onto the porch. "What? You think I should be crying? Maybe I should—she took thousands of dollars from me. Am I sorry about what happened to her? Of course I am. I'm not a monster. But that doesn't change what happened to me. And the fact is that bad things happen to people. You can't spend your life crying about the past."

"No. But you can't bury your feelings so deeply that you end up not feeling anything at all. Marta, you have built such big walls around yourself, how do you expect anyone to get over them?" He ran a hand gently down her arm, looking sadly into her face. "You have come so far since we've been here. I've watched you come out of that hard shell you were wearing. Don't go back into it now. Stay here, with me, and let yourself feel bad. Feel angry, feel sad, whatever it is, just don't squash it down again, please."

She nodded. "I'm a survivor. Of course there were times I wanted to go back, but I didn't."

"Until now."

"Yeah, until now." She turned away. "I still don't know if I can do this. And I'm not sure I want to."

Forty-four

Marta's fingers flew over the keyboard. She looked up when Vasilli moved toward the door. "While you're out, see if you can find a printer, eh? Otherwise, we're going to have to look for one in town."

"Okay. Whatever you need." Vasilli made an elaborate bow in her direction that provoked a grin. She waved a hand in his direction.

"Wait. Ask if we can rent a car. Let's take a little drive this afternoon, get out of this town. What do you think?"

"Do you have any particular destination in mind?" Vasilli asked.

"My aunt lived nearby. They used to be in a village near Konya, not far from here. Or maybe we should wait, until we get these papers signed."

He came back into the room. "Your aunt?"

"I told you. My mother gave the baby to my aunt. She couldn't have any children, so she was happy to take mine. I stayed in her house for about four or five months, until the baby was born, and then my mother came and took me to the airport." She stared off into space.

Vasilli sat on the edge of the bed. "Tell me more."

"My aunt, she was a good woman. She was really my mother's cousin, but my mother thought of her like a sister, and so we called her Auntie. Her husband, ugh." She shuddered. "He was one of those religious fanatics. He kept me locked in a small room in the back of the house, so no one would see me. Believe me, before I went there, I had no idea she was married to such a nutcase. But then it was too late. I couldn't get away, and I had to leave the baby there. I can only hope that my aunt was able to protect her from him. He pretended that the baby was his, but I saw how disappointed he was that she was not a boy." She looked back down at the computer. "There's that male-female thing again. God. I know how that was. I felt it every day I was growing up, my father's disappointment that I was not a boy. Makes you crazy, you know?"

"Yes, I can imagine." He tapped on the top of the screen. "So, we'll find her. How old is she now?"

"Fifteen. She is fifteen, and God willing, she is all right."

"Why wouldn't she be?" he asked.

"Remember when we went to the bank in Ankara? And there was a problem with the accounts? Well, I set up one for my mother, which we now know Sevgi used to finance her education and buy her apartment. Okay. There was another one that I established for my aunt at the same time. And all the money is still there, or most of it. So what the hell happened? Why hasn't she used the money I sent to take care of the girl?"

"I see what you mean." He paused. "Well, maybe your uncle wouldn't allow her to take the money. It could be a pride thing. You know, I've observed that pride is a very important trait in Turkish men."

"Yeah, right after stubbornness." She looked at her watch. "Go—do your scavenger hunt. It may be too late to take a ride today, but let's see what you come up with. I'll finish this document, and we can go back to the house to have another chat with Konstantin."

"He's not there."

"How do you know?"

"I saw a helicopter fly by a little while ago. I am betting that it must be his."

"Okay. Good, that gives us a better chance of finding a printer and getting this stuff ready for our next meeting."

All tasks accomplished an hour later, Marta and Vasilli set out to find a FedEx office. "Or anything like it in this one-horse town," she said.

Probably because of the presence of the Vaso family in town, everything from Western Union to UPS was available. Marta had collected samples from Konstantin's razor, hairbrush, and toothbrush. She also collected saliva on a swab from Vasilli's cheek. The package was posted overnight to Marta's friends at a private laboratory on Long Island.

"Joe said it will take a few days, but he'll put a rush on it," she said, sealing the envelope and handing over a credit card.

"Are you sure this will work?" Vasilli asked.

"Well, it won't stand up in a court of law, but I think it will make a difference to the family," she said. "Can I get something printed here?" she asked the clerk, holding up a thumb drive, which the clerk looked at blankly. "Okay, how about this?" She produced a floppy disk, which was more readily accepted. "Three copies, please."

They walked out of the store, back to the car idling by the curb.

"You couldn't convince them to give you a car without a driver?" she said.

"No, I don't have a proper license or something. I don't know." He held the door open for her, but she walked down the sidewalk.

Back at her hotel, Marta spoke with the manager and placed some cash on his desk. A few minutes later, she slid behind the wheel of the owner's car and Vasilli buckled himself into the passenger seat. "Let's go for a little ride."

Life was different in the villages of Turkey. Things moved slower; people were quieter. The rhythm of the earth was more important than the nightly television schedule, although more satellite dishes were seen on rooftops than would be imagined. Many houses had a single tractor for a vehicle, several goats, and a yard full of chickens—and a cell phone for every adult. This far west, most of the houses had electricity and running water, although few of the children and almost none of the adults had ever seen the inside of a school. Their gaily colored clothing belied the hard lives of the women who did all the manual labor of planting, weeding, and harvesting crops, as well as the cooking, cleaning, and sewing for the family.

"Look, that's what I'm talking about." Marta pointed out the window as she slowed the vehicle to a dusty crawl. "See those women, out in the fields? And look where the men are—hanging off the tractor, watching the women work and waiting to drive them home. This used to drive me crazy." The car, a brilliant blue Opel that had faux-fur covered seats and a beaded bird on a swing hanging from the rearview mirror, captured the attention of most villagers they passed.

Vasilli nodded, peering out the window. A row of females with covered heads and voluminous pantaloons moved slowly through a field, working bent double at the waist. They seemed to be pulling weeds by hand.

"What's that, in the shade there?"

"Babies, most likely. They swaddle 'em up and park 'em in the shade all day long," Marta replied. She tapped his arm. "I bet you didn't think you were going to get a sociology lecture during our little outing, did you?"

"No, but it's fine … I am always interested to hear your take on things. You know that." He leaned back in the seat of the rental car. "It's refreshing to see how your mind works."

"Refreshing. I don't think I've ever been called that before." She sped up and passed an overtaxed pickup truck loaded with dirt. "You know, I am ashamed to say that I never asked Sevgi about my sisters."

"I think you had other things—"

"No, there's really no excuse for it. She said Father remarried. I suppose he has a new family now. I wonder where the girls are. I hope that Sevgi used the money for all of them. She probably did. That's okay then, if she took care of the girls."

"You hope."

"No, I'm sure of it. Unfortunately, she probably turned them all against me, too." She sighed. "But that's okay, as long as they got away."

"As did you."

She smiled wryly. "Sort of. What I know is that you never get away. All those years, all that distance, and look how much effort it took for me to keep everything at bay." They rode in companionable silence for a while, one or the other occasionally pointing out the window at some unusual sight: a red-winged blackbird, a line of mockingbirds balancing on a wire. A plastic playhouse, brilliant in color, stood next to a gray building whose only redeeming feature was a brightly painted wooden door.

"Probably a gift from someone working in Europe," Marta said. "It's common for the fathers to work abroad, mostly in Germany, and send home money or gifts like that."

"It's hard to imagine the poverty," Vasilli murmured. "How can people live this way?"

"They have managed for centuries. It's a hard life, for sure, but it is very common in this part of the world." She pointed to a field of waving wheat. "Turkey has always fed itself. I don't know if that's true any longer, but there were never any food imports when I was growing up, only exports to other Middle Eastern countries."

After some minutes of silence, Vasilli leaned forward in his seat. "What do you think is over there? See that reflection?"

In the distance, she saw a shimmering mirage. Water, a large body of it, emerged from the vision. It was surrounded by forest, interrupted on one side by a large swath of green. And a helicopter was parked next to a wind sock. The road curved around.

"A golf course. Out here." Marta laughed. "See, your nephew knows how to conduct business 'American style.'"

Vasilli frowned. "Should we stop?"

They watched the lone figure swing and then march in the direction of the flag. "He's an interesting character; I'll say that for him." Marta looked at Vasilli. "Do you want to stop? We can, if you want."

He shrugged. "Nah," he said and then turned to study the road ahead. He squinted at the brightness. "Should we turn back? If it gets too late, we may have to spend the night there."

"We can call and let them know we're not coming back," Marta said. "Although the car following us will probably keep him informed of our whereabouts." She chuckled. "Did you think he was going to let us out of his sight?"

"Aren't you getting a little paranoid?" he asked.

"Maybe. But let's see if that little package we sent actually makes it to New York." She chuckled again.

"What is so funny?"

"I would love to see their reaction when they open it up and discover that I sent a tube of toothpaste, a stack of tissues, and a handful of pistachio nuts in a plastic bag."

He looked at her. "You sent a decoy? When did you do that? How did I—"

"The real package is in my bag. We'll mail it in Konya. Less chance Konstantin's people can tamper with it there."

"You sly devil."

"Yeah. I am paranoid. But unfortunately, in these situations, nine times out of ten, I'm right. So you learn to take precautions."

The road was getting busier, more cars and houses crowding the street. "We're getting closer to the city." She looked at her watch. "You know, I think we may just look for a hotel and take our time here. Is that all right with you, or do you want to go back tonight?"

Vasilli shrugged. "Sounds great," he replied. "I'm just along for the ride. Konstantin can wait until I return."

Forty-five

After a satisfying evening spent touring the old city and enjoying its cuisine, Marta and Vasilli rested well in a small but well-appointed hotel. In the morning, after a full breakfast, Marta calmed her nerves by pestering the taxi driver taking them to see her aunt.

"The address I have is old," Marta told the driver. "But maybe if they have moved, the neighbors will know where they are." She perched nervously on the front edge of the seat, Vasilli's large hand patting her back.

"I can't believe our car had two flat tires this morning," she said. "What are the chances of that?"

"And the dead battery was a bit of an overkill, I think," Vasilli replied. "I guess they thought that would keep us under control."

She shook her head, looking around.

"Everything is changed so much," she murmured. "I don't recognize anything." The car skidded along heavily rutted roads, leaving a swirl of dust. Chickens, children, and cats barely cleared the roadway in their path. Motorbike drivers cursed, swerving to avoid the car. Some wagons, heavily decorated and hitched to downcast horses, lined the main drag into town. "Centrum," the sign pointed to the left.

"Go right," Marta instructed. "I hope this is the way."

"You were here fifteen years ago. I'm sure a lot has changed."

"Yeah." She grimaced.

"Marta." Vasilli spoke gently. "The man has an address. Let's see if they are still living there."

The car skidded to an abrupt stop. The driver, whose hand had never stopped hovering over the horn, laid his entire body across the wheel to generate a feeble *squack*. Eventually, he stuck his head out the window and shouted and then left the car entirely, taking the keys and running down the street. Marta looked at Vasilli and then opened the door and stood on the running board to see over the tops of the other cars.

"Looks like a hog-jam," she said, peering back into the car. "There's an overturned truck and about a hundred pigs running all over the place."

"Funny."

"Let's walk."

"What about the driver—the fare?" Vasilli asked.

"Hell, he abandoned us," she said. "I'll leave him a couple of bucks." She tucked some bills into the furry covering of the steering wheel and then took her bag and started down the street. Hat pulled on, Vasilli followed, stopping only when the pigs threatened to soil his beige trousers. He trod delicately around piles of manure and some chickens entering the fray and attempted to keep up with Marta's quick pace. Houses lined the road, some hidden by shrubbery or fencing, but most exposed, windows and doors open to the elements. Some of the livestock were exploring the neighborhood, housewives shooing them out with short-handled brooms or buckets of water.

"Why pigs?" Vasilli asked when he reached Marta's side, past the cacophony of cars, animals, and shouting men. "I didn't think Turks ate pork."

"They don't. But they raise pigs and sell them to the Greeks."

"Oh." Vasilli took out a handkerchief and wiped his forehead. "Anything look familiar?" he asked.

"The problem is no one has any numbers on their houses."

"True. But the mailboxes?" He stopped in front of an ancient galvanized steel post box, jerry-rigged onto a thick slab of wood. "No numbers. There's a name."

They walked past a few more houses. "I think I'm going to have to ask someone."

He grunted a reply and lifted his chin in the direction of a figure removing clothing from a rope line that sagged loosely between two old trees.

"Pardon." Marta walked toward the woman, waving her hands. "Can you tell me where I can find Mr. and Mrs. Uzun? They used to live around here?"

The woman pulled a sheet close to her chest, inspecting Marta as she continued to fold the crisp white fabric.

"Who are you?" she asked.

"I'm their niece." She held out her hand but dropped it when the woman did not reciprocate. "My name is Marta Demir."

"You haven't been here before." It was a statement, an accusation, not a question.

"Yes, once, long ago, with my mother. Her sister lived here. Can you tell me if they are still living here?"

The woman looked over Marta's shoulder, toward Vasilli. "That your father?" she asked.

"No, he's a friend." Marta clasped her hands together. "Please, ma'am, can you help me?"

"Well, the man, Uzun, he left a few years back. The woman, your aunt, she's still here. Down the road, last house on the left. You might not see it. It's way back from the street."

"And their daughter? Is she … there?" The question hung in the air like the yellow sheets flapping between them.

"Not here. I haven't seen that girl since, well, I can't exactly say. She's been gone a long time."

"Gone, like dead?"

"I don't know. You best be asking your aunt to tell you these things." She turned away, throwing garments into a wicker basket.

Marta's knees were weak as they resumed walking down the street. "It's not good," she said. "My uncle is gone, she said, and so is the girl."

"Don't let your imagination get the best of you."

"There." She pointed to a stand of cedars, row after row of thin trees that swayed lazily in the breeze.

"I don't see a house."

"Back there. I remember it now. These trees, they planted them when she was born. It's a tradition in some places, to plant a field of trees when a new child is born. By the time they're ready to marry, the trees will be tall enough to sell. That's how a lot of villagers get the money for a dowry, or to help their sons build a home. The house is back there, believe me." She walked through the field, stumbling once on a rock and then stopping suddenly when the little gray shack came into view.

"How could I have left my child here, in this place?" She clutched her blouse. "I'll never forgive myself if something happened, if that man did anything to her. I swear to God—"

She was interrupted by the sound of a single rifle shot whizzing through the trees. A crack and some branches fell where the bullet hit its mark. Vasilli ducked behind a tree, pulling Marta toward him.

"*Dikkat! Dikkat!*" a low voice cried out the warning. "Danger, danger. Get away from here before I shoot you."

"Aunt, it is me, Marta." She stepped out of the shadows into a patch of sunshine. "Aunt, you remember Marta?"

Another shot rang out, this time whistling high overhead.

"There's a man there. I can see him."

"Aunt, this is my friend. He won't hurt you. Can I come closer and talk to you?"

"You, but not him."

Marta looked back at Vasilli. "Stay close."

"If you don't come out in fifteen minutes, or I hear anything strange, I'm coming in," he said.

She walked toward the house, fading in and out of sight as the light played along the rows of trees. Through the shadows, she could see her aunt, a small woman, wrapped in a white dress that was three times as large as her slight figure. Gray hair stood wild on her head. Her eyes were large and dark and jumping around. Marta slowed down, allowing the older woman to get a good look at her niece.

"Aunt, do you remember me?" she asked softly. She held her arms out and watched the frightened woman lower the gun and take a tentative step off the weathered stoop.

"You look like her, but how can I be sure?" She spoke softly, slurring some words around the missing teeth in her mouth. Her hands loosened around the gun. "Show me something."

Marta fumbled for her wallet and then stopped. She reached into her shirt and pulled the locket carefully over her head.

"This was my mother's. Do you remember it?" She held out the gold chain. "You remember my mother? She was just like your little sister."

The woman narrowed her eyes and then gestured with her chin.

"Put it on the stump there and back away. You could have stolen it. How can I be sure?" she repeated.

"I'm not putting it down," Marta said. She looped the chain back over her head. "My mother gave that to me the day she put me on an airplane to America. I haven't taken it off since that day, and I won't give it to you now. It's the only thing I have left of her." She took a step toward the house. "I left my baby here with you. What happened to her? Where is she? What happened here?"

Throwing the gun down, the older woman began wailing and slumped to the ground. Burying her face in the folds of her apron, she rocked back and forth. Marta could not make out any words, just the piercing cries through the muffling fabric.

"*Tezze-gim*, please tell me what happened." The woman would not be consoled, rocking into a hysteria that Marta could not comprehend. Eventually, she left the side of the figure huddled on the ground and made her way slowly to the house. Signaling Vasilli to join her, she pushed aside the heavily scarred wooden door.

"What did she say?" Vasilli asked.

"Nothing yet," Marta replied. "She's not all there, I think. In the meantime, let's see if there is anything here." She picked her way into the dim room, the only light coming from two unscreened windows. A cat hissed from the corner and then jumped on a sill and watched their progress around the single room. A Formica table, wobbling on a broken leg resting on a stack of newspapers, dominated the space. In a corner, a roughly built fireplace showed signs of recent use. Burlap bags spilled out potatoes, yams, onions, and some other roots that Marta could not recognize.

"Is this how it was back then, when you were here?" Vasilli asked. He lifted the corner of a threadbare quilt that was neatly aligned on a small cot in the other corner. A shelf above the bed held some washed-out cloth that Marta figured must be her aunt's entire wardrobe. A single book, the Koran, was also on the shelf. There were no photographs, no ornamentation. A single light bulb hung from a wire in the middle of the room. Two chairs, not matching, were pushed to the wall next to the table, where another shelf held an assortment of cups, plates, and glasses.

Marta stood at the window and surveyed the room.

"No. Definitely not. I don't remember all the details, but there were two bedrooms, a separate kitchen, and a living room with all the usual stuff—couches, chairs, television. Not like this. Most of the time, I was locked in my room, but I did see the rest of the house a couple of times." She turned around, taking in the entire room. "I can't imagine what happened here."

"Life," her aunt croaked from the door. "Life happened here, girlie. You have no idea how hard life can be." She walked slowly into the room, glaring at Vasilli, who slipped back out the door before she could raise the gun again. Marta saw him move out of sight by the open window.

"Tell me, Aunt."

"Get the fire started, would you? There's some kindling back there, yes. There are still hot coals under there, just stir it up. And the tea is in the tin. Good. You were a good girl, I think. My sister, what happened to my sister?"

Marta moved around the small area, striking a match to the poor sticks of wood she had gathered. Blowing hard, she saw the coals glow and the sticks finally catch. "Water, *Tezze*? Where is your water?"

"There's a pitcher on the stoop. I brought it from town this morning. There's a place there at the mosque—I guess it's for the men to wash their feet, but I think Allah would not begrudge me some water. And I wash there, too. Every day. When I can't get to the brook, I go there and have a little scrub." Marta moved around the room, preparing the tea and wiping out the cups. "I see you turning up your nose. That's just like your mother, too, isn't it? She came here, 'to check on the child,' she said. Never came back, she never did. I guess we weren't good enough for her. I don't know. She kept telling me, 'This is how you hold the baby. This is how you feed the baby,' like I didn't know what to do, like I needed her to come here and show me. Finally, he made her leave. She gave me some papers, said there was money to help with the child, and that she'd be back. But she never came back."

Marta pulled the other chair in front of her aunt and sat down.

"Where is she?" the old woman asked.

"I'm sorry, *Tezze*, I just found out she is dead. She died a very long time ago, probably right after she visited you here."

"How?"

"It looks like my father killed her. He beat her, you know? And the last time, it was too much."

Her aunt laughed. "You look shocked. Tell me, what woman is not beaten by her husband? Let me meet that woman. It's part of life, child. That's how it is." She shook her head and wrapped her arms around her thin chest. "That's life."

"Is that what happened to you, Aunt?"

"That—and more! What do you think? Do you think I like to live like this, digging potatoes from the ground with my bare hands, stealing water and wood? I collect newspapers from the street, cans, and bottles. That's my income. Remember when you came here? The furniture, the crystal that I had? The silver tea service? All gone, just like the house. He left—I have no regrets about that—I sent the girl away, and then he left. He took what he wanted; he took everything. Said I brought nothing to the marriage and so that was what he was leaving me with. 'Stupid cow—can't even have a child,' he said. Hah. How does he know it was me? Hmmm? He married again—no children there, either. But sure, he took it all and left me here in this shack. I have the trees still. Someday, the girl might need them."

"The other rooms?"

"I tore them down, just left this one. All I need. I burned the wood from the others, sold the cinder blocks, the roof tiles. Sold everything I could. Except myself. I haven't gotten that bad yet." She smiled, revealing blackened stubs of teeth. "Think any man would pay for this?" She slapped her breasts and thrust open her legs. Marta pulled back, reacting to the woman's heavy odor. "Yeah, it keeps the men away. Don't want any trouble like that here."

"Aunt, when my mother was here, you said she gave you some papers. What did you do with them?"

"Buried 'em. In the yard. I've got no use for papers, but I didn't want him to get them, so I buried 'em." She looked around and then leaned close. "She gave me some money that day, and I kept it hidden too. When I needed it, I got it," she whispered.

"What did you do with it?" Marta whispered back.

"I, well, I used it to send the girl away. See, he was bad, always yelling and hitting, but then one day, I came back from shopping and I saw it. I saw his look. He was looking at her like no father should look at a daughter, and I knew I had to get her out of here, or she was going to, well, he was going to—you know, I had to protect myself ... and her, oh yes, I had to protect her. So I took the money and I sent her away. And after that, he, well, it wasn't long after that he left, too."

"Did he hurt her?"

"No, no. Not really. Just the usual stuff, you know—discipline. But he didn't ... No, I don't think so. I got her away from him in time, I think."

Marta stood and poured the boiling water into the teapot and then waited while the brew steeped. She concentrated on breathing, catching Vasilli's eye as he leaned into view. "Are you okay?" he mouthed. She nodded.

"Aunt, can my friend come in and sit with us?" Marta asked.

"No. No men in this house. No."

"He won't hurt you, but all right. I'll bring him a cup of tea outside, and he can drink it there." She poured three cups, put two on the table, and carried the third to where Vasilli was perched on a tree stump.

"Have you been able to follow anything?" she asked. "I'm sorry I can't translate for you. She's not very stable, and I want to get as much out of her as I can."

"Sure, sure. What do you know so far?" He nodded and sipped the bitter tea while she relayed the information.

"Sorry there's no sugar. Can you stand it?" Marta asked. They both looked up as the wail of a song wafted through the open window. Marta peered inside. Her aunt was sitting, eyes closed, hands clasped around the teacup, singing and tapping a rhythm with her bare toe.

"She's got a good voice," Vasilli offered.

Marta shrugged and then went back into the house. She waited for the song to end and touched her aunt on the hand. "Can you tell me where you sent the girl, *Tezze*?"

"You know, I think I would like to have some meat. Yes. That's what I want. You will bring me some meat for dinner, and then we can talk about the girl and I'll tell you what you want to know. But first, I want some meat."

"Would you like to go to a restaurant? We can take you ..." Both Marta and her aunt looked at the older woman's clothes. "Well, I could get you some new clothes."

"Listen, girlie, you can't come in here and just buy things and think everything will be okay. This is my life, and you giving me some money or clothes is not going to change it. I just want a decent meal. And then I want you to leave me alone. Can you do that?"

"Yes, Aunt, but—" Marta was cut off.

"No, no 'but' this or that. You get it? I don't want anything from you, except for you to leave me be."

"Let me just say this one thing, Aunt. When my mother gave you those papers and that money, it was from me. I sent you money from New York, every month. It's been sitting in the bank. All you have to do is go there and get it. You don't have to live like this."

"Get out. Go and get me some meat. Don't talk about money or papers, or that girl. If it wasn't for that girl, my husband would still be here. So don't talk to me about papers."

Forty-six

Vasilli offered to go and purchase some food, but Marta needed to walk off her frustration so they both headed down the street, Marta shaking her head and relating her aunt's comments.

"I'm not sure where she sent the girl. I don't even know if she is telling the truth. But she sent the girl away to save her marriage."

"It wasn't her child, so maybe that made it easier."

"She raised the girl from birth. What kind of woman doesn't develop a bond under those circumstances?"

"Marta, she did what she thought was the best thing for the girl. She sent the child away to protect her from his abuse. You have to give her credit for that." Vasilli stopped in front of a small restaurant. "Shall we try this?" They both looked up and down the street. "It looks like our only choice. I just hope they have meat."

Marta tried to engage the woman behind the counter in conversation, unsuccessfully, and then accosted the cook and a young girl who was studiously chopping vegetables. The girl colored a bit when Marta spoke to her but did not raise her face. Marta saw the two adults exchange glances, and she turned back to Vasilli. Speaking loudly in Turkish, she said, "Father, I cannot find anyone who will tell us what happened to my aunt. These good people do not know, and this is our last hope. We have stopped everywhere. After we take our meal, I think we should just return home. We're never going to find anything here." She broke into sobs and threw herself into his arms, whispering, "Play along with me."

He patted her head and took out a large white handkerchief, which he rubbed over his eyes before handing to her.

"Oh, Father, I am so sorry about this. I had hoped we would find your sister before it was too late, but there is no more hope."

Marta continued in this vein, noting the hushed conversation taking place on the other side of the meat counter. The thwack of the girl's knife continued unabated, until a door slammed and there was silence. Marta raised herself up and peered into the back room. No one was there. The smell of meat cooking permeated the room, and she looked at Vasilli, who shrugged and helped her stand. "What?" he started, but stopped when her forefinger brushed his lip.

"Hello, is anyone there?" she said softly.

"Shush." The girl waved Marta over. "They'll be back in a minute. I know your aunt. I remember her daughter. We were in school together for a while. Here ..." She pushed a paper into Marta's hand. "Meet me there in thirty minutes, and I'll tell you what I know. Now get away, quick. They're coming."

Two steaming platters, covered with wax paper, were fashioned into takeout by the woman, incredulous that the pair was not going to eat at the table provided but rather "in a picnic" down the street. She practically pushed them out, flapping her hands at Marta's promise to return the plates later that afternoon.

"Not a lot of takeout in this town, I guess," Vasilli joked. "Do you think she knew?"

"Yep, but here's another example of the woman keeping things from the man. I guess it was easier for her to get rid of us than to have him involved in the transaction."

Marta's aunt was sitting on her front stoop, her gun laid across her lap, picking through a bowl of rice. Once in a while, she flipped a dark kernel to the side, where a group of doves jumped and fought. Her stringy gray hair had been smoothed back into a bun, and she seemed more composed than when they left.

"Do you have meat?" she asked Marta and then narrowed her eyes, lifted the gun, and shook it at Vasilli. "Go away, mister."

"Here you are, *Tezze*," Marta said. "Let me serve you inside. The man will stay out here. You can lower the gun." Marta walked into the house, placed one of the plates on the table, and then returned to where Vasilli was rooted at the edge of the trees. "Sorry," she said. "I'll be back as soon as I can." Taking the second plate inside, she transferred the contents into a heavy skillet and covered it with the wax paper. Her aunt sat before the meal, left hand still grasping the gun, forking food into her mouth with the right.

"Take it slow, Aunt," Marta said. "You'll make yourself sick if you eat too fast. Here, take some bread." She sat opposite the hungry woman and then noticed a dirty gallon of olive oil on the floor near the fire. Sod clung to the rusted sides of the tin, its cover slightly askew.

"Aunt, what's in the tin?"

"Your papers. I dug them up. No more money in there. Just old papers. Some photos. That's all. I don't know what you want from me."

"Is there anything in there that says where you sent the girl?"

She shook her head vigorously. "Nope. Couldn't risk him finding it, finding her."

"Can you just tell me now?" Marta asked.

"No. You'll tell him."

"Aunt, do you know who I am?"

She looked at Marta and then squinted. "One of Neslihan's girls, right? Never could tell them apart. Of course, we only saw you once or twice. Family all over the place, never keeping in touch with each other, only showing up when there was an emergency. What about my emergency?" she cried out. Gravy dribbled down her chin. "When I called, did anyone come to help? No. Just hung up on me, like I was some stranger. Can't count on anyone, no family, nothing." She wiped the plate clean with a heel of bread and looked around for the other plate. "More."

"Save it for later, Aunt, so you don't make yourself sick." Marta picked up the plate, dribbled some water over it, and wiped it clean with a rag. The two dishes in her hand, she turned back to her aunt. "Will you tell me where you sent her?"

"No. Now get out of my way. I want the rest of my meat." She pushed Marta aside and stooped over the pan. "Get out."

Marta backed away, mindful of the gun still gripped by the older woman.

"I'll be back later," she said. "Maybe you'll feel like talking after you've eaten."

They retraced their steps to the restaurant and left the plates on the table in front. The girl was not there, so they hurried down the street looking for the place she'd told them to come. A coffee shop, in a shaded alleyway, matched the address on the paper. The girl emerged from the shadows when she saw them. "*Gel*, come here. I haven't much time."

"My name is Zeynep. I am fifteen years old. I went to school with Nazlan Uzun. This is who you are looking for, yes?"

"Yes. What can you tell me?" Marta's hand unconsciously played with the locket at her neck. "Do you know where she went?"

"About five years ago, she disappeared. And then her father, he left too. So the mother, she just stayed there by herself and everyone says that she went crazy. But she's not crazy, I know. She comes out at night and picks up the cans. She grows some vegetables. She gets water from the mosque. She's not crazy. Okay, she did tear down most of the house and burn it, but it was like a good plan, you know? Not like she set the place on fire or anything.

She pulled it down wall by wall and burned the wood and furniture piece by piece."

"The girl—Nazlan—do you know where she went?"

"I don't know. She was saying something just before she left, like she knew that they were going to send her away soon. She gave away her things to some of the girls. She gave her books, a special seashell, a butterfly she had captured and mounted with pins, stuff like that."

"What did she give you?" Marta leaned forward.

"It's a book. I have it. I ran home and found it. I haven't looked at it for a long time." She pulled a battered blue paperback from her backpack. "Here. It's a funny book. I don't know why she had it. But she was always looking through it, reading stuff to us, making notes in the margins. I don't know why." She pushed the book across the table to Marta, who hesitated. Zeynep pushed it another inch. "You can have it, lady. I mean it."

Vasilli picked up the book and held it in his lap. Marta looked at him and then at the book and then turned back to the girl. "Thank you for the book. So, you have no idea where she went? Nothing at all?" Zeynep shook her head. "Think, please. Was there anything different, anything she said, anyone hanging around?"

"It was a long time ago, you know. I was just a kid. What did we know? One day, she was there, and then she was gone. We thought maybe her father, well, sometimes if she had a beating, then she'd stay out of school for a few days. So we thought maybe that was it. But she never came back."

"He beat her?"

The girl shrugged. "Most of the fathers do, some more than others. Usually they only hit the boys, but sometimes, well, you know. I was lucky. My parents are different. They never hit me. But I am good. I don't do anything to deserve a beating."

"Did Nazlan? Was she a bad girl?"

Zeynep blushed. "Oh no, I didn't mean that. He was a mean man; that's all. He beat his wife. He beat his dog. Once I heard that he beat a donkey to death when it wouldn't do what he wanted. He was a mean man. I'm glad he left. He sort of gave me the creeps. Like he was always watching, you know?"

Marta nodded.

"He left town the summer after Nazlan left. I remember because my mother and some of the other women went to the house to see her. They offered to help her, you know, find a job or contact her family or something. But she turned them away. She threw them out of the house, and after that, whenever anyone went near, she would shoot at them. So no one goes there. She comes out only after dark. I think she sells her cans and papers to the blind man who takes care of the mosque. He gives her eggs sometimes and maybe chicken, I don't know. And that's how she survives. I feel sorry for her, but Mother says that we all make our own choices." She leaned forward. "I think he beat her so much that her brain is messed up in her head. Anyway ..." She stood up. "That's all I can tell you. I hope it helps."

Zeynep turned to go. Marta stared into space. Vasilli kneaded her arm. "Thank you, *yavrum*," he called.

The girl turned back, a look of confusion on her face. "You know, there is something ... I don't remember the details, but a few months before she left, there was a visit from some religious community. They gave a musical performance, some mystical singing, that kind of thing. Then afterwards, they gave a talk about their community. And they passed out brochures. I'm sure that Nazlan took one. She seemed interested, even though the rest of us thought it was horrid. Imagine, living in a monastery like that when you're just ten years old. But I remember now that Nazlan had a funny look on her face. She folded that paper into her pocket and didn't say a word."

"Do you remember the name of the place, the group, anything?"

"No, sorry. But maybe at the school, they might have a record or something."

"Thank you, that's a good idea. Thanks for remembering, and for the book." Marta smiled at the girl. "What are you doing now? Are you preparing for university exams?"

Zeynep looked confused. "No, ma'am. I work for my parents. You saw me. That's my job now. I finished school last year. My parents needed me to work."

"I'm sorry, I thought ... well, you seem so bright, I thought you were still ... sorry. I assumed, you know, that you were still in school." Marta fished in her bag, brought out a card, and scribbled on the back. "Here's my number, in case you remember anything else. Will you call me? Or if I can do something for you, please call me. Will you?"

The girl took the card, nodded, and walked away.

Forty-seven

"Where is there a monastery around here?" Vasilli asked.

"I have no idea." Marta shook the book by the spine, its pages flapping. "And this book, it's mine, I think. I had it with me when I was planning for New York, but I lost it just before I left town. Someone must have found it and kept it. I wonder why it ended up meaning so much to her ... and then, why did she leave it behind?"

They walked back to the main street, and Vasilli sat on a bench emblazoned with the name of a bank while Marta paced the sidewalk, turning to flag a taxi whenever a car approached. "Dammit, we're never going to get a ride back at this rate."

"Can you call someone?"

She gave him a harsh look. "Like who? Konstantin? Sure, they'll send someone to pick us up."

"I'm certain they are already in the vicinity, watching us—probably enjoying the show, too." He patted the seat. "Come sit here. They'll be along shortly, I'm sure."

She sat down heavily. "Let's see that book now," he said, holding out a hand. She pulled the blue volume from her bag and watched as he gently turned the pages.

"Well, some of it is in English—I think she was trying to learn the language—but most of her notes are Turkish. See here, this entire section is filled in with tiny writing. And here, she's underlined some parts, and the margins are full. Look, little drawings."

Marta leaned over and took the book from his hands. "Vasilli, this is her diary," she said. "Here, this section: 'I hope that I can go to college someday and leave this place. I will be the smartest in my class and so I can get a scholarship to go to the United States.'" She continued reading, silently. She looked up at him with eyes brimming.

"What?"

"Listen … 'Last night was bad. I think that he will kill her soon, and then I don't know what will happen to me. Will he kill me too? I am doing exercises every day and practicing my kicks, in case I have to fight. I won't let him kill me, too.' It goes on like that, how she's got a bag packed, ready to run, but she can't leave her poor mother. 'Why doesn't she fight him? Why can't she leave? I would help her. I can go to work, and we would be able to survive without him.' Oh my God, Vasilli. What have I done?"

"What have you done? Marta, that's nonsense. You had no choice. And it seems like your girl was stronger than both of them. She got away. And now we just have to find her."

A car rolled up silently, the window sliding down.

"Need a ride, sir?" Marta shook her head, but Vasilli pulled her to her feet. "Let's go. We can't waste any more time here."

Konstantin was in the foyer sorting through a stack of mail when they arrived at the house. "Uncle, how was your day?" he asked. "Miss, you look like you could use a rest. Perhaps you'll excuse us while we complete some business. I can have someone draw you a nice bath, if you'd like." His smile did not soften the coldness of his dark eyes.

"No, I'm fine. I'd actually appreciate a cold drink. Vasilli, wouldn't you care for a beverage?" They walked toward the sitting room, open once again to the terrace. The screech of a peacock was heard in the distance.

Drinks in hand, the three settled into cushioned seats on the veranda. The flowers and trees, together with the gamboling children on the lawn, created a fairy-tale picture that Vasilli was the first to sully.

"Konstantin, did you have any other uncles or aunts?"

"What do you mean, sir? You and my father were the only children."

"Is that so? What about your mother's side of the family? Anyone there?"

Konstantin's face reddened. "What are you implying?"

"I'm simply asking a question."

There was a long silence, in which the tinkle of ice cubes was the only music. Marta shifted in her seat, met Vasilli's eye, and turned to Konstantin.

"Do you have the papers ready to be signed?" she asked.

"The lawyers …" He made a dismissive gesture with his hand. "Everything is in order, but it takes time, you know."

"Yes, Time." She paused for a sip. "You've pretty much acknowledged that Vasilli is the rightful heir to your father, that he is your legitimate uncle. Haven't you?"

Konstantin shrugged. "Yes, but the lawyers, they require certain forms to be completed."

"But they work for you, no? So you tell them what you need and they do it, right? I have some papers here that Vasilli asked me to draw up for him, which you could sign right now and be done with it. Things can be settled that easily. Hmmm?" She pulled an envelope from her bag and smoothed the papers on the coffee table. "See, you sign here, and Vasilli signs here, and then we file these papers with the courts—and voila! It's done. Simple." She dug a pen from the bag and handed it to him. "Shall we?"

"I can't sign anything without the lawyers checking it over." He put the pen on the table.

"I will sign." Vasilli pulled the papers to his side of the table and signed with a flourish. "Konstantin? Just read them. There's no tricks here, just a simple declaration of our relationship. Surely you don't need a lawyer for that."

"You have a lawyer, no? You brought this woman here with you, didn't you? And you want me to sign things without my lawyers? I don't think so." Konstantin crossed his arms and looked off in the distance. "Uncle, what were you doing in the village today? Who are these people that you have been talking with?"

"That has nothing to do with you," Marta replied. "That's not your business."

"Ah. But you know that everything is my business, in this town and with everyone who works for me."

"I don't work for you." Marta turned to Vasilli. "I'm going for a walk. I need some air." She glared at Konstantin, but he ignored her. "Don't try to threaten me, Konstantin. Just sign the damned papers and let's get on with our lives."

"What do you mean by that? These papers have nothing to do with you; you're just the lawyer, the lawyer who sleeps with her clients, who sleeps with any man, in fact. Maybe you'll sleep with me, too? Or Sami-bey, would you like to sleep with Sami-bey, if that would 'seal the deal'? Hmmm?"

Vasilli stood up, his hand pulled back, ready to slap his nephew. Marta caught his arm, brought it down to her side. "Don't let him provoke you," she whispered. "He's just a scared little man. I've dealt with this kind before."

Konstantin laughed and went to the bar to refill his glass. "Yes, you've dealt with many men before, haven't you? And isn't my uncle just another notch on your belt? What do you think you're going to get out of him anyway? Uncle, how can you be taken in by such a fortune hunter? Such a slut?"

Marta turned away from Konstantin and leaned in to whisper in Vasilli's ear. "Don't fall for it. Don't let him bait you." He nodded, not taking his eyes off the younger man.

"I'm fine. Go for your walk. I'll be here," Vasilli said.

Nervous about leaving the two men, Marta paused on the stairs below the terrace, listening for the sound of voices. None came. She walked quickly through the garden and then headed back to the little church and the graveyard behind it. The new stone for Vasilli's brother Yurgos dominated the yard, but Marta stopped and inspected all the others. Although they appeared older, she noticed a clean white footstone set into the grass nearest the back wall. She scrubbed away at the ivy that half-covered it. The name, Nicolas Vassilios, and the dates engraved there caused her to hurry back to the house.

When she arrived, the two men were sitting silently on the terrace, drinks in hand, watching a gymnastics display by the children.

"Father, watch me! Watch me!" one of the girls shouted. He clapped his hands and then looked around. "Where is your mother?"

"She's dressing."

"Go get her for me. Now." He spied Marta coming up the stairs. "Well, that was a short walk. Would you like to freshen up before dinner?"

"No, I'm fine. What is for dinner anyway?" she asked.

"We have brought in a special fish, caught this morning, just for Uncle."

"Really. How nice." Marta settled into the chair opposite the men. "Tell me, is that what you served your other uncle, before he died?"

"What other uncle?" Vasilli asked. "You said there were no other relatives."

"No other living relatives." Konstantin sighed dramatically, one hand on his brow.

Marta turned and spoke to Vasilli. "I'm sorry to tell you this. Apparently, your mother was expecting when your father left her on the island. She had another son, a son named Nicolas, who was born in 1924. He died just a little while ago, didn't he, Konstantin?"

"He was an old man."

"Why didn't you tell me?" Vasilli turned to his nephew. "I asked you—"

"Uncle, he was born after you left, and he died before you returned. So what is the difference? You never even knew he existed."

"Precisely. I asked you to tell me about your father, and you never even mentioned another brother. Why is that?"

"Uncle, you don't understand. He was old; he lived in Ankara. He didn't have anything to do with us."

"So why didn't you tell me about him? Tell me now, and I will try to understand."

Marta interrupted. "Vasilli, remember those articles I had that described the empire, the Vaso fortune? I wasn't paying much attention at the time, but I remember there was a scandal a few years back, when a younger brother challenged the succession plan that had been announced by Yurgos. Something about him being passed over and then, a suspicious death. Isn't that right, Konstantin? Didn't your uncle die from some kind of bad fish?"

Konstantin rose from his seat, his face red.

"See, Uncle, she's just trying to poison you against me."

"I don't think I'm the one with poison on her mind," Marta replied calmly. "However, Vasilli, I'd recommend that you be careful what your nephew offers. Apparently, if you don't sign away your rights, you could be joining your brothers in the family cemetery."

"Konstantin, sit down and tell me now, tell me about this brother I never knew about," Vasilli said sternly.

Konstantin walked away.

"Honestly, I never put it together before," Marta said. "I went down to the little cemetery, and I found the stone, hidden along the wall. I'm sorry—I should have told you when we were alone."

"No matter. I just don't understand how this could have happened. It's … it's medieval, like palace intrigue."

"Exactly. You remember those stories, from our palace tours, all the brothers plotting against one another, the mothers poisoning the nephews. Only this time, it was the son who needed to get rid of his uncle, to make sure he had control of the family. Complete control. If I were his sister, I'd be nervous."

"Maybe that's why she stays away from here." Vasilli leaned forward, resting his hands on his knees. "But if he wanted to, I could have been dead already. The mugging, the fall down the stairs at Topkapi. Why let me get this close?"

"I'm not sure. Curiosity, maybe?" She put a hand on his. "Maybe we should get out of here, too."

"Let me see those articles, the ones you got from that boy. I want to read more about this before I confront Konstantin again." Vasilli rose and took Marta by the hand. "How long before that DNA test comes back?"

"I'm going back to the hotel. I'll call my friend and see how it's going." Marta paused. "Are you sure you want to stay here, in this house? Don't you see that you could be in danger?"

He shook his head sadly and walked her to the door. "Come back for dinner," he said. "Come back soon."

In her room, Marta couldn't find the envelope with the news articles. She plugged in her laptop and began to search. After a short delay, she got

Vasilli on the phone and told him the papers were missing. "Do you think they came in here, went through my belongings?"

He paused, moving outside to the balcony and surveying the grounds before answering. "What kind of people are these, anyway? My brother would never—"

"You have no idea what your brother would do," Marta reminded him. "The last time you saw him, he was ten years old. But imagine—here he is, with a mother who's pregnant and his father gone, and he has to find a way to support the family."

She stretched, scanning the articles quickly.

"Okay, I've got some articles on the Internet. It says here that he began his business as a fisherman and then started buying and selling the catch of all the other fishermen on the island, then owning their boats, then branching out into the shipping business, and becoming a huge success. All from what he learned at your father's knee."

"Yes, yes. But what about the other stuff," Vasilli urged.

She scrolled through the listings. "Well, he was a great philanthropist," she said.

"Yes, we know that. Get to the brother. What happened to the brother?"

"Okay, here it is: 'Nicolas Vaso, younger brother of shipping magnate Yurgos Vaso, was pronounced dead upon arrival at Istanbul's German Hospital in Taksim. The seventy-year-old, a poet and teacher at Bilkent University in Ankara, was apparently visiting his brother's apartment in Beyoğlu when he was stricken. Conflicting reports about the cause of death have not been confirmed. Apparently, either because of an allergic reaction, a poisonous specimen, or choking on a bone, Nicolas Vaso succumbed while eating a fish dinner with his family. No additional information was available. Mr. Vaso, a widower, leaves no children. His only heir is his brother, Yurgos, who was reportedly distraught at the death.'"

"How long before Yurgos died?"

"A few months, but remember, Yurgos was much older than Nicolas and probably already pretty frail. Oh, there's a picture of them together." She stood up and moved to the window, peering at the street below. She could hear Vasilli scratching his chin as he processed the new information.

"Well, Nicolas lived in Ankara and probably had nothing to do with the family business, so why kill him?" Vasilli asked.

"Maybe it was just an accident, a bone stuck in his throat. Who knows?" Marta replied. "I just find it interesting that Konstantin did not tell you there was another brother."

"Humph. Interesting."

"Now you're getting paranoid," she said. "Let me see what facts we have, and we'll go from there."

"You seem remarkably calm about this. Don't you want to set the record straight with Konstantin, tell him that we are not sleeping together? For someone who's just been accused of some pretty terrible things, you're not even rattled. If I didn't know you better, I'd wonder if you're plotting something yourself."

"I'm calling the States, to check on the DNA," she said.

"Why bother? We know there's no question anymore."

"I'll call you right back." She disconnected the call and then dialed again. "What have you got? I know you just received the package. Well, when can I expect something? When? Can't you … Oh, fine. Just put a rush on it, will you? And send me the bill. I know, I know you will." She paced the room, dialed the phone, and resumed her nervous journey around the carpeted room.

"Nothing yet," she said when Vasilli answered the phone.

"Not yet, the results, or not yet, your plan for revenge?" he replied.

"Oh, I assume you'll be handling your nephew," she said. In the background, she could hear raised voices. "What's going on there?" she asked.

Vasilli moved to the window and saw Konstantin holding his wife's arm bent in a strange angle. She was twisted almost to her knees, sobbing. "It's Konstantin, with his wife," he said. "They're having a disagreement of some kind. Oh, he's got her arm twisted." He sucked in his breath sharply.

"What's going on? Why don't you do something?" Marta asked. "Go out there and break it up."

"She'll be all right," Vasilli said. "I can't interfere in that marriage."

He watched as Konstantin twisted again, just above the elbow, where his wife's arm was already a deep purple color. He shouted at her, his mouth just inches from her face.

"I told you, no dancing, no 'gymnastic' stuff for those girls. And what do you do? You let them jump around, showing their legs to a strange man, showing their bottoms to their father. What kind of mother are you? If you can't handle it, I'll find a school for them, and I'll send them away to learn how to be proper women."

"What's happening?" Marta whispered into the phone. "I can barely hear him."

"It's over, I think," Vasilli said. "He let her go." Konstantin had dropped her arm, and she crumpled to the ground at his feet.

"Please, Konstantin," she pleaded. "I didn't know they slipped outside. I swear, it will never happen again."

Vasilli turned away from the sight of the woman on her knees, begging, clutching her arm.

"I think it's over," he said, stepping back from the window. "I couldn't follow much, but I guess he didn't like the girls running around outside."

"He's a brute," Marta said. "He's not going to change."

Vasilli nodded. "Don't worry about me. You let me take care of it. Just concentrate on finding your daughter."

"You know, maybe Serpil knows something about a monastery in this area. If I could talk to her alone—"

"Don't get involved," he warned. "Don't try to help her—not now. Maybe in the future, we'll be able to help Serpil. Just not yet."

"Be careful what you eat tonight," she said. "I don't want you to have an 'accident' while I'm not there."

Forty-eight

After a bath, Marta changed into a nightgown and climbed into bed with the *Blue Guide New York*—her daughter's diary. She wished for a magnifying glass and looked around the hotel for anything she could use. The bottom of a water glass helped a little, but it was slow going. At 11:00, Vasilli called.

She sat quietly through his report on the uneventful dinner. "I'm glad it went well. I've been trying to read this diary. This kid sure had a lot to say. I just can't make it all out. When I get back to the city, I can take it to a shop and have it enlarged on a photocopier."

"So, tomorrow," he said.

"Yes. Tomorrow, I'm going to try and find this monastery." She pulled up the laptop from the foot of the bed. "I haven't been able to come up with anything online. I'm probably not putting in the right search terms."

"Get some rest, and we'll start fresh in the morning," he said.

Although she agreed, Marta was unable to sleep. Long into the night, long after she'd retrieved the message that Vasilli was confirmed to be related to Konstantin, Marta studied the diary. She flipped around, looking for larger text, noting the sections that were highlighted and illustrated with little characters. Smiling at a scene drawn around the map of Central Park, she turned to the section about Columbia University and started to read.

> Here is the school where I will attend when I have arrived in America. I will be one of the special students who is here, invited to study the great books and learn all about literature. And I will tell everyone about the great Turkish poets, about Yahya Kemal and even Nazim Hikmet … And even now, the modern ones like Orhan Pamuk and Bilge Karasu, not just the ancient writers. I will share with my fellow students the stories about Suleyman the Magnificent and how he brought all the artists and writers and musicians together, and how they produced the most beautiful things in the world.

225

Marta smiled through the tears that flowed down her cheeks. Her daughter. How was she going to find this child and help make her dreams come true? Who knew what had happened to the girl, where she'd been for the past five years, and what kind of horrific things might have happened to her?

"Stop it," she said aloud, wiping her face. "Think positive. It's not too late. I'll find her. It's not too late."

Once again, the pair met for breakfast at the Vaso compound. Shortly after the coffee was served, the sound of Konstantin's helicopter roared outside, whipping the trees and stirring up a great cloud of dust. Vasilli excused himself, running downstairs to ask for a ride to the city with his nephew. Marta watched the two men, earphones magnifying the size of their heads, settle into the back of the vehicle. Vasilli looked out the window and then clutched the seat when the machine started to rise.

"He says he's afraid to fly, and now look at him," Marta said. "I hope they have airsick bags on that thing."

The quiet woman stacking dishes behind her started. "Pardon?" she asked.

"Oh, sorry, I was talking to myself." Marta smiled. Sipping her tea, her thoughts quickly moved from Vasilli to what she'd learned about her daughter. *I wonder what she looks like.*

The woman had returned with fresh tea.

"Pardon," Marta said. "Can you tell me if there is a school for girls somewhere around here? Some kind of monastery perhaps?"

The woman looked at her hands and then mumbled, "No, ma'am." She turned and continued to sort linens. Marta stuffed the *Blue Guide* into her bag, thanked the woman, and left the room. Maybe she would have more luck talking with Serpil, the lady of the house—if she could find her.

Serpil was not very accessible, as Marta feared. Instead, she sat in the kitchen with the cook staff and picked their brains while enjoying another cup of tea and some fresh bread with cheese. Flattery, she soon realized, worked in every country. Comparing the tea to her mother's special brew and declaring the *kaymak* "better than anything she'd ever tasted" and the olives "perfect," Marta managed to relax the women enough so that they joined her in sitting around the huge island. She slathered on the *kaymak*, the thick cream that was a specialty of the town, covering a slab of plain cake. She looked around appreciatively. Often, the real signs of wealth were shown in the kitchen, and in this ancient city, the combination of old and new showed the priorities of its owners. Copper pots of every size and shape hung from the ceiling, and the brick oven contrasted pleasingly with the stainless steel appliances that lined the room.

Her teacup filled again, Marta decided to trust the group and reveal her purpose. "My daughter is here, somewhere, and I want to find her. The last I knew, she was sent to some religious school."

Requisite questioning about why her daughter was here when she lived alone in New York was mostly satisfied when she described the brutality of her uncle and the effort of her aunt to protect the young girl. They nodded. One wiped tears away, and all murmured sympathy for her plight. "I can't let Konstantin know about this," she added. They seemed to embrace her with their assurances that nothing would reach his ears.

"That one, *yinek*," the youngest cook said, almost spitting the word. "Insect." The others nodded and then looked nervously around the room.

"He hears everything, eventually," the one named Sibel whispered.

They scratched heads and frowned thoughtfully, but no one knew of such a school.

"Are they foreigners?" Sibel asked. "I remember hearing about some foreigners that had a place, a religious retreat, in the mountains. But I don't know about any school there. It was just for the religious. They raised bees or made wine or something like that."

"You're making that up," the older woman chided. She looked at Marta. "She makes things up sometimes, mixes up what she reads in the magazines with what she thinks is real. Sorry."

"That's okay." Marta slumped in her chair. "Just in case, where did you think this place might be, if it was really there?"

"I think …" Sibel looked at the reflection in a large pot. "Isparta, I think."

The others laughed. "Isparta! That's in the mountains; it's where her sweetheart went to the army!" They swatted her gently with towels. "Isparta! You're just dreaming about your long-lost boyfriend now. There's no monastery in Isparta, only an army base."

"How far is it from here?" Marta asked. No one answered; they just shrugged and resumed their work. One washed grape leaves that filled a large basket. Gently, she pulled them from the pile and washed each side, inspecting as she worked. Marta imagined that Konstantin would be a hard man to work for, looking for any excuse to dismiss an employee. A brown spot on a leaf could mean unemployment, and in this company town, the options were surely limited.

A huge pile of ground meat was covered with spices and then kneaded by four hands reaching into a giant bowl. Sibel chopped onions, finely, with a huge knife that she rolled expertly on a board. Tears streamed down her face, and she began to sing. Marta watched, fascinated, as her fingers deftly moved the onions and the flashing knife barely missed the tips of them. The warbling song was something new, some kind of new musical genre that combined American country music with what Marta and her friends used to call Turkish "misery music."

Marta found Serpil in the salon, a small glass-enclosed porch filled with exotic orchids. Pale, blond, she looked like an exotic flower herself. Serpil sat up abruptly when Marta entered, picked up her embroidery, and resumed work.

"Can I help you?" she asked coldly. She reached for the servant's bell, her movement stiff and constrained by the injuries to her arm, well hidden under a loose caftan.

"No, I am fine," Marta said. "What lovely work you do! May I?" She leaned over the delicate design, flowers on a linen napkin. "My mother tried to teach me, but I am all thumbs."

Serpil smiled politely. "How can I help you?" she asked again.

"Oh, I was just looking around. Kind of boring, with the men gone from the house. Where are the children?" Marta sat on a rattan chair, sinking slightly into the colorful cushions.

"They have lessons. Upstairs. With the tutor."

"Ah. So they don't go to a regular school?"

"They do, but while we are here … Well, my husband thought it best that we bring in the tutors for now." Serpil had reddened a bit during this exchange, and Marta could tell she was about to lose her. The embroidery needle was idle. It was seconds away from being set aside and her quarry lost.

"Can you tell me something? I traveled here once when I was a child, and I remember there was some kind of monastery around. Do you know about it? Can you tell me where it is?"

"Not near here," Serpil said slowly. "We have the dervishes. That's all we have here."

"Oh." Marta picked at her nail. "Do you know where I can get a good manicure? My nails are in bad shape." She held out her hand. "See?"

"Hmm. My girl does it. I'd be happy to send her to your hotel this afternoon."

"Thanks. So, you don't know about any monastery, some place where they might keep bees, for honey, something like that?"

Serpil shook her head. "No. I can ask Konstantin, if you wish."

"Oh, no, I don't want to bother him. It was probably somewhere else that I was thinking of. It's been a long time, you know."

"There are the tombs." Serpil blushed again. "You know, the ones carved into the side of the mountains. Near Demre, I think."

"You're right. I had forgotten those too. But no one can go near them, right? That's not allowed."

"Well, no. But there is a place, I can't remember the name of it, where the caretakers used to be. They were some kind of religious people. But I don't know if they are still there. I, look, I have to go check on the children. I'll send my girl to do your nails." She looked pointedly at Marta, still sitting in her chair. "To your hotel."

Forty-nine

When finally Vasilli returned, it was by car, not helicopter. Marta stifled a chuckle when she saw that he'd had the upsetting reaction she predicted. Konstantin did not return with his uncle, who arrived looking wan and sheepish in a limousine. He joined Marta on the terrace, where they watched the peacocks strutting below.

"Had a nice morning?" he asked, perching on an ottoman next to her chair. She nodded, a slight smile on her lips. He felt her forehead. "Are you ill? Have they drugged you somehow?"

She smiled again. "No, I'm fine. I'm just ... I don't know. I just had this feeling today, that I'm going to find her. She's going to be okay. I can't explain it." He took her hand, slid a package from his pocket, and placed it there.

"Open it."

She unwrapped the box, artfully folded with heavy pink paper so no tape was needed. Having removed the top, she nodded appreciatively. An ancient coin hung from a heavy gold necklace.

"I hope you like it," he said. "I wanted to give you something, a token of my appreciation for everything you've done for me."

She kissed him softly on the cheek. "It's perfect."

"Well, it's the least I can do," he said.

"Just wait until you get my bill." She smiled and shook her head slightly. "Thank you." She closed the jewelry box and placed it on the seat beside her. "So. Tell me about your morning. Did you and Konstantin have a chance to talk some more?"

Vasilli scratched his ear. "Yeah, we went to his office," he said slowly. "You're not going to like this. But I signed the papers. I gave up my rights to the family fortune." He held up a hand to stop the tirade he expected from her. "I have my own money, and I don't want this to continue to be an issue between me and the family. So I signed it. And now I don't have to worry about getting poisoned or smothered in my sleep."

"All right." She crossed her arms and jiggled a foot. The silence was uncomfortable. Finally, she spoke. "It's your choice. I don't agree with you, but it's done."

"Yes, I told you right from the beginning that I didn't want their money, even before we knew—"

"Fine. You're right. Listen, I'm going to go over to the hotel for a while. I have some things to do. I'll meet you later, okay?" She stood up and held the gray box out toward Vasilli. "Thank you again for the necklace. It wasn't necessary, but it's lovely."

"Please don't be angry with me," he said.

"No. I'm not. Really. It's your choice. And I understand why you did it," she said. "I hope that it works out the way you expect." She touched his arm and left him watching the birds.

Marta spent the remainder of the day reading the tiny handwriting that permeated the guidebook. It was tedious work, but she smiled through the eyestrain as she learned more about the young girl's aspirations. She was not smiling when she came across a section describing the girl's growing discomfort around the man she believed to be her father, however, and had to put down the material for a time to regain her composure.

Late in the afternoon, Vasilli reappeared and they once again explored the streets, hoping to find a decent restaurant. They settled for a small *lokanta*, filled with businessmen and lit solely with brass lanterns that emitted a smoky glow. With the familiar menu and a bottle of local wine, they resumed speculation about the future.

"Do you think that you will stay here?" Marta asked.

Vasilli grimaced. "I don't know. So far, Konstantin has been very—how shall I say?—inconsistent in his attitude toward me. He is polite and respectful, but he is also suspicious and afraid. I hope that now that I've signed the papers, he'll change, but I don't know. Whenever I try to ask him about business, he gets very brusque."

"Yes, I can see that."

They paused to allow the waiter to clear plates stained with lamb juices and stray pilaf. Vasilli refilled their glasses with wine.

"He's very sensitive and unpredictable. So far, the only safe topic is his son, and even there, I have to tread lightly," Vasilli concluded. "Now, tell me some more about your daughter. What is she like?"

Marta grew animated as she described what she had found in the diary. "She's very bright. I can see that. She has ambition, and she is a hard worker.

If only … if only she hadn't been stuck with those awful people. But it's funny, I think she knew that she was not their biological child."

He looked skeptical but did not comment.

"I know it's probably just wishful thinking. But she knew that she had to get away from them, from that place." She paused. "That says something."

When they returned to the house later that evening, most of the lights were on but no one appeared to greet them. A bit tipsy from the wine, neither Marta nor Vasilli was discouraged by the quiet. On the desk in the foyer, however, a FedEx envelope addressed to Marta had been opened, its contents scattered about.

"Nice of them to open it for you," Vasilli remarked. "Saves you the need to do it yourself." He watched her gather the papers. "Nothing out of order, I hope?"

"No, it's the official DNA results. I'm surprised it got here so quickly. Well, whoever opened it knows the truth now. I suppose it was Sami-bey, or one of his ilk. Wonder if Konstantin came back early?"

"You need not concern yourself," a voice came from the shadowy library. "He knows about the test and was expecting the result as it came."

"Are you going to contest it?" Marta spoke to the shadow she knew to be Sami. "Do you want to run your own tests?"

"No, as I said, apparently Konstantin is satisfied that Mr. Vassilios is in fact his uncle. So that question is settled." He flicked the light switch, illuminating the room behind. "Would you care to join me for an aperitif?"

Marta was about to decline when she felt Vasilli's hand pushing her forward. She looked at him quizzically, but he merely smiled.

"What is your pleasure?" Sami stood poised over the bar.

"You know, we've already had quite a bit to drink this evening. Perhaps some coffee would be in order. Marta? Coffee?"

Servants called, orders made, they settled on the chairs and watched Sami light his cigarette and then sip delicately from his glass of whiskey. He was comfortable in a way completely at odds with his behavior when Konstantin was in the vicinity, thus confirming that the younger man had not returned to the house.

"So." He puffed on the fragrant tobacco. "How did you spend your day? Visiting our quaint little town? Did you go to the museum, by any chance? They have a lovely display of ancient artifacts."

They smiled silently.

"Perhaps you took a ride through the poppy fields. They are really beautiful this time of year. Of course, they're cultivated and grown year-round in greenhouses. For medicinal purposes only, you know. But I suppose you couldn't get very close to the growing areas. The army has it pretty well under control, no need to tempt anyone thinking about illicit activities, you know." He sipped again. "So, you must be tired after all your adventures, Mr. Vassilios. At your age, it must be difficult to keep up all this activity."

Still, they smiled. Coffee was served in tiny porcelain cups, blue and red ornamentation highlighted by gold-leaf trim. They sipped. Marta smiled at Vasilli. "Would you like me to read your cup again tonight?" she asked.

"No, I don't feel the need to know my future," he replied. "I'm quite happy with what I have in the present."

"Well, I am happy that you came to your senses," Sami said. "Signing the papers this morning. A sensible course of action."

Vasilli nodded, and Marta concentrated on her coffee. "Well," she said after a moment, "I think I'll get back to the hotel. I want to head south to-morrow." She turned to Vasilli. "Will you be staying on here, then?"

Vasilli hesitated. "I think I will spend some time here, get to know Konstantin and the rest of the family. But if you'll have me, I'd like to come with you tomorrow." He walked her to the door.

"Watch out for him," she said, nodding toward the library. They could hear Sami talking on the telephone.

Back in her room, Marta perched again with the guidebook on her knees, looking for any sign that might show where the girl had gone. Why leave it behind, if not to serve as a road map should someone care to search for her? Marta refused to believe otherwise, especially after she read a long section inscribed over the diagram near the Statue of Liberty.

I don't think that I belong here, with these parents. They are different. They are not like me at all. How can I be the child of two such ignorant people? I love them, but I can't be theirs. Can I? Is this what they call evolution? That two dull people with no imagination, no thirst for knowledge, should give birth to someone who craves it like fish need water? I know other kids think that they must be adopted, too, but sometimes, late at night, when I hear them talking, I feel like they're talking about me, about getting me, and what to do with me, and how I don't fit here with them. Is it my imagination? Or is it only a dream? That the only way I could escape from my fate is if my real parents showed up one day, to take me back where I belong.

It has to be here, she thought. The girl had a brain and a plan, and she wouldn't have left the book behind without thinking it through. She jumped when the phone trilled. The room was bright with sunlight, but the lamp was still blazing. She must have fallen asleep, Marta thought, picking up the telephone.

"Did I wake you?" Vasilli asked.

"I have to go back," she said. "To my aunt. I have to talk to her. I have to make her tell me where she sent the girl."

"Marta, she's not going to tell you." He sighed. "But we'll go, if that's what you want. I don't think it will get you anywhere. Let's just hope she doesn't shoot us for trying."

"You don't have to come with me," Marta said. "I'm torn myself."

"Look, aside from the gun and all that, I'm not sure your aunt knows much of anything anymore. She seems rather … compromised by her situation. Mentally, I mean. So I don't know that she can really help, even if she wanted to." Vasilli paused. "But we'll do whatever it takes to find your girl. I promise."

"Thank you," she said. "I guess you're right. We can always go back to my aunt later, if we need to. I don't think she's going anywhere."

"So," he said. "What do you think we should do next? Should we go to the tombs, where Serpil said there used to be a place? Or somewhere else, something you found in the book perhaps?"

"I didn't find anything in the book, not really. Just the thoughts and dreams of a very bright young girl." She flipped through the pages. "Maybe you can take a look at it. You might see something. I can't look at it any longer. I'll take a shower and meet you in the lobby."

A short time later, Vasilli sat in the passenger seat while Marta navigated the rental car. He thumbed through the pages of the *Blue Guide*, squinting at the tiny handwriting. He checked his old neighborhood and grunted when he saw there was no mention of his coffee shop.

"What kind of snobby guidebook is this, anyway?" he grumbled. Turning some additional pages, he saw the heading for the Cloisters. Instead of a map of the grounds, a different type of paper had been carefully glued into the book. "Marta," he shouted, "I've found it!"

A yellow flyer had been trimmed to fit within the confines of the narrow page. There was a photograph of an ancient building sitting atop a hill with a beautiful vista and the name and address below it. On the back side, there was more tiny writing in Turkish so that Vasilli could not decipher it, a phone number, too.

Marta pulled the car to the shoulder of the road and reached for the book.

"I've found it," he said. "Here, look, she cut out a page and replaced it with the flyer. Look. Clever, clever girl," he said. "Of course, the Cloisters. She's a bright one, this girl of yours. Where did she learn English, I wonder?"

"Wonderful—look at how she did this. Okay, it translates like 'View of Eğirdir.' It's a lake, not far from here. So the place must be in the mountains, overlooking the lake. Around Isparta, I think. It's been a while, but there must be something there." She laughed. "So the onion girl was right, there is a monastery in Isparta."

"Onion girl?"

"Long story, I was talking with the cooks in the kitchen, and this one girl, she said Isparta. The others dismissed her as a flake, but she knew what she was talking about. Let me check the map—I think we're heading in the right direction."

On the road again, the car moved like the wind at the touch of a toe. "We have to be careful on these mountain roads," Marta said. "Cars come flying through these narrow passes, and it can get pretty hairy."

"Gee, thanks for telling me." Vasilli gripped the dashboard. "I assume this thing has air bags and all that?"

She grinned. "They won't help, but sure. Probably GPS too, so Konstantin can watch our progress on his little computer." She tried the radio, but there was nothing but dead air. She turned to look at Vasilli. "Sorry, I didn't mean to freak you out. I just remembered an accident we saw on this road once. Don't worry—the roads are much safer now. They have all these new laws and rules about how fast bus drivers can go and how often they have to sleep, stuff like that. I'm not going to fall asleep at the wheel, I promise you."

"It's okay. I'm not worried. I'm not afraid of dying." He smiled weakly.

Fifty

The road featured beautiful vistas, hairpin turns, and climbs no overloaded truck could make easily. There was not much in the way of traffic. Marta and Vasilli encountered an occasional jeep, an army truck loaded with sullen green-clad passengers, and a single bus going in the opposite direction. At the top, a scenic park invited passersby to stop and look—and buy souvenirs, of course. There were blue glass "evil eye" charms in every shape and size, T-shirts in all colors and sizes, *Nesrettin Hoja* storybooks in several languages, and chess sets carved from onyx, marble, and wood. They had a cup of tea at the obligatory stand, on the same red-and-white-striped melamine coasters, with the same gritty sugar cubes stacked on the side.

"Nice to know there are some things that you can always count on," Vasilli said as he lifted his glass.

"Yes, just like the British, when in doubt, there's always a cup of tea to be had."

"How far are we?" he asked.

She scanned the horizon. "It should be somewhere here, probably not marked on the road. If we see any kind of turnoff or driveway, we'll try it."

"Did you ask the kid if he knows where it is?" Vasilli nodded toward the tea server. "Let me guess; he never heard of it before."

"His words exactly, '*yok, bayan*,' with that annoying little chuck of the chin you so admire in the Turks." She imitated the gesture, and he laughed.

"Only in this country can a nod be interpreted as a negative response," he noted.

"Wait, I forgot to make the tooth-sucking sound that goes with it."

"He's looking over here. Do you think he knows we're talking about him?" Vasilli whispered.

"I don't know, but we better hit the road." They returned to the car, and it was only a short time later that an unmarked road appeared, leading up to the hills. "Shall we try?" she asked, pulling onto the rocky passage. A wooden sign swung from one end of a post, but the writing was worn away and gave no clues.

Around a curve, there was a massive stone edifice surrounded by swaying cypress trees. When they got out of the car, Marta stopped Vasilli.

"Shh, do you hear it? Humming. There are bees here. Do you hear it?" He shook his head, straining to pick up the sound.

They picked a path through the overgrown garden, the wind picking up as they neared the building. "Doesn't look like anyone is here," Vasilli suggested. "Or at least no one who takes care of these grounds."

"There's probably an interior courtyard, where they spend their time," Marta said. "But it does seem awfully quiet."

The large door was barred, and there was no response to their knocking. The pair looked for other possible entrances to the complex. At the south side, they found one. They pushed open a rusty iron gate and ventured through a thick-walled passageway whose walls were thickly covered with moss. The floor was slippery, and Marta grabbed Vasilli's arm.

"This can't be right," she whispered. A turn, and then the courtyard was revealed, bright and filled with flowers of every color. Large and small vines trumpeted with honeysuckle, morning glory, jasmine, and clematis. The humming was louder here, and Marta pointed to the boxes, stacks of them, brimming with bees and dripping with honey. There was, however, no sign of human habitation. A white cat wound its way around Marta's legs before yowling a piteous mewl that drew kittens from several directions.

Vasilli followed her through the courtyard, peering into windows and trying doors as they circled.

"There's no one here," she said finally. "Now what?"

"Well, we go into the town and ask what happened to the people who used to live here," he said. "That's the only logical thing to do."

"We could break a window and go inside."

"I would rather try the other approach first, if you don't mind."

She shrugged. "Chicken."

"I beg your pardon," he said. "Aren't you an officer of the court, Miss Big-shot Attorney?"

"Not this court, not in this country." She picked a flower and then another, twining them into her hair.

"Excuse me," someone called from a shadowed doorway. "Can I help you?"

They rushed over to a short man, the very caricature of a monk, bald-headed and attired in a brown robe, holding a cell phone to his ear.

"Just a moment." He held up a finger. "Yes, I'd like to report a break-in. Yes, at the old monastery. Two people. No, they don't appear to be armed. Excuse me, are you armed? No." He spoke into the phone.

Marta reached over and took it from him, hitting the "end" button and pocketing the device. "Hey," he protested.

"Hey nothing," she retorted. "We're not breaking in. The door was open, and we walked in. We knocked first, but no one answered. Who are you?"

"Who are you?" he asked. "You should introduce yourselves to me, as the intruders."

"All right. My name is Marta Demir, and this is Vasilli Vassilios, and we are looking for a school, a boarding school, I suppose, where my daughter was sent five years ago."

"*Yunan?*" He looked at Vasilli fearfully.

"Yes, he's Greek, but actually more like American. Don't worry; he won't hurt you." Marta crossed her arms and tapped her foot. "So, where are the children? Is this the right place, the 'View of Eğirdir'?"

"Yes, I suppose it is. But there are no more children here. Now give me my phone. I'm expecting a call." He adjusted the cowl of his robe and scowled at her.

"Where did they go, the children? And when?"

"I don't know. I'm just the beekeeper. They left me here, said they'd be back and we'd build things back up again, but no one came for me. I've been stuck here, eating honey, for a long time."

"Fascinating," Marta interrupted. "If we could just check inside, maybe for records of the children, so we can find out where they were sent?"

"No records." He turned around, arms outstretched, laughing at the sky.

Marta rolled her eyes at Vasilli and then raised her voice. "Sir, I'm sorry to be rude, but can you tell me where the children were sent?"

"Oh yes. Well, they were gone before I got here, so I never saw, but ..." He paused and looked around uncomfortably. "They were put to work, is what I understand. When the girls turned thirteen, they were sent to work. As domestics, au pair, that kind of thing. Honorable work, nothing shady about it."

"Who did this?" Vasilli put a restraining hand on Marta's arm. She looked about to strangle the man.

"Some agency, a place on the shore, looking for girls to work in the homes of wealthy foreigners. It was all aboveboard, trust me. The head guy here, he was a real stickler for that. Everything done proper-like."

"He took money for them?"

"Well, yeah, like a broker, you know. The girls couldn't stay here forever, and there was some trouble with the army base, and he decided that once they turned thirteen, out they went. Best thing for everyone. So he made a deal with this woman, she'd come up every spring and get some girls. The ones who were old enough, you know. To work in the homes. And if they did a good job, kept their noses clean and such, they could stay with the family after the summer was over. Follow them to Ankara or Istanbul, or wherever they were from. You know."

Marta stepped forward and grabbed the man by the robe. "And what happened to the girls if the family didn't want to keep them? Did they get sent back here, to wait for the next summer job?"

He shook his head. "I never saw anyone come back."

"I thought you said they were all gone before you arrived." Vasilli tried to remove the man's robe from Marta's grip.

He giggled. "Well, technically, that's true. But they did shut down the school right after I came here. Honestly. And the girls left, and then the other brothers, and then it was just me, taking care of the bees and waiting for instructions."

"I'll give you instructions." Marta spoke through clenched teeth. She turned to Vasilli. "How the hell am I supposed to track her down now?"

"They have to have records of some kind. I think we should go in and look around." He glared at the monk. "What is your name, sir?"

"I don't speak English," the man said to Marta. "And I'm not telling him my name." He spread his legs, crossed his arms, and tried to present a threatening obstacle.

Marta pushed past him. "I'm calling the police!" he shouted, patting his pockets. He looked up in time to see her waving his cell phone over her shoulder and then ran to catch up with the visitors.

The rooms were Spartan, appropriately, and the classrooms empty and echoing. "Office?" Marta barked at the monk, who pointed meekly to the end of a long hallway.

Dominated by a large desk under a stained-glass representation of nature, the room appeared to have been emptied in a hurry. "Looks more like a hasty retreat than a planned closure," Vasilli commented.

"Check all the drawers, in case there's a card or, or something," Marta said. She looked at the monk. "You too, help search. We're not leaving until we find something."

"One thing," he said, finger raised. "Will you take me with you? Back to civilization?"

"Depends."

"On what?" He started sorting through a pile of papers on the floor.

"On what you find." Marta tugged at the central drawer of the desk. "It's locked. I don't suppose you have a key," she said.

He shook his head.

Marta concentrated on her task, working a pen into the opening. Vasilli came up behind her. "Let me," he said. A quick jiggle of an unfolded paper clip, and the lock snapped open. "Voila."

"Cards," she announced and pulled off the elastic. She flipped through the pile. "Come here." She gestured to the monk. "Any of these look familiar?"

"I told you, I don't know who she was. I just know how it worked. How I heard it worked, that is."

"Who are you?" she demanded again. "What is your name?"

"Oh, lady, it doesn't matter. I'm nobody. I'm just the guy taking care of the bees."

She closed her eyes, took a deep breath, and then pushed away from the desk with the cards in her hand. Shuffling through them, she eliminated several that didn't fit her profile. The remainder, she placed in her pocket. She opened all the other drawers, looked under the desk, and then picked up the leather blotter on top.

"Here we go," she said. A brochure, identical to the one pasted in the Michelin Guide, was stuck underneath. When she shook it, several cards rained out of the sides. Those were gathered into her pocket as well.

She looked over at Vasilli who was opening and closing what appeared to be empty file cabinet drawers. "Anything?" He shook his head. The monk paced in front of the door.

"Okay, let's go." She walked toward the door and handed the cell phone back to the monk. "Thanks for your help."

"Wait a minute. You said you'd take me with you," he said.

"No, I didn't. And since I have no idea who you are or what you're really doing here, I'm not taking you anywhere." She pushed toward the door, Vasilli fast on her heels.

"Okay, okay," the man puffed behind her. "Take me with you and I'll tell you whatever you want to know."

"Sorry. No." They walked to the car, the monk loudly pleading his case.

Vasilli opened the door for Marta as the monk followed closely behind.

"You've got a phone, why don't you just call someone to come and get you? Or go down to the road and hitchhike. You're not a prisoner here," Vasilli said.

The monk shook his head, rubbing his eyes. "You don't understand."

"Sorry, I don't."

"Can't you just give me a ride?" he begged.

Marta started the car and waited while the monk pulled himself into the backseat.

"What's your name?" Vasilli asked.

"Oh, sorry, I'm Adam, Brother Adam." He smiled. "Pleased to make your acquaintance." Within five minutes, he was snoring loudly.

Fifty-one

Vasilli looked through the cards while Marta navigated the curvy road. At the peak of the mountain, nestled in a crevasse, the town of Isparta beckoned. Houses perched on each side of the hill, topsy-turvy, most looking like the construction had halted suddenly. They drove through the central avenue, past two mosques, seventeen cafés, and an elementary school, before reaching the end of the town. The highway continued, past the daunting entrance to an army base, heavily fortified with barbed wire and turrets but guarded by two guys resting against the gate, cigarettes dangling from their mouths. "Top security, there," Vasilli noted dryly.

"Yeah, but there're real bullets in those guns. That's what makes me nervous. One of these kids goes whacko and boom, you've got a massacre on your hands."

"Well, that could happen anywhere, right?"

"You're right. It could happen anywhere. It just seems to happen more often here." She signaled and turned the car around, heading back into town.

"You seem to know a lot about this army stuff." Vasilli's comment was answered with silence. "Why does Turkey need such a large army, anyway?"

"They're always ready."

"For?"

"Enemies, imagined and real. It's a long history." She pulled over and parked. "Find anything worth checking in those cards?"

"Maybe. These two." He handed them over. "Marta. The army ... you lost someone?"

She sighed and looked out the window. "Yes, two cousins ... three really. Two were killed; one decided that he liked Cyprus better than Turkey, and so he stayed. At least that's what my aunt wanted to believe. I don't know if they ever heard from him again."

"And?"

She pushed the hair away from her face. "What do you want from me? All right. After I found out I was pregnant, I did try and contact Mehmet again. But he was gone. His mother wouldn't tell me anything, but some friends found out for me. Since he couldn't fight his mother, he went off to do his military service."

"Didn't you say it was a requirement?"

She snorted. "He went early. Wasn't scheduled to go for another year or so, but he just decided that it was better to get it over with. So he left. Came here, I think, or maybe Burdur, the next town over. Anyway, he ran away. And I have no idea what happened to him after that." She opened the car door. "Let's go."

Vasilli gestured to the brown lump asleep in the backseat of the car. "What about him?" he asked.

She rolled her eyes. "Just leave him."

The dusty streets were sparsely populated in the middle of the hot afternoon. Some old men stared out from behind a plate-glass window in the largest of the cafés; a few grubby kids chased a cat along the street and into an alley. Two women, age indeterminate, swept the stoops in front of solid brown apartment buildings. Neither looked up when Marta addressed them.

"Pardon, can you help me find this address?"

There was no response, except for a bit more vigorous stirring of the dust at their feet. One turned and walked into the building, the door slamming shut behind her.

"So much for the famous Turkish hospitality," Marta joked. "Maybe if you ask someone, they'll be nicer."

"Well, according to this card, the address is here, above this bank." He pointed. "Look, there's a sign in the window. Let's check it out."

There was no sign on the door, and no response to the ringing or knocking. Marta tried the number on her cell, and from the dark hallway, they could hear the phone ringing inside. "Well, at least the number is right," she said.

"Maybe we should ask at the school. You know, if these people were recruiting young girls to work, they might have tried the local school too."

Locked up tight, the school was apparently not in session either. "Where the hell is everybody?" she asked. They both looked around, stopping their survey of the town at the spire of the mosque. "Someone has to be there."

In the courtyard of the mosque, an old woman beat energetically at a rug draped over two chairs. After a brief exchange conducted primarily with primitive sign language, she motioned to Vasilli to follow her inside the building. "In the back, I think, there's an office. The imam should be in here."

He raised an eyebrow.

"She's speaking some kind of dialect, I could barely understand her," Marta explained.

"Interesting."

"We'll see if he's there. Maybe she was just telling me how to neuter a bull, I'm not sure."

A small man, young but with an old face, stood when they knocked on the open door of his office. Dark shadows under his eyes and deep creases in his cheeks suggested that the job was not agreeing with the young cleric.

"How can I help you?" He gestured toward the empty chairs.

"Do you speak English?" Marta asked. She introduced herself and Vasilli, who offered his hand to the imam.

"I am Ali, Ali Karsak," he said. "It has been a while since I used my English, pardon for the mistakes I make."

"It's fine. Thank you for trying." Marta explained their journey and the information about the monastery and the employment agency that sent girls to work for wealthy families.

"Yes, I know about this. It was before I arrived here, when the monastery was in operation. It closed, oh, probably three or four years ago. The ministry came, said there was evidence that the girls were being sold for prostitution, and they shut down the whole place."

Marta gasped. Vasilli put a hand on her arm. "Was anything ever proven? Did they find the girls? What happened to them?"

Ali shook his head. "I don't know. Nothing else happened here. Some parents came, I think, and took their daughters back home. The rest of them, I don't know."

"What ministry was involved?"

"The women's bureau, I think, or maybe it was education. I'm sorry, I'm not sure." He fingered the thin beard struggling to grow on his chin. "Can I do something for you? Would you like to pray?"

Vasilli's hand tightened on Marta's arm. "No, I think we're good. Thank you for your help." He started to rise.

"Wait a minute. Is there anyone in town who would remember? Someone who was here at the time, maybe someone who worked there? This can't be a dead end. There has to be someone in this God-forsaken place who can help me."

"'God-forsaken'?" Ali chuckled. "That's a good description. Since I've been here for a year, I have not seen much of God's work being done here. It's a desolate place, without much soul, I'm afraid." He leaned back in his chair, closing his eyes. "There is one person. I've never spoken with her. She seems to have a problem with religion. The bank manager. Her name is Kaderli, I think. She works at the Yetibank on the corner. Don't tell her I sent you. She'll definitely blow you off." He stood, hands tucked into the sleeves of his loose white robe. "Sorry I couldn't be more help. Please come again, if you would like. It's nice to be able to talk with someone for a change."

Marta nodded and walked to the door. "Why don't you transfer, go to another city?"

"Not up to me." He shrugged. "I'll do what I can here. Good luck to you."

The manager at Yetibank was out to lunch, as was the entire staff. "How can they close the entire business for lunch?" Vasilli asked.

"They do. They used to force all the shop owners to close at the same time, so no one could take advantage while the other stepped out for a break."

"Strange."

She shrugged. "Never thought about it. But it's only fair—shopkeepers have to eat too."

A boy approached, selling *simit*, the sesame pretzels. "Are they fresh?" Marta asked, squeezing one of the round pastries. "Okay, we'll take two. Can you send someone over with tea? *Çay?*" She handed him some change, took the two *simit* in squares of newspaper, and handed one to Vasilli. "Lunch. Enjoy."

The tea arrived, the warm drink welcome after the dry snack of *simit*. The rattle of a grate being lifted down the street revealed a small farm stand, fruit glistening in the sun. Marta left her tea with Vasilli and returned shortly, a bag of bright green plums in her hand, cheek full of the sour fruit.

"My God, I missed these," she announced. "Why don't they grow these in the States?" She handed one to Vasilli, who bit into the crisp fruit and then sucked at the saliva that practically ran from his mouth.

"Sour," he gasped.

"Yeah, isn't it wonderful?"

The sign on the bank window flipped to "open," and Marta drained her teacup, stood up, and started to walk across the street. "Coming?" she asked.

Vasilli spit out the pit and looked around for a place to discard it. Finding none, he slipped it into his pocket, wrapped in the ever-present white handkerchief. They entered the bank and soon found themselves sitting in a waiting area, listening to the rise and fall of what must have been the manager's high-pitched voice.

"She must be on something," Vasilli whispered.

"No, that's the typical Turkish female's façade," Marta said. "All bright and feminine and cheery. Just watch out while she sharpens her knife on your spinal column."

"Hello, please come in. Sorry to keep you waiting. How may I help you?" She escorted the pair into her office, a modern room with modular pine furniture that looked straight out of an IKEA catalog. "Can I get you some çay? Mine, cenim, my dear, please bring some tea for our visitors." She settled officiously behind the desk. "Now, how can I help you?"

Marta placed the flyer on the desk. "Miss Kaderli, what can you tell me about this place?"

"Are you reporters?" She was indignant. Her posture became even straighter, her voice more high-pitched.

"No, certainly not." Marta removed the offending flyer. "A member of my family was at this school, and she disappeared. I'm trying to find out about this work program that was in place, to send girls to work for wealthy families. Do you know anything about that?"

The woman sighed heavily. "I'm sorry to tell you that these are just rumors. There was no such thing going on here, I assure you. We provided the financial, ahem, guidance to the directors, and there was no, ahem, untoward business going on there. Nothing at all." She nodded at the girl carrying a silver tray with crystal glasses and silver spoons. Vasilli raised an eyebrow, took his glass, and dunked two cubes of sugar.

"I'm truly sorry if a member of your family is missing, miss. Truly sorry. But the times we live in, sometimes young girls get … how do I put this … distracted? … by the opportunities they see in the big city. And so they go. And they get lost. So unfortunate." She shook her head. "Have you looked in Istanbul; that's where they usually end up. In the jail, the hospital perhaps? I'm sorry to be so brutal."

Marta smiled. "Oh, not at all. I appreciate your candor. But I'm certain that this girl was not distracted. She was, is, a very smart girl and would not be so foolish. Only if someone forced her would she, well, you know what I mean. So, I know there are families that hire girls to work for the summer, and perhaps, if they work out, they go back to the city and stay with the family all year. Taking care of the children, that sort of thing. You know this; I know it. So how do we find these girls? Is someone keeping track, keeping an account, so to speak?"

They stared across the table. No one moved, except for Vasilli, whose eyes continued to scan the desk and shelves around the room. He stood up, placed his empty cup on the tray, and moved toward the window. Before she could intercept him, he picked up a blue folder and looked at the label on the tab. "Would this be something you might want to look at?" he asked Marta, handing her the file.

She turned and read the tab aloud. "Kaderli Employment Service. How lucky! Although it is a rather thin file, don't you think? There must be more than this." She opened it and started turning pages. Miss Kaderli tried to reach over the desk to retrieve the folder and then marched around and stood in front of Marta. Vasilli moved in place by her side. "Don't even think about it," Marta growled. The woman pursed her lips and spun on her heel, returning to her chair.

"Now, I'll give you the name of the girl, and you will look in your other files and tell me where she is. That's how this is going to work. I'm not going to turn you in. I'm not going to report you to the authorities, but you are going to give me a name and address for this child. If you don't, you'll be very, very sorry." She closed the file. "Turn on your computer, and tell me where I can find Nazlan Uzun."

Fifty-two

"Side." She pronounced it See-day.

Marta exhaled loudly, trying to calm her nerves. "Write it down. Everything you know." Her heart pounding, Marta reached for the paper that scrolled out of a printer. She read it hungrily. It was from three years ago. "Is she still there, with them?" she asked.

Miss Kaderli shrugged. "I don't know. They never asked for another girl, so it's possible they kept her. I don't know. I haven't, you know, kept up with the business very much, since the monastery closed and all."

"Pity. You can't exploit any more little girls. Must have been tricky for you, to avoid being connected to the scandal up there. You're a clever woman, I'll give you that." Marta smiled. "If I find out you've been lying to me, I will be back. And I won't come empty-handed."

"Your threats mean nothing to me." The woman sighed. "I'm stuck here in this hellhole of a town, living next to that stinking army base. It can't get any worse than this."

Vasilli opened the door and waited for Marta to precede him from the room. "It can get worse," she turned and whispered. "I can make it worse for you."

They left, closing the door. Something shattered against it, startling the secretary sitting placidly at her computer, playing solitaire. She hit a key, and the game disappeared.

"I wouldn't go in there right away if I were you," Marta said. Kaderli's shout made the girl jump. Marta shrugged, smiled, and walked out to the sidewalk.

"Where is this Side?" Vasilli asked.

"On the coast. They might not be there yet; it's still early for summer homes. But we can look for the family in Antalya. That's the other address she has listed."

Back at the car, Marta spread a map on the roof. "Here we are, and this is Antalya, and this is Side."

"They're not so far," Vasilli commented.

"No, but the roads don't go straight between any of these points. So it's not that short a ride. If we go to Antalya, we can probably get there before dark. Are you game?"

"You sure you don't want me to drive?"

She gave him a look of disgust as she refolded the map. "What's the matter? Does my driving make you nervous?"

"Not yours, just everyone else's."

When he opened the car door, Vasilli checked the back.

"Brother Adam is gone," he announced.

"Well, I hope he finds a new home," Marta said. She slid into the driver's seat, waiting while Vasilli removed his jacket, loosened the striped tie, and climbed in. He adjusted the seat, took the map, and placed a pair of sunglasses on the tip of his nose.

"Let's move." He was asleep before they reached the bottom of the mountain. Marta, lulled by the sound of his snoring, turned on the radio and hummed along with the noise that emanated from the tinny speakers.

A smell, captured on a soft breeze that wafted through the open windows, caused her to inhale deeply. "Eucalyptus."

A scent memory filled her thoughts. *Late at night, when everyone was sleeping, the shimmer of a breeze loosened the eucalyptus trees. It was summer when the baby was born. The trees were in full leaf, and the smell floated on the top of every breeze. Behind the smell of manure, the oily industrial spew during the day, the diesel belch of the trucks and busses passing on the main corridor through town, you could pick it out. At night, when the other scents were cleared away, the sound and smell of the eucalyptus soothed you to sleep.*

It was the only pleasant time, when they left Marta alone. The baby was sleeping, usually with her aunt, "so she'll get used to me." But on this night, she was in Marta's room. There was no explanation. Marta was awake, and she could hear that the baby was too, but not crying; that would bring her aunt running for sure. She was just making baby noises, sucking and cooing, moving around in her tight little bundle.

Marta had tried to object to that, binding up the baby, but she was overruled. Weak from the loss of blood and afraid of her uncle's murderous looks, she kept quiet. But that night, Marta crept to the basket and loosened the blankets until the baby's legs kicked free. In the dusky light, Marta believed that she saw a smile. She took her daughter into her arms.

Nazlan ground her head into Marta's neck. Marta cupped her in the palm of her hands; she was that small. She was strong, though, pushy. She grunted and gave Marta a good kick in the abdomen—thirsty, perhaps.

Marta was not allowed to breast-feed. Her aunt announced, "No sense in starting that nonsense. Formula will do just fine." Her chest ached and leaked a bit when the baby cried. Aunt made Marta tie her breasts with cloth. "Better for you, not to let the milk come down."

Too late, Aunt, Marta had thought as she brought the baby to bed, loosened the constraints, and placed the child at her breast. She gummed around, getting red in the face, until Marta pushed the nipple at her and she latched on. What a feeling. It came straight from her empty womb, the baby pulling and drinking. This was what Marta needed, to feed her child. In the moonlight, the softness of the baby's skin against her own, caressed by the smell of eucalyptus on the soft breeze, they bonded.

Marta fed her until she slept and then checked her little diaper and placed her back in the basket. In the morning, seeing the baby's legs loose and Marta's dreamy face, Aunt decided it was time for her to leave.

"You're all healed up now. Best be going. Best for everyone if you leave now." She wouldn't let Marta touch the baby again. "Best not to. Best be going."

When she walked away from the house, knees shaking with every step, Aunt threw a pail of water across the steps and sidewalk. Uncle's slap reverberated, and Marta turned around.

"You cow," he shouted at his wife. "You only throw water when you want the traveler to return safely." He pushed Aunt into the house where the baby was crying, shut the door, and looked at Marta. "Keep moving, slut," he said. He kicked dirt over the bright spot the water had made. "Keep walking. You're not welcome here anymore."

Marta could hear the baby's squalls as she turned and walked away. Milk dripped through the fabric around her chest. Her heart beat so violently that Marta was certain she would die. It did not slow until she was on a bus headed to Istanbul, first stop on her trip into exile.

The breeze carried different scents as Marta and Vasilli traveled south toward the Mediterranean Sea—some unpleasant farm smells, the occasional cooking odor, and, when they drew closer, the unmistakable scent of the sea. Awake now, Vasilli exclaimed over the extraordinary blue on the horizon as they approached the shore.

The Sheraton in Antalya sat on the edge of a sparkling bay filled with colorful fishing boats, yachts, and the mix of people belonging to both. Strolling tourists, vendors, high-end stores, restaurants, and tour buses, all vied for attention and space on crowded roads and sidewalks. Marta pulled into the driveway, road weary and hungry for something more substantial than tea and *simit*. After showers, a change of clothes, and a brief perusal of the phone book, the pair set off to find a fish dinner that both could enjoy without fear of familial tinkering.

The evening was crystal clear, the waters calm. Marta found it hard to relax, however, as she inspected the face of every young woman who passed by their table. Vasilli held her hand and tried to distract her, but she had shut out his attention.

"Hey, are you in there?" he said. "Talk to me. Don't go all intense on me again."

"I'm sorry." She forced a smile. "I'm just tired and nervous. What if we don't find her? What if she's left the family already? I'll never know. I won't be able to trace her after this. Now that we've come this close, if I lose her, I don't know."

"So we keep looking. We don't know if she's gone. Don't think the worst. I can see you going into protective lawyer mode again. Don't be that way." She attempted a smile.

The noise of a drum attracted the attention of everyone on the street. A small brown bear, lead by a frayed rope around her neck, was dancing on her hind legs to the ragged beat. The drummer stopped, picking a lively rhythm, while the boy holding the rope loosened his grip and allowed the bear to pirouette for the gathering crowd. They applauded; the boy removed his hat and passed it through the audience.

"Barbaric," Vasilli commented.

"You should see what they do with dogs and cats," Marta agreed. "But it's almost impossible to stop them. They live outside of the law." The drumbeat moved down the street, and the crowd dispersed.

"You want to try another fortune-teller?" he asked.

"Nope. I think I'll take my chances with reality," Marta said. "Let's get some rest before starting the search for this guy, Mr. Haluk Sejattin."

In the morning, Vasilli once again attempted to navigate while Marta drove the narrow streets. Once they found the number, they sat parked at the gate and looked up at the house. Vasilli emitted a low whistle. "This is the kind of place that should be a hotel, not a private home," he commented.

"There's probably a place in Istanbul, too, and the beach house," Marta added. "Whatever he does, this guy makes a good living." She sighed, looking at the surrounding houses. "I just hope he's kept his hands off my daughter."

"One step at a time," Vasilli said. "Let's see if she's here before we go accusing anyone of anything."

"So, I guess we just go to the front door and ask for her. The direct approach."

He nodded toward the gates, which were clanking open. A late model, low-slung Mercedes appeared, driven by a young man in a business suit. The gates closed. He never gave them a second glance.

"Well, at least we know the man of the house is out of the way." Vasilli opened his door. "Coming?"

She followed him, hissing. "What's your plan?"

He pressed the buzzer at the gate and turned to her, smiling. "Watch and learn."

After it was quickly established that the visitor had no Turkish and the respondent had no English, the intercom went dead. "Well, that was brilliant," Marta said.

"Wait."

She paced, as he leaned casually against the gate. Something banged and then footsteps approached the gate. He nodded at Marta. "Now it's your turn. We're new to the neighborhood, you're looking to hire an au pair, whatever story you like," he said. "Or the truth, even, might be appropriate here."

A middle-aged woman, dressed in a black uniform with a white apron, approached the gate. She started talking quickly in Turkish, before even arriving within range, waving her arms in a parody of "shoo." When she saw them, she looked from one to the other and then said, *"Git."*

"Pardon," Marta began, speaking just as rapidly as the maid. She shook her head during Marta's entire speech but then stopped abruptly.

"Hayır," she said finally. She put her hands in the air and then shook her head vigorously.

"Is she here?" Vasilli asked.

"I'm not sure. She seems to be afraid to talk about the staff. I guess they've had a few girls over the years. But she's curious, I can tell. Let me try another thing." Marta leaned toward the woman and whispered, "She's about fifteen now, looks like me, I would guess, pretty smart too. Right? She's probably good with the kids, quiet around the adults."

The woman nodded, in spite of herself.

"I don't want to harm her. I just want to make sure she's okay, and then I'll leave her alone. I won't disturb anybody. Just let me see her—from a distance. She doesn't have to even know I'm there. You're a mother, right?" Another nod, slower this time. "So you know how I feel. I've come so far. I just want to know that she is safe. If she's fine and she's happy, I'll leave her be, I promise."

Marta put her hands together in supplication. The woman looked at her and then at Vasilli before responding. "Who's the old man?"

Marta laughed, translated, and replied. "A friend. He's here to help me." The woman raised her eyebrows and then led them around to the back of the house, a service entrance hidden by the massive stucco columns and shrubbery. "Wait here."

In the shadow of the house, Marta shivered. Vasilli draped an arm around her. "I'm glad you went with the truth," he said. "It's usually the best choice."

Thrusting a folded newspaper into her hand, the woman began shooing Marta and Vasilli away from the house. *"Git, git,"* she said. "Go, go."

Marta held up the paper. "What is this?"

"Look inside, the address is written in there. Not here—take it with you. That's where they are, the mistress and the children. Already gone to the beach, getting the house ready for the summer. He's going on the weekend. Now go. I can't talk to you anymore. And don't tell anyone where you got that address, or I'll be fired. *Git!*"

"Let me give you something for your trouble, some money ..." Marta fiddled with her bag, but Vasilli pulled her back down the driveway.

"Let's go," he said. "There's probably a surveillance camera out here. She gave you the newspaper as a cover. Let's go."

Fifty-three

Vasilli drove back to the hotel; Marta's hands were shaking so she allowed him to take the wheel. Her cell phone rang just as they pulled into the driveway, and he took it from her.

"'Alo?" His face changed and darkened. Eyebrows pulled together, he said, "Stop! Be quiet. I won't listen. You ... I'm hanging up now. You may call me back when you are able to speak in a civil tone."

He handed the phone to Marta and then the keys to the valet. "Konstantin is back. Seems he's a little upset that I left town without his permission."

"I know it's easy for me to say, but try not to let him get to you," Marta said. She took his arm as they walked into the hotel.

"He doesn't ... much," Vasilli said. "But I'm going to teach this guy a thing or two. And besides, I have you to keep me grounded in reality. Right?"

She was about to reply when the phone trilled again. This time, she answered, "Yes? Are you prepared to speak respectfully to your uncle? All right then, I'll put him on."

Vasilli took the phone and sat by the window, loosening his tie and kicking off his shoes. Marta watched him, folding her clothes and packing them into her luggage.

"He's coming," she said when he disconnected the call.

"Yes. He asked me if we can sit down and talk about this ... about everything. He wants to know what I want. So he's coming. And he asked me to be here. Can you wait?" He looked pointedly at her bags, sitting by the door. "I want to go with you. I want to be there for you when you meet her. We can go first thing tomorrow, after I see him."

She shook her head. "I need to do this alone. I hope you understand. I've got to go find her, and when I do, I need to face her alone." She stood in front of him, her hands on his shoulders. "Such a dear, sweet man. I'll be

254

all right, you know. I'm going to take my time and see what happens. But I have to go. And you have to stay and work things out with Konstantin. You have to take your proper place in the family. If I'm here, I'll be in the way of that. He has to accept you, and I seem to offend him just by being in the room. Don't you see? Some things we have to face alone. We came this far together, and I appreciate everything you've done for me." She kissed him lightly on the cheek and then moved toward the door. "We'll meet again, maybe here or maybe back in Istanbul. Hopefully, the next time I see you, I won't be alone."

"You're never going to be alone," he said huskily. "I'll always be with you."

"I know, and if you need me, you can always call. Don't forget to recharge your cell phone," she said. "I'll keep in touch." And she was gone.

The Turkish coast, like much of the Mediterranean, is full of exquisite little towns perched along the rocky shore. The road from Antalya, weaving in and out along the coast, presented another challenging ride for Marta, her impatience growing with each passing mile. Two lanes served slow-moving delivery trucks, tourist-laden buses, and passenger cars blending in and out, drivers jockeying to shave a few seconds off their journeys. No one respected the "no passing" signs, and the more daring chose to make their moves on short-vision curves. Everyone used their horns, Marta included. It was the only way to be sure that you were recognized as a player on the road. She stopped for a break at Manavgat, where spring water from the mountains gathered and gushed over a waterfall practically leaping with trout. A restaurant seated diners so close that their glasses and shoes were misted with the cool spray.

Marta felt nervous, and yet, deep inside, she was becoming calmer the closer she came to her destination. *I should have made this trip years ago,* she thought. *I should have checked on the girl and taken her out of the hellish situation before it got out of control.* She'd closed the door on her family, and she was starting to realize that she was also a loser in that equation. If only she'd known about her mother, if only she'd realized her uncle was unstable, if only— She shook her head. As wrong as her refusal to look back for the past fifteen years was, it was worse to start playing the "what if" game now. *Everyone chooses,* she thought. *Now I have to do what I can to salvage this.*

There was only one road to Side, a small town on a little peninsula, surrounded by incredibly white, sandy beaches. Side was the former home of pirates, the center of slaving activity. It was resettled by Cretans when the Greeks expelled their Muslim population in the 1920s. A new breed of pirate, the young and ruthless entrepreneur, ruled the compounds now. There were lots of towns like this one along the Mediterranean and Aegean shorelines. Every village had a ruin or two, its ancient battle scars and rivalries, with a history so deep it was imprinted on the DNA of every breathing creature, from the scorpion to the human.

Marta pulled into a Turk Petrol station, gassed up, and asked for a map. Studying it, she smiled at the rack of *Nesrettin Hoja* books. One in Greek caught her eye, and she bought it for Vasilli, even though he claimed ignorance of the written language.

Luckily, there was a *pension* just a few doors away from the address she had been given by the Sejattin family servant. Checking in, she refused the offer of a meal and headed directly to the beach. Boulders blocked access to the area behind the Sejattin house. Wading into the shallows, Marta tried to look nonchalant as she inspected the house. She saw workers in the back removing winter shutters and washing down furniture, but there was no sign of children or their au pair.

Eventually, she decided to check out the surrounding beaches. She found a small patio with rickety tables behind a mid-level hotel, decided it was a good place to get the lay of the land, and ordered some tea. Her bag, with a towel, some sunscreen, and a paperback, was slung casually across the adjoining seat, to discourage any companions. She walked a bit up and down the shoreline looking at the faces of all the teenaged girls and was disappointed by her survey. After an hour, she moved to the next beach, repeated the exercise, and then tried another.

By the time the sun was dipping low in the sky, Marta was cranky, hot, and discouraged. Back in her patio seat, Marta listened to the music playing from overhead speakers and took in the smell of roasted meat competing with the tang of lemon cologne and something else, something she remembered from beach visits years ago and since then whenever she had the misfortune to be handed someone's child to admire: baby oil. That scent drove her to collect her belongings and begin the long trek back to her *pension*.

When she returned to her room, she called Vasilli. He seemed distant, quiet. "Is Konstantin there?" she asked. "With you right now?"

He answered, "Yes," and she smiled, thinking of how he'd be nodding slowly too.

"So you can't talk to me now. I get it. Well, I'm here. I found the address, but the house looks pretty quiet. I spent the afternoon trolling the local beaches, but I didn't see anyone who looked like, well, like me. I haven't any idea if she's even here, but tomorrow, I'll start early and keep looking."

Silence, then he replied, "That sounds good."

"Listen, don't let him get to you, okay? Call me later if you wish. I'll be here."

"Tomorrow sounds fine with me," he said.

"All right, I'll call you in the morning. Don't let him keep you up all night, you hear me?" The line went dead. "Dammit," she said. She plugged in the cell phone and watched the charger light up.

Although she thought there was no way she'd rest, sleep came quickly, and when she rolled over, the windows were already bright with the new day. Pausing only for a quick shower, she slathered sunscreen on pink, tender shoulders and headed out again. Walking in the opposite direction from her previous explorations, she found a prime seat on the beach. This one was more promising—few tourists were among the Turkish families that arrived and rapidly filled the sand. The water was startling, blue and beckoning. She walked for an hour and then returned to her perch, watching, hopeful. Her calls to Vasilli went unanswered, and her unease about him added to the knots in her stomach as she waited anxiously for a sign that her daughter was nearby.

She took a lunch break, walking into the small downtown in search of a café. Passing the large walls that screened the Sejattin house from the street, Marta was startled when the gates opened and a car nosed out into the street. A young woman with blond hair and designer sunglasses was screeching at the two children wrestling in the backseat. No sign of an au pair—perhaps she had given the girl an afternoon of liberty. Marta hustled back to the beach and resumed her vigil.

Around two, a group of teenage girls appeared, four or five coltish creatures, all long legs and flat chests, bikinied and shy. Marta watched them, but she was too far away to see their faces. She gathered her bag, threw the towel casually over her shoulder, and sauntered along the beach, coming to rest just twenty feet from their encampment.

She spread out the towel, removed her long shirt, and sat down to apply more sunscreen. She felt them watching as she lay down, closing her eyes against the bright sun. It was hot. She couldn't remember the last time she'd been half naked at a beach. After what seemed like hours but was really only fifteen minutes, she stood up, walked to the water, and slowly picked her way into the sea. It was icy against her overheated skin. She shivered, turned back, and saw the girls heading in her direction. She turned around and dove in, began swimming hard, and felt a current ripple nearby. One of the girls passed her and then turned, laughing.

"Sorry if I splashed you," she said, before disappearing under the next wave.

Marta treaded water for a few minutes and then returned to shore. By the time she was back on her towel, the girls had also come out of the water. They walked past her, chattering, looking at her and smiling. She pulled a brush from her bag and started to work the snarls from her hair. The rhythmic brushing soothed her nerves. She dropped the brush, twisted her hair into a knot, and secured it with a single tortoise clip.

She was strangely calm, her movements becoming slow and hypnotic. She felt that one of the girls looked familiar. *She looks familiar because she looks like me,* Marta thought. She took some deep breaths and watched them.

The girl she figured might be her daughter towered above the other girls. Marta was pleased to see that the girl stood straight and tall, not hunched over like she had been at that age. Her long, skinny legs were just starting to fill out, and the knees still looked knobby. Marta smiled as she watched the girl rush gawkily into the sea, emerging dripping and spitting, running to shower the burning salt water from her sunburned skin. She stood for several minutes under the frigid water and untangled her long hair with a bright pink comb.

They slathered baby oil all over each other. Marta felt their eyes on her, just as she had been watching them. When she packed up her things, she deliberately left the expensive sunblock in the sand. She moved to the small café nestled under the shade of the pine trees, settled into a chair, and signaled for tea. When she looked back at the girls, they were examining the lotion and arguing. The girl—dare she call her Nazlan?—stood up and looked around, shading her eyes. She spotted Marta, took the bottle, and waved it in her direction. *An honest child,* Marta thought, as she held up her hand and shook her head. She was not ready to have an encounter with her, but the girl wrapped a towel around her waist and approached the table. Marta's heart began to pound. A bead of sweat rolled down her back.

Nazlan was thin and delicate, still awaiting the curves that would come in time. Marta recognized her in a visceral way and tried to steady her breathing. She had only seen the girl from a distance, and when she walked up to the table, Marta was startled by their resemblance. She flushed and wondered why no one else could see it. Looking at her darkly lashed eyes in the girl's face, Marta smiled a greeting that masked her fear. Nazlan had the same bone structure, green eyes, and heavy chestnut hair. Marta also recognized Mehmet's eyebrows arching in a familiar quizzical way over her face.

"You forgot this," Nazlan said, holding the bottle toward Marta.

"Oh, that's all right," Marta said. "You keep it. It's better for you than the baby oil."

Nazlan studied Marta's face for a moment, and once again, Marta felt light-headed. "Have you been using this cream for a long time?" the girl asked. "You have such young skin."

Marta smiled. "How old do you think I am?" Before Nazlan could answer, Marta continued, "The sun makes you wrinkle, you know. You should protect yourself if you want to keep your beautiful complexion."

Marta saw that she was flattered by the compliment. Still breathless at this encounter, Marta fumbled for something else to say. She had only planned to watch from a distance and felt unprepared for this conversation. Her hands trembled, and she clutched the tea glass nervously. Nazlan looked again at the bottle, hesitating.

"Are you sure you don't need it?" she asked.

"No, I have plenty," Marta replied. She took a breath and took the plunge. "So, do you live here? Or are you on vacation?"

"Oh, I am here with the family I work for," Nazlan said. "We stay here all summer. *Bayan* Sejattin said I could take the afternoon off, so I met up with my friends from last year and came down here." She turned as if to leave but then stopped. "Where are you from?"

Marta was caught off guard by the question and covered by sipping at her tea again. Before she could answer, Nazlan continued, "Your Turkish, it's different," she said. She fingered a piece of hair unconsciously, and Marta was charmed by her direct and observant manner.

"I have been living in New York for a long time," Marta said. "I guess my Turkish is a bit rusty." Nazlan nodded, thanked Marta again for the lotion, and skipped back to her friends.

For a long time, Marta sat watching the group absently. She remembered the first time she saw her daughter. On the day she was born, when Marta held her, the baby had grasped her finger with her own perfect hand. Marta had looked hard into the girl's clear eyes and willed her to remember her mother. She had traced the fine hairs around Nazlan's face with a light touch. Fifteen years later, Marta yearned to hold her again and felt an acute emptiness for all the years she had missed. She put on her sunglasses to cover the tears.

Marta dialed Vasilli again, left a message that she had found the girl, and asked him to call her. She replayed the conversation over and over. Nazlan had a lovely, melodic voice, and Marta wondered if she had inherited any musical ability from her father. The waiter refilled her teacup, pausing to watch the girls on the blanket below. Marta gave him a look that sent him scurrying away. She drank the scalding liquid and allowed herself to fantasize about spending time with Nazlan. She watched and waited.

The girls walked down the beach and returned laughing. Marta watched them try to twist their hair into the same style as hers, and only Nazlan was able to copy it. Marta smiled at that. She was certain then that she would find a way to have a relationship with this girl.

Marta fingered the soft pages of the *Blue Guide*, which she had placed in her bag. She pulled it out, looked at it, and put it back. Was it too soon? She placed it on the table and was interrupted by the waiter returning with a plate of cheese toast. Tucking her wallet away, she was startled by the shadow across her table.

"I am Nazlan." The girl stood with her hand on the back of a chair. With a quizzical expression that quickly turned to alarm, she reached for the blue book. Her green eyes were direct and steady when she looked up at Marta.

"Is this yours? I used to have one just like it," Nazlan said.

Marta swallowed hard and moved her hand toward the book, but the girl picked it up and flipped through the pages. Her eyes grew wide, and she looked alarmed.

"This is mine. Who are you, and how did you get my book?" she demanded. She crossed her arms. "Well?" she huffed.

"Please, sit down. I'll answer your questions," Marta said. "If you look here, in the front, you'll see my name ... see, here it is. Someone must have erased it, but you can still see it. I had this book when I was preparing to go to New York, about fifteen years ago." Marta pushed the book across the table, and the girl lifted it up, peering closely at the faded signature on the title page.

Marta signaled the waiter to bring another cup of tea and then nudged the chair with her foot. "Please, sit." When Nazlan sat down, Marta said, "Your friend Zeynep gave this book to me when I went looking for you."

Nazlan rubbed her face and then picked up the book again.

"Can you please tell me who you are? Why were you looking for me? How do you know Zeynep?" she asked. She clutched the book to her chest and shivered. "Has something happened to my mother?"

"No, *Tezze*—ah, your mother—is fine," Marta replied.

"Is she your aunt?"

"Yes, she's my mother's half sister."

"So you're my cousin," Nazlan said. Her shoulders relaxed a bit. "But why would you come looking for me? I don't even know you."

Marta reached across the table. "I'm sorry. I know you must be confused." She paused. "Look, there's no easy way to tell you ... I'm not your cousin. I'm your mother."

The girl pulled her hand away. "No," she said.

"I'm so sorry. I don't know any other way to tell you this. I know it's a shock. I was young when I got pregnant, and I couldn't take care of you, and so my mother made me give you to her sister. She couldn't have children of her own, and so ... I ... I hope you can forgive me and give me a chance to explain—"

Nazlan stood up abruptly and backed away from the table.

"I need to go. I can't listen to you anymore," she said. Marta watched as the girl ran back to her friends.

Marta sat back in her chair and watched the group pack up their gear. Nazlan shook her head when one of them reached over to her. The other girls stole glances at Marta, but Nazlan steadily avoided her gaze. Marta flipped the phone open when they left, and Vasilli quickly replied.

"That didn't go well," she said, after describing their brief exchange.

"Give her time," he urged. "She'll be back."

She sighed. "I don't know. I think maybe I shouldn't have told her right off … Oh well, it's done." She sighed. "Tell me about Konstantin."

"Well, I finally met his sister. My niece," Vasilli said. "She's a live one. No wonder he wanted to keep us apart."

"Really? In what way?"

"She's a spoiled brat. That's the only way to put it. Covered in jewelry, with a milquetoast husband waiting on her hand and foot. She could care less about the business, and her only interest in me is apparently making sure that I won't be taking anything away from her and her children," he said. "She was totally charming, you can imagine. What a cast of characters in this family!"

"It is so interesting to see what money does to people," Marta agreed. There was a long silence. "So," she said slowly.

"So."

"What are your plans?" she asked.

"I don't really know, to tell you the truth," he said. "What about you? What's your next step?"

"I think I wait," she said. "If she comes back and she agrees, I'd like to bring her back to New York with me … but first, she has to come back. So I'll wait and see."

"Yes, that makes sense." He sneezed twice.

"Are you getting sick?"

"Nah, it's just allergies," he said. "That damned cat." He blew his nose. "Do you want me to come down there?" he asked.

"No. I'm going to sit tight. She knows where to find me, and I think she'll come around. She's curious. I think she was waiting her whole life for this, and now she's got to decide what to do." She smiled. "I saw her copying my hairdo. Before we spoke, I was watching her and her friends on the beach."

"Really?" He sounded skeptical. "What does that mean?"

"She's mine. She's going to be mine."

"And then what?" he asked softly.

There was another long silence. "I have no idea," she said. And then she laughed.

Fifty-four

The next day and the next, Marta sat at the beach and waited for Nazlan. She spoke with Vasilli several times a day, and each shared their frustrations with their situations. While he struggled to get Konstantin to trust him, Marta waited for Nazlan to return to the beach. Occasionally, she took a walk along the boulevard to make sure that the family was still in residence there, just to be sure that Nazlan had not left the resort community. From everything that she could see, it looked like the family had settled in for the summer. Unfortunately, she could not tell if Nazlan was still with them.

By the third day, Marta was certain that she had spoken too soon and scared the young girl away. She purchased a bestselling novel in the hotel gift shop and attempted to read it, but the legal thriller held no interest for her despite the fact that she had once actually met the author in a courtroom battle years earlier.

After a lunch of toast and tea, she returned to the shore and lay in the sun. *It's hopeless,* she thought. *I may as well go home and try to save my career.* She groaned, reached for the sunscreen, and noticed a shadow falling over her legs.

"Merhaba," Nazlan said. "Hello."

Marta squinted, attempting to shade her eyes with her hand.

"Hi," she said.

Nazlan moved a bit and blocked the sun so that Marta could see her.

"Hi," Marta said again. "I'm glad to see you. I was afraid—"

"I needed to think," Nazlan said. "I needed some time."

Marta sat up, patting the towel next to her. "Sit," she offered. The girl dropped gracefully onto the towel.

"It's my fault," Marta said. "I shouldn't have told you everything all at once like that. I was just so excited to finally see you."

"It's okay, really," Nazlan said. "It was kind of sudden. But seeing you with my book, it was very … unexpected. And then, when you said … when you said …"

"When I told you that I was your mother," Marta said.

"Yes, that." Nazlan smiled. "I couldn't take it in. I had to think."

"I understand."

The sun was beating on the sand, raising the temperature sharply while the two continued their halting conversation. "Should we move to the shade?" Marta asked.

Nazlan nodded, stood up quickly, and turned to offer Marta her hand. She smiled when the older woman grasped it firmly, and together they walked into the shade. Marta slipped into her sheer cover-up and sat opposite Nazlan, her back to the sea.

"So, where were we?" Marta asked. "I know. You had to think, I understand. You can ask me anything," she said. "I mean it. I know you must have a million questions, so go ahead. Ask."

Nazlan ducked her head shyly. "I do have questions." She took a deep breath. "Who is my father? Where did you go after I was born? Why didn't you ever come back, or call, or write? How did you find me now? Why?" She held her elbows and took a deep breath. "I'm sorry, but I want to know. I need to know everything."

"Please don't apologize. I'm the one who should be apologizing. And I do, I am so very sorry for all that you have had to live through. I never, ever thought that this would happen to you," Marta said. "So, to begin at the beginning, I met your father when we were both in law school in Istanbul."

"Did you love him?" Nazlan asked, leaning across the table.

"Oh yes, I did. And I think he loved me, too. But his family did not approve of our marriage …"

"You were married?" Nazlan asked.

"No, I … well, we were going to be engaged … I had a ring … but his mother …"

"What was his name?" Nazlan interrupted eagerly.

"His name was Mehmet," Marta said. "We were in love, and I was very happy, but things did not work out."

"I don't understand," Nazlan said.

The waiter, by now familiar with Marta's drink preferences, brought over two cups of tea and some sugar cubes.

"Anything else?" he asked. Both women shook their heads.

"Times were different then, and my father … well, it would take a long time to tell you about my father, but for now, let me just say that my father is

Laz, and he didn't, well, he didn't take it very well when Mehmet's mother refused to agree to the marriage. My father—"

"I know," Nazlan said. "I know about your father. I heard stories all the time, things that my father, er, would say about your family."

"I'm sorry about that," Marta said, warming her hands on the tea. "Oh, I am sorry about so many things—"

"We can't go back," the girl said wisely. "I wish we could, but I survived it. I always felt like I didn't belong to them, but then I thought that it was probably just wishful thinking. In some ways, I'm just grateful to know that I was right."

"You are so much smarter than I was at your age," Marta said. "I wish I had been stronger. I wish I could have kept you, but I thought the only thing I could do was run. I thought you would be okay with them. I am so sorry."

Nazlan got up abruptly. "I need to go. I told *Bayan* Sejattin that I would just be gone for a few minutes ... I can meet you later, after I put the kids to bed. Maybe around 8:00?"

"Of course," Marta said. "I'll wait for you on the street across from the house."

Nazlan smiled and started to leave the café.

"Wait!" Marta yelled. Nazlan turned toward her expectantly.

"What kind of contract do you have with this family?" Marta asked.

"I ... I don't know," Nazlan said thoughtfully. "I just went where the agency told me to go. I never knew the details."

"Do you get paid?"

"I do, mostly just a couple of lira here and there for 'expenses,' clothes and things, you know? They said something about sending me to school, but that was only at the beginning, and I can't remember them bringing it up in the past year or so." She scratched the back of one leg with the opposite foot. "Why do you ask?"

It was Marta's turn to hesitate. "I was just wondering ... if you are allowed to leave or if you owe them a certain time or anything like that."

Now Nazlan smiled as she practically skipped away. "See you later," she called over her shoulder.

Marta waved back. "Yes, see you later," she said, mostly to herself.

She returned to her room, showered, and changed. Several hours of waiting faced her, so she booted up her laptop and tried to discover the requirements for Turkish passports and U.S. visas. After finding several dead ends, she jotted some notes and closed the computer without even checking her e-mail. At six, she ordered room service and placed a call to Vasilli. He did not answer the phone. *He's probably enjoying cocktails with Konstantin,* she thought.

By seven thirty, she was pacing her room and decided to begin the short walk to their meeting place. Nazlan was already there, wearing a pair of blue jeans pressed into sharp creases and a loose white shirt tucked casually into the low-slung pants.

"Hey, you're early," Nazlan exclaimed.

"And so are you." Marta accepted the younger woman's arm through hers. "I couldn't wait. How did you get out early?" she asked.

"Oh, the family decided to go out for dinner together, so I was excused," Nazlan explained. "I told them I wanted to go to bed early."

They walked toward the bustling port area, sidewalks filled with café tables and cajoling waiters trying to attract patrons. "Let's sit," Marta suggested. "Would you like a cola? Something else?"

There was a brief and uncomfortable silence after their orders were placed and the two women once again faced each other across the table.

"I know I didn't answer all of your questions this afternoon," Marta said. "And I promise that I will. I just want you to know that I want to make things right now. I want to take care of you and make sure you get an education and whatever else you want to do. I know it's presumptuous of me, but I want you to know that I intend to make up for lost time. I want to take you back to New York with me, if you are willing to go."

"But I—" Nazlan interrupted.

"Sorry. Maybe you don't want to leave … It's just that I read some of the things you wrote in the book and I thought—"

"Would you let me talk?" Nazlan burst out. "Of course, you know more about me than I know about you. It's not fair, really, but I get it. So you want to come in and save me … I get that too. It's just a lot to take in, you know?"

"Yes, I know, and I am sorry."

"You need to stop apologizing too," Nazlan said. "I don't know what you know, but my life was okay up until a couple of years ago. My dad got all weird when he saw me wearing a bathing suit, and then *Anne* freaked out, and things got kind of crazy. I don't really know why, but she threw him out and then she started following me around. And one day, I came home, and she had packed all my bags. So I was sent to the monastery and trained to be a babysitter … and I ended up with this family. It happened pretty quick, and I never had the chance to go back, so I never really understood why." She paused. "Do you know why she sent me away?"

Marta nodded. "I think so. From what I could understand, your mother was afraid that your father found you … attractive … and when you started growing up, she thought that he might try to … you know, do something to you. So she sent him away. But I think she maybe went a little crazy then, and she ended up sending you away, too."

Nazlan looked confused. Marta continued, "You're a very pretty girl, and I think that your mom was afraid that, well, that your father might think of you in the wrong way."

Nazlan shook her head slowly. "She's okay, right? You said she was all right."

"Yes," Marta said. "I saw her, and she is okay. In fact, I was thinking that we should go back there together. What do you think?"

"Are you going to leave me there again?" Nazlan said.

"No. I wouldn't do that—unless that is what you want." She smiled. "I was hoping that you might want to come back to New York with me. But first, we would have to get your birth certificate and other papers. Most of them are with *Tezze* … your mother."

Nazlan smiled. "Okay," she said. "Let's start with that."

"Okay," Marta replied.

"Um, I need to know something," Nazlan said. "I need to know about my father. I mean, I get that he couldn't marry you, but didn't he ever ask, you know, about me?"

"Oh, baby, I am sorry. I never told him about you. He left, and I tried to contact him, but I couldn't find him and so I never got the chance to tell him that I was pregnant."

Nazlan frowned. "So he doesn't even know that I exist?"

"No. I used to think that if he knew, he would have come for me—for us—and we would have been together. But he disappeared. I guess his family sent him away, and my father was so angry that I had to get out of Istanbul too," Marta explained. "My father wanted to kill me, said I had ruined the family name, so my mother sent me to her sister. And then—after you were born, she put me on a plane to New York."

"You never came back?" Nazlan asked.

"No." Marta sipped her coffee. "I did find out, maybe a year later, that Mehmet had joined the army. That's all I know."

"Can you tell me about him? What was he like?"

Marta looked away. "It's not easy. I can see him in your face and hear him in your voice."

Nazlan smiled. "More."

"I will tell you everything you want to know, but first, I need to ask you. Are you willing to come with me to see your … your mother?" Marta asked. "What do you think?"

Nazlan's smile evaporated. "Yes, I want to go home."

"Home?"

"Yes, to see *Anne*, to hear her tell me this too. I need to give her a chance to tell me all of this too," Nazlan said. "I don't know you. How do I know that you are telling me the truth? I need to hear it from my own mother. So yeah, I want to go with you. As soon as we can."

"Fair enough," Marta said. "We'll go see her tomorrow."

Fifty-five

The following day was filled with joy as well anxiety for Marta. She arrived promptly at 8:00 AM at the front gate of the Sejattin family home, introduced herself to the man of the house, and explained her intention to remove Nazlan from their service. After handing over her business card (the Turkish version, inscribed with high-quality ink and paper), Marta quickly negotiated an agreement that would rescind their contract and release Nazlan into her care.

When they walked away from the house, Nazlan was quiet, her jaw tense and her eyes wide. "Thank you," she stammered.

"Are you okay? I know you must be frightened." Marta put a hand on the girl's shoulder. "I promise that I will not abandon you. Actually, I never did—you just didn't know it." They stopped to hail a cab. "For the past ten years, at least, ever since I got a good job in the city, I've been sending money for you. It's still sitting there, in the bank."

"What? Why? Why would she ... Why did they ...?" Nazlan drew away from Marta, pushing herself into the corner of the cab's backseat. "Why would she take the money and not tell me about it?" she asked.

"I asked the same thing when I went there. Your mother ... well, she didn't trust anyone. She buried the papers in the backyard—I saw them. I know the money was never touched. It's still sitting there, for you."

Nazlan shook her head. "It's all too much," she said softly. "I don't understand."

Marta patted her knee. "We'll sort it out. Hopefully your mother will be able to explain things to you."

"What do you mean? Of course she'll tell me," Nazlan said.

"Your mother, she's not well. I don't want to alarm you, but she seems to have become very paranoid and delusional. She tried to shoot me when I first showed up at the house, and she was not entirely rational when I was speaking to her ..." Marta said.

269

Nazlan frowned. She looked out the window. "And then what?" she asked. "What are you thinking?"

"Well, we'll get your birth certificate, and we'll get you a visa. And once we're in New York, we'll get your school records, and then we'll see about getting you into a decent school." She looked at Nazlan. "How's your English? I think it's pretty good, based on what I read in the *Blue Guide*. What do you think?"

"So you want to take me to New York with you? Just like that?" She exhaled loudly, puffing her cheeks in thought. "Hmmm. Well, I think … I think I can learn very fast. I haven't used my English much, but I can remember some things." Nazlan looked out the window again. "Where are we going now?"

"Oh, to my *pension*," Marta replied. "I have a rental car there, and after I check out, we'll head to your mother's—to my aunt's house."

"Can we … can you give her some money too?" Nazlan asked. She started to cry. "I don't know what to do. How can I just leave her? She can't take care of herself."

"That's what I thought, but apparently, she's very clever. She's managed for the past couple of years, and well, we'll see what we can do when we get there. I did offer her money …"

They arrived at the hotel, where Marta paid the cabbie and settled her bill. The rental car was driven to the front, her suitcases neatly stacked in the back. They placed Nazlan's rucksack in the trunk next to Marta's bags.

"Let's go," Marta said. Nazlan was a quiet passenger, and Marta allowed the sound of the radio to fill the space between them. *It's a lot to process*, she thought, and she did not want to push the girl. She smiled then, giddy at the thought that her daughter was sitting in the vehicle next to her.

"Why are you smiling?" Nazlan asked.

"I can't believe you are here," Marta said. "I can't believe this is happening."

"Neither can I," the girl replied soberly.

Marta reached out and stroked the girl's arm. "I know this is a lot. I know it. We're both going to have some adjusting to do—but I want you to know that I never stopped thinking about you, loving you, worrying about you, and wondering if I did the right thing by letting you go. Now I know it was a mistake, but it's not too late, is it?"

She pulled the car abruptly off the side of the road. Nazlan looked at her, eyes wide with fear and wonder.

"Look." Marta pulled the locket over her head. She opened it and held it out to the girl. "This is your hair. I took this little bunch when you were born, and I've kept it next to my heart for the last fifteen years. Does that mean anything to you?"

"How do I know it's mine?" Nazlan said stubbornly. "How do I know anything you have told me is true?"

"When we get to your mother's house, she'll tell you." Marta closed the locket and replaced it around her neck. She released the brake and eased the car back onto the highway. *You really are my daughter,* she thought proudly.

Marta's cell phone trilled after they had been on the road almost an hour.

"Answer it, would you?" she said to Nazlan. "Go ahead."

"'Alo?" she said. "It's a man, someone named Vasilli," she whispered.

"It's okay. You can talk to him," Marta urged. She listened to Nazlan's side of the conversation, imagining Vasilli's kind voice responding to the girl's questions. Her English was stilted, but she was understandable. After a few exchanges, Nazlan covered the receiver with her hand.

"Do you have anything you need to tell him?" she asked.

"I found my daughter, and I'm very happy," Marta said.

Nazlan repeated these words and then listened intently before disconnecting the call. "He seems like a nice man," she said. "He said to tell you that he's happy too, and he hopes to see you again soon. He said he's going to stay for a while, but he'll call you when he gets back to New York." She put the phone back in Marta's bag. "So, is he your boyfriend?" she asked.

Marta laughed. "No, although I think he'd like to be. I actually met him on the plane. We became friends over here. I helped him find his family, and he … well, he helped me find you."

"And they lived happily ever after," Nazlan announced in English, her accent more British than American.

"Where did you ever hear that?" Marta asked.

"In school, of course." Nazlan laughed.

"Of course," Marta said. "So, what grade did you finish?"

Nazlan frowned. "I finished three years of the secondary school. I was just starting to get ready for the university exams …"

"Don't worry. You're very bright. I'm sure you will make up the lost time very quickly. Do you think you might be interested in going to college in New York?"

"I could never think …" Nazlan hesitated and then changed the subject. "So, what do you do in New York?" she asked.

"I'm a lawyer," Marta said. "I was in Istanbul working on a case."

The traffic slowed around them, horns blaring. The cars slowed and came to a stop. Marta tried to see what was happening on the road ahead of them. She sighed and then turned to Nazlan.

"I thought I told you that I'm a lawyer," Marta said.

"Maybe. I don't remember," Nazlan said. "I just know …"

"What?" Marta asked. "What do you know?"

"I, uh, I'm glad you found me," Nazlan said blushing.

"Me, too." Marta grinned. "Me, too."

Fifty-six

Their smiles were quick to fade, however. When they arrived at the ramshackle cabin, both Marta and Nazlan cried out, "No!" The structure was gone, its remains a tumble of embers and ash. Nazlan ran to the neighbor's house while Marta picked through the wreckage, hoping she would not find any evidence that her aunt had perished there.

It was not much of a search, for there wasn't much left. On the stump where Vasilli had taken his tea, Marta saw the olive oil can, weighed down with a large rock. When she approached, she noticed something protruding from the ground: the rifle her aunt had carried throughout their visit. The papers were still safely in the can, Marta noticed, and there was a short note printed carefully on the back of a flyer about a shoe sale. It was addressed to Nazlan, but Marta scanned it quickly before the girl returned, breathless and agitated.

"Bayan Erden said that there was a fire two days ago. No one could stop it. It happened during the day, when all the men were gone," she said. She stopped to catch her breath, hands on her knees as her eyes scanned the area. "We need to call the hospital. She might be there. She might be hurt ..."

"No," Marta said, her hand resting lightly on the girl's shoulder. "She's all right. Look, she left you a note."

"Where did you find this?" Nazlan snatched the paper from Marta's hands.

"It was here, in the oil can, with your birth certificate and those bank papers I told you about," Marta explained. "She's okay, I'm telling you. Don't worry."

Nazlan had already started reading the short note. She stepped away from Marta, held the paper to her chest, and sobbed. "*Anne*, why?"

Marta waited a moment. "What does it say, *genim*? Read it to me."

"You were right; she is fine. She burned it. She burned down the house. She says, 'I have to start over, and so do you.' She says she loves me, but that she knows you will be a good mother to me." With another sob, she collapsed in a heap on the ground.

Marta wrung her hands together, uncertain of what she should do. *Should I touch her or leave her alone?* She thought. *What's the right thing to do?*

Nazlan looked up at her and wiped her eyes with one hand; the other clutched the note. Her face was smeared with soot. Marta handed her a tissue.

"I don't know what to say," she said.

Nazlan blew her nose heartily and then looked up at Marta again. "There's nothing to say," she said. She held up the letter. "This says it all."

Marta squatted next to the girl. Nazlan's tears had started again, and Marta idly patted her back. "Listen, she loves you. She always did what she thought was the best thing for you. She sent you away to protect you, and she knew that if you came back here to live, your life would be very, very hard. She wants you to have a chance at a better life. I know it feels bad, but this must have been a very hard thing for your mother to do. And she did it for you."

Nazlan hiccupped into the tissue, her sobs abating. "I know," she said. "It's just … it's just too much … all at once."

Marta stood up and pulled Nazlan to her feet. She lifted her chin and looked her in the eye. "You are strong, and you are smart, and you will survive this," she said. "And I'm here to make sure that you do."

Nazlan smiled reluctantly. "Can I have another tissue, please?" she asked.

Marta laughed and gave her the packet. "You can have whatever you need," she said. She looked around. "So, should we get out of here? I don't think there's anything else for us to do here, do you?"

Nazlan shook her head. "I guess not."

"Istanbul then?" Marta asked, placing her arm around Nazlan and turning the girl away from the ruins and toward the car.

"Istanbul," Nazlan said. "Let's go."

When they were in the car and underway again, Nazlan removed the papers from Marta's bag. She studied them silently.

"What do you see?" Marta asked.

"I have two birth certificates, one with you as my mother and another with the names of my parents."

"Hmm," Marta said. "I wonder why they bothered with the first one. It would have been so easy for them to register your birth without ever mentioning my name."

"Well, it looks like that's what they did," Nazlan said. "The one with your name is a photocopy ... yes, it's a photocopy—someone whited out their names and typed yours there. Why do you think she did that?"

"I think that's part of the message that she left you. She wanted you to know about me, and that was the only way she could tell you," Marta said.

They drove in silence for a while. The hum of the road and the heat of the midday sun was mesmerizing.

"Do you have any music in that bag?" Marta asked.

Nazlan pulled out an MP3 player and fiddled with the console. In a few minutes, music filled the car.

"What is this?" Marta asked.

"You like? It's Tarkan." Nazlan started singing along with the music. She had a lovely voice, and Marta's smile made her cheeks hurt.

The long ride was much shorter with the entertainment Nazlan provided. She not only sang along, at times acting out the verses with eyes closed and hands clasped over her heart, but she also provided a running commentary about the songs, the performers, and, after a while, life in general. Marta laughed and interjected the occasional question, but Nazlan required little prompting to continue her chatter for several hours. Although they stopped a few times for tea and bathroom breaks, neither was tired when the car approached the city.

"Where shall we stay?" Marta asked. "Do you have any preference? Anywhere you always wanted to go?"

Nazlan paused, her finger on her lower lip. "I don't know much about the city," she admitted. "I did read about the Pera Palas hotel. Wasn't it the place that Agatha Christie wrote about the Orient Express? Do you know it?"

"Yes." Marta laughed. "I've heard about that. But I never went there. So let's check it out."

The older hotel was in a bustling part of the city, and Marta lost her way several times, prompting Nazlan to laugh and point excitedly at street signs.

"There—go there," she said, pointing down to a busy intersection.

"I thought you didn't know Istanbul," Marta replied, maneuvering the car through a tangle of taxicabs. They narrowly missed being sideswiped by a bus, and both burst out laughing when the driver yelled at them.

"Let's pull over and try to ask for directions," Marta said after half an hour. "I know we've been past this mosque at least three times, so that makes us officially lost."

Nazlan leaned out the window and asked a few different people before one finally came to the curb in response. Gesturing wildly, he offered such complicated directions that finally, he pulled open the back door and jumped in the car.

"I'll take you there," he announced. "Drive."

Nazlan hung over the backseat, introducing herself and Marta to the red-faced man, who identified himself as Hidayet. He grabbed Marta's shoulder a couple of times, shouting in her ear when she should turn. At one intersection, he leaned forward and pressed the horn. She removed his hand and suggested that he calm down.

"You cannot drive this way in Istanbul," he said. "Your daughter knows. You must be fierce. Drive like a lion, not like a lamb." At the next turn, he clapped his hand. "Aha! See! There you are—the Pera Palas. Okay, I leave you now." He was out of the car before Marta came to a complete stop.

"Thank you." She waved out the window. Pulling up to the front of the hotel, she looked at Nazlan. "I think he's right—driving in this city is not for the faint of heart."

They entered the ornate hotel, overwhelmed by the history and grandeur of the place. They were quickly registered and escorted to their room. Marta was pleased to see her highly adaptive daughter slightly disarmed by the elaborate accommodations. Although she'd been living with a fairly wealthy family, Nazlan was appropriately awed by her new surroundings. She jumped on the bed while Marta tipped the bellman and closed the door.

"This is magical," Nazlan announced. "I have never even dreamed of such a place."

Marta joined her on the bed. Both lay on their backs staring at the flowers and carvings in the light fixture.

"Just wait, kid," Marta said. "We are going to have a great time together. I just know it."

She rolled to her feet and hoisted Nazlan's bag to the luggage rack. "This is all you have? Is there more, that the Sejattins are going to send along?"

"No. This is it. I mean ..." Nazlan hesitated. "I had some other clothes, sure, but I never brought much to the beach and really, it was mostly stuff that *Bayan* was getting rid of. Most of it didn't even fit me, but that's what I had so that's what I wore." She looked into the bag. "I'm sorry. I don't want you to be ashamed of me."

"No, I would never be ashamed. You're a beautiful girl. We'll just have to go shopping and pick up a few things for you. I understand there's a wonderful mall nearby," Marta said.

"Oh, I didn't mean that you should buy things for me. I don't want you to spend your money. Really, I am fine with what I have." Nazlan closed the bag hurriedly and shoved it by the door.

"Nonsense," Marta said. "I told you, there's money for your education and for whatever you need. Tomorrow, we'll go to the bank and then, we'll go shopping. But first, I need to make some calls to the consulate, to see about getting you a visa and a passport."

"Passport? I have one." Nazlan dug into her backpack and produced the document. "The family wanted me to be able to go with them when they traveled, so they got this for me. I never had a chance to use it. We were going to Italy in the fall …"

"Great," Marta said. "So all we need is a visa." She pulled out her cell phone and then tossed the hotel directory at Nazlan. "While I'm doing that, how about booking us for a couple of manicures in the spa downstairs? And you look like you could use a good haircut."

Nazlan smiled nervously, checking her hair in the mirror. "Really?" she asked. "I usually just trim it myself—"

"Today, we splurge," Marta announced. And so they did. Hours later, having been shampooed, massaged, trimmed, and pampered, the two returned to their room. There was a large parcel sitting in the middle of the double bed, its contents denting the lush duvet.

"What's this?" Nazlan picked up the box.

"Something for you," Marta said. "Open it."

The dress she had purchased while Nazlan was getting her hair styled was a cool linen shift in a flax color that highlighted the girl's golden tan. It fit perfectly, and she modeled in front of the mirror while Marta changed for dinner.

Seated at a window table in the hotel's dining room, mother and daughter examined the menu. Marta once again had to reassure Nazlan that although the prices seemed unreasonable, she could order whatever she wished. "We're not going to have to do dishes," she said.

Nazlan looked at her skeptically. "Why would we have to do that?" she asked.

"Oh, it's an American saying. If you can't pay the bill, they make you work it off in the kitchen," Marta explained. "It's just a joke. Don't worry."

Nazlan reddened. "Thank you again, for everything." She looked at her polished nails, and Marta reached over and covered her hand.

"I know this is a lot to take in, and I love that you are so independent and mature. But now, for a little while at least, you can enjoy being a kid. You don't have to worry about money, and you don't have to keep thanking me. This is way overdue, and I should be thanking you for allowing me back into your life." She paused. "This is getting too serious!" she said. "How about some good news?"

"Yes?"

"I had a message from the consulate. We can apply for your visa tomorrow—we have to go there in person—and it should be ready in a couple of days. So we can head to New York on the weekend," Marta said. She squeezed Nazlan's hand again. "Aren't you excited?"

Nazlan laughed nervously. "Yes, I am," she said. "I never thought ... I dreamed about it, but I never thought it would happen."

They ate dinner, Nazlan peppering Marta with questions about Manhattan, museums, schools, and architecture. "I love reading about the buildings," she said. "I want to see everything!"

"And you will," Marta said. "I do have to go back to work, but I can take some afternoons to explore with you. Maybe we'll get you into an intensive language program, so you'll be ready for school—"

Nazlan frowned. "Oh," she said.

"Hey, it's still a vacation, but we have to think about your future, right?" Marta said. "Don't worry; I'll make sure you have plenty of time for exploring."

The next days passed in a haze of shopping, taxicabs, and waiting in line—at the bank, at the consulate, and finally at the airport check-in lines. The early morning flight was fully booked, but Marta's connections got them seated in first class. By now, Nazlan was lugging a large suitcase and small carry-on bag, her rucksack having been left for rubbish. As they inched toward the security clearance, Marta made another attempt to raise Vasilli on the phone.

"No answer again," she said, snapping the phone shut. "I wanted to talk with him before we left. But I guess we'll hook up again in New York." She ran a finger idly along Nazlan's chin. "I am so happy," she said. "Are you okay with all of this?"

"I'm great," Nazlan said. "Well, maybe a little nervous. I was never in a plane before ..."

"I can give you some Dramamine, if you want. For the motion sickness," Marta said.

"Nah. I'll be fine. I'm always fine," Nazlan said.

When they were on the plane, Marta once again in her preferred seat with a Bloody Mary on its way to her hand, Nazlan stowed her sweater and bag in the overhead compartment. Marta handed her the laptop bag. "Put this up there, too, would you?"

Denise, the flight attendant, handed Marta her drink. "Not working today?" she commented. "I've never seen you without your computer." She laughed. "Who is this lovely girl?" she asked. "A relative? She looks just like you."

Marta smiled and opened her mouth to reply, but Nazlan interrupted. "I'm her daughter," she said proudly. She leaned back into Marta's shoulder. "We *do* look alike, don't we?"

Marta wiped a tear from her cheek. "Yes, we do."

Denise turned to help a passenger board. "Sir, you should have checked that bag. I'm not sure we have room for it ..." She looked at his ticket. "Well, you're in first class. Sit right here. I'll see what I can do with this." She took his luggage and rolled it toward the galley.

"I was upgraded," the man waved his ticket. "It was a last-minute decision to make this flight and ..." He stopped, looking at the two women squeezed shoulder to shoulder and looking out the tiny window.

"Excuse me." He tapped the younger woman's arm. "Maybe you can help me. I'm looking for a really good lawyer."

Marta and Nazlan turned at the same time to look at the man.

"Vasilli!" Marta exclaimed. "What are you doing here? Meet my daughter—meet Nazlan."

Vasilli took Nazlan's hand and kissed it gently. Still retaining his grip, he smiled at her. "I cannot tell you how happy I am to meet you, my dear," he said. "And how glad I am to see you again!" He nodded to Marta, grabbing her with his other hand. "What a lovely thing to see!"

The air crackled with an announcement from the crew that the plane was ready to move, so Vasilli was hustled into his seat and strapped in. He reached across to Nazlan, who was gripping the armrest until her knuckles were white.

"Don't be afraid," he said. "Flying is easy! You'll love it!" He smiled at Marta. "And you never know who you'll meet on a plane."

Nazlan looked at both of them, smiling. She turned to Marta.

"Happily ever after," she said.

"Happily ever after." Marta nodded. "Let's go home."